THE KNOT OF A KNIGHT

LINDA RAE SANDE

Twisted Teacup
PUBLISHING

ALSO BY LINDA RAE SANDE

The Daughters of the Aristocracy
The Kiss of a Viscount
The Grace of a Duke
The Seduction of an Earl
The Sons of the Aristocracy
Tuesday Nights
The Widowed Countess
My Fair Groom
The Sisters of the Aristocracy
The Story of a Baron
The Passion of a Marquess
The Desire of a Lady
The Brothers of the Aristocracy
The Love of a Rake
The Caress of a Commander
The Epiphany of an Explorer
The Widows of the Aristocracy
The Gossip of an Earl
The Enigma of a Widow
The Secrets of a Viscount
The Widowers of the Aristocracy
The Dream of a Duchess
The Vision of a Viscountess
The Conundrum of a Clerk
The Charity of a Viscount

The Cousins of the Aristocracy

The Promise of a Gentleman

The Pride of a Gentleman

The Holidays of the Aristocracy

The Christmas of a Countess

The Knot of a Knight

The Heirs of the Aristocracy

The Angel of an Astronomer

The Puzzle of a Bastard

The Choice of a Cavalier

The Bargain of a Baroness

The Jewel of an Earl's Heir

The Vixen of a Viscount

Beyond the Aristocracy

The Pleasure of a Pirate

The Making of a Mistress

Stella of Akrotiri

Origins

Deminon

Diana

CHAPTER 1
FORMER LOVERS, PRESENT PARENTS

The afternoon of December 14, 1824 at The Queen of Hearts, Stafford Street, Mayfair

A light snow fell as Randall Roderick, Marquess of Reading, made his way through the brass-framed front doors of the newest gaming hell to capture the attention—and the blunt—of the bored young bucks of London's aristocracy.

At one time, Randall would have been one of those men. Sporting a full purse tucked into his elaborately embroidered waistcoat, Randall would have had thoughts of gambling until the wee hours of the morning. Afterwards, he would have enjoyed a tumble with a courtesan in one of the gaming hell's elegant bedchambers before making his way to his townhouse in Westminster to sleep.

The memory had him scoffing. Thank the gods that at the ripe old age of five-and-thirty, after fathering four bastard sons and a daughter, he had matured enough to swear off his rakish behavior, buy another townhouse—this one in Curzon Street— and had taken a wife.

That had been six years ago.

Constance Fitzwilliam Roderick, Marchioness of Reading, was at this moment home with their youngest boy—one of his two legitimate sons. The other had already started school at

Eton. Before taking his leave that day, he had almost told her why he was paying a call at The Queen of Hearts.

Almost.

Randall stopped and stood just inside the entrance of the gaming establishment, long enough to allow his eyes to adjust to the dim interior. At this time in the afternoon, there were only a few of his colleagues at the faro tables, and no one was seated at the card tables designed for French Hazard.

"What's your pleasure, sir?" a young woman asked as she curtsied. Her red satin gown, so tight in the bodice it barely contained her rising moons, was styled after those from the century prior.

Pulled from his reverie, Randall regarded the young woman who stood before him. She couldn't have been more than his daughter's age, and for a moment, he feared she *was* his daughter. "I need to speak with Miss... *Mrs.* Higgins," he said with as much authority as he could muster. "Violet Higgins. Please let her know Reading is calling."

He had half a thought to ask after his daughter using her name—Rachel—but until he could determine the whereabouts of his only daughter, Randall thought it best he keep her identity secret. He had no idea what plans her mother might have for the young woman who would now be twenty years old.

One brow arching at hearing his request, the young woman dipped another curtsy and said, "She's not here at the moment, my lord, but I can take you to her." She turned and hurried toward the back of the gaming room.

Confused by her comment, Randall stutter-stepped to catch up to the young woman, his gaze darting about to take in the almost gaudy decor of the red and gold gaming hell. Decorative plasterwork coated in gilt covered the walls that weren't papered in red or gold. His footsteps were muffled by a patterned carpet in the same colors. Gaming tables made from mahogany were surrounded by chairs upholstered in rich brocades. Multiple sets of double doors along the walls suggested there were other gaming rooms beyond, and a huge carpeted staircase, currently cordoned off with a thick gold rope, was obviously the means to access the brothel.

When they passed through a set of double doors into a large dining room, he actually paused. The lingering scents of the dinner that had been served the night before had his stomach growling.

"When is the next meal to be served?" he asked before he continued to follow the young woman to the far corner of the room.

"Dinner service begins at eight, but our cook can make you something now if you desire," she replied as she quickly glanced around. She pressed a hand to a paneled wall. A hidden door revealed itself as it opened, and she motioned for him to step through. She just as quickly closed it behind her. "The Queen would appreciate your discretion in not sharing how it was you arrived at her office."

Randall said, "Of course," as he turned to discover that from this side of the wall, the door actually looked like a door.

He continued to follow her up a flight of stairs and down a corridor that suggested they were no longer in the gaming hell but rather in an elegant house. The conservative decor was entirely at odds to what he had just paid witness to in the gaming establishment.

The young woman went through one of the open doors, her conversation within briefly muted until Randall stopped at the threshold. He couldn't see whoever it was she was speaking with, but he recognized the voice of his former mistress. Knew from the sound of surprise that tinged her response that she hadn't expected him on this wintery day.

Well, he hadn't seen Violet Higgins in an age. All their contact over the years had been through correspondence. In his letters, he had made it very clear Rachel wasn't to follow in her mother's footsteps.

Violet had agreed, so long as Randall saw to the tuition for her schooling. Randall had not only covered his daughter's expenses for school, he had funded all of her expenses and most of Violet's until Violet had arranged another protector.

Now that he had seen the size and the decor of The Queen of Hearts, she had apparently arranged a rather lucrative settlement with someone. He knew the funds he had sent her over the years wouldn't have paid for such a grand gaming establishment.

"The Queen will see you now, my lord," the young lady said as she dipped another curtsy and then hurried off down the corridor.

Stepping over the threshold as if he expected a bomb might explode, Randall peeked around the door and allowed a happy sigh. "I rather doubt I would have recognized you if I saw you on the street," he said as he moved farther into the room, his top hat clutched between his two hands.

"Because I've grown old?"

Randall shook his head as he approached the woman who stood behind a massive desk. "Because you're more beautiful than you were when I last saw you," he countered. He reached for her hand, and after a pause, she finally lifted it so that he could lean over the desk and take it to his lips. "How are you, Violet?"

The former courtesan gave a quick curtsy before she sat in a wide chair behind the desk. "I am well. And you?"

"The same."

"And married life?"

He inhaled, determined to tell her the truth even if it might sting. "I find I rather adore it."

"Good," she replied with a grin. "You've obviously received my latest letter."

Randall pulled the envelope from a pocket in his waistcoat. "Yesterday. Is she here?"

Violet scoffed. "Not until tomorrow at the earliest. I thought I made that clear in the note."

"I cannot help it. I haven't seen her in... eleven... twelve years," he complained.

"But I suppose you've seen her twin brother," Violet accused, a note of bitterness apparent in her voice.

Randall inhaled as if he was about to answer, and then let

the breath out. "Not since he was at Eton. And only by a happy accident."

Obviously surprised by his response, any indignation Violet seemed to feel escaped in a long sigh. "How was he?"

Pulling another note from a pocket, Randall held it out to her. "He was quite fine then. His father... his adoptive father... has been good about sending me updates about him on a somewhat regular basis. This was the latest I received from him," he explained as Violet took the letter from him. "You may keep it and feel pride in knowing your son will be graduating from Oxford very soon."

"Oxford?" she repeated in awe. "Not Cambridge?"

"Reginald will go to Cambridge," Randall said, referring to his youngest illegitimate son.

"Will I ever see Richard?"

Randall winced. "If he ever comes to London, and if he should decide to gamble here, then... possibly," he hedged. "Violet, he cannot know about us. Or about the arrangement that was made on his behalf."

"Why ever not?"

"He has been raised as if he is the legitimate heir to a viscountcy," he whispered. "He replaced a babe of about the same age that died shortly after his birth. I made a promise to his father that I would tell no one. That I would never claim him as mine."

Violet dipped her head. "I do appreciate that you allowed me to keep Rachel."

"I was never going to take her away from you," he murmured. "Now, what have you heard from her? Was she able to hire a companion and travel after she completed finishing school?" He had sent funds when Violet mentioned Rachel's desire to visit Italy prior to her return to British shores.

"I do not think she enjoyed the experience," Violet replied. "Which is why she's coming here sooner than I expected."

"Sooner?" he repeated.

"She was going to wait until the Season was about to start."

"Ah," Randall acknowledged. "I am rather excited for her.

She must be so happy to finally be making her come-out. She'll no doubt have a line of young bucks ready to court her—"

"Randall," Violet interrupted. "Let's get her back to England before we go making plans for her to wed. She may not even want to marry just yet. She's only twenty," she reminded him.

He took a deep breath. "Of course. But do know that I have every intention of funding her gowns and such for her come-out. I can even arrange for a sponsor if you don't wish me to do the honors."

Violet allowed a slight grin. "You can do the honors," she replied in a whisper. "But please don't expect she'll marry well."

"Why ever not?"

Angling her head to one side, Violet spread her arms out, her palms up. "I was a courtesan. I own a gaming hell—"

"A rather lucrative one, it would seem."

"It is," she agreed, her stance softening somewhat. "But Rachel is doomed to suffer for my choice of occupation."

"But she's my daughter, too," Randall argued, as if his rank could counteract Violet's place in society. "Perhaps there is a man out there that will appreciate her for *her* and not for who her parents are."

Violet rolled her eyes, as if she thought him naive. "Perhaps," she replied. "But you must also prepare for the possibility she will not wish to marry at all."

Randall looked so stricken, Violet feared she would have to locate a vinaigrette to revive him. The thought had a huge grin splitting her face. "Oh, Randall, you needn't look so frightened," she scolded.

His expression didn't change, and his next words had tears brightening Violet's eyes. "Does she remember me, do you think?"

"Of course she does," Violet replied. For a moment—and only a moment—she regretted her decision to send her only child to the Continent for school. She hadn't seen Rachel in several years, either, and only then because of a windfall that had allowed her to travel to Switzerland and to buy the building that eventually housed The Queen of Hearts.

"She'll be here tomorrow?"

"She's due on a ship bound from LeHavre," Violet replied. "I think it's expected to arrive mid-morning. But, please, don't be there. I have a bodyguard seeing to her whilst she's on this trip. He'll pound you to a bloody pulp should you attempt to go near her," she warned.

Randall sighed loudly. "When, then?"

Amused by his enthusiasm, Violet said, "The day after. Perhaps we'll have dinner together," she suggested.

"In that dining room downstairs?" he asked hopefully. "Your cook must be—"

"French, yes, and no, you can't have him," Violet said with a smirk.

"How long have you been... The Queen of Hearts?" Randall suddenly asked.

"Three... nearly four years now," Violet replied.

He gasped. "That long?"

Violet tittered. "My, marriage really has changed you if you were unaware of my establishment," she accused.

He nodded. "It has, Violet. I am a different man than I was. A better father, too. And I wish to be that for Rachel."

Tears once again threatening, Violet inhaled deeply and said, "Well, I shan't get in your way, but know this. She's my daughter, too."

"Understood," he agreed.

With that, Randall, once again bowed over her hand before taking his leave of The Queen of Hearts.

He had no idea his exit was witnessed by anyone of note.

CHAPTER 2
SECRETS OF A GAMING HELL

*M*eanwhile, at *The Jack of Spades, St. James Street, Mayfair*

Sir Randolph Roderick stepped into the dimly lit gaming hell that had at one time been a bastion for faro and *vingt-et-un* players. Their dealers, most of them young women of questionable virtue, were known as the best in the business. The odds of the card game usually favored the player, but with a skilled and beautiful operator, the house broke even and instead made its money on the other offerings of the typical gaming hell—liquor, high-stakes card games, and the brothel on the second floor.

Once Frank O'Laughlin had installed a billiards table in a space that had at one time acted as a smoking room, the clientele changed.

So did reports of foreigners attempting to pass counterfeit currency.

Randolph knew Frank bought his liquors from a reputable source, a broker who had a royal charter from the Crown. But when his deposits into the Bank of England started to include notes of questionable authenticity, he went on notice.

Allow an agent of the Crown to investigate by acting as a client, or shut down his establishment.

Frank agreed to not only host an agent to investigate, one who would act as a frequent gambler, but he went one step further. "I'll supply an apartment in which he can live and a reward for when the damned frogs are caught," he claimed.

At no point had the suspected source of the problem been mentioned, although early intelligence reports did suggest a French connection. The Napoleonic Wars were a distant memory for most, but that didn't mean the treachery of the French had been forgotten.

Although Randolph was glad for the offer—there were times when he played billiards until well past three in the morning—he only took advantage of the apartment a couple of nights a week. He had a more than modest townhouse in Westminster, courtesy of the Reading marquessate, where he preferred to spend his nights.

Even if Barbara no longer lived.

The reminders of her were everywhere. In her bedchamber, where his gifts of an ivory comb and brush from Floris still decorated the dressing table and her gowns still hung in the elaborately decorated dressing room.

In the breakfast parlor, where the sideboard featured an array of delicate pottery from Wedgwood, pieces she had personally chosen while on a trip to Stoke.

In the dining room, where the Waterford crystal goblets added brilliance to his otherwise dull dinners.

In the nursery, where Charlie's bassinet sat in one corner and her oak rocking chair stood in another.

And in the parlor, where her portrait, commissioned by her father upon her betrothal, still hung above the fireplace mantel.

Twice he had ordered its removal, and twice he had stayed the order before the butler could see to carrying out the mission. "My son will wish to know his mother's likeness," he had said, usually after he recovered from his hangover.

Thank the gods he could still play billiards when he was half-foxed. *Vingt-et-un* and French Hazard, not so much.

He couldn't seem to add numbers when his brain buzzed from too much alcohol.

. . .

The burly dunner at the front door of The Jack of Spades gave Randolph a nod and checked the time on his chronometer. "You're early," he accused.

Randolph waved a hand down the front of his body. "I need to change into different clothes," he replied, annoyed by the guard's comment. If the large, bald dunner, whose primary job was to collect the debts owed to the hell, knew his usual arrival time, then his marks might have noticed as well. "Next time, I'll be late."

Randolph knew the men he was after were down a side street at The Ace's Hole, a seedy public house that offered rancid meat pies, sour ale, and games of chance that definitely favored the house. The dice were loaded, as was the director who kept tabs on the proceedings.

He knew because he had just come from there.

Before that, his marks had been at Crockford's, a hell that featured a varied clientele and existed for the sole purpose of separating their players from as much of their money as possible. Although a sharp eye could catch Crockford's operators' frequent attempts at cheating—their operators employed sleight of hand along with waiters that made sure to distract a player's attention when a cheat was in progress—there were few when the drinks were encouraged and kept full.

Randolph was glad his assignment was based primarily out of The Jack of Spades. If cheating happened, it wasn't because Frank O'Laughlin encouraged it. In fact, the owner employed a number of crowpees to watch the play, not only to catch customers who might be cheating, but to keep an eye on the employees as well. Frank had just the week before fired a clerk and an operator for taking a baron for all he had, most of it through sleight of hand.

Both were now employed at Crockford's.

Frank also didn't employ any puffs. "I don't want decoys playing with high stakes," he had said when his director—the superintendent of the play—suggested it one night when the floor was quieter than usual. "Cheating will not be tolerated at the Jack," he had added in a hiss. "You want to cheat? Go to Crocky's."

Dressed in his most pedestrian clothes—worn trousers, a plain brown wool waistcoat, and a top coat from the turn of the century, Randolph appeared as if he were a down-on-his-luck farmer who gambled for the sake of his paltry existence.

The deceiving appearance meant he now had over fifty pounds in his pocket, probably all of it counterfeit.

After he changed into the garb of a well-to-do member of the gentry, he intended to win far more from the targets. He had overheard their plan—to finish their night at The Jack of Spades.

Besides the difference in his clothes, he would change his overall appearance by wetting his wavy hair and combing it back from his face, shaving, and then donning a pair of spectacles that would have him perceived as a gentleman fresh from the country.

He made his way through the gaming hell to the back and up the stairs to the first floor. His room, all the way at the end of the hall and facing the street, required he pass the doors of rooms belonging to *vingt-et-un* operators, crowpees, bartenders, waiters, and the gaming hell's cook, a cranky old woman known for morning meals that rivaled an aristocrat's wedding breakfast.

Randolph looked forward to those breakfasts on the two or three days a week he woke up in the gaming hell. If he didn't respect Frank so much, he would have made an offer to Annie to be the cook at his townhouse.

His apartment was one of only two that featured windows that looked out over Stafford Street. Not that the view was particularly pleasant. Although poverty wasn't rampant in Mayfair, desperation was for those who hoped to earn a shilling or two from its residents.

A young woman who looked as if she hadn't slept for several days was attempting to sell wilted flowers to anyone who passed on the street. A three-legged dog followed his charge, a young boy pulling a cart filled with limp vegetables.

But the one sight that had Randolph pausing before stripping off his cheroot smoke-laden clothes was that of a familiar man taking his leave of a gaming hell across the street.

The Queen of Hearts was anything but—a gambling den lined with red velvet walls and faux gold gilt decor that made most of its money from prostitution. The girls they employed were considered the equivalent of courtesans—well-dressed young women who were the daughters of courtesans, educated and trained in the bedroom arts from the time they were old enough to be bedded.

The owner, fairly new compared to the owners of the other gaming hells and men's clubs that lined the street, was an older matron who sported a mouche on one cheekbone and a white wig that was tall enough to house a colony of mice.

So what had his father, Randall Roderick, Marquess of Reading, been doing in there?

CHAPTER 3
A WIDOW LEFT ALONE

he following afternoon, in Bradley House, Curzon Street, Mayfair

Despite the bleak, gray skies outside her first floor parlor window, Xenobia Dunsworth was smiling for the first time in an age.

There were callers in her parlor.

And she wasn't wearing black, lavender, or gray.

In fact, she had instructed her lady's maid to find the brightest colored gown in her wardrobe so that she might greet her callers looking her very best. "Something that portends the holiday," she had said in response to her lady's maid's query earlier as to what she might like to wear that day. "Christmas is only a week away, Sullivan, and although I no longer have a husband with whom to share it, I intend to celebrate."

She was fairly sure Sullivan looked as if she were about to faint at hearing her proclamation. "Don't faint on me now," Xenobia warned.

"Oh, I wouldn't dare, my lady," Sullivan replied. She was quick to pull out a frock in a color that could best be described as poppy red, except that some draper thought it better to use the French term, *coquelicot*.

Xenobia didn't care. The gown had a blush appearing on her

pale cheeks and enhanced lips she had surreptitiously dabbed with a bit of color.

"*N*ow that you are out of mourning, we shall expect you at all the entertainments," Julia gushed as she helped herself to another Dutch biscuit. Lady Julia Comber, a cousin by way of her mother, had been Xenobia's closest friend since the death of her husband, Baron James Dunsworth. James had been Xenobia's very best friend her entire life.

"It is too bad there are so few here in London during the winter months," Lady Pettigrew lamented. The elderly viscountess, an inveterate gossip, eyed the remaining cakes as if she were keeping count of who had consumed which ones and how many.

"April is not too far away," Lady Caroline Chamberlain remarked. Despite his age, her husband, Viscount Matthew Chamberlain, was the head of the Foreign Office.

"I fear I have been forgotten by the *ton* as it has been so long since I attended even the theatre," Xenobia lamented. James had died in November of 1823, which meant she had essentially been out of sight for over a year.

And out of sorts.

To lose her very best friend to pneumonia had been devastating. Then, to suffer alone for so long, with only Julia with whom to spend time when her cousin could manage to be away from a growing family, had her stitching and needlepointing until her fingers bled. She had taken up drawing, although her efforts had yet to look like whatever it was she was attempting to draw. A wish to escape her reality had her reading every novel she could borrow from the circulating library.

The Gothics kept her awake at night. The mysteries were predictable. The humorous stories barely made her smile.

"Well, I really must be going," Lady Pettigrew announced suddenly.

"So soon?" Xenobia replied, a quick glance at the mantel

clock showing the viscountess had only been in her parlor for half-an-hour.

"Yes, well, I must pay a call on your neighbor. She is so rarely in town," she replied, referring to Countess Middleton.

"Of course. I'll see you out," Xenobia offered as she moved to stand up.

"Oh, there's no need. Look. Chesterfield is here," the older woman said, referring to the butler. With that, Lady Pettigrew sailed out of the room, the butler quickly escorting her down the stairs and to the front door.

Xenobia realized then that Eugenia Pettigrew had arranged for Chesterfield to interrupt them after exactly thirty minutes. She turned her attention on Julia and Caroline. "I do hope you're not going to leave, too," she murmured.

Julia angled her head. "Not for a few more minutes," she replied as she helped herself to another cake. "Now that she's gone, I feel as if I can speak freely and *eat.*"

Dipping her head as she attempted to suppress a knowing grin, Xenobia did the same.

Caroline grinned as she took another cake. "I'm of the same mind as you, even if I am not eating for two any longer." Despite her age, the viscountess had given birth to her third child just a few years earlier. "Besides, Chamberlain said he would be late for dinner this evening."

Julia and Xenobia exchanged quick glances. Xenobia knew first-hand what a comment like that could mean. Caroline caught their concerned looks, though, and leaned forward.

"It's not an *affaire*, unless you're referring to his devotion to his job. He's got his men after counterfeiters now," she whispered hoarsely. "Apparently, there are about to be some arrests made." This last was said in a manner suggesting she was sharing a secret.

"Counterfeiters?" Julia repeated. "You mean, fake bank notes? I thought that had been solved a few years ago? All those women they put to death?"

Xenobia cringed at remembering the Bank of England's efforts to stop counterfeiters. Their agents had caught mostly women passing the bank notes—many of whom had no idea they were doing so. Those making the counterfeit notes were rarely discovered and prosecuted. "As long as there is paper money instead of coin, there will always be counterfeiting. At least, that's what James used to say," Xenobia said before refilling Caroline's teacup.

"Chamberlain would agree with that," Caroline replied. "Apparently his agents are after some foreigners who are bringing it in from another country. I'll just let you guess which one."

Julia inhaled. "France?"

Caroline nodded.

"But, how are they passing them?" Xenobia asked.

"In gaming establishments. Here in Mayfair. In St. James Street, in fact," Caroline replied. "That street has become nothing but men's clubs and gaming hells," she complained. She suddenly glanced at the clock over the fireplace mantel. "And speaking of St. James Street, I must head in that direction. I've an order in Jermyn Street to pick up."

Julia and Xenobia said their farewells to the viscountess and returned their attentions to their tea.

"I received a letter from the Continent a few days ago," Xenobia murmured, reaching for a folded missive that rested on a side table.

Furrowing a brow, Julia seemed to consider the comment a moment before her eyes rounded. "From Rachel?"

"Indeed. She's returning to London. I expect she'll arrive this week," Xenobia said with some excitement. "I have missed her so."

"Is she well?"

"Very, although I am under the impression she did not enjoy her attempts to travel after she finished school," Xenobia commented. "Italy was too hot and France was too cold. Spain was too sunny and... well, I don't think she was prepared for just how long it took to get anywhere of note."

Julia winced. "I share her thoughts on that matter," she

replied. "And I am glad she is returning. But where will she stay?"

Unfolding the letter, Xenobia leaned over and showed Julia the address Rachel had included with her missive. "Well, at least it's in Mayfair," Julia murmured. Then she grimaced. "She doesn't wish to marry, though, does she?" she asked in a whisper.

Xenobia swallowed. "I rather doubt it. I believe she intends to be an independent woman, even if her father probably has other plans for her."

"I am glad she has kept her expectations low. Although..."

"What?" Xenobia asked, once it was apparent Julia wasn't going to finish her comment.

Julia shook her head. "Oh, it's nothing. Just a fleeting thought of some men who have yet to marry," she murmured. "So it's true the Earl of Middleton still lives next door?" she asked, remembering Lady Pettigrew's comment about paying a call on the Countess Middleton.

Xenobia furrowed a brow. "Yes, as does his wife when she is in town," she replied, hoping Julia wasn't thinking to pair Rachel with the much older earl. The man had sired two sons, though. Luke Merriweather, Viscount Wessex, was already married and had a son while his younger brother, Mark, was still unattached—and probably too young to consider matrimony.

"It's been an age since I've seen any of them," Julia remarked.

Frowning at her cousin's words, Xenobia thought it best not to ask what Julia had in mind. From the time they had been young girls giving their governesses a difficult time, Julia had excelled at causing trouble. She'd even gained her husband by way of accepting a wager. Believing he was merely a groom in her father's stables—and not knowing he was the second son of an earl—she had agreed to make him into a gentleman in time for a ball.

Alistair Comber probably had no idea what he was agreeing to when he accepted her offer to make him into a gentleman.

Julia had succeeded, but only because Alistair was already a gentleman. Despite how cross the two had been with one another during those few weeks of him learning to dance, dress, bow, and speak, they ended up happily married to one another.

"Are your children well?" Xenobia asked, deciding it best she change the subject.

Waving a hand in the air, her cousin Julia rolled her blue eyes and gave her head a shake. Every last golden blonde strand remained in place. "Everyone is fine. Juliet has decided horses will be her life—and her father is doing nothing to disabuse her of the idea."

"Perhaps he shouldn't," Xenobia countered. "By the time she's old enough to wed, there will be men who will appreciate a fine horsewoman more than they do now."

Julia allowed a shrug. "Perhaps." The word didn't hold much hope.

"What of your son?"

"Jamie has a head cold, but he's the last to have it. Alistair says there will be four new colts in the Harrington House stables this spring. And this one..." She paused and leaned back as she placed a hand over her rounded belly. "Has learned how to kick." She straightened as much as she could. "I am worried about you."

Xenobia's eyes widened. "Why?"

Julia sighed. "You're all alone. You've lost your best friend—"

"You needn't make it sound as if I misplaced him."

"—and you're still young enough to find another and become a mother. You've always wanted children," Julia went on, ignoring the interruption.

"I am nearly five-and-twenty years old," Xenobia said in protest.

"But you're not *dead*."

Xenobia blinked. The words had sounded as if they were a scold.

"I was recently introduced to a gentleman whom I think you should meet."

"Julia,—"

"My husband thinks the world of him, I believe because he knew what to do with Jupiter."

"Jupiter?" Xenobia repeated, thinking she referred to the planet.

Whatever could a man do to Jupiter?

"His horse, of course. Now, I'm going to see to it you two meet—"

"Julia!"

"Just give him a chance, Xenobia," Julia insisted. She paused a moment and dipped her head. "I believe he has suffered much like you have, given his wife died in the childbed."

Xenobia relaxed into the settee. "Is... is he an aristocrat?" She struggled to recall if she had heard or read anything about a lord having lost a wife to childbirth in the last year.

Julia angled her head as if she were attempting to solve a math problem in her head. "He is certainly related to one," she finally hedged.

"But I haven't met him?"

Her cousin shook her head. "Doubtful, unless you've been at Tattersall's or the race track."

Xenobia rolled her eyes. She hadn't been to the Derby or the Ascot in years, and she had never been to the auction house featuring horses. "You know I have not."

"Well, then. It's settled," Julia announced as she struggled to stand up, the evidence of her pregnancy making itself apparent. "I'll send you a note as to when you can expect him. I'm off," she said, at the very moment Chesterfield once again appeared on the parlor threshold.

"Thank you so much for coming," Xenobia said as she watched her friend take her leave. "And Happy Christmas!"

Allowing a sigh, Xenobia regarded the tray of cakes and helped herself to the last one. With no one to watch, she ate the entire piece with a second cup of tea as she considered Julia's comment.

CHAPTER 4
A CALL MOST CURIOUS

*M*eanwhile, at Middleton House in Curzon Street, Mayfair

Having endured an hour of listening to gossip shared by four older harpies in his mother's parlor, Mark Merriweather nearly kissed Pennyworth when the butler appeared on the threshold and indicated with a crooked finger that his presence had been requested elsewhere.

Feigning annoyance at the interruption, Mark bowed to the assembled ladies, made his apologies, and joined the butler at the door. For the first time in nearly an hour, he inhaled air that wasn't scented with the heavy perfumes the women seemed to favor. "I cannot convey just how happy I am that you thought to save me," he whispered, breathing deeply once again in the hopes to rid his nostrils of the last vestiges of the cloying scents.

Pennyworth furrowed a bushy brow. "I fear I cannot take credit for the interruption, sir. You have a caller."

Mark straightened. "I do?" No one ever called on him. They called on his father, the Earl of Middleton. They called on his mother, the Countess of Middleton. They sometimes called on his brother, Luke, apparently not knowing he had moved to his own townhouse in Westminster upon his marriage to Analise Lancaster six years ago.

The only person he could recall ever asking for him was

Christopher, Earl of Haddon, and then only because they were scheduled to play cards at The Queen of Hearts, and Haddon had offered to drive.

He had accepted the offer—Haddon had a phaeton that was the envy of every young buck in Mayfair—but would never do so again. The ride to Stafford Street had been as frightening as it had been exhilarating. Not once, not twice, but three times Mark was sure he would be thrown from the bench as the earl took the turns entirely too fast. They had made it to the gaming establishment in one piece, but Mark was sure he had aged a year that night.

At hearing Pennyworth's throat clearing and a quiet, "Sir?", Mark shook himself from his reverie.

"You can bring him to my study," he instructed.

The butler cleared his throat again. "Your caller is Lady Comber, sir."

Mark blinked before his brows furrowed. He knew of Lady Comber, of course. She was married to Alistair Comber, the man who saw to acquiring horses for the various Middleton equipages through his work at Tattersall's. Mark might have danced with her at a few balls over the years, but at no point would he expect her to pay a call on him. "You can bring her to my study," he said, not sure where else they could meet given the parlor was still in use.

"Yes, sir."

Pennyworth headed for the main stairs while Mark took the corridor in the opposite direction and used the servants' stairs to get to the ground floor. He entered his office only a moment before the butler's knock. "Come," he called out as he settled behind his desk.

He grimaced when he realized a week's worth of correspondence and invoices was scattered about the desk's polished surface.

Well, that's what happened when he didn't have a man of business, he supposed. The week before, he had discovered Mr. Traynor had been stealing from him.

Embezzling.

The amounts were not a lot—small enough to hide in the accomptant's overly frequent pay vouchers—but over the course of a year, they had added up to nearly a hundred pounds!

Too embarrassed to discuss the matter with his father, Mark had simply given the man his notice of dismissal and warned him that should he discover any more funds missing from his account, he would report him to the magistrate.

Mr. Traynor pretended ignorance on the matter until Mark held up the sheets from the ledger containing the damning information, and Traynor quickly took his leave.

Without a man of business to see to his business—a public house in Westminster—Mark might become buried in papers.

Pennyworth opened the door and announced his caller.

Lady Comber sailed into his study before dipping a quick curtsy. Mark stood and moved to the side of his desk. He bowed and reached for her gloved hand. "This is a surprise, my lady," he said before brushing his lips over the kid leather.

"For me, as well, Mr. Merriweather," Julia said as she settled into the only chair on the other side of the desk.

Mark blinked, not bothering to hide his expression of confusion. The effect was amplified by the lock of hair that dangled onto his forehead, apparently too stubborn to remain with the rest of the dark hair atop his head. "Would you like tea?"

She shook her head. "No, thank you. I've just come from having tea with Lady Dunsworth," she replied.

"Ah, the widow next door," Mark replied. "She is no longer in mourning?"

"She is not, but *she* is not why I've come to see you," Julia said. "I've come about you."

"Me?"

"And your lack of a wife."

Mark blinked as he exhaled, her comment nearly as effective as a punch to the gut. "My lady?" he managed as he wondered what his mother might have arranged behind his back.

She was usually the one to bring up his lack of a wife.

Without preamble, Julia asked, "What exactly are you looking for in such a creature?"

Knowing his jaw was left slack from her first comment, Mark made sure to clamp his mouth shut upon hearing her second. "Truth be told, I didn't know I was looking, so I'm not sure what I would want." He had to resist the urge to roll his eyes when he heard his white lie spoken aloud.

"Oh, poppycock, Merriweather," Julia countered. "I've known you for... how many years now?"

Mark finally settled in his chair and gave her query some thought. "Nearly our whole lives, I suppose," he murmured. Even if they were only acquaintances, they were nearly of the same age. When the earl was in town for Parliament, they attended the same entertainments.

"Is there a reason you haven't yet wed?"

Scoffing, Mark stared at her. "I don't really believe that's any of your concern."

"Of course it's not," she agreed.

The admission had Mark shaking his head.

"But tell me anyway," Julia insisted.

Furrowing a brow, Mark asked, "Why?"

Julia angled her head to one side in a manner he supposed she used on her husband when she grew impatient with him. "I come with news that you might find... *useful*," she whispered.

Mark stared at her a moment, his gaze darting to the papers scattered across his desk. The only news he would find useful at the moment was word of an available man of business. Or a secretary.

Well, he could write his own correspondence. He'd been doing so since he finished university.

News of an available bookkeeper, though? That was news he could use, and he decided to tell her so. "Does she do book-keeping?" he asked.

Julia blinked before she seemed to think on his query. "I rather imagine she could," she replied. "She was always very clever when we were younger," she added. "And all women are raised to keep household accounts, of course."

Mark's eyes widened. "You are?"

Once again angling her head to one side, Julia huffed. "It is part of the responsibility of running a household," she replied. "Now, when were you thinking to buy or let a townhouse of your own?"

That sensation of being punched in the gut once again had the air going out of Mark. "My lady, I haven't given it any..." He allowed the sentence to trail off when he remembered that only a half-hour ago, when he was trapped in the parlor with his mother's callers, he had wished for his own place.

Nothing too elaborate. Bachelor quarters in The Albany would do, although he thought the leases there were a bit too expensive. He sighed and amended his response. "I suppose I could look into the matter. With an agent," he added.

"Good," Julia said as she gave him a brilliant grin. "Now, tell me what you'd prefer in a wife. Besides the skills to keep your books?"

Without thinking of how she had outmaneuvered him, Mark shrugged and said, "Well, she'd have to be amiable and not insipid. I cannot begin to tell you how insipidness has ruined the current crop of young ladies."

"Of course," Julia said, finding she couldn't disagree. "Go on."

"Well, I suppose it wouldn't be too much to ask that she be... attractive?" he hedged.

"Not at all," Julia agreed. "In fact, I have reason to believe she's quite beautiful. What else?"

About to ask who the beauty was, Mark instead began to wonder if Julia was going to charge him for matchmaking services. "Not too tall," he said, momentarily allowing his mind's eye to capture a vision of the woman he would like on his arm. "She has to be able to ride a horse."

"Oh, I'm quite sure she can do that," Julia mused.

Visions of a dark-haired beauty, her long locks spread out on a pillow beneath her head and her entire body beneath his had Mark's cock responding with an arousal he hadn't felt in a very long time. "Long hair," he whispered. "Not too young. Twenty, at least. Educated, if possible. I should like to carry on a conversation of some import over dinners."

Julia watched as the second son of an earl put voice to his desires. He seemed lost in his thoughts as he recited the traits of his perfect wife while the entire time, Julia tried to imagine what Rachel Roderick looked like now that she was eight years older than when Julia had last seen her.

"I suppose I should mention the need for a modest dowry. Something I can use to ensure she and the children are taken care of when I die," he said with some awe, as if he had never before given a thought to his own mortality.

"And if it's more generous than that?"

Mark stared at Julia for a full five seconds before he gave a start. "All the better I suppose, but now you have me worried."

"Why? So far, she fits all your criteria," Julia claimed, even though she didn't know Rachel's height or if she could do arithmetic well enough to do his books.

"She does?"

Julia lifted one of her shoulders.

"There's a catch, isn't there?" he said.

Unable to keep a wince from appearing, Julia finally sighed as she held up her thumb and forefinger and pinched them together. "*Oui, petite*," she replied in a whisper.

Mark pounced. "I knew it. There's always a catch," he said with good deal of disappointment. "Out with it," he added on a sigh.

"She's an aristocrat's daughter," Julia stated, noting how he seemed surprised to hear it. "But she was born on the wrong side of the blanket." Staring at Mark for a moment, she was surprised when he still seemed to be contemplating a possible match.

"When can I meet her?"

Julia blinked. "Well, I have reason to believe she might have arrived in London today, and if that's the case, she'll be..." She winced again, attempting to remember the address in the letter Xenobia had shown her. She was fairly sure it was on the back side of The Queen of Hearts, which made sense if Rachel was going to live with her mother for a time.

"Where? She'll be where?"

Julia jerked back at hearing the desperation in the man's voice. "The Queen of Hearts. Or at least, the owner there has a room reserved for her in a... a private residence. She won't live in the gaming establishment, of course," she stammered.

Julia wasn't really sure of any arrangements Rachel's mother might have made on behalf of her daughter, but she knew Rachel would be under her mother's roof for at least the first few weeks of her stay in London.

What happened after that depended on if Julia could find a husband for her.

For a moment, Mark looked confused, and then he slowly frowned. "So, she is or is she not an employee of The Queen?"

Her mouth dropping open at the insinuation her friend might be a prostitute, Julia quickly stood and said, "She is most certainly *not*." A wave of light-headedness had her wavering at the very moment Mark had joined her in standing. When his eyes widened at seeing her momentary distress, he was about to step from around the desk and make an attempt to break her fall should she faint. Julia put up a hand to stop him. "I momentarily forgot I'm not to do that," she whispered.

"Do what?" he asked in alarm. "Faint?"

She gave him a quelling glance. "Stand up quickly. The baby doesn't like it."

"Baby?" The note of surprise in his voice had Julia rolling her eyes.

"Fear not. I won't be giving birth anytime soon," Julia replied. "But I will take my leave. It looks as if you've quite a lot of business to see to," she added as her gaze swept over his paper-littered desk. "Do give my regards to Lord Haddon when you see him this evening."

Mark shook his head. "How is it you know I'm playing cards with Haddon this evening?"

Once again, she gave him a look of disbelief. "It's Wednesday," she replied, and with that, she dipped a curtsy and took her leave of the study.

Left standing with his mouth open and his brows furrowed, Mark contemplated his caller's words and decided he and Haddon really needed to change their ways.

It seemed they had become predictable.

He had become predictable.

Settling back into the desk chair, Mark regarded the papers on his desk and decided to do what he could with them.

All the while he saw to his correspondence, he imagined a dark-haired beauty and what it would be like to be married to her.

It was nearly an hour later when he realized Lady Comber hadn't told him how much he would owe her for her services as a matchmaker.

CHAPTER 5
A DAUGHTER'S RETURN TO LONDON

*M*eanwhile, at *The Queen of Hearts, Stafford Street, Mayfair*

With a bit of trepidation, Rachel Roderick opened the door to the bedchamber her mother had said was hers. Given the gaudy decor she found in the gaming hell two stories below—red velvet trimmed in faux gilt—and the preponderance of pink in the parlor, she expected to find a similarly outrageous situation behind the dark wood-paneled door.

Instead, the bedchamber was a model of restraint in the art of decorating.

A deep blue velvet canopy draped from the ceiling above the blue velvet-clad bed. The furniture was French, although Rachel couldn't say from which King Louis it took its style. The drapes matched the counterpane while sheer white ruched fabric separated them from the two clear glass pane windows.

Beneath her feet was a carpet that looked as if it had never been trod upon.

Tempted to remove her slippers—as much to test the thickness of the rug as to ensure she didn't track anything onto the floor, Rachel instead moved quickly to the bed and set her valise upon its smooth surface.

"Will this do?"

Rachel whirled to find her mother, Violet Higgins, standing

on the threshold. As shocked as she had been to see the owner of The Queen of Hearts in her high white wig and scandalous red satin gown upon her arrival at the gaming hell only the hour before, Rachel was equally surprised to see Violet looking a decade younger and dressed far more conservatively now. "Mother?" she guessed.

Despite her age—she had to be at least forty—Violet giggled and moved to pull her daughter into a hug. "You needn't tease me," she scolded.

"I didn't recognize you," Rachel replied. "You look... so young. Slimmer. And your hair—"

"Is not white, it's true," Violet acknowledged as she waved to her coiffure, her natural brown hair streaked with chestnut strands and coiled into a fetching bun atop her head. A number of curly loose strands decorated the back of her neck and her temples.

The tops of her breasts had barely been contained in the bodice of her red satin gown. Now they were hidden beneath a sprigged day gown. "What I wear as the owner of this establishment is merely a costume," Violet explained as she motioned for Rachel to join her in one of the blue floral upholstered chairs in the adjacent sitting room.

Rachel took a moment to open her valise and remove a few items before she pulled out a fabric-wrapped box. She moved to the chair her mother indicated, but she paused to offer the box to Violet.

"What's this?" her mother asked as she gingerly reached for the box.

"A gift. I wanted you to have something from Switzerland."

Violet examined the fabric covering, her eyes brightening with tears. "You didn't need to—"

"Mother. You're not crying, are you? It's merely a gift," Rachel whispered. "Although maybe you will cry when you see what it is," she added as she settled into the adjacent chair. She sighed at how comfortable it felt, especially considering the seats she had been forced to sit in during the course of the past fortnight.

After the rocky coach ride from Zurich to Le Havre, the tumultuous trip across the Channel, and the hackney ride from Wapping, Rachel welcomed the sensation of not moving.

The tall, muscled chaperone who had accompanied her was blessedly quiet for most of the trip, but Rachel had decided it was more because he didn't speak French. He obviously knew English, though, for she had been shocked the first time he spoke to her, sounding not at all like a full-grown guttersnipe, but rather a refined gentleman.

Violet removed the fabric wrapping and then used a fingertip to trace the seams of the box until she discovered the well-hidden hinges and then turned it around on her lap. Gripping what she determined to be the lid, she lifted it an inch and peered inside, as if she feared whatever was in there might come popping out.

"It won't bite, Mother," Rachel said with a chuckle.

The sound of chimes—several of them, all different—had Violet giving a start, and the lid dropped back down. She gasped and then opened it completely, staring at the revolving cylinder that played music as small pins plucked its surface. "I've always wanted one," Violet breathed when the tune came to a stuttering halt. "How do I...? What makes it play?"

Rachel reached over and pointed to a small protrusion. "Just turn that until it feels tight, and then let go."

"I'll break it, I'm quite sure," Violet countered as she passed the box to Rachel. "Will you?"

Shocked at hearing her mother's claim, Rachel took the box and wound the stem several turns. "You won't break it, and even if you do, any watchmaker in town can fix it," she claimed. Rachel held the box for Violet until the older woman took it from her. "Tell me, is it true what you said in your letter? About a come-out for me this Season?"

Violet blinked at hearing the change in subject. "Well, of course. You're twenty now, and it's well past time you had a Season."

Rachel experienced the familiar sensation of excitement

coupled with fright. As much as she wanted a Season, she knew it could be fraught with issues.

She was the illegitimate daughter of a marquess and a courtesan. A madame. Although her father had recognized her and given her his name, she had no idea if he would welcome her should she meet him at any of the social events. She was under the impression he had funds set aside for her dowry, but she had no idea of its value.

"Do you think Richard will attend any of this Season's events?"

Violet dipped her head. "I really couldn't say," she whispered. "I've not seen your brother..." She allowed the sentence to trail off.

How had she allowed Randall Roderick to take her son from her all those years ago?

As many times as Violet asked herself the question, she always knew the answer.

She wouldn't have been able to raise twins.

Randall knew it—had known it once he learned she would be having twins. He had made the arrangements for Richard to be raised in an aristocrat's family while Rachel had been left with Violet.

At first, Violet doubted she could raise even a single child, although she had done it—quite successfully, given she had funds from Randall to pay for Rachel's expenses as well as her own—until Randall arranged for Rachel's finishing school on the Continent. Then Violet was suddenly by herself once again.

At least she had a burgeoning business to run. A reputation as a celebrated courtesan to maintain. The life of a gaming hell queen to live.

Even if she did most of that living coiffed and garbed as she was now, unrecognizable to most everyone. The anonymity allowed her a quiet life when the demands of the gaming hell didn't interfere. It also meant she could freely move about London without the possibility of some unwelcome rake propositioning her or a lady of the *ton* giving her the cut direct.

• • •

"*W*ill I require a new wardrobe?" Rachel asked. Violet had always seen to it she had fashionable clothes while she was in Zurich. There were times she wondered how much it was costing Violet for the finishing school as well as her living expenses.

She wasn't the only boarder at the school, of course. Many of her fellow students were from England. Each year a number of girls returned to British shores more refined than when they had left, ready to rejoin their families and for their introductions to Society.

The school's reputation—and therefore its price—rose with each new graduate. Rachel had feared her mother wouldn't be able to afford this past year's tuition, and so she was surprised when funds arrived by way of a courier that not only paid for the school, but afforded her a generous allowance.

She set aside some of it and used the extra funds to hire a companion with whom she could travel when school wasn't in session. Although she had enjoyed forays into France and Italy, she soon tired of the time it took to get anywhere of note.

Glad to be back on British shores and in London, she vowed she would remain in town for the foreseeable future.

And she could foresee that being a very long time.

"We'll have to take a look at your gowns before we make that decision," Violet replied. "Something tells me you've a trunk full of clothes far more fashionable than anything you'll find here in London." She had watched as two of the gaming hell footmen had removed not just one but two large traveling trunks from the hackney upon Rachel's arrival.

"Oh, I rather doubt that," Rachel replied. "I paid witness to a number of well-dressed ladies when I disembarked the ship."

Violet had ordered her caddy to watch for the arrival of the ship in Wapping. When he confirmed through his contact—the chief mate—that Rachel was on board, he had quickly made his way back to The Queen of Hearts and informed Violet. Knowing Rachel's chaperone would see to her daughter's quick transport to the gaming hell, Violet had only an hour's notice before the hackney arrived.

"Well, it matters not. Your father has been most generous over the years, and he'll be seeing to the costs of your come-out, as well."

Rachel inhaled softly. "My father?" Her mother's words surprised her. "He's been paying for everything?"

Violet allowed a shrug. "Well, of course. He's been doing so since you were born."

Blinking, Rachel considered all the times she had thought her mother had been the one to fund her expenses. "Every bit of it?"

A grin appeared on Violet's lips as she nodded. "I apologize if you thought otherwise. Randall... Lord Reading, rather, has always seen to it I had the funds for whatever you required."

"And you?"

Violet angled her head to one side. "Many of them. At least those from when you were still living with me. After that... I was able to see to earning my own fortune. As I did before you were born."

"As a courtesan."

It wasn't a question, but Rachel noticed her mother's wince, and she regretted having put voice to the words. "I apologize—"

"You needn't. It is how I make—*made*—my living for many years," Violet admitted. "I was a mistress to several very generous men, two of whom loved me very much." She swallowed, as if she were attempting to overcome a sob. "May they rest in peace. But now I own this business. I make a good deal of money, and I am a fair employer. I pay the girls well. I pay my protection well. But despite all that, I am fearful of how *you* will be received in Society because of me and my business. To that end, I think it best you stay here in the residence. If you're seen with me, and I am garbed as The Queen, then there should be no mention we are related."

Wincing, Rachel asked, "And if you are not garbed as The Queen?"

Violet allowed a tentative smile. "Then I think it would be safe for you to be my daughter."

Rachel nodded her understanding before a brow furrowed. "Does that mean my father will be seeing to my come-out?"

Violet's eyes darted to the side. "I spoke with him about it yesterday."

"What?"

"You needn't be concerned. He knew you were expected back in London at any time and hoped you might have already arrived. He's desperate to see you again."

Looking as if she might faint, Rachel gave a small shake of her head. "But, what if I don't wish to see him?"

Violet blinked, her brows furrowing to make her appear much older. "Oh, Rachel. Why wouldn't you? He's a good man. He's been a good provider for you."

"He fathered four bastards!"

Grimacing, Violet whispered, "Five." Randall Roderick, Marquess of Reading, had fathered four boys and Rachel. Aloud, she added, "And he has two legitimate sons. He married about six years ago—"

"About time," Rachel said with derision.

"Rachel," her mother scolded. "He knows he was a rake. He never implied otherwise. But... he has changed."

Rachel scoffed.

"He has," Violet insisted. "He dearly loves his wife. Like him, she's a horsewoman. Understands horse breeding and racers. Grew up with a father who raced horses. She's perfect for him."

"And you were not?" Rachel argued.

Violet winced. "I never would have been accepted as a wife to an aristocrat," she replied. "Nor would I have wanted to *be* one. Even the promise of a coronet could not have persuaded me to pursue such a life."

"And yet you want me to."

Sighing, Violet settled back into her chair, as if she knew she was losing an argument. "I want you to have the chance, of course," she replied. "Whether or not you marry will be your choice. Randall... Lord Reading... is not going to *force* you to accept an offer."

"He said that?"

"He did. When he was here yesterday."

"But... there's a dowry?"

Violet's eyes narrowed. "There is," she affirmed. "Quite generous, I think."

"So... if I didn't marry, would it be enough for me to live on as an independent woman?"

Stricken at hearing the query, Violet gave a start. "I suppose so, yes, but... I really hope you'll consider any suitors you might meet during the Season's entertainments."

"Won't they only be interested in me for my dowry?" Rachel countered.

"Well, some, yes," Violet agreed. "But others are looking for a wife. For a mother to bear their children. For a helpmate to assist them with their business. Most have their own fortunes and will not be in need of yours," she explained.

Rachel inhaled before she finally nodded. "Very well." She paused before she said, "I sent a letter to Xenobia before I left Zurich. I gave her this address—"

"And she has replied," Violet said with some excitement. She pulled a missive from a pocket in her gown. "Thank you for mentioning Lady Dunsworth. I nearly forgot. It arrived a few days ago."

Leaning over to take the envelope from her mother, Rachel gave a tentative grin when she recognized the writing. "Did you have to pay for its delivery?"

"Of course not. A footman delivered it," Violet replied.

Rachel huffed. "Xenobia was always a bit of a skinflint. I think her marriage to Dunsworth only made her more so," she explained as she slid her thumb beneath the red wax seal.

Violet sobered at the mention of Lord Dunsworth. "Apparently they were very good friends," she murmured.

"Oh, the very best," Rachel replied as she unfolded the letter, "but he was not much of a husband."

Inhaling sharply, Violet regarded her daughter with shock. "She told you of his infidelities?"

Rachel lifted her gaze to her mother's and then furrowed a brow. "Was he a client of yours, Mother?"

Shaking her head, Violet said, "No. I would not have... *entertained* him," she murmured. "But he had his favorites here, I will admit."

Not surprised at hearing the admission, Rachel sighed. "Did he know you were my mother?"

"Of course not. No one here even knows I have a daughter," Violet assured her. "And for the time being, we should ensure that remains the case. So as to not spoil your come-out."

Nodding, Rachel said, "Understood," before she scoffed. "If not your daughter...?"

Violet considered how they could keep the secret. "My... bookkeeper? I suggest it only because I could really use some help with the ledgers. I had a clerk who was supposed to be handling the business funds, but I discovered he was cheating me—"

"Embezzling from you?" Rachel asked in alarm.

"Indeed. He's been arrested. Apparently, The Queen of Hearts wasn't the only business he stole funds from, so it's likely he'll be transported after the trial."

"How much, Mother?"

Violet blinked. "How much, what?"

"Money! How much did he steal from you?"

Her shoulders sagging when she hesitated to respond, Violet finally whispered, "About ten-thousand pounds."

Rachel's mouth dropped open, and she struggled to take her next breath. "Have they recovered any of it?"

"My banker has been working with... well, with his banker, which is rather fortunate since they seem to be related to one another somehow, and I may see a thousand pounds before the year is out," she said as lightly as she could. When she saw how Rachel looked as if she might be about to cry, though, Violet leaned forward and added, "You needn't worry for me, darling." A wan grin appeared. "'Twas maybe a month's profits."

"Maybe?"

Violet sat very still a moment before she said, "You see, this is why I need someone I can trust to keep the books."

Rachel blinked. "Well, I am good with my numbers," she admitted. "And it will give me something to do until the entertainments start this spring."

"I'll pay you, of course," Violet replied. "I don't ever wish to be cheated again by some clerk out to line his pockets with my income. My girls' income."

Tiredness seemed to overwhelm Rachel just then, apparent in the way she seemed to have trouble remaining upright in her chair. Her ramrod-straight back no longer seemed able to remain so. "Apologies, Mother, but I think I am in need of sleep."

"Of course you are," Violet replied, noting the dark circles beneath her daughter's eyes. She couldn't help but feel as if Rachel was disappointed with her, and that attributed to her weariness. "I'll take my leave and have my lady's maid help you with your buttons—"

"I can see to them myself," Rachel insisted, her gaze briefly darting to Xenobia's letter. At some point, she would read it, but not until she was alone.

Wincing, Violet allowed an audible sigh. "You needn't. I've a trusted woman lined up to be your lady's maid. She's been employed here at The Queen for several years and could use a new position."

Rachel gave a start, realizing her words had sounded as if they were a rebuke. "I apologize. I didn't mean to sound ungrateful," she said in a quiet voice. "I am grateful. For everything."

"But you are overtired," Violet whispered, relieved to hear her daughter's words. "Get some sleep and do come down to the dining room for something to eat when you're ready. Cook is making an excellent dinner this evening."

Rachel nodded and struggled to stand. "Do I need to... sneak about when I'm outside this room?"

Violet's eyes widened, as if the query was offensive. "Of

course not! This floor is off-limits to patrons. There's only the one set of stairs, and those lead down to the parlor and a dining room on the ground floor. And the private entrance from Piccadilly Street, of course," she explained. "You could live an entire life in this building unaware there is a gaming hell facing Stafford Street," she added proudly.

Nodding her understanding, Rachel moved to the bed and settled on it, sighing as the soft mattress gave way. A moment later, and she was sound asleep.

Allowing a grin, Violet leaned over her daughter and kissed her forehead. "Sleep well."

She made her way to her own bedchamber, knowing it was past time she don her evening disguise as The Queen of Hearts. Two men were due to arrive for a meeting, and she had no intention of allowing them to see her as anything other than The Queen.

CHAPTER 6
AN ARRANGEMENT TO MEET
IS MADE

eanwhile, at Tattersalls'

"Who?" Randolph asked as his best friend's wife talked of a woman she'd had tea with earlier that afternoon.

Outside the stables, an auction was about to start. He had clients in the crowd to whom he had made recommendations. Should they end up the owners of the mares he had raised and trained and then been charged with selling, he stood to earn a good deal of blunt from the commission.

"Lady Dunsworth. She's Baron Dunsworth's widow," Julia Comber explained. "And one of my dearest cousins. Would you be a darling and go meet her?"

Randolph finished brushing the Cleveland Bay mare that stood before him just as Alistair Comber entered the stables. "Ah, my sweet. What brings you here?" the second-son-of-an-earl asked as he stopped to give his wife a peck on the side of her head. His gaze changed to one of worry. "Are you all right?" he asked as one of his hands moved to her middle.

Julia gave him a brilliant grin. "I am, and so is the babe," she assured him. "But I am on a mission to seek Sir Randolph's help."

"Help?" Alistair repeated, giving her and his friend a dubious glance. "What are you about, my sweet?"

"Lady Dunsworth's filly," she replied. "She's a timid thing, and apparently Xenobia has been unable to find someone to break her. Why, if Sir Randolph was successful, she'd be forever in his debt."

Intrigued, Randolph moved the mare into her stall and regarded Julia with a furrowed brow. Most of the horses he raised in his father's London-based stables were temperamental colts, work horses that would eventually pull all manner of equipage. To train a filly from a young age, perhaps for riding, would be a welcome change.

"It will be such a pleasant surprise for Lady Dunsworth," Julia gushed. "To learn there is someone who might help her in this situation. Of course, her late husband would have seen to such things if he were still alive," she added, apparently to make sure he understood the baroness was a widow. "I always felt a bit sorry for her whilst they were together. He was her very best friend—"

"Best friend?" Randolph interrupted. "Why ever would you pity her for that?"

Julia's eyes widened and her mouth clamped shut. Her head nodded, though, as if she was sharing a secret. "There was no... *passion* in their marriage. Just friendship, I think. Which is probably why she never bore him a child. The barony went to his cousin, which is just as well."

Curiosity had Randolph listening more intently. He had been married to a dear friend. Barbara had known he was a bastard before they wed, and yet she had happily accepted his suit. Welcomed him into her bed—insisted he remain there for the entire night, sometimes—and then was giving birth to their son when it all went so terribly wrong.

He had buried her three days later, and he hadn't thought of bedding another woman since. Thank the gods his father had offered his nursery. Besides the assurance his son was receiving the best of care with Mrs. Foster, his son had a playmate in the form of an uncle who was only a year older.

When would he have had the time to consider female companionship?

When he wasn't minding horses or paying calls at his father's townhouse to spend time with his son, he was answering to the head of the Foreign Office.

Although it had been some time since he had been sent on a mission in another country—the Foreign Office couldn't always afford the costs of travel for their agents—he was on an assignment that occupied him most nights after London's gaming hells opened.

"Well, it is unfortunate her husband died," was all he could say when reason returned and he was able to think clearly. "She lost both a husband and her best friend."

Julia dipped her head, her gaze dropping to note his large fists. "Indeed," she replied before lifting her eyes to meet his. "I know it's probably not appropriate for you to pay a call on her at Bradley House, but would you consider doing so? Mourning has kept her home for over a year, and although she could have enjoyed a bit more freedom these past few months, she hasn't taken advantage. She's practically a hermit."

For just a moment, Randolph wondered if Lady Comber was attempting to play matchmaker. She was telling him things about Lady Dunsworth that had nothing to do with her timid filly. But then he held his tongue when she waved a hand and asked if he might be able to see to the baroness' filly later that evening.

"Tonight?" he countered in surprise.

"Why, yes," Julia replied, her voice having softened to nearly a whisper. "From what Alistair has said, I know you are far too busy to meet with her during the day. Bradley House isn't far from Reading House at all. It's in the same street, in fact. Would you be available at nine o'clock perhaps?"

The time had Randolph furrowing a brow, although the suggestion was a relief since his afternoon would be spent at Tattersalls'. Then there would be dinner with his father, Randall Roderick, Marquess of Reading, and the man's marchioness, Constance. If their townhouse was just up the street from Bradley House, he decided he could make the appointment.

Besides, his other position didn't require he attend a gaming hell on this night. His marks weren't known to gamble on

Wednesday evenings, instead choosing to attend the assemblies at Almack's when they were open. If the young ladies who accepted dances from them had any idea of their true reason for being in London, Randolph was sure they would faint.

He did have an appointment at one of the hells, though. With any luck, his meeting with the proprietress of The Queen of Hearts and the investigator hired by the Bank of England would be quick, and he could be on his way to dinner with his father.

"I will pay a call on her at nine o'clock," he said then, giving Julia a bow before he headed to another stall.

"This will be such a great relief for her," Julia replied. "I will send her a note and let her know to expect you."

Her husband, Alistair, returned to her side whilst leading a large draft horse. "Are you dabbling in matchmaking?" he asked in a whisper.

Julia's eyes widened before she turned to be sure Randolph was out of earshot. "My darling, I don't *dabble* in anything," she replied with a mischievous grin.

CHAPTER 7
A MISSIVE MOST WELCOME

An hour later, at The Queen of Hearts

Rachel awoke with a start and held her breath, her heart hammering in her chest. The bed didn't seem to move, nor did she hear conversations through the walls.

I'm no longer on a ship, she thought with relief as she remembered where she was. She looked about for a clock, finally focusing on the one on the fireplace mantel. Giving a start, she sat up.

Five o'clock at night?

She hadn't meant to sleep so late, but once she had settled onto the comfortable bed for a nap—probably the most comfortable on which she had ever slept—she was overcome with tiredness.

The series of vivid dreams, no doubt amplified by her travels that morning, had her remembering the parade of people she had passed while on her way to The Queen of Hearts. Although she was sure she could have found her way without the burly chaperone, she had been glad of his company when they departed the ship. His imposing size had prevented her from being crushed by the crowd of people on the docks—passengers, dockworkers, drivers and pickpockets—and saved her from having to use the point of her parasol to poke a rather insistent costermonger who attempted to sell her a shrunken orange.

At least, she'd thought it was an orange.

The incident reminded her she was once again in the largest city in the world. The protection she'd been afforded while attending the finishing school in Zurich, a much smaller city and far different from London, was long gone. If she was to have a come-out this Season, she knew she would have to prepare for the possibilities of what—and whom—she might face.

Although there were no candle lamps or gaslights lit, her bedchamber wasn't yet dark. The sound of paper rustling with her movements reminded her there was a letter from Xenobia she hadn't yet read.

Finding light turned out to be easy—her mother had apparently had the building plumbed for gas, for a simple push of a button had the chandelier above coming to life with a circle of flames. She admired the trick for a moment before turning her attention to the crumpled parchment.

My Dearest Rachel,

I am in receipt of your most welcome letter and cannot wait for your arrival in London. I do hope your travels are not a trial but rather an opportunity to see the places we heard about whilst studying our geography. Alas, I have not yet made it to the Continent but someday hope to visit Italy.

My mourning period is coming to an end, and I have had quite enough of wearing black and gray. I will even begin hosting callers soon.

I have invited my cousin and several ladies to join me for tea the week before Christmas. I also intend to decorate Bradley House with as many red and white flowers as the hot house is able to deliver. With Dunsworth's death coming at such an awful time last year, I did not have a happy Christmas.

This year I shall, and learning of your imminent arrival makes it all the more happy.

I should like very much for us to renew the friendship we had whilst at school. Will you favor me with a call at Bradley House? Or may I pay a call on you at the address you provided? I shall be

*very curious as to where you are staying as you finally prepare for
your first Season.*

Lifting her attention from the letter, Rachel thought immediately to dissuade Xenobia from coming to see her, but then
she remembered her mother's comment about the residence.
With its private entrance from Piccadilly Street, there was no
way to know that it was part of The Queen of Hearts. Perhaps
she could host callers in the parlor on the ground floor.

She turned her gaze back on the parchment.

*Should you need a sponsor for your come-out, I am up for the
challenge. As a young matron and widow, I am perfect for the
position. (You know I will turn the other way should some dashing
young man decide to kiss you.)(Unless you want me to beat him
with my fan and warn him off, which I can also do.)*

Rachel grinned as she read this last bit, rather glad Xenobia
still had her sense of humor.

*I look forward to your return to London and to your favourable
reply.*
   Sincerely,
   Lady X

Grinning at seeing Xenobia's simple signature, Rachel
refolded the letter. She glanced about the room, wondering if
there might be an *escritoire* or a desk with paper, but her search
proved fruitless. Surely there would be some in the parlor.

About to take her leave of the bedchamber, she caught sight
of her reflection in the cheval mirror, heard her stomach growl
in complaint, and then once again noticed the time.

The letter would have to wait. She needed to dress for
dinner.

CHAPTER 8
A MISSIVE MOST CURIOUS

*M*eanwhile, *at Bradley House*

Xenobia finished a Christmas greeting to her late husband's mother and regarded the parchment with a critical eye. She never knew what to write to Agnes Dunsworth. The dowager baroness still lived on the barony's estate in Kent, and although she had written to invite Xenobia to join her there on a permanent basis—*in the event you find Town too much to bear*—Xenobia knew better than to accept the invitation.

No amount of desperation would have her moving to a country estate in Kent, no matter how beautiful or how vast. She didn't wish to feel more alone than she already did.

Chesterfield appeared on the threshold of her salon the very moment she finished folding the letter. "This was just delivered by a footman," he said as he held out a silver salver.

The white note emblazoned with only her first name had Xenobia frowning—until she recognized Julia's handwriting. "Very good, Chesterfield. And this one is ready to post," she added as she finished addressing her letter. She placed it on the salver and helped herself to Julia's missive, unfolding the note as if it might contain an explosive device.

Before the butler could take his leave, she asked, "Have the Christmas flowers arrived yet?"

The butler nodded. "They have, my lady. However..." He paused and allowed a pained expression.

"What is it?"

"There are far more of them than there is room in the parlor," he murmured quietly.

Xenobia considered how she had placed the order with the hot house in Chiswick. *Enough red and white flowers to fill a barrel.*

Goodness. How large was their barrel?

"I'll come down and arrange them in a moment," she replied. "In the meantime, gather up every available vase from around the house, and have a footman go up to the attic. See if he can't find the table that used to be in the hall near the base of the stairs."

She had always been curious as to why her father had ordered all the furnishings in the hall be removed at some point before his death. Although he didn't live long enough to explain it to her, her mother had simply waved a hand and insisted it was nothing. Besides, she and her mother didn't live at Bradley House, but rather in a dowager cottage on the grounds of the Pendleton estate. Xenobia had moved into Bradley House upon her marriage to James Dunsworth after learning she had inherited it from the army captain.

"Yes, my lady," Chesterfield replied before he quickly took his leave.

Smiling at the thought of fresh flowers filling Bradley House, Xenobia turned her attention to Julia's note.

My dearest Cousin Xenobia,

It has taken my very best behavior and all my cleverness, but I have managed to secure an appointment for you to meet with him at nine o'clock. I know it is a terrible time, but he will pay a call on you, so there is no need for you to go out.

Xenobia glanced up.

He? Him? Who?

She scanned the note again for a name and found none. Reading the rest of the missive was of no help, either.

Please do not dismiss him out of hand. I just have this incredible sense of wonder that you two might enjoy one another's company. Of course, that may be because the baby has spent the entire morning kicking me senseless. I do hope this one is a boy, or I will be doomed to have a hoyden. The horrors!

    Do let me know how it goes.

    Julia

Xenobia dropped the note on her *escritoire* as if it were on fire.

Nine o'clock.

Well, she was usually awake well before then, but not always dressed for the day. She would make an exception, of course, and have her lady's maid do her hair in something more appealing than a top knot or a bun at the back of her head. She could wear the poppy-colored gown and hope that it would account for how red her face would be when the mysterious man arrived.

I don't know his name. We've probably never even been introduced, she thought as a bit of panic swept through her.

Then she remembered what Julia had said about Jupiter. About Tattersall's and the races.

She hurried down to the library and scanned the foiled titles of her late father's collection of books. When she found one with the word 'horse' in the title, she pulled it from the shelf. *A Treatise on the Breeding of Thoroughbred Horses* was printed on the title page.

Finding no other books about horses, she reluctantly placed this one in the crook of her arm and then stepped into the ground floor salon. The scents of hot house flowers assaulted her as she paused on the threshold, stunned to discover pasteboard boxes of flowers stacked about the room.

"Oh, dear," she murmured. A watering can and a number of vases were set up on the low table, and she quickly assembled several arrangements, passing them off to a housemaid and Smith, a footman, for placement in all the public rooms.

She still had several boxes of flowers remaining when the last of the vases was filled. "Chesterfield, I need the punch bowl," she announced when the servant appeared on the threshold.

"Right away, my lady. Colburn has just informed me that there are no tables in the attic," he said, referring to the other footman. "But he says that the table that used to be in the hall is now in the study. As are the caryatids that used to be in the hall between the doorways."

Xenobia blinked. She tried to recall ever noticing a round table in there—she was only ever in the study to pay bills—when Chesterfield added, "It's more of a... gaming table, my lady."

"Is it round?"

His eyes darting sideways, Chesterfield finally gave a nod. "Somewhat. The top is covered in felt, my lady. For playing cards."

"Well, it will have to do until I can have a proper one installed," Xenobia replied, knowing she would probably never spend the money on such a table. If the gaming table fit in the space, it would have to do. "Please see to its placement in the hall. We'll put the punchbowl on it, and given the number of roses, no one will be the wiser."

Although he seemed reluctant, Chesterfield finally gave a nod and took his leave.

With nothing to do until the punchbowl was delivered, Xenobia made her way to the study. She immediately found the four caryatids—they had been in the study as long as she could remember—lined up on one of the short walls behind a leather sofa.

The gaming table was at the opposite end of the room. Featuring a huge tripod base of carved mahogany, the round surface was covered in a deep red felt. Although it was a bit scuffed, the fabric wasn't torn, and the wood's smooth finish was a testament to its frequent cleaning.

Bending down, Xenobia studied the edges of the table, her

fingertips traveling over the curious ornate carvings and inlaid wood patterns. From their shape, she was sure they had some purpose other than decoration. She was about to sit in one of the accompanying chairs to gain a better vantage when two footmen arrived to move the table.

She took her leave so that the servants had room to work and then resumed her flower arranging in the salon.

By the time she had the punchbowl filled with white roses, it looked like a snowball when Smith placed it on the red felt-topped table.

"Vera appropriate, my lady," the housekeeper remarked when she paused on her way between rooms.

"Thank you, Barclay. These flowers may have to do for decorations this year. I haven't yet arranged for any evergreens for Christmas Eve. I wonder if it's too late?" She hadn't bothered with any Christmas celebrations the year before given her husband's death.

"I can find out for you on the morrow, my lady. Cook and I will be going to market. If I find a tree cutter, I'll make the arrangements. We can have the footmen see to bringing them into the house the morning of Christmas Eve."

"Very good," Xenobia replied, taking a deep breath when she realized the floral scents had already begun to fill the hall. "I love roses," she murmured, the familiar odor reminding her of her youth. Of when her mother would receive bouquets from men who admired her.

Once Xenobia had confirmed all the flower boxes were empty, she retrieved the book on horse breeding and made her way to the upstairs parlor. She rang for tea and settled in for another late afternoon of reading.

When dinner was served, Xenobia took it in the parlor, looking up from the pages only to take a bite of food. By the time Colburn retrieved the dishes and a maid had delivered tea, she had read over half the book, and the floral scents from no less than three vases filled with red roses had permeated the room.

If she had any intention of raising horses suitable for the

Derby or one of the other horse races run under the auspices of The Jockey Club, she was fairly sure she knew what she was looking for when it came to horseflesh.

As for riding a horse, she hadn't done so since she was a child. She was fairly sure she owned a riding habit, but it was no doubt long out of fashion. Perhaps she would see to a new one and buy a horse. An Irish walker or a Welsh pony. Something gentle that wouldn't toss her off if it was frightened by another animal.

As to racing her own horse in such a spectacle as the Derby, she found she wasn't the least bit interested.

Despite knowing of several aristocrat's wives who owned stables of racing horses—the Marquess of Reading's wife, Constance, came to mind—the horse racing circuit was most definitely a man's world.

Xenobia was thinking of this and more when she heard her butler make an odd comment from somewhere downstairs. Daring a glance at the mantel clock, she furrowed a brow and then murmured, "Damnation," when she noted the time.

It was exactly nine o'clock.

At night.

CHAPTER 9
EXPLORATION AND EAVESDROPPING

early three hours earlier, at The Queen of Hearts
Opening one of her trunks, Rachel rifled through the fine gowns her maid in Zurich had packed on her behalf. Knowing her father had paid for their creation—rather than her mother—had her regarding them in a new light.

For years, she had thought her father as simply one of a string of her mother's protectors. Men who contracted for her services as a mistress for some period of time and then moved on to another.

That she had been given a surname different from her mother's was not so unusual—to this day, she wasn't sure her mother's real name was Violet Higgins.

She pulled one of the darker dinner gowns from the trunk and shook it out, relieved the folds in the fabric hadn't creased too much. As she changed into it, her thoughts went back to her earlier conversation with her mother. Went back to the words they had exchanged about her father.

I must have sounded like an ungrateful brat, she thought with some concern. She remembered her time as a young girl. A time when she still lived with her mother in a fine townhouse in Green Street.

Her mother had frequently spoken of her father. Told her

how they had met—at the theatre—and how handsome he was. So young and quite popular. He could drive four horses one-handed and ride a Thoroughbred like no other.

A twinge in her chest had her blinking back a tear when she remembered the gift she had received from him when she was but five. A Welsh pony. Gray with white stockings and the most gentle disposition. She had named him Richard because her mother frequently spoke of a Richard. She knew now why she did so, but at the time, Rachel had had no knowledge she was a twin.

Along with the pony, her father gave her a white pasteboard box containing her first riding habit. Wrapped in a layer of tissue, the hunter green wool coat trimmed in black and featuring black frog closures down the front had fit her perfectly, as had the black riding boots included in the box.

She remembered hugging the man. Remembered being lifted into his arms and settling her head onto his shoulders. Remembered the scent of his cologne and the shaving cream his valet had used that morning. Remembered his comment about what a lovely young lady she was turning out to be.

She had liked him. She certainly hadn't feared him, for he had been familiar to her for as long as she could remember. She would wrap her arms around his cravat-clad neck and hug him. Despite her mother's warning that she would crush the silk, he would silence her protests with the wave of his free hand and share secrets with her in his hoarse whisper.

"You're my favorite daughter," he would say.

Grinning with delight, she would hug him again and then kiss his cheek, her bowed lips making a quiet smacking sound. Then she would giggle, and he would laugh, a hearty, guttural laugh as he tightened his hold on her.

Sometimes, she fell asleep as he held her. She felt that safe in his arms.

Rachel shook her head, at first unaware tears were streaming down her face. She quickly dropped the gown onto the open trunk and stepped back lest her tears stain the watered silk.

Pulling a hanky from her pocket, she quickly wiped away the tears and took a deep breath. Faith! She hadn't given her father more than a single thought in all the years she'd been in Zurich.

She had thought of that pony, though, for Richard had been the reason she wanted to remain in London when her mother told her she'd be taking her to the Continent for school.

She had bawled when they had boarded the ship bound for LeHavre. All because she couldn't take the pony with them.

What had happened to Richard?

How long did ponies live?

Determined to discover the pony's fate, Rachel donned the dark blue dinner gown and saw to repinning her hair into a simple bun atop her head. A quick glance in the dressing table mirror had her wincing, though. She took the time to leave some dark waves loose at her temples and redid the style into something more appropriate for dinner.

Tucking her feet into a pair of slippers, she practiced a curtsy in front of the mirror before making her way out of the bedchamber.

*A*s her mother had implied, the corridor leading to the back stairs was empty. On her way down the carpeted steps, a housemaid passed her going up, her arms laden with bed linens.

"Good evening, my lady," the maid said with a warm smile. "I'm Baker, but you can call me Gem. I was just about to knock on your door to offer assistance."

"Oh, that's rather kind of you," Rachel replied. She hesitated. "Might you take a look at my buttons? I'm not sure I got them all," she said as she turned her back to the maid.

"There's one that needs fastening," Gem said. "Let me put these down here in this bedchamber…" she opened a nearby door and hurried to place her burden in the middle of a bed. Rachel followed her, her gaze taking in the elegantly appointed room.

"Does anyone use this chamber?" Rachel asked.

"Oh, not for a long time," Gem replied as she stepped behind Rachel and fastened the button. "The Queen used to let rooms here, but she prefers the peace and quiet of having no tenants," she explained.

Rachel nodded her understanding. "I shall endeavor to be very quiet," she whispered.

"I didn't mind the hub-bub," Gem said on a sigh. "I used to cook for all them. Breakfast and dinner," she said as she brushed a piece of lint from Rachel's shoulder.

"How many lived here?" Rachel asked.

Gem considered the query a moment. "I'm not sure, but with the servants and all, I was makin' meals for twenty or thirty every day."

Rachel's eyes widened. "So you must be the cook for the gaming establishment now?"

Giving her head a quick shake, Gem said, "I would have loved to continue, but The Queen finally got her Frenchie, so I just assist in the kitchens when he asks for help and pretend to be a maid when he doesn't."

"It sounds as if you miss your old position," Rachel murmured.

"Oh, I do. But I like working for The Queen, so I do what I must." She dipped a curtsy. "Which means I best get back to it, my lady."

"Rachel," she said as she curtsied.

"Vera good to meet you, my lady." The maid returned to the bedchamber to collect the stack of linens as Rachel resumed her walk down the corridor.

She wondered how many servants worked for her mother. From the number of doors along the corridor where her bedchamber was located, she thought there were at least six bedchambers. Perhaps the servants quarters on the floor above numbered eight or ten. The next floor down seemed to have only four doors along the corridor, although several were open.

Instead of continuing her descent, Rachel headed down the hall toward the first open door. She peeked in to discover a spacious parlor. A fire was set in the fireplace, and a housemaid was busy dusting. Before the servant could spot her, Rachel ducked out and went to the next open door.

Through the opening, she determined the room was a library, but without going all the way in, she couldn't discern the size of its collections. On the opposite side of the corridor, she heard voices coming from the only other open door. She paused and almost hurried to the stairs, but her mother's voice was interrupted by a male voice, and she paused.

"I assure you, my lady, the investigation is nearly complete."

"You said that the last time you were here," her mother replied, exasperation evident in her voice.

"Two days ago, yes—"

"I hardly think it's fair that you're removing these notes without providing me reimbursement," Violet complained.

"You will be compensated, I assure you." The male voice was different from the first one she had overheard, and Rachel furrowed a brow.

Just how many men were with her mother?

She angled her head toward the opening, realizing the room must have been a study or an office of some sort. Two gentlemen were in chairs, their backs to the door. She dared not lean too far over, or she knew her mother would see her from where she sat behind a desk.

How odd, Rachel thought. Her mother had positioned a rather large mahogany desk across the corner of the room rather than along one of the walls. From where she sat, her mother had a clear view of the door while her callers did not.

Rachel could imagine how, despite the large desk, her mother could appear imposing whilst garbed in her bright red Queen of Hearts costume and huge white wig.

"I've heard that before," Violet said with a huff. "Are we to have someone on the floor tonight?"

"Not tonight, my lady," the first man said. "However, I will be at the Jack of Spades on the morrow. If our utterers are still in London, as I expect they are, they will no doubt end their evening there in the billiards parlor."

"Billiards?" Violet repeated.

"Mr. O'Laughlin has found it's not as lucrative as his other offerings, but it pays more than using the space for a smoking room."

Utterers?

Rachel blinked. She recognized the term. Anyone who had heard of fake money—counterfeit notes—knew utterers were those that passed the bills. The ones who may or may not have known they were using counterfeit money to purchase goods or services.

Having come from Europe's banking capital, she was well aware of what the banks did to those found in possession of counterfeit notes.

Had these men determined her mother was an utterer?

A jolt of fear shot down her spine. Utterers were arrested. Tried. Transported. Some even put to death. At least, that had been the way of it back when she lived in London as a young girl.

Worried for her mother, Rachel was about to enter the office when she heard the sounds of the men rising from their chairs.

"We appreciate your cooperation, Mrs. Higgins. Please be assured you will not suffer the consequences of these men's actions."

"You will not be arrested for what they have done at your business," the first man added by way of a clarification. His voice was pleasant. Familiar. Comforting in a way that had Rachel deciding she didn't need to fear for her mother.

"I had better not," Violet replied, obviously indignant. "It's enough that I'm still dealing with the unfortunate aftermath of Mr. Traynor's misdeed." She seemed to calm down, though, for her next words were entirely at odds with her rebuke. "Now, Cook has made an especially fine dinner for tonight's patrons. Will you be joining us in the dining room, gentlemen?"

Rachel blinked before she scoffed. Her mother was obviously a forgiving woman if she could offer her callers hospitality after *that* particular conversation.

"I appreciate the offer, my lady, but I must depart. I have a dinner engagement."

That had been said by the man who Rachel decided was the younger one. His manner of speech was refined, as if he were to the manor born. She couldn't miss his use of "my lady" when he addressed Violet, though, as if he afforded all women the honorific.

The other, obviously older gentleman said, "Much obliged. Missed luncheon, and I'm on duty here tonight to watch over the faro tables."

His manner of speech wasn't nearly as refined—more like a tradesman. *An investigator*, Rachel thought. Probably a Bow Street Runner, if they still had such a thing in London.

Realizing she had to make it back to the stairs before the men left the office, Rachel hurried to the end of the corridor and grabbed the stair rail. From the way their voices—and her mother's—suddenly increased in volume, she knew they were already out of the office. If they were looking in her direction, they would have already spotted her. If not... She leaned over the bannister and glanced down.

Deciding she wouldn't make it over the stair railing—she might have as a child if she had sat upon it and glided down the polished wood—she merely acted as if she had just come down the last flight of stairs and was about to descend the next.

She caught herself before she could say, "Mother?" These men probably didn't know Violet Higgins had a daughter, and Rachel remembered their earlier conversation. Violet Higgins didn't want anyone in London to know her true identity, nor did she think it a good idea that anyone knew she had a daughter.

Rachel dipped a curtsy. "My lady," she said.

"Ah, I do hope you had a good nap. These gentlemen are just about to take their leave," Violet replied. "I'm going to escort Mr. Wilson to the dining room. Mr. Roderick would probably prefer leaving through the private entrance?" she half-asked as she turned her attention to the younger man on whose arm hers rested.

"I would. Much obliged," the taller, younger man said as he gave a nod in Rachel's direction. From the way he regarded her, she had the impression he was attempting to place where he might have seen her before. He looked familiar, but she was sure she hadn't seen him before.

Rachel blinked and then remembered her mother's words from earlier. The private entrance led to Piccadilly Street. "I can see to it," she offered. At least she hoped she could. Although she had probably come in that way, she hadn't yet had a tour of the residence to know its floor plan.

Violet gave her a brilliant smile as she placed a hand on the older man's arm. His gray topcoat wasn't of the latest fashion—not like the younger man's—and his paunch suggested he enjoyed his food and drink.

For a moment, Rachel wondered if the man was one of her mother's clients, but the thought was so repulsive, she visibly winced.

The two headed down the stairs, already engaged in quiet conversation, while Rachel regarded the man she was to lead to the private entrance. His dark hair was longer than what she'd seen on the men she had passed that morning, but his eyes were kind and his clothes fit him to perfection. "This way," she said as she motioned to the steps.

"Of course," he replied as he offered an arm. "I've not seen you here before," he remarked as they made their way down the steps.

"That's because I haven't been here before," Rachel replied, realizing he was angling for an introduction.

She wasn't about to provide him with one.

"So, you're new here?"

Rachel felt a bit of panic. Did he think she was one of the doxies? Or did he think she was an employee?

The last thought had her deciding she could at least pretend to be. "I am."

"The Queen runs a tight ship. She's to be commended."

The relief Rachel felt just then at hearing his comment had

her relaxing, especially after the discussion about the embez-zlement.

"More so than The Jack of Spades?" Rachel countered, remembering his mention of it when he was speaking with her mother.

"Frank O'Laughlin is as conscientious as The Queen," he replied. "Nothing for the Crown to be concerned with. Crocky's, not so much."

"Crocky's?" Rachel repeated. *And what did the Crown have to do with gaming hells?*

"Crockford's," he quickly amended.

"Ah, I shall be certain never to darken their door," she said as they reached the bottom of the stairs. She had no idea what Crockford's was, but she was sure she would learn soon enough.

Her mother and the man she was escorting had already disappeared behind a door at the end of the ground floor corridor—the dining room, no doubt—so Rachel hesitated before she determined which way to turn.

"Do you gamble?" the young man asked, apparently surprised by her response.

"Of course not," she replied as she headed for the vestibule. The sight of sidelights and a transom above the door had her feeling relief. "Here you are. That's Picadilly Street," she said as she opened the door for him.

The young man held his top hat between his two gloved hands and gave her a slight bow. "Thank you, Miss...?"

"Rachel," she said as she curtsied. "Good day, sir."

Apparently aware he was being dismissed, the man gave her another nod and took his leave. From the sidelight next to the door, Rachel watched as he waved to someone he obviously recognized, and in a moment, a fine town coach pulled up to the curb, and he disappeared inside.

A coach-and-four.

Not a hackney.

Stepping away from the sidelight lest she be seen by the young man, Rachel made her way through the vestibule and beyond a hall until the scents of food reminded her she hadn't eaten all day.

Her last thought before going through the door was of the gold crest that had been on the coach-and-four.

Why did it seem familiar?

CHAPTER 10
A DINNER WITH A FATHER
AND STEPMOTHER

Seven o'clock, at Reading House in Curzon Street

Constance Fitzwilliam Roderick, Marchioness of Reading, watched as her maid added another curl to an already elaborate hairstyle. "Really, Simmons. There will only be three of us for dinner this evening. Randall and I aren't even planning to leave the house afterwards."

Simmons paused, a hairpin held between two fingers as she regarded her mistress in the dressing table mirror. "Three?" she repeated, apparently unaware they were to host Randall's oldest son for dinner.

"Randolph will be joining us. In fact, I expect he might be here by now," Constance replied, hoping her lady's maid might be finished. "He's probably in the nursery, tossing his son and his brother about."

Simmons' reflection in the dressing table mirror showed her widened eyes. "Tossing?" she repeated.

Constance couldn't help but grin. "He claims his father did it with him when he was a child, and I have paid witness to Reading doing it with Robert when he doesn't know I'm watching," she explained. "As much as it frightens me to see my youngest son thrown into the air, his giggles are so delightful. Reading seems to enjoy it as much as Robert does," she claimed.

"He probably did it with Raymond as well," she added, referring to their six-year-old son.

Simmons had never had children of her own, but she probably wouldn't have allowed baby tossing. "I believe I might have heard a commotion in the nursery earlier, my lady. I've just one more pin to place." The hairpin was quickly inserted into the last curl and Simmons stepped back. "Will there be anything else, my lady?"

Constance rose from the small chair and regarded Simmons for a moment. The maid had been her companion for several years before her marriage to Randall Roderick. Back when she still lived at Fair Downs in Sussex. Despite living in London and near Reading for all the years since, Simmons still hadn't adapted to their new lives. "Not tonight. In fact, I expect I won't have need of you after dinner."

At least, she hoped not. With any luck, her husband would be undoing the fastenings on her scarlet dinner gown. He was finally over a head cold, and she had every intention of spending the night in his bedchamber.

Simmons' eyes widened. "Very good, my lady." She dipped a curtsy and moved to the door. When she opened it, she let out a squeak.

"Ah, Simmons, I didn't mean to startle you," Randall Roderick, Marquess of Reading, said as he glanced beyond the lady's maid. "My oldest son and I have worn ourselves out playing with the boys, and I've come to collect my lovely wife."

Simmons dipped a curtsy and hurried out the door as Constance afforded her husband a brilliant smile. "I am so happy you are feeling better," she said as she allowed him to kiss the back of her hand and then her lips.

"As am I. Did you dismiss her for the night?"

Constance eyed him through lowered lashes. "Should I have?" His look of disappointment had her smile returning. "I did, of course. If you think I would spend another night alone in bed—"

The rest of her comment was cut off when Randall kissed

her again. "I nearly came to your bed last night," he whispered. "I wanted you..."

The rest of his comment was cut off when Giles, the butler, appeared outside the marchioness' door and cleared his throat.

"What is it?" Randall asked, struggling to keep annoyance from sounding in his voice.

"Sir Randolph has finally taken his leave of the nursery. I put him in the downstairs parlor, sir."

Constance and Randall exchanged quick glances. "This must be a night to celebrate," he murmured, one of his bushy eyebrows lifting in delight. "I think he was in there for nearly an hour. His son is going to grow up thinking he's a bird."

"And our youngest won't?" she teased, giggling when she saw how he reacted.

"He's grown too heavy to throw up into the air. I'm reduced to spinning him around by his arms until I'm dizzy," he explained. "Children are hard work," he added, sounding as if he was complaining. The expression on his face said he was teasing, though.

"I do hope Randolph did well today," Constance said as she placed a hand on her husband's proffered arm. They made their way down the carpeted stairs.

Her husband did his best to hide his first reaction at hearing her words. Had Constance somehow discovered his oldest illegitimate son's true occupation? There was a reason Randolph had been knighted by the king, and it had nothing to do with training horses.

Then Randall realized she referred to that day's auction at Tattersall's. Two mares that Randolph had raised and trained since their birth were set to be sold. "He would not have come for dinner if he had not," Randall replied, his manner having sobered. "But that doesn't mean you should ask him if he's courting anyone," he warned.

"I wouldn't," Constance replied, feigning shock. "What has *courting* to do with how he did today at the auction?"

Randall ignored her query. "Although I favored his wife, I never thought Barbara was good enough for him."

Constance knew better than to argue. Barbara Hancock had been a perfectly acceptable young lady for Randall's oldest son. The daughter of a tradesman, she had been petite and pretty and didn't seem to mind she was marrying a bastard. He was a knight, after all, so she could style herself a lady.

But after a year of being subtly reminded of his illegitimacy—and his tendency to labor in horse stables—by those who hosted her for tea or the occasional garden party, Barbara's good nature changed. She grew resentful, as if she was feeling trapped by circumstances over which she had no control.

When Barbara died giving birth to their son, Randolph found himself a widower at the ripe old age of two-and-twenty.

Randolph's son, Charles, shared the upstairs nursery with Randall and Constance's son, Robert, Viscount Roderick. The older son, Raymond, Earl of Farringdon, had been breeched two years before, spent a year with a tutor, and was now at Eton.

"I heard that, Father," Randolph said from where he stood just inside the parlor, referring to the marquess' comment about Barbara. "You should know better than to speak poorly of the dead."

Randall feigned regret. "Noted," he murmured as his son bowed and then kissed the back of Constance's hand.

"I'm so glad you could join us this evening," she said, just before she moved to her favorite chair. "Does this mean the mares sold for a fair price?"

"Constance!" Randall scolded.

She gave him a quelling glance. "*You* would have asked if I had not," she countered.

Randolph allowed a brilliant grin. "They did. And for well over the expected price," he said as he moved into the parlor. He waited until both his father and stepmother were seated before he took a chair near the fire.

"Spirited bidding?" Constance guessed.

Randolph angled his head. "Truth be told, I think it was a case of mistaken impressions." He accepted a cup of coffee from a footman and helped himself to a few walnuts from a proffered bowl.

"Oh, now you really must explain," Constance urged. Having declined the offer of coffee, she was able to place a hand on his arm to reinforce her words.

Her stepson grinned. "Alistair Comber's wife came to the stables at Tattersall's while I was brushing one of the mares," he explained. "Comber was there, of course, but she was there to ask a favor of *me*. Apparently the buyer was watching from the door. He saw Lady Comber, dressed all fine like she always is, and he thought she was interested in the nags as a Christmas gift, so he bid high from the start, and the other gentleman who was bidding didn't seem put off by the price, so he upped the bid several times."

Having taken a sip of his coffee, the marquess furrowed his brows. "Lady Comber? What was she about?"

Giles appeared at the threshold and announced dinner.

Relieved he didn't have to answer the query, Randolph set down his coffee and offered an arm to Constance. "Might I have the honor, my lady?"

Constance allowed a grin. "Yes, but if you think for one minute *I'm* not going to ask the same question—"

"Connie," Randall said in a mock scold. "Let the man at least get through the first course," he teased.

Randolph dipped his head in Constance's direction. "She was there to ask if I might consider taking on the training of a filly."

Randall and Constance exchanged quick glances. "Surely not one of her father's horses," Constance commented. Lady Comber's husband, Alistair, saw to the Earl of Mayfield's stables at Harrington House, including the training of the colts.

Giving his head a shake, Randolph said, "One belonging to a Lady Dunsworth." He led Constance to her chair and pulled it out for her. "Are you familiar with her?"

The name had Constance jerking her head to look up at him. "Xenobia Dunsworth?"

He shrugged as he took his seat opposite of hers while his

father sat in the carver. He didn't recall if Julia Comber had mentioned the woman's given name. "Apparently she has a timid filly in need of training. I told Lady Comber I would pay a call on Lady Dunsworth after dinner this evening."

Once again, Constance and Randall exchanged curious glances. "*This* evening?" his father repeated, as a footman poured wine and another delivered the soup course. "I had hoped we might play a game of billiards."

"Lady Comber assured me nine o'clock wouldn't be too late," he replied. "But where exactly might I find Bradley House?"

Randall seemed to count in his head as he regarded the chandelier above the table. "Tenth house east of here, same side of the street," he murmured.

"She has wrought iron balconies on the second and third stories," Constance added. "With flower boxes, although of course they are empty now. And a bright blue front door."

Randolph nodded his understanding as he regarded his soup. "My lady, are you acquainted with Lady Dunsworth?"

Constance finished a sip of wine before saying, "I am, although not well. Since her husband died last year, she hasn't been paying calls for some time. Perhaps that will change now that she's out of mourning."

"An older lady then?" Randolph guessed.

Pausing in the midst of bringing a spoonful of soup to her lips, Constance shook her head. "Not at all. I rather think she's younger than me. Perhaps by five or six years."

Since he had no idea how old his stepmother was—he was terrible at guessing people's ages—Randolph made a mental note to ask his father when they would be alone later that evening. "Do you think her agreeable?"

Constance set down her spoon. "I do." She narrowed her eyes. "Are you... considering courting her?"

Randall let out a guffaw as Randolph displayed a suddenly reddened face. "I am not," he said with a shake of his head. "I am just trying to be sure I am... *prepared* for when I meet with her. I'd like to make a good impression. Perhaps her good opinion will then be shared with others who are in need of a horse trainer," he reasoned.

A grin lighting her face, Constance leaned forward. "I apologize. I could not help myself. She's such a sweet woman. I cannot imagine how the loss of her husband must have affected her. They were such good friends, you see."

Randolph remembered Julia Comber's description of Lady Dunsworth, remembered her making a similar comment. At least Constance corroborated what his friend's wife had said about the woman. He still wondered about her parting comment, though.

Just let yourself in. The footman is only there during the days, and the Dunsworth butler is very old. He probably won't hear your knock.

About to ask about the servant situation at the Dunsworth house, Randolph didn't have to when Constance said, "The baroness really should hire a younger butler. I really don't know how Chesterfield manages all the stairs. He is a hundred years old if he's a day."

Randolph blinked. "Thank you for your insights," he said as he returned his attention to his soup. When his father asked about the auction, Randolph was glad for the change of topic.

The three spent the rest of dinner discussing horses, the stables that one of his three younger half-brothers managed in Reading, and horse racing.

*L*ater that evening...
The third to the last billiard ball careened off the side of the billiards table and into a leather pocket. "You are far too good at this," Randall groused as his son straightened and moved to set up his last shot. They hadn't even been in the billiards room for ten minutes, but it was beginning to look as if Randall might not get a chance to sink a single ball.

"I have been practicing," Randolph said as he leaned over. "And apparently you have not."

Randall set aside his leather-tipped cue stick and crossed his arms. "I have better things to do at night these days."

His shot having sunk the second-to-the-last billiard ball, Randolph regarded his father with a furrowed brow. "A new mistress?" he guessed.

The marquess' eyes widened. "God, no!" he exclaimed. "I'll have you know I am a happily married man." When his son didn't look convinced, he added, "I'm spending my evenings with Connie, of course. And my spare heir and my grandson. I've no desire to spend them with anyone else." There was a pause before he added, "You excluded, of course."

Randolph seemed to finally believe his father's words when he sunk the last ball. "Can you afford her?"

Randall let out a guffaw that had his son straightening in alarm. "Afford her? Why, Connie is the most frugal woman in all of England," he replied. "She'd be sewing her own clothes if I didn't require she use a decent modiste. Even then, she chooses the least expensive fabrics, which I then surreptitiously have to have replaced before the modiste starts any gown for her," he complained. "Your brother and your son would be riding in a perambulator previously used by another's heir if I hadn't insisted on a new one."

Retrieving the billiard balls from the six pockets around the table, Randolph considered his father's description of his marchioness. He had worried that when Randall Roderick finally decided to marry and sire legitimate children, he might end up with a fortune seeker for a wife. Instead, it sounded as if Constance was a skinflint.

"May I ask how old she is?"

Randall narrowed his eyes. "Eight-and-twenty, so, yes, there is more than a decade betwixt us, but she is..." He allowed the sentence to trail off as his face displayed a quizzical expression.

"More mature than you?" Randolph guessed with a grin.

His father pretended offense. "Yes, but only because she lived so long without assistance," Randall replied. "Poor thing saw to a household and stables for years and did so on funds she found hidden around her late father's house in Fair Downs," Randall explained.

"Hidden blunt?"

"She thought her mother had left it for her to find, since her father gambled away all his horse racing winnings, but I later learned from one of the servants that her late cousin, Norwick —David, not Daniel—would go to Fair Downs when he knew she wasn't there and leave coins under the floorboards and at the bottom of containers and vases, under mattresses and inside her favorite books."

Randolph stared at his father. "You said that with such glee, I have to wonder if you are doing the same thing now?" he half-questioned.

His father's eyes drifted up and to the side. "If you could see the delight in Connie's eyes when she finds a five-pound note tucked under our son when she picks him up from his bed, you would do exactly the same thing."

Furrowing a brow, Randolph asked, "What if the nurse discovers it first?"

Randall shrugged. "Unlikely, since Connie is always the first in the nursery in the morning, but if she did, then I have delighted a faithful servant and ensured she will be with us for the next babe," he replied. "Which I think may be on the way."

At that moment, Randolph's opinion of his father went up a notch, and not because another sibling was in his future. Despite the fact that his father had seen to every expense Randolph had incurred since birth, he had thought the marquess a selfish, entitled man. Now he questioned everything he had ever thought about his father. "How did you know she was right for you?" he asked as he arranged the balls on the green felt.

Randall allowed a shrug before he started to respond. He stopped and then said, "I met her in the park whilst on an early morning walk. She was with Simmons, her lady's maid, and..." He remembered her bearing and the intelligence she had shown. How she had captured his interest. Once he learned she raised horses—that she was familiar with horse racing and all that it entailed—he was hopelessly in love.

"And?" Randolph prompted, just before he took the first shot. The billiard balls scattered about the green felt, one of them falling into a corner pocket.

"Exactly how much have you been practicing?" Randall complained as he watched his son line up his next shot.

"Nearly every night at The Jack of Spades, but only because I'm on an... an assignment," he stammered, hesitant with how much he admitted. "At a couple of gaming hells, actually."

Randall furrowed his brows as he considered the hint. "Is one of those The Queen of Hearts, perhaps?"

Randolph paused before preparing for this next shot. "I will only say that I just came from there, and all will be well." He watched as his father visibly relaxed, and a sense of disappointment settled over him. He yearned to ask him more about The Queen of Hearts—the woman, not the business—but his father was regarding him with amusement.

"Foreigners passing counterfeit blunt?" Randall guessed. "Or gaming hells serving smuggled liquor?"

Randolph sunk another ball into a side pocket. "Yes," he replied with a smirk, and then his expression sobered as he missed the next shot.

"About damned time," Randall murmured, positioning himself to finally take a shot. "Thought I'd never get my chance." He leaned over, hit the white ball, and watched with satisfaction as the ball it collided with landed in a side pocket.

"Good shot," Randolph remarked, but sighed when he saw his father's next attempt go off at a bad angle.

"It's nearly nine o'clock," Randall said, his attention on the mantel clock directly across from where he stood. "As I recall, you have an appointment with Lady Dunsworth."

Randolph straightened from his missed shot and allowed a sigh. "I should be off then," he said, his expression showing indecision.

"Son, I just *knew*," Randall stated then, in answer to Randolph's earlier query. "I cannot admit that it was love at first sight, for I believe I was merely *intrigued* with Connie at the start. But I could not imagine finding a better woman to be my wife. My marchioness. The mother of my two youngest sons."

Allowing a nod, Randolph gave a slight bow. "I'll see myself out and discover what I can about this timid filly."

He took his leave of the Curzon Street townhouse and made his way east, counting doors until he reached the tenth one with the blue door.

Following Lady Comber's advice, Randolph opened the door and let himself in.

CHAPTER 11
DINNER WITH THE QUEEN

*M*eanwhile, at *The Queen of Hearts*
Rachel gingerly opened the door to the room she hoped would be the residence's private dining room and stopped short.

Beyond the white paneled door was indeed a dining room, but it was nothing like any she had seen before.

A restaurant, was her first thought as she nearly stepped back in surprise. The room was huge. There were at least twelve round tables dressed in red table linens and set with white china. Most had well-dressed men seated around them, and young women garbed in red satin gowns moved about carrying trays of food and drinks. Another young woman sat at a pianoforté, expertly playing but not singing.

"There you are," Violet said, suddenly appearing at Rachel's elbow. "You must be famished."

"I am," Rachel replied as she nodded.

"I've a table for us in the far corner. We won't be bothered there," Violet said as she indicated a table for two.

Well aware of the stares that followed them as her mother led her to the table, Rachel stiffened. "I was expecting a regular dining room," she whispered.

"Of course you were. And one day I might have one, but until then, this is where we shall take our meals." Violet was about to pull a chair out from the table, but a young man's hand intersected hers and did the honor.

"Allow me, Your Highness."

Rachel's eyes widened as the well-dressed man hurried around to her side of the table and pulled out her chair as well.

She gave a nod. "Thank you, sir." Pausing, because she hadn't yet decided if he was part of the wait staff or a patron, Rachel decided to err on the side of caution. She dipped a curtsy to his slight bow.

The young man stared at her. "You're welcome, my lady," he replied. His gaze didn't waver, even as Rachel lowered herself into the upholstered chair. "May I be permitted to say that your gown is most lovely? As are you?"

Rachel blinked, nearly scoffing at hearing his words.

Were all the men in London this forward?

"Now, sir, you cannot say such things," her mother admonished the man. "At least, not before you've been introduced."

The young man finally tore his gaze from Rachel's. "Apologies, Your Highness. I could not help myself."

Violet gave him a prim grin. "Your apology is accepted."

When he turned his gaze back to Rachel and continued to stare at her, Violet audibly sighed. "Rachel, may I have the pleasure of introducing you to Mr. Me—"

"Mark, please," the gentleman said as he bowed.

Violet arched a brow while Rachel was forced to offer her hand. He bowed over it, and Rachel stifled a gasp at the sensation his lips created on her bare knuckles.

"Rachel is a lovely name. It means first-born daughter, does it not?" he asked.

Remembering her mother's comment about keeping their relationship secret, Rachel nodded. "It does indeed, sir." She dared a glance at Violet before she added, "It's very good to make your acquaintance, sir. We were just about to enjoy this evening's dinner. Would you care to join us?"

Mark's eyes widened, and for a moment, Rachel thought she might have committed a *faux pax*. A quick glance in her mother's direction had her thinking otherwise. Violet appeared rather proud, one of her perfectly coiffed brows arching.

"Alas, I have already partaken of Chef Jean Claude's magnificent meal this evening," Mark replied. "I have warned Her Highness that I shall one day outbid her for his services."

Rachel dared another glance at her mother and found Violet displaying an impish grin.

"When you have your own kitchens, then I shall grow concerned," Violet remarked with a smirk.

One of his gloved fists pounded onto his chest and Mark let out a sound suggesting her *bon mot* had wounded him. "I already do, Your Highness. And although I have a cook, I would prefer Chef Jean Claude making the meals."

"Then I have been warned."

Mark turned his attention back to Rachel. "May I inquire how it is you have come to be at The Queen on this fine evening?"

Rachel's eyes widened. They hadn't yet discussed how she was to answer such questions, but she decided it was best if she kept her answers as close to the truth as possible. "I have just accepted Her Highness' offer for the position of bookkeeper here at The Queen," she said.

It was Mark's turn for his eyes to widen, which had Rachel feeling the heat of a blush creeping up her neck and onto her cheeks. He had obviously assumed she was one of Violet's light-skirts. One of the doxies that lived on the second floor of the gaming hell.

"Bookkeeper?" he repeated. His expression showed his indecision as to what he would say next. "Forgive me. I have interrupted what is undoubtedly your celebratory dinner."

Violet was quick to say, "You're forgiven, of course, Mr... Mark." She seemed to struggle to say his given name, as if she knew exactly who—and what—he was. "Now you'd best return to your card game. Who knows how much Haddon has cheated since you took your leave?"

The young man's eyes narrowed. "He does not cheat, Your Highness. Not like his father," he argued. "But I shall heed your advice." He once again turned his attention on Rachel and bowed deeply. "My lady," he said before he stepped backwards. "I do hope this isn't the last I shall see of you." Then he made his way out of the dining room.

Rachel noticed he afforded her one more look before he disappeared through a set of double doors, no doubt the entrance to the card room.

"Who was that?" Rachel asked at the same moment a young woman appeared with a menu board and a bottle of champagne.

She poured the bubbly into crystal glasses already at their place settings as she said, "It's an honor to serve you this evening, Your Highness, Miss."

"Thank you, Marjorie. We'll have the chef's dinner this evening."

"Very good, madame." The waitress dipped a curtsy and hurried off to another table.

Rachel frowned. "The chef's dinner?" she repeated.

"Beef medallions in a sauce unlike anything anyone else serves in this town," her mother replied. "It's divine."

Lifting the glass of champagne to her lips, Rachel paused when she noticed how her mother regarded her. "What is it?"

Violet gave her head a shake and held up her own glass. "A toast to you, my darling. I am so glad you are back in London." She lifted her glass into the air and then sipped from its brim.

"I am glad to be back," Rachel said. She took an experimental sip of the champagne and then allowed a smile. "It's delightful."

"I only serve the very best, even if it is sometimes hard to acquire."

Rachel furrowed her brows. "Is it legal?"

A grin once again lifting the corners of her mouth, Violet said, "Oh, yes. I am sure to stay within the law when it comes to... *everything* about running this place."

Rachel felt a good deal of relief at hearing her response. For a time, she had wondered if The Queen of Hearts might operate outside the realm of law, but then she remembered the comments of the man she had escorted to the door. "Not like Crockford's?"

Violet's eyes widened. "What do you know of Crocky's?" she asked in alarm.

"Only what that young man told me. The one I saw to the door after your meeting."

Staring at her daughter for a moment too long, Violet said, "I suppose he asked you if you had seen your father?"

Rachel blinked. "He did not."

"He didn't introduce himself?"

"He did not."

"And you did not offer your name?"

Angling her head to one side, Rachel wondered at her mother's query. "Should I have?" Then her eyes rounded as she tried to determine who he might have been.

An aristocrat of some renown? An important official with the city? How could she be expected to know anyone in London?

Violet sighed and glanced around the dining room before she leaned over the table and said, "Randolph Roderick."

Staring at her mother, Rachel's first thought was she shared a common last name with the young man. But then her eyes widened once again. "He's one of my... *brothers?*" she guessed.

"The oldest," Violet affirmed. "If Mr. Wilson hadn't been there, I would have introduced you."

Rachel allowed her mind's eye to replay their interchange. At no point did he look at her as if she might be a relation, but now she understood how he had seemed so familiar. "He looked like Father did when I was a child. When he gave me the Welsh pony for my birthday."

Violet's sigh was audible, as if she was surprised Rachel would remember that day. If she hadn't already been under contract with another, Violet might have begged Randall to take her back. His attentiveness to their daughter had her heart clenching. Even now, she remembered wishing they could be together.

Perhaps she had been in love with him. Or perhaps she had

been too young to know what love was. In the interim, she hadn't felt the same toward any of her other protectors. She had felt fondness for a few of them, but nothing that could be considered love. Now that she had The Queen of Hearts, she had no need of a protector. No need to be someone's mistress.

"He does bear a remarkable resemblance to Reading," Violet murmured. "That was the second time I have met with him and his colleague, and both times, I have been struck by the sensation that I know him when I do not."

Rachel wondered at her mother's words until she surmised she was speaking of the intimacy she had shared with Randolph's father. "You do not bed him, though," she replied.

Violet's reaction was so quick and so filled with shock, Rachel had a hard time suppressing a grin. "I rather doubt he even knows I was employed by his father. Besides, I am old enough to be his *mother*," Violet claimed. "And although he is as handsome as his father was at that age, he is... *was* married. Why, he even has a young son."

The oddest sensation gripped Rachel's chest. A twinge accompanied by a deep desire to meet the tyke. "I'm an aunt?" she whispered. She let out the breath she held as a grin split her face. "I have a nephew." Then she suddenly sobered. "What do you mean when you say he 'was married'?" she asked.

Violet leaned back as the first course of the dinner was delivered. The soup sent up wafts of deliciously scented steam as it passed before them.

Had she not attended nearly ten years of finishing school in Zurich, Rachel would have lifted the bowl to her lips and drained the contents, she was so hungry.

"His wife died in the childbed," Violet explained as she lifted a spoon and ladled some of the thin broth into it. "About a year ago."

Rachel tested the soup, finding it far more delicious than its appearance would suggest for a broth. Her mother's words surprised her, though. "Mr. Roderick does not seem old enough to have been married, let alone be a father," Rachel replied. She took another taste of the soup and understood why the man who had introduced himself as Mark would wish to outbid her mother for the cook's services.

She thought of the reasons why a young man would marry, and a sense of disappointment settled over her. Randolph had probably followed in his father's footsteps, but had done so with a young woman whose father had discovered his indiscretion. "He had to marry her?" she guessed.

Violet shook her head. "Not at all. Randolph is nothing like Reading was at his age—other than in appearance. He married for love, or that's what his father claimed." She sighed. "Just yesterday, Reading admitted he didn't like Barbara. Always thought Randolph should have aimed higher with his choice of wife."

The words implied Barbara wasn't the daughter of an aristocrat. "He is a very handsome man," Rachel murmured.

Violet's brow arched. "Well, he's off-limits to you, but I rather imagine he will be in search of a wife. It's been a year and his son needs a mother."

"A nursemaid sees to the babe, then?" Rachel asked, wondering how she could angle for an introduction to her nephew.

"Reading's nursemaid, yes. Reading's youngest boy and Randolph's babe share the nursery at Reading's townhouse here in Mayfair."

Rachel dropped her spoon into her soup. "I have more brothers," she said, remembering what her mother had told her whilst they were in her bedchamber.

"You have six all told," Violet agreed, returning her attention to her soup. "But I only know of the whereabouts of Randolph."

"Oh?"

"He has dinner every Wednesday night with his father and stepmother at the Reading townhouse in Curzon Street," Violet said with an arched brow.

Rachel remembered the town coach she had seen pull up to the curb in Piccadilly Street. Remembered the gold crest that had been painted on the glossy black door.

The Reading crest, no doubt.

For a moment, she wished she had offered her name and wondered how Randolph would have reacted to hear she was Rachel Roderick.

Would he have acknowledged her as his sister?

Did he even *know* he had a sister?

She vowed that when she saw him again—and given his avocation, she was fairly sure she would—she would introduce herself and request an introduction to her nephew.

CHAPTER 12
AN UNANNOUNCED
ARRIVAL

A moment later, in Bradley House

There was no knock at the door, no indication a caller had come to Bradley House. Chesterfield only discovered the intruder because he was on his way to secure the front door for the night.

Finding a man at the base of the marble stairs had him pausing. He might have let out a shout to summon a footman, but both Colburn and Smith had left the house earlier that evening. Seeing the manner in which the intruder was dressed had him instead giving a slight bow. That and the way he was gazing up, as if he were staring at someone at the top of the stairs.

A quick glance up assured Chesterfield his mistress wasn't standing there. Nor was anyone else, for that matter.

"On whom do you pay a call this evening?" Chesterfield asked.

Randolph dared another quick glance up the stairs, noticing that the railing was decorated with red velvet ribbons. Coupled with the huge bouquet of white roses that adorned the odd hall table, he knew the mistress of the house was looking forward to the holiday. He turned his attention to the servant. "Your question implies there is more than one master or mistress in residence. I understood there was a single mistress," he replied. "I've been told I am expected." He didn't offer a card, though, nor his name. Lady Comber had implied the butler would be deaf to his arrival.

Chesterfield bristled, his immediate dislike of the gentleman sounding in his response. "Sir, I must ask you to leave. Lady Dunsworth isn't receiving callers this evening," he said, waving his hand toward the small vestibule.

His gaze once again going to the top of the stairs, Randolph allowed a smile and a deep bow. "Good evening, my lady."

Having heard the conversation from the first floor parlor, Xenobia now stood at the top of the stairs and regarded her caller with a combination of curiosity and caution. "Good evening, Mr...?"

"Roderick. We've an appointment. I was sure it was for nine o'clock," he said, just then wondering if Lady Julia Comber might have meant nine o'clock *in the morning*.

But what lady of the *ton* was up and about at nine o'clock in the morning?

"Yes. Yes, of course. I apologize. I didn't realize the time had grown so late. Do come up," Xenobia said as she waved a hand to reinforce her words.

Randolph paused for only a moment before ascending the stairs, his polished Hessians barely making a sound on the carpet runner. His voice had echoed in the nearly empty hall, and he took a moment to discover the hall had no furnishings. No caryatids. No chairs along the walls. No statuary.

There was just the round table sporting a huge ball of white roses. Even if he hadn't been able to ascertain what kind of flowers they were by their appearance, the scent of roses wafted around his nostrils. As for the table, he could swear it was a gaming table, but he didn't have a chance to look at it more closely.

He paused at the top of the stairs to reassess the situation. Lady Dunsworth was not at all what he was expecting.

Even though his stepmother had said Lady Dunsworth was younger than she, Randolph had imagined the baroness as a far older woman. He had imagined her hair gray and her body more frail.

Instead, she was a comely young woman with honey blonde hair and eyes the color of aquamarine gemstones. The teal blue dinner gown she wore only accentuated the striking eye color.

Once he could see her more clearly by the light of the hallway sconces, all of them sporting red ribbons around their brass fixtures, he knew his imagination had conjured an entirely different creature.

Lady Xenobia Dunsworth was indeed a beautiful woman. Not young, exactly, but not old, either. Five-and-twenty perhaps at most, her once youthful appearance replaced with an ageless elegance. Her hair was caught up in a neat bun atop her head with loose tendrils at her temples.

Still dressed in her dinner gown—a velvet skirt with a pleated bodice and short sleeves void of decoration—she looked far more elegant than most widows. The collection of jewels between her breasts and the two that hung from her plump earlobes merely enhanced her regal bearing.

Caught up in the crook of her arm was a copy of *A Treatise on the Breeding of Thoroughbred Horses*.

A jolt of excitement passed through Randolph at the thought that her filly might be a Thoroughbred.

He reached for her hand, startled at how cold it felt in his. He brushed his lips over the back of her bare fingers, sure he felt her reaction in how her hand shook in his hold.

Perhaps she hadn't been touched in a long time, which had him wondering if she had eaten alone that night. "Sir Randolph Roderick. It's a pleasure to meet you, my lady," he said, once again bowing before her.

CHAPTER 13
DUTIES CALL

*M*eanwhile, at *The Queen of Hearts*

Rachel regarded the dessert plate that had been placed before her and then nearly giggled. "I do not think I can eat another bite," she said in a quiet voice. "Besides, it's so lovely. I cannot imagine ruining it," she added as she admired the perfectly formed *fleur de lis* on a white china plate. The mousse was surrounded by a circle of raspberry sauce and decorated with chocolate curls. She looked up to find that Violet had already delved into her dessert, an expression of delight touching her lips along with a hint of the chocolate.

"Oh, do. It's light and ever so delicious," Violet encouraged her. One hand lifted a locket from her bosom, and with a press of her thumb, it opened to reveal a chronometer. Her eyes widened. "Oh, dear. It's later than I thought. I really must do my rounds before long," she murmured.

Startled, Rachel glanced around to discover the dining room was nearly empty. "Are they done serving for the night?"

"Oh, no. We serve dinner until one o'clock in the morning," Violet replied.

Rachel blinked. "How late is The Queen open?"

Violet chuckled. "There are times when it seems as if we do not close," she replied. "But most are gone by three or four, and so that is when I have my director lock the doors."

Usually unable to stay awake that long, Rachel found she felt rather refreshed from her long nap and wondered if she could remain awake until then. "Perhaps I could take a look at the ledgers? Get a start on what it is you'd like me to do? I'm not the least bit tired."

Surprised by the request, Violet leaned back and regarded her daughter a moment before she allowed a grin. "Very well. I'll take you to the study and show you what I need. But don't feel as if you must do anything just yet. It's your first day back in London."

Rachel shrugged. "It's not as if I'm going anywhere this evening," she countered. "I should like to pay a call on Xenobia tomorrow, though."

"Of course. I can arrange for the town coach to take you," Violet replied before she finished her dessert.

Rachel dared a taste of the mousse and closed her eyes in appreciation. "If I could, I'll take this with me. I don't wish to keep you from your duties."

"Of course, darling. And take your tea, too," she urged as she stood and led them to what appeared to be a wall. Near the corner, Violet pressed her hand against the paneling, and the door opened to the private residence. She held it open as Rachel passed through and then closed it.

"I did not realize there was a door there, it was so well hidden in the wall," Rachel said in awe.

"There are many such doors in the gaming hell," Violet replied as they made their way up the stairs. "They hide the corridors that allow my employees to access the kitchens and the counting room without bothering my patrons."

"Clever," Rachel commented as they entered the study. "Do you not keep this locked?" she asked when Violet was able to simply turn the handle, open the door, and lead them in.

"I should, I suppose, but I trust my staff. Besides, only a few maids work here in the residence."

"And that door from the dining room?"

Violet inhaled softly. "I suppose I should see to securing it," she murmured. She moved around to the other side of the desk and pulled a large leather-bound journal to the center of it. Then she lifted a thick stack of receipts, bills of lading, and invoices and dropped them next to the ledger. "I used to update the ledgers every day," she said on a sigh. "Then I decided to do it weekly. Now I'm more than a month behind—"

"Show me what to do and I shall see to it they're caught up," Rachel encouraged her.

Violet sighed and opened the ledger to a page half-filled with entries. "Please don't think ill of me—"

"I won't."

"The invoices are paid. At least, all but these," she said as she indicated those in the pile. "The invoices must be matched with whatever paper proves their item has been delivered before I pay it. I refuse to pay if there's no proof of delivery," she explained.

"So, I match these bills of lading with their invoices," Rachel said as she rifled through the stack and found an example.

"Exactly," Violet murmured. "Then, you enter the invoice in the ledger and mark the number of the cheque that was used to pay the bill."

"Where do I find those?"

"Oh, well, I have to make them out and sign them. Then I have a footmen deliver them," Violet explained.

"Perhaps I can make them out and leave them for you to sign," Rachel offered, understanding from just how many invoices were in the stack why it was her mother had fallen behind in her bookkeeping.

"You would do that?" Violet asked, obviously surprised by the offer.

Rachel lifted a shoulder. "Why not? I've nothing else to do, unless you're going to require me to do needlework?" she asked with a visibly pained expression on her face.

"I wouldn't. Ever," Violet promised her as she withdrew another book from a desk drawer. "Here are the cheques. The next time I go to the Bank of England, I'll take you with me so we can arrange to have you added to my accounts."

"Oh, I hardly think I should be on your accounts," Rachel

argued as she thumbed through the papers and pulled out several sets of matching invoices and packing lists.

"You should be, Rachel," Violet said, sobering as she regarded her daughter. "Should something happen to me, I do not want The Queen to end up lost, or in the hands of some scoundrel."

Rachel's eyes widened in alarm. "Are you expecting something to happen to you?"

"No, no, not at all. But if I learned anything from your father, it was the importance of responsibility," Violet said in a quiet voice. "For you, and then for my business," she added.

Giving a start at the mention of her father, Rachel stared at her mother. She was about to ask about him again, but The Queen had already continued putting voice to her thoughts.

"Even if you decide you do not wish to keep The Queen upon my death, you will at least have the ability to sell it... or arrange for someone to run it on your behalf. It's become quite a lucrative venture." She paused and then waved a hand over the ledger. "At least, it was the last time I worked on this."

Lowering herself into one of the chairs that faced the desk, Rachel regarded her mother in an entirely different light. Whilst at finishing school, she had never told anyone her mother was a courtesan. Never mentioned she owned a gaming hell. Why suffer the embarrassment?

But after having enjoyed one of the best meals of her life served in an elegant dining room by an efficient staff, and after taking a look at the balance in the ledgers, Rachel realized her mother wasn't simply a popular courtesan. She was a successful businesswoman. Someone for whom Rachel should feel pride.

"You've become a rather remarkable woman, haven't you?" Rachel asked in a whisper.

Violet's eyes rounded before she fell into her desk chair. "Oh, darling," she whispered before she let out her breath in a huff. "You're going to make me cry," she added as tears brightened her eyes.

"Mother, don't cry," Rachel said as she leaned forward and placed one of her hands over Violet's. "I am just happy for you.

That you've found your calling and seem to enjoy it?" she guessed.

Violet gave an impish grin. "I do, actually. There are days when I feel as if I am the most powerful woman in all of London."

Rachel's gaze went to a stack of papers, the top one containing a sum of money followed by a signature. "Would those be documents of what is owed to you?" she asked.

"Acknowledgements of debt by some of our more avid gamblers, yes," Violet agreed before she rolled her eyes. "*Vowels,* they're sometimes called."

"What happens if they're not paid?"

Another impish grin touched Violet's lips. "I become the owner of whatever it is they have offered in place of repayment."

Chuckling, Rachel finally allowed a nod. "So you really *are* the most powerful woman in all of London."

Leaning over the desk, Violet said, "Only when the real Queen of England isn't in town." She inhaled softly. "And on that note, I really must be getting down to the gaming floor. Don't spend all night here," she said as she took her leave.

Rachel watched her mother go before she settled herself in her mother's chair and began her work.

Engrossed in entering numbers and notes into the ledger, she didn't notice when she was no longer alone.

CHAPTER 14

A MYSTERIOUS MAN PAYS
A CALL

eanwhile, at Bradley House
A bit dismayed her caller had appeared at exactly nine o'clock *at night*, Xenobia found she couldn't be cross with him. He was punctual, and not at all what she expected. She knew this because she had spent her entire dinner imagining the man her cousin had described in her letter.

Xenobia noted the expectant expression he displayed and remembered his pleasantry. *Sir Randolph Roderick. It's a pleasure to meet you, my lady.*

"And you as well," she said as she motioned to the open door just beyond the first sconce. "We can speak in the parlor," she offered, rather glad the servants had placed several vases of flowers about the room.

The floral scents of roses and lilies helped to mask the odor of disuse she had noticed the day before—unfortunately only moments before her callers had arrived for tea. The addition of red velvet bows on the door handles and red ribbon along the top of the mantel had been her meager attempts at decorating for the upcoming holiday.

"Very good, my lady," her visitor responded, as he followed her over the threshold.

"Should I ring for tea?" she asked, cringing at the thought

that another servant would discover she was alone with a strange man. "Or would you like some brandy, perhaps?"

"Only if you wish some for yourself," Randolph replied, waiting until she was settled into a chair near the fireplace before he lowered himself into the adjacent chair. "I must admit you are not quite what I expected."

That odd sensation skittered down her spine again, along with a flash of annoyance.

What had *he* expected?

"For some reason, I thought you would be much older. Not so... beautiful," he added.

The words were said so matter-of-factly, Xenobia was left staring at him. But of course he would say such a thing. He was probably expecting to be paid for putting voice to compliments, although she still hadn't decided if she would go through with any kind of arrangement with the man.

Why, oh why had she allowed Julia to talk her into this? Julia had never actually employed this man—she had merely arranged this meeting. However did she even know about him?

Had one of their mutual friends paid him to keep them company?

Company probably wasn't exactly what they enjoyed. Her gaze dropped to his thighs, their muscled shape straining his Nankeen breeches. She briefly wondered if his tailor had to double-stitch the seams to keep them from splitting.

Besides the double-stitching of his breeches, his tailor could be commended for the perfect points of his shirt, a tasteful waistcoat and a topcoat made of superfine. A valet had obviously seen to and tied his immaculate cravat. He was dressed better than most gentlemen.

"I have not been in the company of an unmarried woman— without a chaperone—for some time," Randolph said in low voice. He appeared to wince, apparently because he sounded like a dandy for hire. One of those men who were paid to accompany older women to all the events of the Season and then entertain those very women in their bedchambers until the wee hours of the morning.

Or until they were sound asleep.

"I am hardly in need of a chaperone," Xenobia countered, sure he said such things to all his potential clients. Flattery was rather effective with women. "But thank you for the kind words." She paused before she dared another glance in his direction. "You're not at all what I expected."

CHAPTER 15
AN ALMOST UNWELCOME VISITOR

*M*eanwhile, in the office at *The Queen of Hearts* Rachel regarded the first few lines of entries she had made in her mother's journal. Her mother's instructions had been easy to follow, and having kept such a ledger for her own expenses whilst in finishing school, Rachel already had experience at how to fill in the information. She double-checked her addition before she turned her attention on the remaining papers in the stack of invoices and bills of lading.

And then on the person who stood in front of the desk.

She gave a start, immediately recognizing the man from the dining room. "Mark?" she said as she quickly stood. Momentary fright had her wishing the door were closer. That she wasn't behind a desk and he in front of it.

"I apologize," Mark said as he dipped his head. "I didn't mean to frighten you. You were just so... *engrossed* in what you were doing that I didn't wish to—"

"How did you get in here?"

The young man actually turned his body and pointed to the open door. It was at that moment that Rachel had a chance to study him. He was still a young man—mid-twenties, perhaps—and he sported dark hair with an errant lock up front that couldn't seem to decide if it was to hang upon his forehead or point in the direction of his forward movement.

His clothes were impeccably cut and his shoes... well, she couldn't see his shoes given how close he was standing in front of the desk, but she could imagine they were of the finest quality.

"I meant, how did you get into the private residence?" Rachel quickly amended.

Mark inhaled and then sighed. "I saw The Queen come from there, and when you weren't with her, I thought to come find you."

Rachel might have felt frightened by the intruder if she hadn't been so indignant at hearing his response. "What ever for?"

His hands moving behind his back, Mark seemed at a loss for words before he finally said. "Two reasons, really. It seems I am in need of someone of your... talents."

Rachel gave a start. "Talents?" She immediately grimaced, not intending to repeat anything he said lest she sound insipid.

"Bookkeeping," he quickly clarified. His eyes darted about before he moved to shut the door and then returned to stand before her.

What she had thought about his shoes was true. They were rather fine.

Her eyes rounded. What if someone should discover them? Together? Rachel was about to put voice to a protest when Mark seemed determined to settle into one of the chairs in front of the desk. Deciding he wasn't about to accost her, Rachel sat down and remembered how her mother had dealt with him. She regarded him with an arched brow. "You are without a man of business?" she asked.

Mark seemed surprised by her query. "I did have one, but I had to let him go."

"Had to?" Rachel repeated, wincing at hearing her response. Mark would think she was a parrot if it happened again. "Explain." She could imagine her mother saying the word with the same hint of impatience.

He nodded. "Given your... profession, you're no doubt familiar with the act of embezzlement?" he half-asked.

Stiffening—that was the second time this day she had heard the word—Rachel straightened. "I am."

"My man of business was... pilfering. From me. He must have thought I couldn't add. Or maybe he didn't realize I was reviewing his work to ensure he was completing my ledgers correctly, but I discovered what he was doing—"

"Which was?"

"Seeing to it he was paid more than his due," he claimed. "By adding the missing monies from some accounts to the amount he was writing on the cheques he made out to himself every week."

Every week? she almost repeated. Who ever heard of being paid weekly? Instead, she asked, "By how much?"

Mark suddenly seemed reluctant to share any more information. "The amount matters not."

Rachel blinked. "Sir, it matters quite a lot. Your man of business needs to be reported to the authorities."

"I think it best this be kept quiet."

"So someone else can hire him?" Rachel asked in disbelief.

"I let him go without a character," Mark countered.

"But he can still claim he worked for you," she argued. "That might be enough to convince someone to hire him without the benefit of a character."

"Then that will be their mistake," he replied curtly.

"But your good name will be at risk."

Mark stared at her. Not having considered that possibility, he allowed a long sigh. "I shall pay a call on the magistrate on the morrow," he murmured. When he noticed how her attention was no longer on him but on something in her mind's eye, he furrowed his brows. "It seems I've lost your good opinion, have I not?"

Rachel blinked and regarded him a moment before she gave her head a shake. "Not at all. I was just thinking about how this might have been handled in Zurich."

"Zurich?"

Grinning—she couldn't help it given her words had him

repeating one of them—Rachel nodded. "I rather doubt embezzlers dare operate there."

"Zurich, as in Switzerland?" he asked.

"Indeed. I have lived there most of my life," she explained, managing not to wince at having exaggerated her length of stay on the Continent. She decided to withhold the fact that most of that time had been spent in finishing school.

"But... you're English," he said, as if he knew for certain.

"I am. I've only just returned to British shores to... to accept this position," she claimed, hoping he wouldn't see through her white lie.

"I'll pay you double," Mark stated.

Rachel blinked again. "What?"

"Come be my bookkeeper, and I'll pay you twice what The Queen pays you."

Her eyes rounding again, only because she was so stunned by his desperation, Rachel gave her head a shake. "I hardly think it would be prudent of me to accept an offer and then give my notice all in the same day," she argued. Besides, she didn't even know what her mother planned to pay her, although she had mentioned she would be paying her.

"The Queen will not mind."

Rachel was ready to demand he take his leave, but she found she was curious to know more about him. "Tell me... Mark. What is it you *do* that requires you hire a bookkeeper of my skills?"

He leaned back in his chair, as if he already knew he would secure her services. "I don't really *do* anything," he replied proudly.

Rachel fought to keep an impassive expression on her face. The response was in keeping with a typical gentleman. Thoughts of her father flitted across her mind's eye. Gentlemen didn't work. They didn't do manual labor.

But they owned land. Hosted tenants who did the farming or mining. They amassed wealth from the labors of others. They were aristocrats...

Blinking at the realization a peer of the realm might be

sitting across from her, Rachel angled her head to one side. "My lord—"

"Mark," he corrected her.

"My lord, I would have you tell me the truth," she whispered, her eyes wide and her heart beating a tattoo she was sure could be heard across the desk.

Slumping in his chair, Mark allowed a long sigh. "Oh, if I must." His eyes went skyward before he straightened and said in a somewhat mocking tone, "The Honorable Mark Merriweather, owner of The Three Bells, at your service." At her arched eyebrow, he added, "Middleton is my father."

Despite her determination not to react, Rachel inhaled sharply.

The son of the Earl of Middleton—an heir to the Middleton earldom—sat across from her.

And he had offered her a position.

CHAPTER 16
EXPECTATIONS

*B**ack in the parlor at Bradley House*

Randolph straightened in the chair, not sure from the tone of her voice if Lady Dunsworth was disappointed. He had no idea how Lady Comber had described him. That she had even agreed to recommend him to Xenobia Bradley Dunsworth was a testament to the exuberant woman who charmed everyone with whom she made an acquaintance.

"No?" he replied, thinking he would have to scold Lady Comber when next he saw her.

His usual confidence with a new acquaintance faltering, Randolph considered Lady Dunsworth's words.

You're not at all what I expected.

Well, he was dressed in the clothes he had worn to dinner at his father's, and although he really should have worn shoes, he had instead donned his Hessians. His shoes weren't shined and the boots were.

Besides, his stepmother, Constance, claimed to prefer seeing men in boots. She had already seen to it his two-year-old half-brother, Robert, had a pair of black riding boots for when he rode his Welsh pony—with a footman's assistance, of course. Constance was as much of a horsewoman as his father was a horseman, after all.

Had Lady Dunsworth expected he would show up wearing the clothes he wore whilst working in the stables?

Or was she referring to his physique?

He was a bit taller than most, a bit larger in the arms and across his shoulders, but then most in his profession were. Lifting bales of hay and saddles all day along with pushing horses into place in front of various carriages had a tendency to strengthen arms and legs.

Had she thought she might have recognized him? There was certainly a glimmer of something in her eyes when she first saw him standing at the bottom of the stairs.

They could have met for a ride in the park, a time he was learning to appreciate given he could exercise a different horse from his father's stable every afternoon in Hyde Park.

He didn't care if he wasn't recognized. As a bastard son of a marquess, he didn't expect it, even if his father had acknowledged him as his son when he was but a babe, paid for his upbringing and education, and was seeing to a generous allowance every month.

Although he attended this initial meeting with little in the way of expectations, he wanted it to go well. If Lady Dunsworth recommended him to her friends, and they then made mention of him to their husbands, he might gain more clients at Tattersalls'.

"May I inquire as to what you expected?" Randolph asked as he settled deeper into the floral upholstered chair.

He wanted to impress this particular woman.

Especially now that he thought she had a Thoroughbred.

Xenobia tore her attention from her caller and briefly regarded the flames in the fireplace. Besides the beauty of their hypnotic waves and ever-changing colors, the warmth they provided was also welcome. "I expected you would be a fop," she finally replied, once again daring a glance in his direction.

She almost hoped he would be.

At least then she could easily dismiss him out of hand.

When she noted his furrowed brows, Xenobia continued. "A dandy, wearing heeled slippers and rings on every finger. A powdered wig on your head and a mouche on your cheek. Dressed in puce satin pantaloons with a matching tailcoat, and an embroidered waistcoat with more flowers on it than anything in my wardrobe." A smile lightened her face then as her description grew ever more ridiculous, despite her having described what her late husband looked like on the nights they attended the theatre.

She didn't want to think about him. Didn't want to think about how best friends could grow apart after a few years of marriage.

At first confused, but then amused by her words, Randolph allowed a grin. "Oh, my. I do hope you're not disappointed," he murmured, appreciating her attempt at humor.

She shook her head. "If you had been a fop, I would have had Chesterfield show you to the door."

If he had looked anything like James, she would have retrieved her small pistol from the dressing table in her bedchamber and shot him in the head.

Both of them.

At least Sir Randolph was handsome, in a rather brutish sort of way. His body wasn't anything like her late husband's, although his clothes seemed to fit him to perfection. His dark hair, wavy and a bit too long in the back, would not have worked in any of the Roman styles currently favored by men in the nobility. His jaw was entirely too square, his nose didn't include a hook at the end, and his dark brows framed eyes that were so blue, she was sure she would be caught staring if she so much as looked in his direction.

Randolph blinked. "I thank you for seeing me then," he replied. "Lady Comber gave me just a brief description of the situation. What are your expectations?"

Xenobia inhaled softly, not sure if she could admit just why it was she had agreed to this meeting. Julia's note was so unexpected and yet described exactly something her cousin would do. "May I ask first what others say in response to that question?"

Angling his head slightly, Randolph wondered at her hesitance. From what he had learned of her from his discussion with Lady Comber, she was a widow just recently out of mourning. She had no children. Just a filly in need of training.

"Well, we usually discuss the expected amount of time it might take. It varies, of course."

Xenobia blinked. "So, you are paid according to the amount of time you spend with a... a client?" she struggled to get out.

He nodded. "I am, but I am very good at what I do, and I'm usually able to break a filly in a couple of weeks at most."

Xenobia blinked again, never having heard the term used to describe a full-grown woman before. "Break a filly?" she repeated, a stab of fear causing her heart to race. "Do you often equate the female sex to a... a horse?" she asked in confusion.

It was Randolph's turn to blink. "Rarely," he replied. He held up a finger, as if to make an exception. "I might have. My father has said many times that he is married to a 'spirited filly.'"

"And if your... *client*... is not *spirited* as much as she's simply in need of... *company*, what then?"

Randolph's gaze darted to the fire as he parsed her words in his head. "There are no other horses in your stable?"

Understanding his query as a metaphor, Xenobia said, "The only stallion died more than a year ago." As she gave her own metaphor further consideration, she thought she should have referred to her late husband as a gelding. He certainly hadn't done his job as a stud, given he never got a child on her. "And other than the two shires that pull my barouche, there are no other horses in the mews. That belong to me, at least."

Angling his head to one side, Randolph displayed an expression of disappointment. "There is no *timid filly* in need of attention?" He thought of the book she'd had in her arm.

Still had in her arm.

She hadn't set it aside when they took their seats, and now he wondered if she'd kept it in the event she thought she might need it as a weapon. Something to clobber him with should he attempt to take liberties with her.

Randolph took a deep breath and held it a moment before he straightened in the chair in which he had become far too comfortable in Lady Dunsworth's parlor.

CHAPTER 17
A SECOND OFFER

*B*ack in the office at *The Queen of Hearts*

"You're the Earl of Middleton's heir?" Rachel asked in disbelief.

Mark shook his head. "Merely the spare," he replied. "The second spare, actually. My brother, Luke—Viscount Wessex—he has already married and sired his heir. Hence, I am the spare's spare."

Rachel exhaled. "Well, that's a relief," she murmured. At least the Middleton earldom wasn't in danger of this man becoming its title holder given what had happened with his man of business.

Furrowing a brow, he asked, "And why is that?"

Rachel rolled her eyes. "I've been calling you *Mark* all evening. Hardly appropriate if you're a peer." Under her breath, she added, "Hardly appropriate no matter the circumstances." She huffed then and leaned forward. "Why did you insist on being introduced as *Mark*?" No wonder her mother had given him such an odd look when he had approached their dining table.

Allowing a grimace, Mark sighed. "It provided anonymity of sorts," he replied. When Rachel merely stared at him, he added, "I admit, I approached your table because when I saw you, I knew I hadn't seen you before, and..." He gritted his teeth, almost mentioning the visit he'd had from Lady Comber.

"You thought I was one of the lightskirts," she accused, her eyes widening in horror.

He shook his head as he said, "No. You're dressed far too fine to be a lightskirt."

"A courtesan, then?"

The space between his brows narrowed. "I could see that you were a woman of quality long before The Queen introduced you."

Rachel relaxed a bit before she asked, "Then why?"

"Curiosity, I suppose," he finally said. "I've lived here in London exclusively since I reached my majority—"

"So, a few months?" Rachel guessed. The man couldn't be more than five-and-twenty.

"Nearly four years, actually," he countered, obviously bothered by her gentle teasing. "I was given my inheritance upon the occasion of my twenty-first birthday."

"But your man of business took it all."

Mark scoffed. "He did not. He was never allowed access to *those* funds," he stated, his manner suggesting he was thoroughly offended by her remark. "Only those of The Three Bells."

At that moment, Rachel knew she had gone too far with her gentle ribbing. She had learned long ago from the way her mother interacted with her clients that English men had egos that could be easily bruised. During her time in Zurich, she had discovered European men weren't nearly as bothered when teased. They saw the jabs as challenges and did their best to prove them wrong.

"I apologize, Mr. Merriweather," Rachel said quietly. "It's not my place to make comments about your financial situation."

Caught by surprise at hearing her apology, Mark lifted a hand to his face and scrubbed his jaw. "It *would* be if you were my man of business. And please, call me Mark."

Realizing he hadn't yet told her the second reason he had come to her mother's office, Rachel ignored the comment and asked, "Why *did* you follow me here?"

His eyes darting to the side, Mark seemed to slump in his chair. "I admit, it was because I was intrigued."

Rachel blinked. She was about to repeat the last word but she caught herself in time. "By?"

"Well, *you*, of course. I've never seen you before."

"I have been in Zurich for a long time."

"Which is why I haven't seen you before."

"Are you intrigued by all the woman you haven't seen before?"

"No, of course not."

"Then why me?"

He cleared his throat before he said, "You're gorgeous."

The comment was so unexpected, Rachel could feel the heat of her blush even before it reached her face. "Thank you, sir," she replied, not sure how else to respond.

"You're not insipid."

"Insipid?" Rachel repeated, wincing at not catching herself in time. For a moment, she wondered if that's how she should be behaving now that she was back on British shores. Perhaps young ladies here were raised to be insipid. *Expected* to be insipid.

Mark leaned forward, as if he was about to impart some important state secret. "It's as if all the gels in the *ton* are raised to be insipid," he whispered. "As if they're *expected* to be insipid."

"Poor things," Rachel replied, sure she was still displaying a bright pink blush on her cheeks.

"My thoughts exactly," he replied with a raised finger. "You, however, have obviously avoided such rigorous training—"

"Or ignored it," Rachel said under her breath.

"And have decided you wish to be a woman of the world."

Inhaling as if she intended to respond, Rachel found she didn't know what to say to such a pronouncement. She had always thought a woman of the world was someone who traveled extensively. Someone who had adopted the habits and manner of speech of those she met along the way. Someone who didn't require a paid companion but who saw to her own arrangements and her own happiness.

Having failed at traveling—she despised the time it took to get from here to there and the modes she had to employ to do it —Rachel could hardly consider herself a woman of the world.

"I am not ashamed to say it's not a title I'm able to claim," she said quietly. "Travel and I do not suit."

"But it sounds as if you tried." It wasn't a question.

Rachel angled her head to one side. "I did. The Kingdom of the Two Sicilies was very hot, and a volcano kept erupting—

"Etna," Mark said in wonder.

"Vesuvius," she corrected. "Then Ferdinand the Third died—"

"Didn't he used to be a duke?"

"Grand Duke of Tuscany, yes," Rachel replied, impressed he knew. "The Greeks were at war—"

"They want their independence," Mark affirmed.

"And Lord Byron died of a fever during one of the campaigns he led for them," she went on with a sigh. "Such a loss. Although now he is a hero of war to them."

When Mark didn't say anything about the poet, she arched a brow, hoping it appeared the way her mother's did when she employed it.

Apparently it did, for he finally cleared his throat and said, "Yes, well, I do hope you weren't one of his conquests."

"Conquests?" Rachel asked in surprise. This time, she didn't wince at having repeated his last word, but she did gasp before saying, "I assure you, I was not."

"Good, because all his affairs ended in..." He was about to mention venereal disease but thought better of it. Rachel might have been a woman of the world, but that didn't mean she should know about such things.

"Heartbreak?" she guessed, her brows furrowing when she realized almost immediately that Mark meant something entirely different. "Yes, well, he won't be spreading the effects of his love any longer now, will he?"

It was Mark's turn to blush. "No, my lady." He stared at her a moment before he said, "I would call you Miss Last Name, but I don't know your last name."

Rachel blinked several times before she decided she could finally share the information. If he recognized she was related to the Marquess of Reading and therefore illegitimate, then perhaps he would take his leave and she could get back to working on her mother's ledgers. "Roderick. Rachel Roderick."

Mark said, "It's very good to meet you." Then his eyes widened. "Lord Reading is your father?"

Inhaling softly, Rachel finally nodded. "He is."

"I went to school with your brother, Randolph," he claimed with some excitement. "Or I should say 'Sir Randolph'," he amended. "He's a knight now. Earned his title for service to the Crown."

Rachel's eyes rounded as she once again mentally sorted which brother Randolph was. "He's the oldest," she said, not adding that she had seen him just that day but hadn't known it was him.

"Oh, yes. I suppose there are others," Mark murmured.

"Three others, yes. That I know of." Sure Mark would take his leave now that he knew the truth about her, Rachel inhaled deeply and glanced down at the ledger.

"Have you even met him?" Mark asked, his query filled with concern.

Rachel shook her head. "I haven't met any of my brothers. I understand I have six now."

Mark's head bobbed once before he said, "Randolph is an honorable man. Widowed now, you must know—"

"I just learned of his loss earlier today," Rachel murmured. "He's not that old," she added, remembering almost immediately that his wife had died in the childbed.

"Has a boy. Sees to the Reading stables here in London, and he trains horses, too," Mark went on. "Sold a pair today at Tattersall's for a very good price. I would have bid, but..."

"Your man of business stole all your funds?" Rachel teased, a grin brightening her face.

"Now see here," he said with a matching grin. "Just for that, you have to come with me for a ride in the park," he demanded.

"It's terribly dark out there right now. Won't we be accosted by footpads?" she asked, struggling to keep a straight face.

"Ha ha," he said with a grin. "Tomorrow afternoon."

Rachel shook her head. "Sir, you've just learned I was born on the wrong side of the blanket. I rather doubt you wish to be seen with me."

"You'll have to wear warm clothes, of course," he said, ignoring her comment. "Is there... someone I need to speak with to gain permission to take you? Your father, perhaps?"

For a moment, Rachel understood why so many of the young women with whom she had attended finishing school carried around vinaigrettes in their reticules, for at that moment, she thought she might require one.

She might faint at any moment.

"Perhaps," she finally acknowledged.

"I'll come for you at two—"

"Four."

"Four?"

Rachel was relieved to hear *him* repeat a word. "Half-past three. I must pay a call on my dearest friend, Lady Dunsworth, on the morrow. I expect I'll be at Bradley House about two o'clock."

Mark nodded his understanding. "Shame about Dunsworth. They were the best of friends, I hear."

Well aware of Xenobia's relationship with James Dunsworth, Rachel struggled to refrain from telling Mark what she knew about Baron Dunsworth. Keeping secrets was easy when she'd been in Switzerland. For the past few years, none of her fellow students had even met Xenobia. They had no idea who her mother was or anything about the man she had married.

"They were very good friends, yes," Rachel acknowledged.

The space between Mark's brows narrowed. "But *you* were not friends with *him*," he said in a voice suggesting he thought there was some horrid reason for her dislike of the baron.

Rachel shook her head. "I never met the man."

"But you didn't like him."

Her mouth dropping open, Rachel stared at Mark. "I admit that my poor opinion of him was based only on what Xenobia wrote about him in her correspondence."

Mark seemed to think on her response for a long time before he finally said, "I'll come for you at half-past three o'clock."

"What if my father doesn't give you permission?"

He inhaled slowly as if he was giving her question a good deal of thought. "Then I shall still pay a call to let you know of his decision."

"What if I don't have a horse?"

A raucous laugh escaped Mark's throat.

"Why are you laughing?" she asked in dismay.

Mark broke out into laughter again before he sobered. "Forgive me, but I find it very amusing that the daughter of the Marquess of Reading doesn't own a horse," he said, his voice filled with humor. "I shall bring one for you," he promised. "A beast who is not too large and is as gentle as they come."

"You don't even know where to call on me," she argued.

"If not here...?"

Rachel gave him the address in Piccadilly Street for the private residence, secretly glad he didn't seem to recognize it was the back of The Queen of Hearts.

He stood up and reached for her hand. "I look forward to it," he said before he kissed the back of her bare hand, lingering over it a moment longer than was polite. He pointed to the ledgers. "Do give my offer some thought." Then he bowed deeply and took his leave of the office.

Staring at her hand for several seconds after he left, Rachel wondered how a simple kiss could leave her entire arm tingling in delight.

CHAPTER 18
MIXED METAPHORS

S *till in the parlor at Bradley House*
Timid filly?

It was Xenobia's turn to wonder at their strange conversation. Was the term in reference to a horse? Or to her? As far as she knew, no one had ever called her a timid filly.

Rachel had secretly called her a skinflint due to her hesitance to buy things she could easily afford.

Her husband had called her "Dear Heart" whether he was pleased or vexed by her.

Her mother called her "Bea" when she'd had too much to drink.

Her cousins sometimes referred to her as "Lady X," although never in public.

So what had Julia said to this man?

"I do not own a filly," Xenobia stated. "Both of my shires are old and gelded," she added, her mind racing with how she might gracefully dismiss Mr. Roderick and then hide in her bedchamber for the next decade.

But she noted the change in his expression, as if he had just realized exactly what she had just come to believe.

Julia Comber had obviously played a trick on him.

And on her.

"Forgive me, but I am left with the impression you think

me something I am not," he said quietly. When Xenobia turned her gaze on him, as if she expected him to say more, he added, "I am not a... fancy man for hire, my lady."

Lady Comber had obviously given her that impression.

When he noted the look of confusion that crossed the widow's face, he dipped his head. "I will admit, that once, a very long time ago, before I was married, of course, I accommodated a widow who was looking for a tumble. And I escorted a baroness to the theatre. Once." He paused, remembering Lady Dunsworth was a widowed baroness. "She was old enough to be my grandmother and was in want of another man in her box in order to even out the sexes of those whom she had invited that night.

"But I am nothing like my father once was," he quickly added.

When he watched her for what appeared to be signs of approval, as if he hoped her estimation of him had gone up just a fraction, her steady gaze gave away nothing of her thoughts.

*X*enobia finally blinked twice, deciding for certain that she had completely misunderstood Julia. Misunderstood why her friend had insisted she meet this Mr. Roderick. He probably thought her a Merry Widow, fresh out of widow's weeds and in search of a man to warm her bed every Tuesday and Friday night.

And why would he assume she knew anything about his father?

Who was his father?

"I must apologize, Mr... uh, Sir Randall, did you say?"

"Randolph," he replied, a wince crossing his face.

She allowed her mortification to show in her expression. "I am so sorry, but I think my cousin Julia might have..." She allowed the sentence to trail off as she considered how to save face with the young man. "She may have misrepresented my situation when she asked that you pay a call. With you as well as with me."

Instead of appearing annoyed as he had every right to be, Randolph allowed a wan grin and then sighed. "I had just come to that very conclusion as well, my lady."

"Oh, dear. I feel awful. I've taken your time—"

"It's not your fault, my lady," he said with a shake of his head.

"I plan to be very cross with Julia when next I see her," she said. "I cannot believe she would do this. May I... may I at least offer you compensation for your time? Or... or arrange for a coach to take you home, or wherever you would prefer to be? Your club, perhaps?"

Randolph stared at her. "No. No, my lady. That's not necessary. My coach is parked just down the street." He moved to get up, but saw how agitated she appeared. How tears were on the verge of falling from her bright eyes. "Please, don't cry."

"You must think me a... a wanton." She dropped the book she was holding onto the adjacent side table and fished a hanky from inside the sleeve of her gown.

Settling back into his chair—hard—Randolph stared at her. "Hardly," he said. "Lady Comber obviously made me out to be something I am not when she spoke of me with you, and then led me to believe you were in possession of a timid filly. A terrible trick for which I shall take a whip to her when next I see her."

As he expected, Xenobia's eyes widened as she gasped. "You wouldn't!"

He allowed a smirk. "Of course not. But her husband might once I tell him what she's done," he argued.

"Oh, please don't," she begged her eyes still wide.

His brows furrowed at how frightened she looked. At least tears no longer brightened her eyes. "You are not angry with her?"

The air seemed to leave her all at once. "Ever since my husband died, Cousin Julia—Lady Comber—has been one of the few who has continued to pay calls on me. To ensure I haven't joined my husband from the sheer boredom of mourning," she explained with a sigh. "So, yes, I will be cross with her, but I will ensure we will still be friends once she has heard my complaints."

Randolph considered her words and allowed a sigh. "Comber wouldn't raise a hand against her, nor a whip," he murmured. "He loves her too much."

"But he will be cross with her," Xenobia said with a grin, rather liking his last comment. "Until she reminds him that she's carrying his child, and then all will be well."

Chuckling, Randolph said, "Much like my father would be with his wife, I suppose." He remembered his father's mention that he thought another babe was on the way. "For the very same reason."

Xenobia noticed the change in her guest's expression, how he seemed unsure of how he felt when speaking of his father. "Pray tell, is there a chance I might have been introduced to your father or mother?"

Randolph dipped his head. Lady Comber obviously hadn't mentioned his relationship to the couple who lived just down the street. "I suppose there's a chance," he replied. "Lord Reading. Are you acquainted with him or... or with his marchioness?"

The word 'Reading' had Xenobia blinking. There was only one man she knew of that went by that moniker. "Your father is the Marquess of Reading?"

Randolph nodded. "He is."

The Rake of Reading, Xenobia almost said out loud. At least, that had been the man's reputation before he had finally, at the age of five-and-thirty, married Constance Fitzwilliam. That reputation as a rake had been well-earned. Four bastard sons by four different women, although Randall Roderick had seen to it all were raised by good families.

She had only ever met the daughter. Despite the four years' difference in their age, she and Rachel had become fast friends over their similar circumstances.

"I am the oldest," Randolph said, as if he could read her thoughts.

Xenobia blinked. How had she not realized he looked like a

younger version of Randall Roderick? No wonder he seemed so familiar! His father lived only ten doors down in Curzon Street. Before her husband had died, Xenobia had been a guest in the marchioness' parlor many times. She had even visited the nursery. Held the babes and remarked on how much she wanted one of her own.

Then she realized why his coach would be parked just down the street.

Not because he had thought to save her from gossip, but because he had probably come directly from the marquess' townhouse.

"Were you at Reading House this evening?"

Randolph wasn't sure if he was relieved or bothered that she was familiar with his father. Given her age, it was unlikely Xenobia had ever had an *affaire* with the marquess, but given Reading's reputation as a rake prior to his marriage, it wasn't outside the realm of possibilities.

"I was there, yes," he admitted finally. "I had dinner with him and his marchioness, so it was not at all an inconvenience to pay a call on you." Despite his opinion of Constance having changed considerably over the past year, he still found it impossible to refer to her as his stepmother in conversation.

Xenobia wished she still held the book. She desperately wanted to hug it to her chest—hold it before her as if it was a shield. To pick it up from the table now would only draw more attention as her expression displayed a look of horror. "Oh, dear. I've just now realized Lady Comber was playing at *matchmaking.*"

For a moment, Randolph wished he had accepted the offer of a brandy. This was the one night during the week when he could imbibe and not be concerned about whether or not he got too drunk. "Has she been led to believe you want another husband?"

Stunned, Xenobia held back a rebuke and considered how she might answer. The question would come up the next time she took tea in someone else's parlor—if not directly, then in some roundabout fashion that would no doubt leave her embarrassed. "I don't know that I wish to marry again. At least, not so soon," she finally admitted.

"If not marriage, then what would you like to do next, my lady?" he asked. From her manners, he knew she hadn't given a thought to the life of a Merry Widow. She was far too meek.

Too timid.

When she seemed confused by his query, he said, "Your status as a widow allows you a good deal of latitude." When her eyes widened, as if she intended to scold him, he quickly added, "You can travel, for example. Move to a different town, or live in the country. Take a holiday to Brighton, or enjoy the waters in Bath."

From the way he had qualified his question, Xenobia knew he did not ask what she wanted in order to satisfy his own curiosity, but rather to suggest she think about what she wanted for herself.

"Companionship at first, I should think," she blurted. "Before I would consider traveling anywhere." At seeing his gentle nod, she added, "A friend. Someone with whom to attend the theatre or a soirée. Someone to invite for dinner."

"So, the death of your husband has left you... lonely?"

She nodded. "He was my best friend. For nearly my entire life. But after we married..." She allowed the sentence to trail off.

"Not so much?"

Xenobia once again looked as if she might cry. "I found him annoying. The boy I knew hadn't grown into a man but rather into a... a fop," she whispered. "There were nights he was far better dressed than me, in shoes far more ornate than mine."

Randolph regarded her a moment as he considered his own situation with Barbara. Although he hadn't known her his entire life—or hers—he had thought the two of them were well suited when he proposed marriage. He had thought they were happy together. To discover Barbara had not shared his sentiments had been both a shock and a disappointment.

Given her pregnancy, he had hoped she might grow fond of him once the child was born.

He hadn't considered the alternative.

*R*emembering something of what he had said at the beginning of their conversation, Xenobia said, "You mentioned being married." She held her breath, hoping the floor would open up beneath her.

Surprised by the sudden sadness that had him clearing his throat in order to reply, Randolph said, "I was. My wife died shortly after giving birth to our son, Charlie." He winced at hearing the harsh words spoken aloud, and then swallowed hard as he tried to avoid his hostess' look of astonishment.

"I'm so sorry for your loss," Xenobia replied, her words at odds with the sense of relief she felt just then. At the thought that she had already met Charlie. Held him, in fact. "A friend, too?"

He nodded. "She was a good friend, and yet I still thought it remarkable that she agreed to marry me knowing I was illegitimate."

Xenobia struggled to maintain an impassive expression. "But your father has recognized you as his own, has he not?"

Then she remembered how he had introduced himself. *Sir Randolph Roderick*. As a bastard, it was doubtful he was a baronet. The only other means of acquiring his title was if he were a knight.

"Oh, he has," Randolph replied, and then because he was feeling rather annoyed with the man—especially because he had seen him leaving The Queen of Hearts the afternoon prior—he added, "Me, as well as three other bastard sons. From the day we were born." When she didn't react—he was sure he had scandalized her with the comment—he dipped his head. "Barbara seemed fine with it, but after a time—"

"Society reminded her."

Grimacing, Randolph angled his head to one side, as if he was about to say something. Instead, he finally nodded. "Every day, it seems. I could not change what I am, and Barbara seemed less inclined to accept the situation for what it was."

"And then she died," Xenobia murmured.

The simple words felt as if a door had slammed shut. Randolph inhaled, the scents of various flowers tickling his nostrils. His gaze darted to a vase of red roses and then to another of lilies. Both were reminders of the parlor in his own townhouse at Christmas time. Reminders of Barbara.

He was about to make his excuses and take his leave, but the expression on his hostess' face—her eyes were wide, as if she couldn't believe what she had just said—had him reconsidering. "I think you could do with a brandy, my lady. I know I could use one."

"Oh, dear," she replied. "I think you may be right," she added as she moved to stand. Randolph held out a staying hand. He rose from his chair in an instant and quickly moved to the sideboard where the crystal decanters of various liquors were lined up on a large silver salver.

As Randolph reached for the brandy, he wondered if the decanters had been touched since Dunsworth's death.

CHAPTER 19

A HEART TO HEART WITH A MOTHER

*M*eanwhile, in the office at *The Queen of Hearts*
"You're still here?"

Startled by the sound of her mother's voice—she hadn't heard the office door open—Rachel nearly upended the ink pot as she quickly stood. "I am," she replied. Her gaze darted about in search of a clock, and when she didn't find one on the desk, she glanced at the single candle lamp she had been using to supplement the overhead gas lighting.

The lamp oil was nearly gone.

"It's past one in the morning, dear heart," her mother gently scolded. "I didn't intend for you to put in a full day's accounting in one evening," she added as she moved to stand before the desk. The stacks of invoices and bills of lading were no longer where she had left them. In their place was a stack of cheques made out to various vendors. "You've already finished?" she asked in awe.

Rachel settled into the desk chair as she said, "I have, but I wished to review the arithmetic to ensure I didn't make any mistakes."

"And I interrupted you," Violet said on a sigh.

"Oh, it's all right. I am certain of my numbers now," Rachel replied, noticing a parchment her mother held in one hand.

"The matched invoices are here," she said as she placed the flat of one hand on a neat stack of papers. "I wasn't sure where to put them."

"I'll see to those tomorrow afternoon," Violet said as she waved the hand that held the paper. "I file them away in those cabinets over there." She pointed to a row of wooden drawers with brass handles.

"How?" Rachel asked.

Violet furrowed a brow. "By vendor."

"I'll see to it in the morning. Before I go to pay a call at Bradley House."

"Oh, you needn't," Violet tried to argue, but Rachel had already turned her attention to the next stack of papers.

"These require your signature," Rachel continued, pointing to the cheques. "And these," she pulled another stack to rest atop the ledger, "Don't have matching invoices."

Violet's eyebrows arched in appreciation. "I rather expect they will when the morning's post is delivered," she said with a grin. She crossed her arms and sighed. "I must go back out to the gaming floor for a few hours before I retire for the night," she said. "But I do not expect you to wait up for me. In fact, you should get some sleep. You must be looking forward to seeing Lady Dunsworth."

"Oh, I am," Rachel replied. "She's out of mourning now, and I expect we'll be plotting how we wish to live the rest of our lives as a widow and a spinster."

"Rachel," Violet said in a not-so-gentle scold. "You're not going to be a spinster. Why, I expect you'll have a gentleman calling on you before the Season's entertainments even start."

Her eyes widening at the thought that Mark Merriweather might have said something to her mother, Rachel said, "I told him he had to ask father's permission before he could take me for a ride in the park."

Violet blinked. "He who?"

The air seemed to go out of Rachel all at once. "Mr. Merriweather." From the way her mother stared at her, Rachel regretted having mentioned him.

"He was here? In here?" Violet asked in alarm.

Rachel nodded. "Mr. Merriweather was watching us when we left the dining room together, and when I did not reappear when you did, he came... exploring." When she noted how her mother's coloring reddened, she quickly added, "He was the perfect gentleman, Mother."

"But you were alone with him."

"I was," Rachel reluctantly affirmed. "He offered me a position."

From Violet's widened eyes, Rachel wondered if her mother imagined exactly what she had upon hearing the young man's initial words. "Not as a mistress, Mother. As a bookkeeper."

"How dare he?"

"It seems he had the same trouble with his man of business as you did with yours."

Violet's eyes narrowed. "No doubt because we had the same one," she murmured.

"You did?" Rachel asked in surprise. "He didn't mention a name."

Violet huffed. "I don't suppose *he's* reported Mr. Traynor to a magistrate?"

"He said he would," Rachel replied. "After I warned him his good name would be used even if the cur didn't have a character from him." She paused and then added, "Did *you* report Mr. Traynor to a magistrate?"

Violet seemed to think on her daughter's query before she said, "Not directly. But I assure you, he was reported and has suffered for what he did. I couldn't do it directly, you see, because I cannot afford to look as if someone has taken advantage."

"Mother!"

"I am the only woman running this kind of establishment in this part of town," Violet said in hushed tones. "I would look weak if anyone knew an employee had embezzled funds from me."

"You do have protection?" Rachel half-asked.

"Of course."

"Surely Father would use his influence should you require it." When Violet's eyes darted to the side, Rachel sighed. "You have not called upon him for that," she whispered, not making it a question.

"I would have to be very desperate to involve Reading in any of my affairs these days," Violet claimed. "And when I say *affairs*, I do not mean..." She stopped and exhaled a loud sigh.

"But you could," Rachel whispered.

"I will when it comes to you. I had to promise him that," Violet admitted. After a pause, she said, "And as for Mr. Merriweather, it's quite evident he's sweet on you. Offering you a position seems like an odd way of showing it, though." She paused before she added, "Now what's this about a ride in the park?"

Rachel nearly giggled. "He wants to take me for a ride in the park, but I told him he had to have father's permission—and I'd need a horse to ride—so I rather doubt I'll ever see him again."

Leaning forward in her chair, Violet said, "You told him Reading was your father?"

"I did."

Violet's eyes darted to the side. "And he still asked you to accompany him?"

"He did."

Apparently impressed, Violet said, "Well, Mr. Merriweather may be more honorable than I would have thought."

"Given Lord Wessex already has his heir, Mr. Merriweather isn't in danger of inheriting the Middleton earldom," Rachel said with a shrug. "But whatever is The Three Bells?"

Giving a start, Violet blinked. "How do you know about The Three Bells?"

Rachel scoffed. "I don't, which is why I asked what it was."

"It's a public house. But how is it you know its name?"

It was Rachel's turn to give a start. *Why would an earl's son own a public house?* "Mr. Merriweather mentioned it."

"He's not planning to take you there?" Violet queried, her manner most guarded.

"He is not. But, pray tell, why is it you looked so surprised when *I* mentioned it?"

Violet shook her head. "They've been after my French cook. Ever since I opened. He receives offers nearly every week from a number of households, but The Three Bells is the most insistent."

Rachel remembered her mother's comment about the cook when Mark had come to their table. "Didn't Mr. Merriweather ask about him at dinner?"

"He's another one who threatens to take my dear Jean Claude from me," Violet said on a sigh.

Now aware her mother didn't know Mark was the *owner* of The Three Bells, Rachel now wondered if her mother and Jean Claude were having an affair. She was about to ask when Violet rolled her eyes.

"I am not having an affair with my cook," she stated. "Although..." She allowed the sentence to trail off as she seemed to contemplate the possibility.

"Mother!" Rachel scolded.

"I know. I never mix business with..., well never you mind, but I shan't be entertaining Jean Claude in my bed. Besides, I rather think his heart is already engaged."

"Anyone you know?" Rachel asked, thinking her mother might have sway from a different front.

"No, but he's gorgeous."

Rachel blinked several times before she cleared her throat. "There are times when I am glad I do not have to be concerned about such matters."

Violet's face fell at hearing her daughter's comment. "You needn't lower your expectations for a husband just because you were born on the wrong side of the blanket," Violet said softly. "Your father has recognized you. You have his name, a dowry—"

"I'd be perfectly happy should I never marry, Mother." Wanting the subject changed, Rachel indicated the paper her mother still clutched in her hand. "What have you there?"

Violet glanced at the note as if seeing it for the first time. "Oh, this is the total for yesterday's receipts. The amount I took to the bank earlier this afternoon. It needs to be added as a deposit on the ledger."

Rachel studied the number, her mouth dropping open in surprise. "Mother! This is for... for one day?"

"We have been doing rather well," Violet admitted. "Probably because we're known for not cheating anyone."

"Like they do at Crockford's?"

Violet gave a start. "What do you know about cheating at Crockford's?"

Rachel inhaled and said, "That man you had me escort to the front door? The one you said was my brother? He made mention of it when he was extolling your virtues as a gaming hell owner. It's true what you said about being known for not cheating anyone."

Violet blinked. "I still cannot believe he didn't introduce himself to you."

Rachel shook her head. "He did not. I think he was hoping I might introduce myself, but I thought better of it. Perhaps I'm being too cautious?"

"Probably for the best," Violet murmured, her attention on her mind's eye. "I would have introduced you if Mr. Wilson hadn't been there. Such a toad, that one."

For the second time that day, Rachel wished she'd had a vinaigrette on her person, for a momentary light-headedness had her seeing gray at the edges of her vision. "Randolph seemed... *nice*," she whispered. "He looked so much like how I remember Father."

Sighing, Violet nodded and said, "He is a nice man. And I'm quite sure you'll meet him again very soon. Now. To bed with you, and do help yourself to breakfast in the morning. Jean Claude will have made something delicious for those who work the morning shift."

Rachel thought to argue, but weariness had her deciding it was time to return to her new bedchamber. "Very well. Good night, Mother. I'll come back here to the office before I leave to pay a call on Xenobia. See to the posts and such."

Violet watched her daughter go before she slumped into one of the chairs in front of the desk. Although she would have liked to keep her daughter to herself for a few more days, she knew she would have to share Rachel with others on the morrow.

CHAPTER 20
BRANDY MAKES IT ALL BETTER

eanwhile, at Bradley House

Xenobia watched as Randolph poured a finger's worth of brandy into two crystal glasses. He had mentioned having brothers, but he hadn't mentioned his sister, Rachel, and she wondered at the omission. Perhaps he wasn't on good terms with her. Xenobia sighed and then angled her head as she considered a safe subject. "What of your child?"

Randolph's face brightened, and for the first time that evening, Xenobia thought him handsome. She wondered what he might look like freshly shaven in the morning, with his hair trimmed a bit shorter.

"Charles is just past one and quite a handful," he said. "I expect he'll be walking at any moment. He's living in the nursery at my father's house."

"Growing up with his..." Xenobia paused to consider the relationship. "Uncle?"

"Indeed," he said with a grin as he handed her a glass.

"Thank you. Are you able to see him often?"

"As often as I can. Usually a few times a week, and always Wednesday nights, like tonight."

Xenobia was sure if she had a son, she would have to see him far more often. Every day. Several times a day. "Well, I am glad it was a short walk for you this evening," she murmured.

"And a rather pleasant one," he said as he leaned forward in his chair.

"Even in this wintery weather?"

Randolph lifted a broad shoulder. "It's a bit chilly, but it wasn't snowing when I was on my way here," he replied. He held out his glass. "In a few days, we shall see more greenery decorating doors, and it will be even more pleasant. Now, what shall we drink to?"

Xenobia considered how to respond. "New friendships?" she offered, holding her breath in anticipation of what he might say.

A grin appeared and seemed to further soften Randolph's harsh features. "New friendships," he agreed before lifting his glass in salute. He took a sip, nearly purring with appreciation of the fortified wine.

Lord Dunsworth might have been a fop, but he certainly had good taste in liquor.

"I know I shouldn't, but I find I do like brandy," Xenobia said, just before the tip of her tongue touched the edge of her lip.

That little gesture had Randolph blinking. For a moment, he imagined her doing that immediately following a kiss, as if she wished to retain the flavor of it. "I find it a civilized drink," he agreed. "Too many of my acquaintances have begun drinking scotch from up north. Can't say I have an appreciation for the stuff," he added with a grimace.

"I've heard of it, but never tried it," Xenobia replied. "I rather imagine men of leisure appreciate all sorts of spirits, though."

Randolph furrowed a brow as he wondered if she had deliberately put voice to a double entendre. "Not being a man of leisure, I cannot say from first-hand experience."

Her eyes widened. "May I inquire as to your... work? Or are you referring to the horse training?"

From the way she asked, Randolph knew he had surprised her. She had assumed that as a son of a marquess—even a bastard son—he did not have to work for his living.

He didn't—not really—but he wasn't about to admit it.

"I am in charge of one of my father's stables. The one just west of town," he replied. "I train horses and arrange for the sale of those we do not need for the marquessate, usually at Tattersall's."

As for his other employment, he could have admitted to working for King and Country, but he knew she would ask by which office he was employed. He didn't want to lie to the young matron, but there were some secrets he needed to keep.

"So, you were not at all surprised when Lady Comber asked if you might consider training my horse?" she asked.

He shook his head. "Not at all. I would have welcomed the commission, actually, in the hope that I might secure future employment from others."

"From my recommendation?"

Randolph was struck by how quickly she sorted his reason for meeting with her. "Or your husband's, if you'd had one."

Xenobia dipped her head. "I am terribly sorry about the misunderstanding. For the inconvenience this has caused you."

Randolph finished off his brandy. "You needn't be."

"I'm happy to pay you for your time. For the... consultation," she stammered.

"No need, my lady." He noted her expression. Besides being embarrassed, she seemed at a loss as to what to say or do next. He had already determined she wasn't an empty-headed English miss, but she surely was timid. The last thing he wanted was for her to feel as if Lady Comber's machination was her fault.

He cleared his throat. "It's unfortunate the Season's entertainments will not begin for a few months, but once they do, may I expect to claim a dance with you, my lady?"

"You wish to dance with me?"

Straightening in his chair, Randolph regarded her a moment. She reminded him a bit of Barbara, although where Barbara's innocence about the world had been feigned, Lady Dunsworth's seemed genuine. "I do."

Xenobia's question had left her bow lips slightly parted, and Randolph's thoughts of innocence were suddenly replaced with thoughts of what those lips would be like to kiss. At the moment, they would no doubt taste of brandy. Perhaps there would be a touch of the wine she had drunk with dinner. A hint of sweetness from whatever dessert her cook had created. The tang of salt from a tear.

It would be easy to pity the poor woman, but he was determined to see her as something more than an inexperienced widow. More than an innocent young matron.

Thoughts of what she might be like in his bed flitted at the edge of his thoughts. Would she become a tigress? Purring as he pleasured her and then pouncing when it was his turn to be pleasured?

His manhood hardened behind the fall of his breeches, and Randolph struggled to erase the carnal thoughts.

The last of Xenobia's brandy made its way down her throat, its warmth combined with his words emboldening her. "Pray tell, do you have any evenings free for the likes of me?" she asked. "I mean, to spend like this, of course," she quickly qualified. "Drinks and... conversation. Perhaps on nights after you've said good-night to your son? I fear I have become a bit of a hermit this past year, and I could really use the practice."

Randolph stared at her before his gaze dropped to the empty glass she held. Apparently, the brandy had loosed her tongue.

And her timidity.

He allowed a shrug. "I... I suppose I could return next Wednesday evening. It would have to be after dinner with my father, of course."

"Oh, of course," she replied. "We can enjoy a glass of brandy, and you can tell me more about your son." Since she had already met the babe, she was curious as to how he was getting along.

Randolph allowed a grin. "My stepmother thinks he will grow up believing he is a bird, since I'm inclined to toss him into the air so much."

Xenobia leaned forward, her face brightening. "Oh, how

delightful. I suppose his giggles can be heard throughout the nursery."

"Oh, I think down to the second story," he replied with a chuckle, just then realizing he had referred to Lady Reading as his stepmother.

Well, there was a first for everything, he supposed.

"At some point, he will grow too heavy, and I will be reduced to entertaining him by spinning him around as I hold onto his arms. That's what my father was doing this evening with my brother, Robert." He resisted the urge to blink when he realized he had referred to Robert as his *brother* rather than his *half-brother*.

Glancing into his glass, he wondered from where the brandy had come. If he knew, he would see to stocking it at his townhouse.

Xenobia's face lit up again as a hand went to cover her mouth. "I cannot imagine it. The Marquess of Reading playing with his son."

"It is a sight," Randolph replied as he sobered. "One I did not experience as a child, I assure you."

"Which means you were not rendered dizzy."

"True," he acknowledged, a grin once again returning to his lips and a dimple appearing in his right cheek.

Kissable lips.

Xenobia resisted the urge to blink, wondering why she would think such a thing just then. Why she suddenly imagined what it might be like to be kissed by this man, his firm lips sliding over hers until she opened her mouth to his questing tongue. Even as he suckled the pillows of her lips, she could imagine the tip of his tongue sliding over her teeth, tangling with hers, tasting the brandy she had finished, and perhaps the wine she had had with dinner.

Would he also taste the sweet dessert?

Or merely taste the salt from her tears?

She was contemplating this last when Randolph asked, "Did you wish for me to pour you some more brandy?"

Blinking away her reverie at the same moment she noted

how aroused she felt, Xenobia shook her head. "Oh, no. I would be left foxed," she replied with a grin, rather liking how her knees no longer seemed to be part of her body. There was a slight buzzing in her head, as well, a rather pleasant sensation she had only ever experienced when she drank too much champagne at balls. Her eyes widened, though, when she thought perhaps he had asked because *he* wanted more. "But do help yourself."

Randolph considered teasing her—perhaps she intended to get him drunk and then have her way with him—but he knew it was too much to hope for. "You will not mind?" he asked as he stood and moved to the sideboard.

Xenobia watched as he made his way, his long legs topped with wide thighs covering the distance in only a few strides. Although the tails of his coat hid what was atop those muscular thighs, she imagined he sported a firm bottom. Not the flabby ass Dunsworth had possessed.

Knowing she had to clear her mind of his person, Xenobia thought to clarify a few things before the buzzing in her brain rendered her mute. "May I ask how it is you know Lady Comber?" He had mentioned it, she was sure. But for some reason, she couldn't remember the details.

Randolph turned from the sideboard, the brandy glass held in one hand while the other rested on his hip. He allowed a grin, the very slightest of dimples appearing in his right cheek.

Xenobia swallowed, struck by how the expression made him seem younger. Not nearly as severe as she had first thought him. His resemblance to Lord Reading was now unmistakeable.

"As well as anyone can know their best friend's wife, I suppose," he hedged. "I have known Alistair Comber for some time because he runs his father-in-law's stables—the Earl of Mayfield's stables. I took on the management of one of my father's London stables when I finished my studies at Oxford."

Nodding her understanding, Xenobia angled her body in his direction and asked, "It sounds as if your father's stables are large. Is there a reason he owns so many horses?" She imagined a man who owned a fleet of hackneys or who provided the horses for the mail coaches.

Randolph allowed a shrug. "He and my stepmother raise racehorses, actually. My brother sees to the stables in Reading—that's where most of the Thoroughbreds are—while I see to the horses we use for all the various equipage and the horses we use for riding in the park."

Thoughts of his father's reputation had Xenobia curious. "You're not following in his footsteps, are you?" she asked, her voice quiet.

"If you mean by being a rake or... or a rogue, then no, my lady. He, um, he was quite adamant that none of his sons behave as he did," he stammered. If she'd been a man, he would have mentioned the pasteboard box filled with French letters he'd been given upon the occasion of his sixteenth birthday along with the stern warning they be used.

A profound relief fell over Xenobia, enough so that she knew she had been far too bold with her queries on this night. "Forgive me for having asked if you would be available to keep a widow company," she whispered, knowing a blush colored her face.

Disappointed by her words—Randolph thought she might be about to dismiss him—he said, "There is nothing to forgive, my lady."

Once again, Xenobia wished the floor would open up and swallow her whole.

However was she going to end this gracefully?

Randolph returned to his chair. "I do admit to feeling concerned that you would allow me entry into your home when you thought me something else."

Xenobia dipped her head. "It was foolish of me, but Julia recommended you so highly. She insisted in her note to me that we meet."

Randolph dipped his head. "She was as insistent with me," he replied, remembering Alistair's comment that he thought his wife was up to something.

Matchmaking, he had said, as if to warn him off. Well, there was no doubt of that now.

Xenobia sighed and remembered why she and James had grown apart those last few years. Never expecting to see her caller again, she asked the question that had bothered her for so long. "Tell me, Mr. Roderick. Since you no longer have a wife, do you then employ a mistress?" She gave her head a shake. "I do not ask to judge you, of course. I merely ask out of... curiosity. And because I think I'm experiencing a bit of brandy brain."

Randolph was torn between frowning and chuckling. Lady Dunsworth was proving even the meekest of young matrons could be shocking when she'd consumed a bit of alcohol. "I do not. I... I admit I had thought about it. Once. But I hear tales of how much they cost, and how demanding they can be, and I think I would rather just have a wife." His gaze had gone to her left hand, where her gold wedding band still graced the base of her fourth finger. "Do you ask because your husband employed one?"

Xenobia dipped her head again. "The last two years of our marriage. I was terribly jealous of her."

Randolph frowned. "Because...?"

She allowed the latent anger to help keep the tears at bay. "The time he spent with her instead of with me. Doing things with her that he claimed he could not do with me. To me."

"Because you were his best friend."

All the air seemed to go out of her at once, and her back suddenly settled against the stiff upholstery. His words weren't an excuse, exactly, but merely a statement of fact. "Yes," she whispered. "But... why? He assured me he did not hurt her."

Randolph swallowed, wishing he didn't have to be the one to explain a man's desire for dark carnal pleasures. "I have reason to believe it is a consideration among married men who might have more... more carnal appetites than what they think their wives should have to abide," he tried to explain.

"That they cannot treat their wives with as much considera-tion as they do their mistresses?" she countered, her anger once again apparent. "As if they are doing us a favor?"

"That they cannot do to their wives the *unspeakable* acts that they can do to their mistresses. Because they pay coin for the privilege," he shot back, thinking she sounded terribly naive.

For the first time that evening, Xenobia felt a red-hot flush color her throat and cheeks. The role of a mistress had never been explained in such bald terms before.

Had James thought her too fragile? Too timid for what he wanted when it came to sexual relations? If so, he had never put voice to his concerns. Never asked her if she would object to more adventurous antics in her bedchamber.

Or in his.

The thought had her remembering once again that Julia had been referring to *her* as the "timid filly" when she had spoken with Mr. Roderick earlier that afternoon.

Apparently, he had already come to the same conclusion.

"Is it wrong for me to want... companionship?" she whis-pered. "Please do not tell me to hire a young woman capable of conversation."

Randolph shook his head. "It is not wrong, nor would I suggest a paid companion for you," he replied. "You are far too young for such an employee." He paused. "But, besides what you mentioned earlier, what exactly *do* you want?" He reached for her hand, intending to provide comfort, but he hissed as he took it into his. "Your hand is still cold," he murmured. He set down his brandy glass and reached over to hold her hand between both of his.

She nodded. "I cannot seem to get warm this winter," she replied. "Especially at night. Which is partly why Julia asked you to come, I think."

Randolph regarded her for a long moment, his suspicions confirmed. Lady Comber had been acting as a matchmaker, which meant he could do one of two things.

Take his leave of Lady Dunsworth and never see her again, or make an attempt to get to know the lonely widow. Perhaps take her up on her invitation to spend his Wednesday nights in her company. For drinks and conversation. The quality of the brandy alone would be enough of an incentive for him to return.

"Would you be amenable to a ride in the park?" he asked.

Xenobia's eyes widened. "I... I haven't been on a horse in an age," she replied.

Wincing, Randolph amended the query. "A ride on a phaeton in the park, perhaps? I have a shire in need of exercise as well as the experience of pulling a phaeton by himself." He had several horses he needed to train, but he couldn't imagine she'd be interested in riding every day of the week.

Her face breaking out into a radiant grin, Xenobia dipped her head. "I have only ever ridden on a phaeton once," she claimed, deciding it better she not describe Julia's driving skills —or lack thereof. "It was most exhilarating."

"It can be," he affirmed, a grin once again youthening his appearance. "I will come for you at half-past-three o'clock tomorrow."

Xenobia blinked. "And if it is snowing?"

Randolph shrugged. "Then I suggest you bring an umbrella."

With that, he stood while he still held onto her now-warm hand, and brushed his lips over the back of it. "I will see myself out, my lady," he said. He gave a bow and took his leave of the parlor.

Xenobia watched as he strode over the threshold. Heard his descent as he made his way down the carpeted stairs. Heard him pause and then climb back up the stairs, as if he might have forgotten something.

When he reappeared on the parlor threshold, he paused and then said, "Whatever you do, don't scream." He crossed to her in three strides, placed his hands on either side of her waist, lifted her to her feet, kissed her quite thoroughly, and then he settled her back in her chair.

He must have known her legs wouldn't support her.

"Why ever would I scream?" she asked in confusion.

His eyes darting to the side, Randolph finally shrugged and said, "Why, indeed?" He bowed and once again took his leave of the parlor.

This time, Xenobia wasn't aware of anything except the sound of the front door closing.

For the first time in a very long time, she made her way to her bedchamber with a smile on her face.

CHAPTER 21
A FATHER'S SECRET
REVEALED

A few minutes later

His thoughts scattered in a thousand directions—the two brandies had thoroughly addled his ability to reason—Randolph made his way west in Curzon Street. One topic he could handle was the question of where he would spend the night.

For a moment back at Bradley House, he knew he would have been welcome to spend the night in Lady Dunsworth's bedchamber. Her response to his kiss was that enthusiastic. That passionate.

But he was sure she would be mortified in the morning.

Even if he left her in the wee hours before dawn, she would spend the entire day wishing a floor would open up and swallow her whole.

Probably the floor on which she stood when he arrived to take her for the ride in the park at half-past three o'clock.

Randolph had decided he would spend the night at his father's townhouse. He had an apartment there, although he rarely used it. He thought it enough that his father's wife allowed his son to live in the nursery with her son. He didn't wish to prevail upon his stepmother's hospitality overmuch.

And there it was again.

Stepmother.

He once again wondered at the brand of brandy that could have him changing six years of thinking in a matter of sixty minutes.

His thoughts of Constance had him wincing when he remembered his father's earlier claim that he was spending his nights with his marchioness. He had spied the man leaving The Queen of Hearts—in the middle of the day!

Randall Roderick's claim that he was no longer a rake rankled.

Why did he lie to me? Randolph wondered.

The question had him wondering the same about Lady Comber. Did she really think it was necessary to make him believe Lady Dunsworth needed a horse trainer when all she wanted was for the two of them to meet?

He focused his thoughts on the woman who had no intention of hiring him to train a horse.

He had come to realize that it was *she* who was the timid filly.

The very last thing he wanted to do was to break her.

The butler, Giles, answered the door after only one knock, which had him wondering if the servant had been told to expect him. "Much obliged," he said as he handed Giles his hat. "Pray tell, do you know if the nursery is quiet on this night?"

The butler allowed a rare grin. "I've not heard a peep from the third story since you took your leave, sir."

Embarrassed—the sounds from the nursery were probably quite audible when he'd been up there earlier—Randolph dipped his head. "Has my father retired for the night?"

Giles said, "He did and then... well, he's in his study now, sir," he hedged in hushed tones.

Randolph frowned, quite sure his father expected to spend the night with Connie in her bedchamber. Had she asked him to leave? "You should retire for the night," he suggested to the butler. "I can see my way."

"You're not in need of a valet, sir?" Giles countered.

"Not tonight." He rarely had the services of such a servant, preferring to shave himself as well as dress himself in the mornings. He did arrange for one to shine his shoes and boots and see to his laundry, however. "I will avail myself of breakfast in the morning, however."

"Ah, the master and mistress are usually down by nine o'clock," Giles replied.

"Can I expect those in the nursery to be awake before then?"

The butler allowed a grin. "Undoubtedly."

Randolph gave the servant a nod. Although he was used to being up long before nine in the morning, he had a groom and a stableboy who could see to the stables if he wasn't there.

He made his way to his father's study.

"Ah, I'm so glad you returned here," Randall said as Randolph peeked around the edge of the open door. "I feared you might take a hackney to your townhouse."

"I came in the town coach tonight, but I'm too tired to make the trip to Westminster," Randolph admitted. "I told Downley to park it in the mews and spend the night with your grooms," he added, referring to his driver.

"Glad to hear it," his father replied as he indicated an overstuffed chair.

A memory of seeing his father emerge from The Queen of Hearts the day before reminded him of Randall Roderick's claim that he was no longer a rake. A claim that now rankled.

Why did he lie to me? Randolph wondered again before he said, "Which has me wondering why it is you're not in my stepmother's bed?"

Randall sighed. "I plan to return there shortly. But I hoped I might have your company for a few more minutes before you retire. You were gone longer than I expected."

"Lady Dunsworth and I had much to discuss," Randolph replied as he moved to take the chair in front of his father's massive mahogany desk. "What is it?" he asked, his manner brisk.

"Connie confirmed this evening that she is indeed breeding," his father stated.

Randolph allowed a shrug, not the least bit surprised by the comment. He always expected there would be more siblings. More brothers. "Congratulations." When Randall didn't acknowledge the sentiment, his brow furrowed. "Or... or not?"

"Oh, I am... over the moon, of course," Randall said, allowing a huge grin. "I rather enjoy fatherhood. But I will be two-and-forty by the time this one is born. *Two-and-forty*," he repeated, as if the number were somehow a curse.

His frown deepening, Randolph moved forward so he was perched on the edge of the chair. "Four years younger than Torrington was when his twins were born," he countered, hoping he could assuage what he realized was his father second-guessing his mortality. "Grandfather lived to be sixty... sixty-two, did he not?"

"That's not the point," Randall argued, although he couldn't help the sense of relief that swept over him at learning his oldest son had known Randall's father.

His mother would have been the one to have seen to it.

The fifth Marquess of Reading had been an amiable aristocrat, friendly to all and not the least bit proud while ruling over a huge estate on the edge of Reading. His tenants had been loyal, and his lands had produced crops that could be counted on to keep the coffers full.

His interest in horse racing, although expensive, had paved the way for the string of winners that the sixth and current marquess continued to oversee with the help of his marchioness.

"He was sixty-two," Randall acknowledged. "I don't know why this has me so worried, but... should something happen to me, I want *you* to act as regent until my oldest is of age."

Randolph's eyes widened. "Me?" He gave his head a quick shake. "But... I cannot take your place in Parliament," he argued. "I've only been granted a knighthood." Even if his father petitioned the Crown to elevate his status so he might inherit a title, it was unlikely he would ever become a peer of the realm.

"I know. I just... I want you to be sure Raymond and Robert are raised right."

"You don't think your marchioness will see to that?" Randolph argued. "She's a damned good head on her shoulders, Father," he added suppressing the urge to add, "Better than yours." When he saw that his words didn't seem to change the marquess' mind, he allowed a sigh. "I will see to it, of course," he finally agreed. "I just... I do not think it will be an issue."

Randall dipped his head. "As my heir, Raymond will inherit all the entailed properties, of course, but I intend to settle you and Connie with most of the unentailed properties."

Randolph stilled himself. "What... what of my half-brothers?"

His father displayed a look of offense. "I have already seen to suitable allowances for two of them," he replied. "Along with some small properties on which they can live or lease, depending on their preference."

Furrowing his brows, Randolph asked, "What of the third?"

"I am not allowed to meddle in Richard's life. At all."

"Why ever not?"

Randall stared at his son before he stood and moved to close the door. "Because he is..."

"Is *what*, Father?"

"Heir to a viscountcy."

Understanding finally dawned on Randolph. A baby secretly placed where one had either died or never existed. A babe that could be declared an heir if those in the know merely kept the truth hidden. "I will keep the secret, of course," he whispered. "Not that I would even know who he was," he added with a roll of his eyes.

"Oh, if you ever saw him, you would know," Randall said on a sigh.

"Looks like you, does he?"

Randall scoffed. "Looks more like you. He's only a few years younger. Just as tall."

"So you've seen him? Recently?"

His attention on his mind's eye, Randall nodded. "He's at

university. I saw him quite by accident. It's not my place to be… proud of him, but I cannot help it. He's doing well. He'll make a fine addition to Parliament when his father dies."

"I shall try not to stare should I come across him," Randolph said on a sigh.

"Good. So, I can count on you to see to the other sons, then?"

Randolph considered his father's motivation. "Why are you doing this?"

Randall allowed a shrug. "Truth be told, I hadn't given it much thought, but after our discussion at dinner tonight, I thought you might end up settled with an aristocrat's daughter after all. Or… an aristocrat's widow, perhaps?" he hinted, as if he hoped there might be a courtship in the offing. "There's no reason for you to expect you can only court commoners, son. You are a knight, after all." Randall reached across the desk and plucked a small box from atop a pile of papers. He set it down in front of Randolph.

"What's this?" Randolph asked as he gingerly took the hinged box in hand. He popped open the lid and stared at the gold ring. Clusters of round diamonds hung from either side of a large garnet.

"Just in case you don't have one on hand. I saw to ordering a few when I was last in Ludgate Hill. Thought to make sure you and your brothers were prepared."

Blinking, Randolph regarded his father in surprise. "I am not courting anyone, Father," he stated, at the very same moment a flash of Lady Dunsworth and their kiss came to mind.

"But you will. At some point, you will want a mother for your son. You will want another son. Maybe a daughter or two," he replied. "I want to be sure you can afford them. That you will not be limited by your lot in life as a bastard son."

Clearing his throat, Randolph said, "I have never felt as if I were limited by my 'lot in life'," he argued. "Besides, I have a position."

"That pays shite," Randall countered.

Memories of what Barbara had said to Randolph in the last months of her pregnancy had at one time brought forth doubting thoughts. Reminders that she thought he had no business living in the world of aristocrats despite having been acknowledged by his father. "Nevertheless, you keep reminding me that I am not limited," he added.

"There's another matter," Randall said in a quieter voice. "But, after this evening, I suppose you already know."

Randolph straightened in the chair, about to agree. About to blurt out his frustration at his father over what he had witnessed from his apartment at The Jack of Spades the day before. And then, because the brandy had loosed his tongue as much as it had Lady Dunsworth's, he said, "Would it have anything to do with why you were at The Queen of Hearts yesterday afternoon?"

Randall gave a start. "Were you following me?"

"My room at The Jack of Spades looks out on Stafford Street."

Allowing a nod, Randall's eyes darted sideways before he sighed and said, "I had hoped to see your sister—"

"*Sister?*" Randolph repeated, his voice loud even in his own ears. "How... how long have I had a *sister?*"

"Shhh," the marquess replied, holding a finger to his lips. "Although I don't mind all of Curzon Street knowing, I rather doubt they wish to learn of it at eleven o'clock at night."

Eleven? Randolph almost countered. He was sure he had been at Bradley House for only an hour. Pulling his chronometer from his waistcoat pocket, he frowned when he realized it exactly matched the clock on the fireplace mantel. He had obviously been with the widow far longer than an hour!

Randall's brows furrowed. "I was sure Xenobia Dunsworth would have mentioned her when she learned who you were."

Wondering if he'd had more than two glasses of brandy, Randolph stared at his father. "Why would *she* know I have a sister?"

Lifting a shoulder, Randall said, "Because Lady X

befriended her. They attended the same finishing school together for a time before Lady X returned to London."

His father's reference to Xenobia as 'Lady X' had Randolph wincing. "Did you find her?" Although he had a dozen other questions, such as why Lady Dunsworth hadn't mentioned her, he knew his father wouldn't know the answer to that one.

Randall angled his head first to one side and then the other. "Her mother told me she'll be returning to London any day now. She might have arrived today."

Dumbfounded, mostly because of the brandy, Randolph finally asked, "Do *I* know her?" The mention of the mother then had him wondering if she was a prostitute at The Queen of Hearts. "Or her mother?"

Furrowing his bushy brows, Randall said, "I should hope not in the biblical sense. Her mother is The Queen at The Queen of Hearts. Violet Higgins."

Randolph blinked. Several times. "The one with the wig large enough to accommodate a colony of mice? I just had a meeting with her before I came here for dinner this evening."

His brows furrowing until they made up a long caterpillar, Randall sighed and said, "When I first met Violet, she was but twenty and a brunette. I assure you, there were no vermin. But I do know what you mean about the wig."

Trying to imagine what the woman might have looked like two decades ago had Randolph's brain serving up images that were entirely inappropriate. Violet Higgins was blessed with remarkable charms that were nearly always on full display given how tight her corset was tied and how low cut her modiste made her gowns. "And my sister? Would I know *her*?" Randolph hadn't availed himself of a prostitute in an age, but the mere thought that he—or any of his fellow students—might have bedded the young woman had him glancing about in search of a chamber pot.

"Doubtful. She's actually Richard's twin sister," Randall replied. "She's been attending finishing school on the Continent and traveling a bit, but she's finally returning to London for her come-out," Randall stated.

The memory of the young woman who had escorted him to the back door of The Queen of Hearts suddenly came to mind, and Randolph stared at his father. "I saw her," he murmured.

"Today?"

"Yes. This girl you're talking about. She was about twenty and dark of hair. Familiar, and yet not. And she kept looking at me as if she recognized me."

"Did you introduce yourself?"

Randolph shook his head. "No. It wasn't my place, and Mrs. Higgins was occupied with my colleague, and..." He allowed the sentence to trail off. "I feel like a prize idiot."

"You needn't," Randall countered. "How could you know? Anyway, I met with Violet yesterday—"

"The Queen?"

"Yes. To ensure all was well. Although Violet was a good mother, she is more than willing to allow me to see to it Rachel has—"

"Rachel?"

Randall rolled his eyes. "I had nothing to do with naming her or Richard," he said in his own defense. At the rate the given names beginning with the letter R were being used in the family, there would be duplicates occurring soon enough.

"You think she can make a good match? Despite having a... a *madame* as a mother?" Randolph asked in disbelief.

"I do," his father replied. "Like my other sons—except for Richard—she has my name. She also has a generous dowry. Which I expect *you* to see to if I'm not around to settle it upon the man she marries."

An ache had begun to develop behind his temples, and Randolph couldn't decide if it was due to the brandy or his father's news. "Really Father, this obsession you have with your mortality is—"

"A sign of responsibility. A trait I did not adopt until I met your stepmother. A trait I made sure you had in spades."

Sobering at hearing his father's statement, Randolph considered what he was being asked to do—simply act in his younger brother's stead until such time as the boy was old enough to take on the marquessate and see to it Rachel's dowry was settled on her husband.

"I'll see to it, of course," he finally acquiesced.

Randall regarded his son for a moment. "In the meantime, will you be taking on the training of a timid filly?"

An image of the look on Xenobia Dunsworth's face just after they had kissed came to mind.

He had tried to erase it from his memory during his walk from her house.

The look of wonder.

The look of awe.

As if he had introduced her to a pleasure she had never before experienced.

He was quite sure she would have done whatever he had asked of her just then. That's the moment when he had almost—almost—asked if she would accompany him to a bedchamber so that he might do for her what her late husband had never done.

Pleasure her until her toes curled. Until her breaths caught and her mewls turned to cries of delight. Until she begged for him to take his own pleasure inside her.

The mere thought of Xenobia begging for him had him holding his breath.

Barbara had never begged for him.

The thought brought him out of his reverie in an instant, but reminded him they were speaking of responsibility. Of promises.

Furrowing a brow, Randolph stared at his father a moment before he said, "I will see to her, yes," he murmured. "But I will not need to break her." Between married life with a best friend who sought his carnal pleasures elsewhere and societal expectations, the breaking of Xenobia Dunsworth had already been done.

Randolph had every intention of undoing the damage.

"Oh?" Randall replied, his brows rising in question.

"Just the opposite. It's high time she enjoy a more exciting life, I should think."

His father blinked. "Are you speaking of the filly? Or of Lady Dunsworth?"

"Both," Randolph replied, realizing that brandy no longer had his brain buzzing.

He was stone cold sober.

CHAPTER 22
REFLECTING ON A KISS

eanwhile, back at Bradley House

Xenobia stood in her parlor for several minutes after Sir Randolph Roderick took his leave, one hand raised to her lips.

The man's kiss had been so heated—so passionate—she was sure he had left a mark in the form of a brand on her tender flesh. Her insides seemed to tumble about, in a way that had frissons dancing beneath her skin.

She could not recall a single time where she had been kissed like that. All of her husband's kisses had been chaste. Pecks on the cheek or her forehead. Quick smacks on the lips that hadn't held the passion that could be found in a pinky finger.

Surrounded as they had been by the scents of roses and lilies, of the hints of the coming Christmas holiday in the red ribbons that decorated the mantel and the bows and bells on the door handles, that moment of kissing had been truly magical.

If it were the only gift she received this season, that kiss would still make for a Happy Christmas.

Her long moments of reflection might have continued deep into the night but for the appearance of her butler.

"My lady?" Chesterfield asked as he regarded her from the threshold, a look of concern etched on his face.

"I'm going to bed now, Chesterfield. *Sir* Randolph will

return tomorrow at half-past three," she stated, emphasizing the man's title. "Please be sure to allow him entry."

The butler lowered his head. "As you wish, my lady." He bowed and disappeared beyond the door.

Xenobia didn't take her leave of the parlor just then. She made her way to the sideboard and poured a finger's worth of brandy into a crystal glass. Holding it up to the gaslight from the room's only chandelier, she stared through the fortified wine for a moment before she drank it down in just a few gulps.

She enjoyed every last drop.

The very last thing she wanted to feel was guilt on this night.

CHAPTER 23
A STEPMOTHER'S ADVICE

The following morning at the Reading townhouse

After a few minutes in the nursery in the company of his son—the babe was awake and already garbed in a new nappy when he arrived—Randolph made his way to the breakfast parlor. He expected he would be alone this early, so he came to a halt on the threshold when he saw that Constance was already seated. A selection of foods were set before her, and she held a cup of steaming tea in one hand as she gripped a quill in the other.

"Oh, pardon me," he said.

"Whatever for?" Constance asked, when she finally lifted her eyes to meet his.

"I... I didn't mean to disturb you," he replied.

"You are not. In fact, you might be saving me from finishing this insipid list," the marchioness replied with a grin. "I'm never sure what to include on the menus. How are you this morning?"

Despite the brandy he had imbibed the night before, he felt surprisingly good, and he said so.

"Can any of your good cheer be due to your meeting with Lady Dunsworth? Did she... hire you?"

Randolph winced, fairly sure his stepmother knew there was no timid filly in the Dunsworth stable. "She did not, but I'm quite sure I will be hired should she ever actually *own* a timid filly."

Constance blinked. "Oh, dear. Was there a... a mix up of some sort?"

Randolph regarded her with a suspicious glance. "You knew she didn't have a filly," he accused.

Her eyes darting to one side, Constance said, "I wasn't completely sure, but... oh, was it terribly uncomfortable for her?"

"*Her?*" Randolph repeated as he gave her a quelling glance. He filled a plate at the sideboard and gave his drink order to a footman. "More for me, I should think. Lady Comber set me up."

Constance very nearly beamed in delight. "And?" she encouraged.

Randolph pulled out the chair across from hers and sat down. Hard. "I'll be taking her for a ride in the park this afternoon."

Looking every bit as if *she* had been the one to arrange the dalliance, Constance set down her tea and leaned forward. "Thank you. I do hope this isn't a hardship for you. Xenobia needs this."

"*This?*" he repeated, wondering if she thought he was going to be doing more than just taking the baroness for a ride in the park.

He could imagine other rides that might happen. Her riding him, for example. Astride whilst naked, her honey blonde hair flowing in waves past her shoulders.

Randolph closed his eyes, at first wishing the image hadn't formed in his mind's eye and then deciding he rather enjoyed it.

So did his manhood, which had decided to rise to the occasion and take up every bit of available space in his already form-fitting breeches.

He shifted in his chair and grimaced. "What do you mean by... *this?*"

"A reminder of what life can be like when it's lived," she

replied. "She's been in mourning for more than a year, and you've been working far too much."

"I don't consider my time at the stables as work, really," he replied before he tucked into his meal.

He wondered if Lady Dunsworth was awake yet. If she was eating breakfast. And if she was enjoying her morning meal, was she doing so in her bed or in the breakfast parlor?

Perhaps she ate in her salon whilst she wrote her correspondence. He imagined she was probably diligent about writing to Rachel if they'd been such good friends at school. To her late husband's mother. To her own mother.

Which had him wondering who that might be. He had no idea what family she had been born into. Who she was before she married Baron Dunsworth, not that it mattered too much.

He remembered the dinner gown she'd been wearing. How it matched her eyes. How those eyes had stared up at him when he had finally finished their kiss.

Having left her without making mention of the kiss would only mean that his arrival for this afternoon's ride would be awkward. Lady Dunsworth was probably mortified. In fact, he half expected to receive a note claiming she had a megrim and would be unable to join him for the ride.

That was probably the subject of the correspondence she was writing in her salon.

"I was referring to your *other* position," Lady Reading said in a quiet voice, as if she feared being overheard.

Randolph blinked. "How...?"

"Don't be angry with him," she pleaded. "He wasn't going to tell me, but I threatened to..." She gave her head a shake. "Well, never mind. Your father would never survive a torture of any kind."

"Long tongued, is he?" When Randolph saw her brighten, he feared she had found humor in his possible double entendre. "Don't answer that."

"If it helps, I don't know any details other than which department you report to."

Randolph winced. "And if you didn't know which department?"

She considered the query a moment. "I might have thought you were a Bow Street Runner or a... an investigator of some sort. Working for one of those agencies that people employ when they wish to learn things about someone, or when they've lost something of value and want it to be found."

Well, even if she hadn't learned he worked for the Foreign Office, his stepmother certainly had guessed the manner of his position.

"I find the work diverting," he finally said, just as the footman returned with his coffee. He took a long drink, reveling in how much better it tasted than the dreck that was served at most of the corner coffee houses in London. "And it has allowed me to perfect my billiards game."

"Which has your father quite vexed," Constance complained. "You might have let him win a game last night."

Randolph jerked his head up, surprised at her words. His father hadn't seemed too terribly upset at having lost the night before.

He had seemed more annoyed that he barely had a chance to play.

Randolph finally allowed a grin. "I had no idea. But if he for one moment thought I was letting him win, he would put voice to a scold the likes to which I have never been subjected," he added with an arched brow.

"You know me too well, son," Randall said as he appeared on the threshold. He gave his wife a deep bow and then rushed to her side to kiss her on the cheek at the same moment Randolph quickly got to his feet. "As do you," Randall whispered in his wife's ear.

"Darling, not at the breakfast table," she admonished him. "We have a guest."

Despite appearing as if his attention was on his plate, Randolph used his skills at observation and watched their interplay through his lowered lashes for signs of artifice. He found none. The two seemed genuinely in love.

Randall sighed and turned to regard his son. "Please, be seated, son. You needn't come to attention just because I've arrived for a meal."

"Yes, sir," Randolph replied as he retook his seat.

"I suppose you've already been up to the nursery?" Randall asked as he settled himself into a chair next to his wife. From the way one of his arms moved, Randolph was sure he had a hand on his marchioness' thigh.

"I have," both Randolph and Constance said in unison. She tittered. "Our son is trying very hard to talk, but I cannot for the life of me understand a single word he blabbers. Well, other than 'mum' and 'dada'."

"Nonsense. He can say 'horse' and 'pony'," Randall countered.

"Which is all he'll ever need to know," Randolph offered. His grin was wide enough so a dimple appeared in his right cheek, and Constance blinked.

"You have a dimple," she murmured in awe. "Just like your son."

Randolph quickly sobered. "I believe he inherited his from me."

"And your father," she added as she turned her attention on her husband, beaming in delight.

A footman set a plate filled with eggs and several rashers of bacon in front of Randall before he shoo'd the servant away and turned to grin at his wife. "He inherited his from me," he said before he lifted one of her hands to his lips and kissed the back of it.

Constance blushed as she dipped her head. "Eat your breakfast, darling," she whispered.

"I will, once I learn from my son how his meeting with Lady Dunsworth went last night. I might have won a game had he stayed another quarter-hour." He turned his attention to Randolph. "Is her filly a Thoroughbred?"

Randolph straightened in his chair, his gaze briefly darting to Constance. His father's query was obviously a means to cover the fact that they had already had this discussion in the study the night before.

Constance was suddenly intent on her list, though. "No," he replied. "Just a... a timid filly in need of... some attention," he stammered. "I'm taking her out this afternoon. To the park. With one of ours. See if some company will help."

Randall arched a bushy brow. "That's capital," he claimed. "And I must say, it's a relief to know she doesn't have a contender for the Derby."

"Indeed," Randolph replied, noting how Constance had a hard time keeping a straight face. Once he left the parlor, he was sure she would tell his father that it was Lady Dunsworth he would be taking for a ride in the park rather than her filly.

Or perhaps his stepmother would keep that little secret to herself.

Apparently she was good at keeping secrets.

CHAPTER 24
A REUNION MOST WELCOME

Two hours later at The Queen of Hearts

Having enjoyed the enormous breakfast served in the dining room of The Queen of Hearts, Rachel made her way up to the office at precisely ten o'clock. She knew the morning mail had already been delivered—a maid had seen to collecting the envelopes and paying the postman whilst Rachel was making her way down the steps. One of The Queen's footmen had stopped at her table to let her know he was available should she require any correspondence be delivered.

"I'll be in the office shortly," she had replied, realizing her mother had already informed her employees of her position as the new bookkeeper.

Except for the stack of mail on one corner of the desk and her mother's signatures on the cheques she had made out the night before, Rachel found the office as she had left it.

Knowing the footman would arrive soon, she tucked the cheques into long envelopes, addressed them, and sealed their corners with wax. Applying the only seal she could find into the hot wax—a Q with an ornate tail—Rachel grinned. She could imagine her mother ordering such a seal, its shape reminiscent of the symbols found on the playing cards used in the club.

Turning her attention to the mail, she opened only the

missives that were obviously for the business, leaving the ones that appeared to be personal for her mother to open.

The footman arrived, bowing before she gave him the cheques. "You've done this before?" she asked.

He nodded. "Aye, miss. Used to do it every week, but it's been nearly a month since the last time The Queen had anything for me to deliver." He leaned forward and lowered his voice. "Is The Queen in some sort of trouble?"

Rachel furrowed a brow before she realized he had probably seen the gentlemen her mother had been meeting with the day before. "Not at all. She's working with the authorities regarding..." She paused, wondering if she should be sharing any details. "Their investigation."

His eyes widening, as if he'd been provided some important *on dit*, the footman nodded. "Well, that's a relief."

"I expect we'll be back on schedule now," Rachel said as she indicated the wad of envelopes he held.

"Yes, miss. Should I... report back here when I return?"

Given the number of cheques she had given him and the varied locations of the vendors, Rachel thought he might be making deliveries until midnight. "No need. I rather doubt I'll still be here in the office." She hoped she would be otherwise engaged with either her mother or with Xenobia. Even if Mr. Merriweather didn't come for her at half-past three o'clock, she didn't intend to return to the office until that evening.

He bowed and took his leave, and Rachel concentrated on the new mail. She grinned when many of the bills of lading that had been left over from the night before now had matching invoices. About to start entering numbers into the ledger, she looked up to discover she once again wasn't alone.

She stood up with a start, inhaling sharply at the sight of a man she barely recognized. He didn't look exactly as he had when she'd last seen him over ten years ago—he had aged in the face, and although he wasn't portly, he was thicker through the middle—but he was most certainly the man she knew as her father.

"My lord," she said as she remembered her manners and dipped a curtsy.

"Oh, Rachel, we'll have none of that," Randall Roderick said as he rushed forward with his arms spread wide.

Rachel grinned and stepped from behind the desk. Reminded of how she behaved when she was younger, she stepped into his hold and rested her head on his shoulder. "Father," she whispered. The scent of his cologne was the same as she remembered, and she inhaled deeply. "You still smell the same."

Randall chuckled as he almost released her. He held her at arm's length. "Old habits, I suppose," he murmured. "You've grown into a beautiful young woman, but I shouldn't be surprised given your mother's beauty." He admired her gown. "You obviously found a good modiste in Zurich."

Rachel blushed, secretly glad she had already donned the gown she would wear to pay her call on Xenobia. "Thank you for paying for it all. The gowns as well as my schooling. Room and board. Had I any idea you were footing the bill, I would have sent my thanks to you directly."

The marquess allowed a shrug as he indicated one of the chairs in front of the desk. "Shall we sit?"

Remembering the parlor across the corridor, Rachel suggested they move there. "I think I can ring for tea," she said, hoping that would be the case.

"Have you thought of where you'd like to live now that you're back in London?" Randall asked as they settled in upholstered chairs in the parlor. Once again, a fire had been set and the tastefully decorated room was warm despite the chill outside.

Appearing confused for a moment, Rachel asked, "Can't I stay here? I've a bedchamber here in the private residence."

Randall was about to respond when a maid appeared with a tea tray.

"I only just rang a moment ago," Rachel said in awe.

The maid set the tray on the low table. "The Queen left

instructions that this be delivered to you. She thought you would have a caller about now," the servant said with a wink. "Will there be anything else, miss?"

"No, thank you," Rachel replied, allowing a slight chuckle when she noted how her father watched her. Once the maid had left the room, she said, "Mother has been so accommodating."

"Your mother has always been a hospitable woman," Randall agreed as he took the teacup and saucer she offered him. "An exceptional woman of business. She's always understood what's required to please her clients."

A bright pink blush colored Rachel's face, and she struggled to hide it as she poured a cup of tea for herself. "Father," she scolded.

"I didn't mean to sound cheeky," he replied. "But it is the truth. Although I would like to believe she has no plans to introduce you to her line of work—"

Rachel inhaled sharply. "She does not."

"—I think it best if you don't live here at The Queen."

"Father," she said quietly. "I assure you, I have no plans of becoming a... a courtesan... or a mistress."

"Yet, it seems as if you've become an employee," he said as he motioned in the direction of the office.

"For lack of anything better to do," she replied. "I'm seeing to the bookkeeping. With the investigation going on, Mother has fallen a bit behind is all." As soon as she finished the comment, she regretted having said it.

"Investigation?" he repeated, his brows furrowing with worry.

Rachel inhaled a long breath before she said, "Apparently some counterfeit money has been used to gamble here at The Queen. As well as at other nearby gaming establishments."

Randall nodded. "So I was able to discover from your oldest brother last night. I think you may have met him without knowing it?"

Staring at her father with rounded eyes, Rachel finally nodded. "Mother told me about him last night. He seemed terribly familiar. Because he looked so much like how I remembered you looking," she murmured. "Does he know? Do my other brothers know? About me? About Mother?"

"Randolph does now," Randall replied. "I told him last night. I'd like for you two to meet as soon as possible. Especially since..." He paused. "Well, let's just say he has a new acquaintance in Lady Dunsworth."

Rachel's eyes widened. "Oh?"

"He met her last night. Apparently Lady Comber arranged for them to meet about a horse."

At the mention of Lady Comber, Rachel's eyes lit up. "Julia and Xenobia are cousins," Rachel said, secretly glad to hear Julia was still in town. "And the best of friends. I plan to pay a call at Bradley House in a while. When the time of day is appropriate, of course."

Randall's face brightened. "I should like to be a fly on the wall when she tells you about their meeting. Just be sure you don't go too late this afternoon."

"Oh?"

He leaned forward and lowered his voice, as if he were sharing a secret. "Randolph is taking her for a ride in the park at half-past three o'clock, which brings up an entirely different matter."

Rachel blinked. From Xenobia's last letter, she had assumed the widow hadn't yet been receiving callers—or suitors. "Are you saying my brother is courting Xenobia?"

Randall shook his head. "I am not. At least, I'm not sure, actually. I'm not sure he knows, either," he added before he took a sip of his tea. "Perhaps you will learn more when you see her today. And then you will share what you know with me?" he added with a grin.

Rachel smiled. "I will." She offered to refill his teacup and then did so, before she asked, "Will your marchioness allow me to meet my baby brothers? I understand you have two heirs."

Beaming in delight, Randall said, "I shall introduce you to them with the warning that Raymond is already six and in school at Eton, and Robert is..." He paused before he chuckled. "Too heavy to toss."

A faint memory of having been thrown into the air had Rachel blinking a moment before she grinned. "Is he walking?"

"Oh, yes. Has been for over a year. He's just two and has a clear command of the word 'no'. Which he employs frequently since he shares the nursery with his nephew, Charlie."

"Randolph's son," Rachel whispered.

"Indeed. Randolph's wife died in the childbed, so we keep Charlie in our nursery," he explained.

"I'm so sorry for him," Rachel murmured.

"At the risk of sounding as if I've a stone for a heart, I do believe he's better off without her."

"Father!" she scolded.

Randall held up a staying hand. "Barbara was not good enough for him. Complained bitterly about her lot in life, especially after she decided Randolph's illegitimacy was a problem."

Rachel winced, knowing full well her own illegitimacy would be seen the same by some members of the *ton*. "I told Mother I would probably end up a spinster—"

"*That's* rather unlikely," Randall said, helping himself to a biscuit from the plate Rachel held for him.

"Why do you say that?"

The marquess rolled his eyes and settled back in his chair. "Besides the fact that I have arranged a generous dowry for you, I had a caller this morning. Just after breakfast."

About to ask who it might be, Rachel remembered her conversation with Mark Merriweather the night before and said, "He didn't."

Her father stared at her for a full five seconds before he said, "If you're referring to Mark Merriweather, then, yes, he did."

"I cannot believe it," she murmured in awe. "I didn't expect he would actually..." Rachel allowed the sentence to trail off as her opinion of the odd young man went up a notch.

"He claims he wants to take you for a ride in the park at half-past three o'clock. Asked for my permission to take you."

"That's because I told him he had to," she replied.

Randall arched a dark brow. "Since you only just arrived in London yesterday, I of course was rather curious as to how he had already met you when *I* had not yet had a chance to see you."

Rachel gave a one-shouldered shrug. "He came to our dinner table last night to introduce himself and then later found me in the office. Offered me a position."

"Oh, did he now?" Indignation was apparent in Randall's words. "No chaperone in sight?"

"As a bookkeeper," Rachel clarified, ignoring the rest of his query. "Apparently, he and Mother employed the same embezzler to do their books."

Randall frowned, obviously unaware Violet Higgins had suffered a loss due to embezzlement. "She didn't say a word of it to me when I saw her a couple of days ago," he murmured.

"Then please don't mention I said anything," Rachel pleaded. "I think she was embarrassed, although she obviously caught it before Mr. Traynor got away with too much."

"Why do you say that?"

Rachel again lifted a shoulder. "I worked on her books last night. I saw the amount of her deposits from the day before yesterday. Her deposits from prior weeks. It would seem her bank balance is quite substantial," she explained.

"It's a relief to hear," Randall murmured. "Had she need of an investor, I would have been happy to provide some funds." He paused. "What are your thoughts on your mother? Now that you are of an age to understand how she makes her living?" he asked with concern.

Rachel bristled at the suggestion she should be anything but proud of what her mother had accomplished. "I am not ashamed of her—she has become an excellent businesswoman," she claimed. "And from what I overheard at breakfast this morning, she's well liked as an employer."

"But she must have a huge payroll," he countered, his attention on his teacup.

"There do seem to be a lot of people working here. Maids in the private residence as well as all the dealers and other people who work the floor, the footmen, her cook and the kitchen maids, the girls who wait tables in the dining room, and then the..." She stopped speaking and swallowed the rest of what she was about to say.

"Lightskirts, yes," Randall said under his breath. "And therein lies why it is I would like for you to live in a more respectable house."

Rachel's shoulders sagged. "I understand, but where am I to go?" Her eyes rounded. "Are you expecting me to move in with you?"

Randall seemed to think on the query a moment before he said, "Of course not, although you would be most welcome."

"I rather doubt your marchioness would agree."

Helping himself to another biscuit, Randall shook his head. "Actually, Connie, your stepmother, was quite excited to learn she has a stepdaughter," he countered, remembering the look on the marchioness' face when he had told her about Rachel. He supposed the news that he had actually fathered a girl had her happy.

There was a possibility she could give birth to a girl instead of another boy.

"She hopes she has an ally in a family of all males," he added with a grin.

"Two against... seven?" Rachel whispered, thinking of all the boys her father had sired as well as her father.

"Well, eight, if you include Charlie. Which means the odds are even," Randall said with delight. "Now. As to a house for you, let me review what properties I have here in London with my man of business. There must be a townhouse you can have."

"An entire townhouse?" she asked in awe.

He shrugged. "Well, yes. I can't imagine how I'd give you half of it," he added with a grin.

"My own house," Rachel murmured. "I thought it would be years before I would be running a household of my own."

"Given your come-out will happen in just a few months, it stands to reason you'll have more suitors besides Merriweather. Marriage proposals. I expect you won't have use of the house for long should your husband already own something," he explained.

Rachel's eyes widened. "I must say, I am surprised both you and Mother think I will receive offers of marriage. Given the circumstances and all."

His eyes rounding, Randall stared at her in disbelief. "Of course you will. You're my daughter."

"And The Queen is my Mother," she whispered.

Looking as if he'd been slapped across the face, Randall sobered. "Having attended finishing school on the Continent should help overcome any stigma of having a gaming hell owner as a mother," he countered.

Deciding not to add that her mother had been a celebrated courtesan, Rachel decided it best to change the subject. "May I ask what you told Mr. Merriweather when he called on you? I should have liked to have eavesdropped on that particular conversation," she said.

"Ah, yes. The second son of Middleton," Randall said with a hint of consternation. "He seems genuinely impressed by you."

"Impressed?"

"Likes that you speak your mind. That you're not insipid. Doesn't like being teased, though, but finds your manner of it more amusing than annoying."

About to scoff, Rachel quickly cleared her throat. "I did tease him," she admitted. "But only because he seemed ripe for it."

"Good. Keep it up," Randall said with a wink.

Rachel's mouth dropped open in shock. "Father!" She once again grew serious when she remembered Mark's reference to his business. "Tell me, Father. Are you familiar with a public house called The Three Bells?"

Randall furrowed a brow. "Of course. I've taken luncheon there many a time. It's close to Parliament."

"So... it's a *respectable* establishment?" she asked.

Allowing a shrug, her father said, "Very. They could probably use a better cook, but then, isn't that the case with most restaurants these days?"

Rachel dipped her head in an attempt to hide her humor. At least her mother's dislike of The Three Bells had to do with their pursuit of Jean Claude and nothing more nefarious.

She would be furious with Mark Merriweather if she had learned otherwise.

"When you spoke with Mr. Merriweather, did he mention I required a horse for this afternoon's ride?" she asked.

"Said he had an Irish Walker that you would make look gorgeous, is how I think he put it," he replied. "But I've arranged an appropriate mount for you." He pursed his lips before he asked, "Now, he intends to collect you at half-past three. Do you have a riding habit?"

"I do," Rachel replied. "Thanks to you."

"With any luck, you'll run into your brother and Lady Dunsworth whilst you're riding."

"Indeed," she replied, glad there would be another topic she and Xenobia could discuss when she paid her call on the widow. The talk of riding reminded her to ask about something else. "Father?"

"Yes?"

"When I was five, you gave me a Welsh pony."

"Yes, I did," he acknowledged, his eyes widening. "You remember that?"

"Oh, as if it were yesterday," Rachel replied. "He was gray, and I named him Richard. Whatever happened to him?"

A huge grin split the marquess' face. "You'll have to discover for yourself when you visit my London stables," he teased.

"He's still alive?" she asked in surprise.

"Of course, dear heart. He was maybe two or three when I gave him to you. Randolph sees to his care."

Rachel chuckled. "If I see Sir Randolph in the park this afternoon, I will be sure to arrange an appointment," she promised.

"See that you do. And while you're at it, you might want to have him introduce you to your nephew, Charles. In the meantime, we'll have you for dinner so you can meet your newest brother and your stepmother, too."

"I still cannot believe you told your marchioness about me."

Randall furrowed a brow. "She knows all about all of you," he replied. He opened his chronometer and growled. "I see time has gotten away from us. You'd best be on your way to Lady Dunsworth's. I've an appointment at the bank," he said as he stood.

Rachel was on her feet quicker, moving to embrace him. "I can see you out the Piccadilly Street entrance," she offered.

"Good. Because that's the way I came in," he replied as he arched a brow. "I do hope that's the way you're going in and out of this building."

"It is," she replied.

He offered his arm and they made their way down the steps. "Remember, I want to know all," he said before kissing her on the forehead.

"Yes, sir."

"May I see you to Lady Xenobia's house? She lives only ten houses down from me," he added before Rachel could put voice to a protest.

"What about your appointment at the bank?"

"Even if I am late, they will still accommodate me," he replied.

"Give me a moment to fetch my coat and reticule," she said as she dipped a curtsy and then disappeared from the vestibule.

Randall watched her go and then turned his attention on the only other person in the front hall. "We did well with that one," he said.

Violet Higgins rose from the settee in which she had been sitting. She had been reading her correspondence since his arrival. "We did," she agreed with a nod. "Please don't take *her* from me, too."

Sighing, Randall pulled her into his arms and held her a moment. "I won't, but remember, she's old enough to leave us both," he gently warned. "If we play our cards right, she'll remain in London," he added.

Wiping a tear from her cheek, Violet nodded. "Agreed." When she heard Rachel's footfalls coming down the stairs, she gave the marquess a deep curtsy and hurried off to the door that led to the gaming hell's dining room. She disappeared before a breathless Rachel rejoined her father.

A minute later, and the two were headed in the direction of Curzon Street.

CHAPTER 25

A HUSBAND APOLOGIZES
ON BEHALF OF HIS WIFE

eanwhile, at the Reading stables east of London
Alistair Comber pulled back on the reins of a
matched pair of greys, his phaeton coming to a stuttering halt
beyond the large double doors of the Reading stables. He
wrapped the ribbons around the pole next to his seat and
hopped down from the black equipage. All the while, his gaze
stayed on the huge white stucco building trimmed in dark red
that stood before him.

"'Bout time you came out here," Randolph said from where
he stood next to a bay brood mare. The horse was obviously
pregnant, which seemed odd to Alistair. It was far too early for
horses to be dropping colts. Christmas was still a few days away,
and horses didn't usually foal until the later spring months.

"Exactly how many do you have in there?" Alistair asked as
he made his way to Randolph's side.

"There are eight in there now," Randolph replied. He waved
to the adjacent fenced pasture, a thin layer of snow providing a
white blanket on which there were at least a half-dozen more
horses standing about. "I'm nursing a couple of lame bays and a
shire," he added as he gave the mare a pat on the side of her
neck. "And this one, who always seems to drop her foals three
months before everyone else."

"That would be because your stud—"

166

"Yes, I know *why*. It's just she's been like this since her first foal. She was in heat before any of her sisters her first year, which means she is always early," he complained. "I have to keep her newborns in the stable for their first couple of months to make sure their ears don't get frostbit."

He motioned for Alistair to join him, and they made their way into the barn, new-fallen snow crunching beneath their boot heels.

"I'm so jealous," Alistair breathed as he took in the sight of sixteen stalls, all recently cleaned. Tack was neatly hung from hooks along the front wall, and hay was stacked nearly to the ceiling along another. Above, in the loft, was more hay. Although most of these horses were used for pulling carriages and coaches, there were a few saddles spanning a trestle.

"Don't be. I don't have room for the number of horses you do," Randolph said with a grin, referring to the Harrington House stables. "What brings you all the way out here?"

Alistair jerked a thumb over his shoulder. "Got a pair that needed some exercise, and I owe you a huge apology."

Randolph furrowed a brow. "Whatever for?" He picked up a brush from a nearby table and moved to the nearest stall.

"Lady Dunsworth and her timid filly," Alistair spat out.

Rolling his eyes, Randolph said, "There's no need. Truly. It's fine." He opened the stall, where a Cleveland Bay stood.

"My wife wasted your time—"

"She didn't. Lady Dunsworth's brandy was most excellent," Randolph said as he began brushing the horse. A quiet nicker followed the first stroke of the brush.

Alistair sighed. "I swear, if Julia wasn't with child, I would have sent her to bed without dinner and..." He shook his head. "I don't know what else I would have done."

"You wouldn't strike her, I hope?" Randolph asked in alarm, his arm pausing in mid-stroke. The horse's head swayed, and his neck curved as if he seemed about to complain.

"No! Never. But she needs to understand she cannot go about playing matchmaker under false pretenses. No matter how much..." He clamped his mouth shut.

"How much... what?" Randolph prompted.

Alistair crossed his arms, his head dipping to indicate the horse. When Randolph didn't continue with the brushing, Alistair reached over and took the tool from his hand.

"What?" Randolph repeated.

"Have you considered courting someone?" Alistair asked in a quiet voice, his attention on the horse as he drew the brush from its withers to its flank. "Your son... he needs a mother."

Randolph blinked. "He has plenty of attention. He has a nurse, and my stepmother dotes on him almost as much as she dotes on my little brother," he argued, hardly noticing his use of the words 'stepmother' and 'brother.'

"You need a wife."

Randolph nearly took a step back, and would have if the stall wall wasn't directly behind him. "Says who?"

Alistair paused mid-stroke, which had the bay giving a loud and long whinny of complaint. "Damnation. Do you spoil these beasts?"

"No, but they do have expectations when they're forced to stand still," Randolph remarked as he indicated the rope that tethered the bay to a pole in the corner of the stall. He smirked when he noted how the horse gave Alistair a side-eye. Randolph was sure that if he'd been able, the beast would have hit Alistair with his head—hard.

Alistair quickly resumed brushing the bay. "I had a long discussion with Julia last night. She's convinced she did the right thing, even after I scolded her."

Randolph winced. "Did she cry?"

"No," Alistair replied with a sigh. "She only seemed more... determined. That was before she..." He sighed again.

"Dismissed you from her bedchamber?" Randolph guessed. He rolled his eyes. From his experience with Barbara, he knew how a woman with child might demand a husband's attentions. Despite Barbara's growing displeasure with him, she still desired him—or at least his cock—until the last month of her pregnancy.

"Something like that," Alistair admitted. "She must have

missed me, because I woke up with her in my bed this morning," he said in a quiet voice. "Although I'd like to think it was because she forgave me, I rather think it was more because the fire had gone out in her bedchamber, and she wanted to sleep somewhere warm."

Randolph tried hard to suppress his smirk. He knew all too well of nights like that.

Winter nights.

Nights like last night.

Nights like what was to come tonight.

He had a fleeting thought of Lady Dunsworth. Of how cold she might become should her fire die down before the maid had a chance to add more coal to the fireplace in the early morning hours. How warm she would be if she were tucked against his body.

How warm he would be.

Overwhelmed by tiredness—he had awakened far too early that morning and most others these past few weeks and been staying up far too late—Randolph fought the desire to simply settle into the corner of an unoccupied stall and close his eyes. Perhaps he could settle onto a bed at Bradley House while he held onto Xenobia, warming them both whilst they napped.

The thought was so welcome, he practically moaned. He quickly cleared his throat, his gaze focusing to discover Alistair staring at him. "What?"

"Just... think about it."

Furrowing a brow, Randolph said, "Apparently, I've been doing nothing but."

Alistair's expression matched his own. "What are you saying?"

Randolph blew out a breath. "I'm taking Lady Dunsworth for a ride in the park this afternoon. He's going to pull the phaeton," he said as he indicated the horse Alistair was absently brushing.

"Oh," Alistair replied. "Well."

"Whatever you do, don't tell Lady Comber," Randolph warned. "It's just a ride in the park. Nothing more." He might want it to be more. With any luck, he might end up in Xeno-bia's bed. But the last person he wanted to know that was Lady Comber.

"When are you going?"

"I'm going to fetch her at half-past-three."

"It'll be dark by the time you return," Alistair remarked.

"I'm going to stay in town tonight," Randolph replied, patting a waistcoat pocket that bulged with full a purse.

"Hazard?" Alistair guessed.

"Billiards. I'm hoping to lighten the purses of a certain Frenchman and his Belgian counterpart." He didn't add that he had turned over his last haul to the head of the Foreign Office just two days before.

A few hours after he had spotted his father leaving The Queen of Hearts.

By now, the legitimacy of the bank notes would have been determined. It was possible an agent would be dispatched as soon as this evening to arrest the two for passing counterfeit notes. With any luck, they were also the ones creating the blunt, in which case, their arrest would mean a new assignment for Randolph.

If not, then Randolph would have to discover the source of the counterfeit money.

Alistair winced at the mention of Belgium. Only a decade ago, he had spent many a cold night in the Belgian countryside —behind enemy lines—spying on Napoleon's forces. As an earl's son, he was an officer in the army, but he preferred his undercover work to leading troops.

"The pay must be shite," Alistair remarked.

Randolph furrowed a brow. "Playing billiards? Hardly."

"Working for the Foreign Office," Alistair said. "Chamber-lain never did have much of a budget."

"And how would you know?"

Alistair gave him a quelling glance. "It's no secret. During the wars with Napoleon, we relied on the intelligence of reporters who worked for *The Times*. They had the blunt to send investigators to the Continent. We didn't."

Randolph's frown deepened. "How long did *you* work for Chamberlain?"

"I wasn't aware we could stop," Alistair replied with an arched brow. He gave a long sigh. "That's not true. He hasn't employed me for..." He paused mid-sentence, although he continued to brush the horse.

"Since you married."

Alistair gave a start. "True. I suppose I am of no use if he cannot in good conscience send me across the Channel."

"I was sent to Calais. Once," Randolph remarked. "Had to follow a shipment of wool that was used to pay for illegal liquor. Worst time ever on a ship." He feigned sea sickness by rubbing his mid-section.

"Wool?" Alistair repeated. This time he did stop brushing the horse, and the resulting complaint was long and loud. "Were you on the *Molly*?" Outfitted to look like a pirate ship, the *Molly* had been a vessel in service of the British navy. Now a ship of the Foreign Office, it was dispatched to intercept ships carrying smuggled goods and illegal liquor.

Randolph laughed as he pulled a carrot from his great coat pocket and offered it to the annoyed horse. "The one and only. Damn thing is still seaworthy, if you can believe it, and a more motley crew you'll never find."

"Good men, though," Alistair said. "So... this ride with Lady X—"

"Lady X?"

Alistair rolled his eyes. "Her name is Xenobia. She's actually one of Julia's cousins. She and their friends always called her Lady X, partly because of her given name and partly because she was such a skinflint."

"A skinflint?" Randolph repeated. The thought of how much the woman must have spent at hot houses for all the roses she'd had on display in her house didn't exactly illicit thoughts of thriftiness.

"She was always crossing out items on her shopping lists, claiming she didn't really need them," Alistair explained. "That was before she married Dunsworth, of course."

"Who was her father?" Randolph asked, deciding anything he could learn about the young matron before he took her for a ride would help with conversation. They wouldn't have the benefit of brandy to help loosen their tongues.

"Oh, you would have to ask that," Alistair complained as he moved to the other side of the horse. "Do you know how many Harrington daughters there were?"

"Five, if you're referring to the sisters of the current Earl of Mayfield."

Alistair blinked. "Oh. Well. She's the daughter of Edith, the Dowager Duchess of Pendleton."

Randolph took a moment to sort the relationship. "The Duchess of Pendleton? Xenobia is a *duke's* daughter?" he asked in disbelief.

"No," Alistair quickly replied. "Pendleton died more than a year before Xenobia was born. At least Edith had already given him his heir."

Wincing, Randolph knew the Dowager Duchess of Pendleton hadn't remarried, instead enjoying the very public life of a Merry Widow. With her red hair and bright green eyes, she was said to bewitch gentlemen into her bed. Given her beauty, Randolph sorted casting spells wasn't required.

The timing of Xenobia's birth meant she was illegitimate.

"So... Dunsworth did her a favor?" Randolph murmured, referring to his marriage to Xenobia.

Alistair seemed to think on the comment for a time before he said, "I suppose. I believe her father was a captain of some sort. Alton Bradley. Not sure if he was in the army or a ship's captain. Anyway, the townhouse she lives in was once his, so that meant Dunsworth didn't have to put out any blunt for a house in town."

"Hmm," Randolph murmured as he considered the possible topics for conversation during their ride. She already knew he was illegitimate, although it did help that his father had publicly acknowledged him as his son. He had done so with all of his bastards—or at least the three boys who had his name. "It could be worse, I suppose," he said suddenly.

Alistair's head popped up from the other side of the horse. "What do you mean?"

"She could be my sister."

His eyes darting sideways, Alistair finally allowed a guffaw. "I don't think Reading is capable of fathering a girl," he replied.

Considering he now had five brothers, Randolph would have agreed—if his father hadn't just told him the night before that he had a daughter. Randolph cleared his throat. Loudly.

Alistair raised his head from the chore he had taken on as a sort of penance for his wife's machinations and stared at Randolph. "You have a sister?"

"Rachel Roderick. She was a twin. Apparently she was in finishing school with Lady Dunsworth on the Continent. They may have been friends before that."

"How old?" Alistair asked, his eyes wide.

Randolph allowed a shrug as he did the calculation in his head. "Twenty?"

Alistair blew out the breath he'd been holding. "That's a relief," he murmured. "No, I don't know her."

Randolph gave him a quelling glance. "Does the name Violet Higgins ring a bell?"

"Only if you're referring to The Queen of Hearts," Alistair replied. "I lost more than my fair share of blunt under her former roof before she opened The Queen of Hearts. When I was younger, of course. Why do you ask?" He paused his brush strokes. "Is *she* under investigation by the Foreign Office?"

"No. She's Rachel's mother. Had a boy at the same time, too."

Alistair blinked. "I cannot... I cannot even imagine her—"

"Nor can I," Randolph said, cutting off his friend's comment. "According to my father, she was a brunette and quite a beauty at one time."

"But surely she didn't raise the babes."

"Not the boy," Randolph agreed. "On the one hand, I want to meet her, but on the other..." He allowed the sentence to trail off as he gave his head a shake. "Turns out, I actually saw Rachel at The Queen yesterday. She'd just returned to London."

"Is someone providing protection for her?"

Randolph nodded. "Since Father's arranged for her dowry, I rather imagine someone is."

"You needn't feel guilty for not wanting to make her acquaintance," Alistair reasoned.

"I've met all my brothers but one. Not nearly as awkward as I was expecting those introductions to be," he countered.

"Do you think she'll live in London?"

Randolph shrugged. "I suppose. I'm sure my father knows."

"And your stepmother?"

Straightening, Randolph considered the query a moment. "I don't know. Father was very keen to let her know about all of us before he asked for her hand in marriage. Perhaps he told her about Rachel then."

"If he knew about her."

"Oh, he knew about the twins," Randolph argued, remembering he couldn't say anything about the boy's fate.

"Then why not tell you before last night?"

Randolph gave his head a shake. "Why not, indeed?" he countered. "Now, if you're finished, I'd like to get this beast hitched up."

"Yes, sir," Alistair replied as he handed over the brush. "I would wish you luck, but something tells me you're going to do this the hard way."

"Wish me luck."

"Good luck." Without another word, Alistair made his way back to his phaeton and in a moment was gone from the premises.

Randolph turned to the Cleveland Bay and found his eyelids mostly closed. "Oh, no you don't. If I can't sleep, then neither can you," he scolded.

CHAPTER 26
COUSINS CONTEMPLATE

*M*eanwhile, at Bradley House

"You don't hate me?"

Xenobia gave her cousin a quelling glance. "Of course not," she replied as her lady's maid pinned up her honey blonde hair into a style suitable for her carriage gown's matching hat. She had already clipped off its longer peacock feather, sure she would impale poor Sir Randolph should she turn her head too far to the side whilst they rode on his phaeton.

"Alistair scolded me. It was awful."

Staring at Julia's reflection in her dressing table's mirror, Xenobia's eyes widened. "He didn't...?"

"No," Julia replied. "He wouldn't do anything to *hurt* me, but I was so vexed, I... I told him to leave my bedchamber."

Xenobia blinked. Given the stories Julia had put voice to over the years she had been married to Alistair, Xenobia wondered if this might have been their first tiff. "Did he?"

Julia sighed. "Yes. I had to go to *his* bedchamber when mine grew too cold. I blame this all on the baby, of course."

"Julia!"

"I'm normally not like this," Julia insisted. "But it matters not, since you've received an invitation to ride out of it."

Xenobia allowed a grin as she watched her lady's maid finish styling her hair. "That will be all, Sullivan," she murmured.

The lady's maid dipped a curtsy and hurried from the bedchamber. Xenobia was sure she would spread the news to the other servants that her mistress was going for a ride in the park. At no point had she said with whom, nor did she intend for them to know.

There would be gossip, though, but for once, she didn't care. She'd had quite enough of caring what others thought of her.

"You might have mentioned he is Rachel's brother," Xenobia whispered when she turned to regard her cousin.

Julia gave a start. "I... I didn't think of it. I know you mentioned you had received a letter from her, but I haven't *seen* her in years."

"That's because she hasn't been in London since... I think it's been eight years now," Xenobia countered.

"Where has she been all this time?"

Xenobia leaned closer to Julia and said, "As you know, she stayed at finishing school in Zurich a few years after I left and has been traveling for the past year or so. I can hardly wait to see her." She didn't add that she thought the reason Rachel had been kept away from London was because Rachel's mother had become too well-known as a madame. Rachel's latest letter had mentioned her mother's ownership of The Queen of Hearts, an apparently popular gaming establishment, which didn't help the situation.

The Marquess of Reading had probably been the one to arrange Rachel's move to the Continent in the first place.

Frowning, Julia considered the timing. "A bit old for a come-out, is she not?"

"Twenty?" Xenobia offered. "I suppose, but that's not what has me bothered." At Julia's questioning glance, she added, "Last night, when we spoke of his family, never once did Sir Randolph mention her, or ask about our friendship."

Julia allowed a shrug. "Perhaps he doesn't know you were friends."

"He mentioned his brothers, which has me wondering, does he even *know* he has a sister?"

Arching a brow, Julia regarded Xenobia for a moment, her

mouth rounding into an 'o' as she considered the possibility. "Different mothers. Different classes. Sir Randolph's mother is a member of the *ton* while Rachel's mother is not," she reasoned. "Perhaps he doesn't know."

"Do I mention her whilst on this ride? Should I ask about her?" Rachel queried, a pained expression crossing her face.

"Do," Julia replied. "Then you'll know if he knows about her."

Xenobia gave her cousin a quelling glance. "You're incorrigible. I'd rather not be the one to inform him he has a sister." She might have chided Julia a moment longer but she had other concerns. Given what had happened the night before—just before Randolph Roderick had departed the parlor for the second time—Xenobia had spent the day in a constant state of anxiousness. She looked forward to the ride, of course, but facing Sir Randolph after his scorching kiss would have her cheeks flaming red.

In an effort to blame the coloring on her clothes, she had elected to wear a red carriage gown coupled with a darker red redingote for their ride.

"You look as if you're ready for Christmas," Julia remarked as she fingered the Merino wool of Xenobia's gown.

"As long as I don't look like a gift-wrapped present," Xenobia replied.

"What's that supposed to mean?"

Sighing, Xenobia turned from her dressing table and said, "I'm not sure about Sir Randolph's intentions. I cannot help but think he's only doing this because he feels sorry for me—"

"He's not doing this to score an invitation to your bed, if that's what you're worried about," Julia insisted. "Although the thought of a man unwrapping you like a present paints a rather delightful—"

"Julia!"

Her cousin giggled but quickly sobered. "Alistair says he's too honorable for that. Says he's not one to follow in his father's footsteps when it comes to dalliances."

"You mean Sir Randolph is not a rake?" The query came out more like a statement.

"Exactly! Which is good, but only to a point," Julia replied, still beaming in delight.

Xenobia had already surmised that Randolph wasn't angling for a tumble. Why, if he'd wanted one the night before, she probably would have been the one to lead them to her bedchamber. Let him have his way with her. If for no other reason than she was curious.

Too curious.

What would lovemaking be like with someone who wasn't her best friend?

But she hadn't yet determined his motive for the invitation to ride in the park with him. Given the weather—it was cold, but it wasn't snowing—surely they would have to be bundled up in quilts or a blanket on the bench of the phaeton.

"Do you know what he'll be driving?" Julia asked. "A barouche, perhaps?"

"A phaeton. He said he needs to exercise the horse that will be pulling it."

Julia's face lit up in delight. "When was the last time you rode on a phaeton?"

Xenobia blinked. "The *only* time was when you took me to New Bond Street last year." She recalled the harrowing drive with fright. "You nearly dumped me at the corner of Oxford and New Bond," she accused.

"We did take that corner a bit fast, didn't we?" Julia replied in delight.

"*We?*" Xenobia chided.

"You'll have to hang onto Sir Randolph's arm. Thread your arm through his elbow," Julia explained, a huge grin on her face. "And be sure to sit close. You'll have to, as there's very little room on a phaeton bench."

Xenobia's eyes darted sideways. "Surely I can hang onto the edge of the bench."

"Not if your hands are in a muff," Julia countered.

Inhaling deeply in an effort to calm her nerves, Xenobia was about to claim she wasn't going to take a muff when Chester-field appeared at the door and cleared his throat.

"Yes?"

"There's a Miss Rachel Roderick to see you, my lady," Chesterfield said. "She did not provide a calling card."

Julia and Xenobia exchanged quick glances, both grinning.

"Bring her to the parlor," Xenobia ordered. "And have another tea tray brought up."

"Yes, my lady." The butler hurried off as Xenobia nearly squealed in delight.

"Now we can learn what she knows," Xenobia whispered.

Sighing loudly, Julia shook her head. "You can. I cannot stay," she said sadly. "But I must admit I am tempted to return later this afternoon. About half-past-three o'clock," she teased.

"Don't you dare," Xenobia replied with a look of horror.

"Oh, I won't," Julia said with a shake of her head. She didn't add that she wished she could watch from a vantage overlooking the hall, though. "Good luck," she added.

Before Xenobia could respond or even offer to join her on the descent down the stairs, Julia was out of the bedchamber and bounding down the stairs in a most unladylike manner.

CHAPTER 27
FRIENDS REUNITE

A moment later

Xenobia stepped out of her bedchamber and was about to close the door when what sounded like squealing came from down below. She giggled, realizing Julia and Rachel had crossed paths, probably outside the parlor.

The cries of delight reminded her of the times they had spent together as young girls. The time she had spent with Rachel in finishing school.

If only Julia had been able to join them in Zurich instead of remaining in London.

If only I had been able to remain in Zurich another year or two. But when she was seventeen, her mother had insisted it was time Xenobia return to London and prepare for a presentation to the court. Prepare for a come-out. Prepare for a Season of entertainments.

Prepare to find a husband.

Her court gown had been exquisite. Her mother had worn it for her own presentation, but a modiste had expertly refitted it for Xenobia and embellished the sleeves and bottom ruffle with embroidered leaves and flowers.

A maid had seen to fashioning her long hair into an elegant chignon with a jeweled comb. Her gloves had been a perfect match for the gown. Her mother's heeled velvet shoes had actually been comfortable.

Despite what she wore, despite her perfect appearance, despite her expertly performed curtsy—the day had been the worst in her entire life. Even now, her cheeks flamed when she recalled how the king pretended to ignore her. She wished his wife had been there, for she was sure Charlotte would have afforded her a glance.

A duchess' daughter given the cut direct in front of so many other young women also making their come-outs that Season.

How humiliating.

No wonder she had welcomed her friend's attentions. Lord Dunsworth's attentions. Accepted his offer of marriage after only a few balls.

Rachel would be older than Xenobia had been for her come-out—by three years. Perhaps she would be spared the humiliation of a presentation at court. Given someone would have to sponsor her—someone who had already been presented at court —it was unlikely she would have to endure the trauma.

These thoughts and more had Xenobia struggling to put on a pleasing expression when she entered the parlor. Immediately, the scent of roses surrounded her, and she inhaled deeply. The reminder of the approaching yuletide put her into a much more pleasant frame of mind, and she found smiling was easy.

Once she caught sight of Rachel standing next to the fireplace, her fashionable carriage gown a reminder of her time in Zurich and her gloved hands gripping a fabric-covered box, all the terrible memories of her own come-out flew from her head, and Xenobia beamed with happiness.

"I am so glad to see you," she gushed as she hurried to pull Rachel into her arms.

"Xenobia!" Rachel countered, giggling when she had to struggle to keep her feet. "What an unexpected surprise to see Julia here. I do hope I did not interrupt her call on you."

"Not at all. She had to get home. She's a mother now—"

"With another on the way—"

"And has a husband who adores her. She's been such a good

friend whilst I've been in mourning. Please..." She motioned to an upholstered chair. "Do take a seat. I want to know everything that's happened since you left Switzerland. Everything that's happened since your last letter."

The pasteboard box Rachel held in one hand bumped against Xenobia as she stepped back, and she quickly pulled it against her waist. "Apologies. I shouldn't wish to bruise you with my gift for you," Rachel said.

"Gift?" Xenobia repeated.

Rachel held it out to her. "You must open it now," she said, at the same moment a maid delivered the tea tray. Her attention went to Xenobia's ensemble and her brows furrowed. "You look as if you are about to go out."

"Oh, not until later this afternoon," Xenobia replied, almost mentioning Sir Randolph. She would have, but Rachel again held out the box to her.

"I cannot stay long, for I've an appointment at half-past three," Rachel warned. She inhaled deeply. "I adore the scent of roses. Are they from an admirer—?"

"I had them delivered for Christmas," Xenobia quickly put in. Her gaze went to the box. "It's so kind of you to think of me," she whispered as she took the box and settled onto the settee. She began unfolding the fabric from around the pasteboard box. "Did you bring this back all the way from the Continent?"

"I did. I have thought of you often this past year," Rachel replied. "Had you not been in mourning, I would have insisted you join me on my travels."

"I would have loved to go with you to Italy," Xenobia said as she opened the box and then inhaled sharply. "Is it...?" she asked as a grin appeared.

"Is it *what*?" Rachel teased as she watched Xenobia extract the music box from its packaging. "I fear you may already have one, since this one looks suspiciously like the box you have on your mantel," she said as she pointed to a hinged walnut box above the fireplace.

"A music box!" Xenobia said excitedly as she turned the box

over and located the key. She began turning it. "It's true I have one, but I rather doubt this one plays the same melody." She opened the lid and listened as the cylinder turned and the tines plucked the raised metal nubs to create the notes of a lullaby. "It's sounds beautiful," she whispered. "You're such a dear."

In the meantime, Rachel had stood and moved to the fireplace. She lifted the lid of the music box and looked inside. "I do not believe these are meant to hold mementos," she murmured. "It's preventing the metal cylinder from turning."

"Whatever do you mean?" Rachel asked, rising to join her. She peered inside the box and frowned. Reaching in, she pulled out a wad of paper and began unfolding it.

"Now you've taken to hiding your money in music boxes?" Rachel teased when she recognized a bank note. "I see you have not changed your frugal ways."

"I did not put that in there," Xenobia claimed. "Twenty pounds!" she added, before her eyes widened and she grinned.

"One of the many treasures your father left for you?" Rachel asked as she turned the key on the music box. When she let go, the notes of a lively sea shanty erupted from the box. "Definitely not the same tune as the one I gave you," she said with a grin.

"I much prefer the lullaby," Xenobia said as she stuffed the bank note into a pocket. "Now, do you still take milk in your tea?"

"Of course. And sugar, if you have it."

"Oh, I do." When she noted Rachel's teasing expression, she added, "I admit, I am still frugal at times, but not when it comes to sugar."

"Have you been terribly lonely since Dunsworth died?"

The query wasn't entirely unexpected, but Xenobia was still struck dumb.

"I apologize—"

"I was," Xenobia finally acknowledged. "For a time. But I hosted callers yesterday, and it was as if this past year hadn't happened," she murmured as she poured the tea.

"And Dunsworth?"

Xenobia poured milk into the cups and considered how to

respond. "I believe I am better off without him," she finally said. "That last year with him was... well, let us just say that I may as well have been a widow, for he spent far too many of his evenings with his mistress."

An expression of sadness settled on Rachel's features. "I have learned from your marriage. I shall never wed," she announced.

Xenobia rolled her eyes. "Oh, but Rachel. There is a man out there right now who wants you," she chided.

"As a bookkeeper," Rachel replied. Then her eyes rounded. "Who told you?"

Blinking, Xenobia straightened on the settee and stared at her friend. "No one." Then her eyes widened. "A bookkeeper. Who is it?"

Rachel huffed as her shoulders seemed to shrink into the back of her chair. "Mr. Merriweather."

Xenobia furrowed a brow before she said, "Mark Merriweather?"

"Do you know him?" Rachel was suddenly leaning forward in her chair.

"He lives next door," Xenobia replied. "At least, I think he still does," she added.

Rachel boggled a moment before she said, "He's coming to take me for a ride in the park at half-past three. I expect he's going to give me the particulars of the position."

Xenobia blinked. "In the park?"

It was Rachel's turn to blink. "Well, I expect so. He insisted. He's even bringing me a horse to ride. Which is why I cannot stay too long. I must return to Mother's house to change into a riding habit."

Her eyes sparkling in delight, Xenobia said, "Perhaps I'll see you there. Although I have no idea where Sir Randolph is planning to take me. We're going on a phaeton."

Rachel stared at her hostess a moment, her teacup held between her two hands and suspended halfway to her lips. "You did say 'Sir Randolph'?" she half-asked.

Xenobia nodded. "Randolph Roderick. I wondered... *is* he your brother?" she asked, her question quiet.

The teacup in Rachel's hands lowered as she regarded her friend. "He is," she replied. "How long has Randolph been courting you?"

Her head quickly shaking, Xenobia said, "I don't know that he is."

Frowning, Rachel asked, "How long have you *known* him?"

Xenobia lifted a locket from her bosom and pressed a tiny button on the side of it. The lid flipped open, and she studied the chronometer within. "About fourteen hours," she replied with a smirk. Before Rachel could put voice to more questions, Xenobia added, "It's all Julia's fault. She sent him here under false pretenses. Told him I had a 'timid filly' that needed training," she explained. She straightened. "The real question here is why *you* never told me you had such a handsome brother."

Seemingly perturbed, Rachel placed her teacup and saucer on the low table between them. "I would have had to have been *told* about him. Before yesterday. Before this morning."

Xenobia inhaled sharply. "*You* didn't know?"

Rachel sighed and settled back in her chair. "I've always known I had illegitimate brothers," she admitted. "I just... I've never been introduced to any of them," she whispered. "Randolph was actually at The Queen of Hearts yesterday for a meeting with my mother. I escorted him to the door, but I didn't know who he was. No one introduced us—"

"I know exactly how awkward *that* must have been," Xenobia whispered, thinking that there had been no one to introduce her to him when he had arrived the night before.

Then Rachel's other words came to mind.

At The Queen of Hearts... a meeting with my mother.

The oddest sensations gripped Xenobia just then. Disappointment and despair. Anger and sadness. Disbelief and resignation. "I suppose he is a client of your mother's?"

Rachel's eyes widened as she quickly shook her head. "Oh, no. He's... he's some sort of investigator. On assignment to see to it some... I'm not exactly sure what they are guilty of, but... they're bad men in need of arrest," she stammered. "He was simply there for a meeting with Mother."

Xenobia blinked. "An investigator?" she repeated, remembering some of what he had said the night before. "Horse trainer by day, investigator at night, and a father, too," she murmured as all the other emotions that had coursed through her the moment before dissipated.

She could hardly believe the relief she felt.

"His babe is adorable."

Inhaling sharply, Rachel stared at her. "You've already met Charles?"

"Oh, when he was still quite small," Xenobia answered, understanding why Rachel would seem so surprised. "When I was having tea at the Reading townhouse. It's but ten doors down from here," she added. "And your father's marchioness is quite a pleasant woman. Not one to put on airs, at all. You'll find Connie quite agreeable."

Rachel stiffened. "My father paid a call on me this morning."

A smile slowly appeared on Xenobia's face. "You must have been so happy to see him again," she murmured. "Was he as you remembered him?"

Tears brightened Rachel's eyes before she nodded. "He is. Still wears the same cologne," she replied. "But he has two legitimate sons now, and his marchioness is increasing with another. He wants me to have a come-out this Season." She grimaced. "I tried to beg off, but he's sure there is a man who will wish to wed me."

Xenobia was about to ask if her father intended for her to be presented at court, but thought better of it. "Mr. Merriweather, perhaps?" Xenobia teased.

Rachel's cheeks bloomed with color. The memory of how he had hurried up to the dining table the night before, of how her mother had reacted to his arrival, had Rachel wondering about his motives. He hadn't known she had agreed to see to her mother's books when he was angling for an introduction. *She* had only just offered to take a look at them moments before.

So what had been his motive, if not to gain an introduction?

To arrange a tumble?

Perhaps he had thought her one of the lightskirts who worked on the first floor. But even after he was told what she was doing there, he seemed intent on spending time with her.

Rachel glanced up to discover Xenobia watching her with a grin. "What?"

"You were thinking about Mr. Merriweather," she accused.

"I was thinking about why he wanted me to go riding with him," Rachel countered. "I am jaded enough to believe this ride has nothing to do with scribing numbers and everything to do with him trying to arrange something entirely inappropriate."

"Rachel!" Xenobia scolded. "I do not believe Mr. Merriweather is like that," she said. "The Earl of Middleton is quite strict with his sons, especially after what happened to their sister."

Rachel's eyes widened. "What happened to Eleanor?" The earl's only daughter was a couple of years older than Rachel and only a year younger than Xenobia.

"The Earl of Wakefield," Xenobia stated.

Her eyes rounding in horror, Rachel said, "He's one of my father's friends. He's a... he's a *rake*," she added. "Or, at least, that's what I remember reading in the gossip sheets from London." She might have been living on the Continent, but gossip sold nearly as well there as it did in England.

"Well, he *was*," Xenobia agreed. "Seems after he ruined Eleanor, he mended his ways. They're quite happy now, but I know Middleton was not at the time."

Rachel gave her head a shake. "Perhaps my father is right in wanting me to live in my own townhouse," she murmured.

"What's this?"

Rachel recounted her conversation with her father. "The private residence at The Queen of Hearts is mostly separate from the establishment, but Father fears it's still too close for comfort. He wants me in more respectable quarters."

"I cannot blame him," Xenobia replied. "Besides, you'll have your own household to run. Isn't that what you've always wanted?"

Nodding, Rachel allowed a grin. "Indeed. Except I had imagined it in Zurich," she added wistfully.

"You're not glad to be back in London?" The sound of disappointment in Xenobia's query could not be missed.

"Oh. I am glad to be back in England," Rachel countered. "Now that I've seen my father, and you, and Julia. Mother, of course." The comment about her mother did not sound as enthusiastic as it might have, and she dipped her head. "I love her. I do. And so do all those who are employed by her at The Queen of Hearts. I only wish..." She sighed.

"That her choice of employment did not stain you," Xenobia finished for her. "I am of the same mind when it comes to my mother."

"Xenobia!" Rachel scolded. "Your mother is a duchess!"

"Who did not inform my father of my very existence until well after I was born," Xenobia countered, remembering the story Captain Bradley had told her when she was still small and perched on one of his knees.

Even now, she could remember the smell of his cologne and the feel of his whiskers when he kissed her cheek. Remember the sparkle in his eyes as he would tell her of the buried treasures to be found in the house. Of the treasures he sought each time he captained his ship to some faraway port to collect them on behalf of Wellingham Imports. Of the treasures he delivered to clients scattered around the Mediterranean. "Father proposed marriage—a half-dozen times at least—and Mother stubbornly refused him."

A grimace appearing at hearing the rebuke in her friend's voice, Rachel finally shook her head. "You know she could not have married him. She would have not been allowed. The *ton* would have skewered her."

About to counter the claim, Xenobia allowed a long sigh. "I suppose I do know," she whispered. "At least I can live the rest of my life as a widow and do what I wish." A memory of Sir Randolph's kiss filled her mind's eye, and a frisson shot through her body. She briefly wondered if they might do it again during their ride that afternoon. A satisfying warmth spread through her entire body as she considered what might happen.

"You obviously have something in mind to keep you entertained," Rachel teased.

About to put voice to a protest, Xenobia instead said, "I can hardly wait for you to meet Sir Randolph, and I hope it's this afternoon."

"The last I remember, Hyde Park was rather large."

"True, but the King's Road is still where most go riding. I rather expect that's where we'll be," Xenobia said. "And if not today, then tomorrow."

"You like him," Rachel accused in a quiet voice.

Xenobia blinked. "I do. He's..." She sighed and pondered how to describe Rachel's oldest brother. "Considerate and honorable and... *handsome* in a sort of rough way that's entirely the opposite of what Dunsworth was like."

"He kissed you."

Her eyes widening in surprise, Xenobia asked, "Who told you?"

A huge smile split Rachel's face as she held up a finger. "You just did." She leaned closer. "And?"

Xenobia inhaled and then finally exhaled when she didn't know how to respond. "He took his leave."

Frowning, Rachel straightened in her chair. "He kissed you and then he left?"

A blush colored Xenobia's face. "Well, it was a good-bye kiss, I suppose," she murmured.

At the hearing the word 'good-bye', Rachel inhaled sharply. "Oh, dear. What time is it?"

"It's nearly half-past two."

"I must say my 'good-bye', but I'm only going to kiss you on your cheek," she teased as she stood. She regarded her friend before she gave her head a shake. "I'm not sure if I should wish you good luck or tell you I will pray for you."

Xenobia giggled. "I will pray for *you*," she teased. "Or perhaps I should pray for poor Mr. Merriweather."

Rachel leaned over and kissed Xenobia on the cheek. "And I

shall pray for my *brother*," she replied. "I'll see my way out," she added before she hurried from the parlor.

Xenobia watched her go, a grin lighting her face. Reminded she still had an hour to wait until Sir Randolph arrived, she moved to retrieve the book on Thoroughbred horses and continued to read from where she had left off the night before.

An hour later

"There's a Sir Randolph to see you, my lady," Chesterfield said as he held out a calling card. "Should I let him know you are in residence?"

Pulled from her book at the very moment she was reading about the mating rituals of stallions, Xenobia managed to affect a look of boredom when she replied, "You needn't tell him anything. I'll be down after I put on a hat."

When Chesterfield disappeared from the threshold, Xenobia hurried to her bedchamber and grinned at her reflection as she pinned her red felt hat into place. Then she donned her dark red redingote.

Perhaps Julia was right. She did look as if she was a Christmas package ready to be unwrapped. The thought had a cascade of frissons coursing through her as she took her leave of her bedchamber, fastening the black frog closures down the front of her redingote as she did so.

CHAPTER 28
A RIDE IN THE PARK

*M*eanwhile, downstairs

Randolph knew from the moment the butler answered the door that the servant did not like him. He supposed after what had happened the night before, Chesterfield had every right to be annoyed with him. Given his lack of much sleep the night before, irritation sounded in his voice. "*Sir* Randolph for Lady Dunsworth," he said, emphasizing the 'sir.' This time, he held out his calling card.

Chesterfield took the white pasteboard, not once giving it a glance. "Wait here, sir. I'll see if she's in residence."

Prepared to wait for at least ten minutes—Barbara had never been ready to leave at an agreed-upon time—Randolph made his way to the hall's only piece of furniture. The scent of roses surrounded him as he glanced first at the huge arrangement of white roses in the middle, fairly sure their stems were in a punchbowl, and then at the red felt surface of the table. He knelt and studied the carved edges of the gaming table, his gaze taking in the perfectly matched seams of the inlaid wood.

The imperfectly closed drawers.

"That's odd," he whispered as he nudged one open. Given its small size, he expected to find it containing a deck of playing cards, or perhaps some playing chips. Instead, he boggled at the sight of money.

Twenty pound bank notes, and lots of them. The drawer was so full, it could barely be shut.

He straightened and moved to where another player might sit at the table. It took only a moment to locate a second drawer, this one filled with five-pound notes. He quickly shut it and moved to the next, finding ten-pound notes, but only a few. The next drawer held the deck of cards, and under that, a folded note. He glanced about to be sure no one was watching him as he opened the missive and began to read.

Blinking twice when he finished, he quickly refolded the letter and stuffed it back into the drawer. He was closing it and about to move to another when his attention was captured by the woman descending the stairs.

Xenobia Dunsworth appeared the very definition of Christmas, her carriage gown and redingote in the shades of red that could be found in holly berries and hot-house roses. The red felt hat, pinned at an angle on a coiffure that must have taken her maid at least an hour to create, was the perfect topper to what he wished was his very own Christmas present. The sight of her reminded him that he hadn't yet purchased a present for his son.

He moved to the base of the staircase and gave a deep bow. "Good afternoon, my lady," he said as he reached for her gloved hand. The red kid leather glove was soft in his hold. He brushed a kiss over her knuckles, his nearness to the bottom step preventing Xenobia from taking the last step down.

"Sir Randolph," she replied. "I see my servants haven't yet put a cloth on the table," she added with a frown as her gaze darted to what had held his attention as she descended the stairs.

"It's a magnificent gaming table. I shouldn't think you would want such beautiful carving hidden," he remarked, glad to see that she wasn't displaying embarrassment over their kiss from the night before. He offered his arm, and she took it once she was off the last step.

"I wanted to locate the hall table that should have been there, but this was the closest the servants could find. It was in the study," she explained. "You see, my delivery of flowers arrived for Christmas yesterday, and I'm afraid I may have ordered more than I could accommodate."

They made their way to the front door, Chesterfield pulling it open for them. He handed Xenobia a fur muff, and she took it despite remembering Julia's comment about how she would have to thread an arm around Sir Randolph's elbow in order to hang on for the tight turns.

"I don't think a house can have too many flowers, my lady," Randolph remarked as he led them to the phaeton. "The roses in your parlor are quite lovely."

"It's kind of you to say," she replied, just before her attention went to his high-perch phaeton and the horse that stood snorting in front of it. "Oh, what kind of horse is this?" Xenobia asked as she hurried to stand in front of the huge bay. "It's far too large to be a Thoroughbred," she added.

Randolph grinned at her comment, remembering the book she had been holding the night before. "This is Hermes. He's a Cleveland Bay, and he's usually paired with another the same size as he is. Unfortunately, Aries has come up lame."

"Will he be all right?" she asked, her expression displaying her concern.

"Hopefully. I have his foreleg wrapped, and I'm holding off on exercising him for a few days," he replied. "You can... touch him, if you'd like," he added, continuing to grin at her enthusiasm.

He wondered how long it had been since she was last out of the house. She fairly nearly bounced with excitement, as if she'd been locked away and held hostage for a long time.

A year, he realized, remembering how long wives were expected to mourn their dead husbands.

"How do I do it?"

Randolph moved to stand behind her, and he took one of her gloved hands in his. He guided it until her hand was above the horse's nose. "Just smooth it straight up," he whispered, letting go of her hand. "In the direction of how the hair grows."

She followed his instructions, grinning when Hermes lowered his head so she could better reach the space between his ears. He nickered softly. "He looks so clean. Like he's just had a bath."

"He had a good brushing earlier this afternoon," Randolph said, secretly glad she had noticed the results of Alistair's time spent with the beast. "Let me help you up."

Xenobia regarded the step on the side of the phaeton with widened eyes. "It's terribly high," she said, her gaze going up to where there was a handle she could use to help hoist herself onto the bench once she was up the single step.

"Do you trust me?" Randolph asked.

She turned her gaze onto him. "I... I do."

"Place your hands on my shoulders," he ordered. He moved his hands to her waist and, when she had her gloved hands in place, he lifted her up until she was mostly on the bench seat.

"Oh, this is terribly high," she said, but her expression of delight belied the complaint.

Randolph hurried around to the other side, barely pausing to take the step up and onto the bench. He adjusted his great coat and then pulled a thick quilt from a rack behind the seat. He spread it out over their laps. "Are you warm enough?"

"I am," she replied with a smile. "It's rather considerate of you to bring the blanket."

Randolph unwrapped the reins from around the short pole in front of the bench. "I wish I could claim I thought of it just for today, but I admit to keeping it here on the phaeton throughout the winter months," he replied as he took the ribbons in one hand. "Before I let Hermes loose, I suppose I should warn you that we'll be moving at a fast clip. You'd best hang onto me. I shouldn't wish to lose you on one of the turns."

Xenobia didn't argue, but did as Julia had described, shoving her hands into the muff once her arm was securely wrapped about Randolph's elbow. "Like this?"

"Perfect," he replied, noting how she didn't hesitate to secure her arm to his, or attempt to shift too far away from him on the bench. He flicked the reins, and Hermes pulled them into Curzon Street. "If you get cold, please let me know."

Even if she'd been chilled to the bone, Xenobia wouldn't

have complained. She had never ridden so high in her entire life, and she made certain Sir Randolph knew it.

"However do you get about town?" he asked.

"Town coaches and a barouche," she replied. "Mother never drove. I don't think she knows how, so of course I was never allowed to learn."

"Your mother? Does she live here in town?" He feigned not knowing anything about her family in the hopes she would share her side of what he had learned from Alistair. He felt her hold stiffen around his arm, and he dared a quick glance in her direction.

She quickly looked away from his gaze. "Only on occasion," Xenobia replied. "I think she's on the Continent at the moment. Somewhere in the Kingdom of the Two Sicilies. The Dowager Duchess of Pendleton likes to spend Christmas in Rome," she added, referring to her mother by her title. She didn't add that her mother was probably sharing a count's bed at night and flirting with a duke during the day.

"Having a duchess for a mother must be rather interesting," he remarked. "And what of your father?"

Xenobia relaxed her hold on him just after they made the turn onto Park Lane. "Captain Bradley died when I was eighteen." At his sharp glance, she added, "I don't think he ever completely recovered from his battle wounds. He fought in the war against Napoleon, you see. He was in the navy and then captained ships for commerce."

"You are proud of him, I hope?"

"Oh, I am," she affirmed. "I found him to be a very generous and amiable man. He gave me his house even before he took his last breath, along with an allowance. Made sure the title to the house was in my name, and that it could not be taken away from me should I wed."

"The house you live in now?" Randolph asked.

"Yes."

He frowned. "Did he think you would wed an opportunist?"

Xenobia seemed to think on the query for a time before she

said, "I do not believe he thought I would marry at all, given the circumstances."

Slowing the horse for the turn into Hyde Park—a move that would prevent Xenobia from being pressed overmuch into his side—Randolph furrowed a brow. "Circumstances?"

Tightening her hold on her escort, Xenobia considered how to respond. She had always just assumed everyone in London knew she was an illegitimate daughter of a duchess. That her mother, known for her exploits following the death of her husband, had come to be known as the Dowager Duchess of Debauchery.

At least Edith's time with the captain had been long enough to ensure Xenobia's parentage. Had the duchess discovered she was with child a year or two later, Xenobia—and her mother— might not know the identity of her father.

"Like you, I am illegitimate," she finally replied, deciding he would eventually learn more about her if she didn't offer the information first.

"Then I am in the very best company," Randolph replied. "And it sounds as if our fathers were both honorable in that regard."

"Indeed," Xenobia agreed, deciding it was safe to bring up Rachel. "Your sister paid a call earlier this afternoon. I am so happy she's returned from the Continent."

Randolph jerked his head to regard her with a raised brow. Now he wondered if his father had only told him about Rachel because he had been sure Xenobia would mention her. "You... you know Rachel?"

Nodding, Xenobia said, "We were at finishing school together in Zurich. For several years. Kindred spirits, you might say, despite the difference in our ages."

Randolph seemed at a loss for words. "I only discovered I had a sister last night," he finally admitted. "When I returned to my father's house after leaving you."

Xenobia considered his admission and wondered at the sense of relief she felt at hearing it. "Your father never told you?"

He shook his head. "Even though Rachel is my youngest

brother's twin, she was raised by her mother, Mrs. Higgins, whilst the boy lived with someone else. Apparently, Father lost track of Mrs. Higgins for a time, but has since found her. He's made arrangements for a dowry and a come-out for Rachel."

Xenobia leaned toward him. "I am relieved for Rachel. Her mother always called herself The Queen of Hearts, and Rachel said it was because she was always breaking them."

Randolph furrowed a brow. "She owns the gaming hell of that name," he murmured. "In Stafford Street. I think my father feared Rachel would follow in her mother's footsteps."

"Oh, she wouldn't," Xenobia insisted. "Rachel always knew who her father was. Knew how important it was she remain chaste. We both knew that." She thought to tell him about the possibility they might come upon Rachel and Mark Merriweather whilst on their ride, but thought better of it. She had no idea if he even knew Mark Merriweather.

Dipping his head, Randolph said, "Thank you for telling me about her. I look forward to meeting her knowing you are her friend."

Xenobia allowed a heavy sigh, as if a huge weight had been lifted from her shoulders. Her gaze went to where the foundations for a row of Ionic columns and several arches had been constructed. Huge blocks of stone were scattered about the grounds. Before long, the newest additions to the park would welcome riders and walkers alike onto the King's Private Road. "I hope you are not angry with your father for having kept her a secret."

Randolph took a deep breath. "I wasn't, exactly. Disappointed, perhaps, until he explained the circumstances. I cannot say I would have done it differently." He glanced over to find her regarding him with admiration. "I rather imagine your father was better at the job," and then he grinned at seeing how a blush deepened the color on her already rosy cheeks.

"I truly loved Captain Bradley," Xenobia admitted. "He doted on me when my mother would take me to his house for a week or two every year," she explained, remembering how her parents seemed to rekindle their fondness for one another during those visits. "He allowed me to go into any room, especially the library, and he said that if I were to discover a treasure buried in a box, it would be mine to keep."

His attention captured by this last comment, Randolph remembered the story his father had told him about Constance finding hidden money in her house in Sussex. "And did you find one?"

Her face lit up as she giggled. "I thought so, the day I discovered a beautifully decorated pasteboard box filled with cheroots in the study. I remember him laughing because I didn't know what they were. I didn't know that they were the reason his wool coat always smelled the way it did." She leaned towards him again, inhaling the scent from his coat. "Like yours." Her lips trembled at the memory. "I always remember those weeks as if they were an adventure, because he said he didn't want there to be any secrets between us, and I was always determined to discover what he meant."

Randolph furrowed a brow at hearing the reference to secrets. He wondered what kind of secrets a naval captain could have, especially a wounded one. "Pray tell, when did you move into the house?"

Her eyes darted to his for the briefest of moments. "Not until I married. James... Lord Dunsworth... he didn't have a house here in town, so my ownership of Bradley House saved him from having to let one for us."

Bristling at the thought that Dunsworth might have married Xenobia just so he would have a place to live in London, Randolph had to bite his tongue or risk speaking the sentiment out loud.

He was about to ask if she had siblings when she suddenly said, "But I suppose that's why he had the blunt to let a townhouse and hire a mistress."

Randolph directed the horse to the side of the road and slowed him to a stop. He regarded Xenobia with a look of shock. Her eyes were bright with tears.

Before he gave a thought to what he was doing, Randolph pulled his arm from her hold and then gathered her into his arms, pulling her hard against the side of his body. "Xenobia, no," he whispered.

"I'm terribly sorry. What a horrid thing to say about the dead," she murmured into his wool coat, once again inhaling the scent of cheroot smoke and cologne.

"It's not horrid, my lady," he countered as he readjusted his hold on her. "Even if it is the truth." He held her for another moment, his gaze sweeping the area around them to determine if anyone was watching. He knew if they were seen like this, tongues would wag. "Come. Let's go for a walk," he said as he gave up his hold on her. He stepped down from the phaeton and hurried around to lift her from the high perch.

"But... what of the phaeton?" she protested. Given the weather, no young boy hurried up to mind the gig in exchange for a coin.

"Hermes must learn patience," Randolph replied as he secured the reins to the pole. "And we won't go far."

Xenobia made her way to the front of the horse, reaching up to smooth a hand over his cheek.

Randolph joined her and pulled a small apple from his coat pocket. He offered it to her. "You'll be his friend for life—or at least the rest of the day."

Her face once again brightening, Xenobia took the apple and offered it to the horse. She let out a gasp when it disappeared from her hand, and then laughed at the crunching sound as Hermes devoured the fruit.

Randolph held out his arm. "Shall we?"

Xenobia realized immediately why he had chosen this particular location to stop the phaeton—privacy. A crushed granite path, dusted with a layer of snow, led from the King's Private Road north toward the east end of the Serpentine. Most of the path was lined with hedgerows and covered by a canopy of maple trees. Although their branches were mostly bare of leaves, they were coated with snow. "I've never been on this path during the winter," she said in a quiet voice, almost as if she feared the snow would fall from the branches if she spoke too loudly.

"I've only been once," he replied, remembering how Barbara complained about the cold and the wind off the Serpentine. "I recall it was quiet." He slowed his steps when he spotted a park bench nestled against the bushes. "Will you sit with me?"

"Of course."

"Even if my motives are not honorable?"

Xenobia stared up at him, noticing how weariness showed in the corners of his eyes. "Would you think me wanton if I was more inclined to do so because of what you just said?"

A huge grin split Randolph's face. "Possibly," he hedged. He used a gloved hand to wipe away the dusting of snow that covered the bench. "Actually, I brought you here because of what you said a few moments ago. About your... your husband and his mistress."

Xenobia attempted to hide a frown. "What of him?" she asked as she took a seat, disappointed at hearing the reason for their walk.

He struggled to form his words. "I fear that now that you are out of mourning, you may embark on a lifestyle to which you are unaccustomed," he replied as he sat down next to her. "As if you intend to seek revenge for having put up with Lord Dunsworth's preference for a mistress."

Xenobia inhaled sharply. "I rather doubt that," she said, almost too quickly. "I am not my mother's daughter, if you were inferring I would become a Merry Widow."

He nodded his understanding. "While I am relieved to hear it, I am also torn."

Inhaling softly, she stared at him. "Why?"

Randolph dipped his head, his gaze going to his clasped hands. "After last night, I thought more on your wish to have companionship. I could not help but think you referred to wanting more than just... *conversation*. That you were in fact speaking of taking a lover."

About to deny his claim, Xenobia could not when one of his arms encircled her shoulders. His lips were on hers only a moment later, lips that were cold at first, but soon heated as he claimed her mouth.

Randolph pulled her closer, his lips leaving hers to trail featherlight kisses along her jaw to her ear. Had his hat and hers not prevented him from doing so, he would have kissed the area behind her ear and then moved his kisses down her neck.

He heard her ragged breaths and finally pulled away. "I would ask that if you are considering such a thing—"

"Such a thing?" she repeated, looking ever so addlepated.

"Taking a lover."

Her eyes widened. "I... I wasn't. At least... not before."

"Before?"

Her eyes darted sideways. "Before you seemed to indicate you wished to be the first one in a very short line."

"A line of only one, I should hope."

Xenobia felt a rush of excitement. "Are you that one?"

He nodded. "Despite the circumstances."

Xenobia's brows furrowed. "Circumstances?"

"Besides my responsibilities at the Reading stables, I have a position. One that requires me to work most nights," he stammered. "I can be your lover on Wednesday nights after dinner—"

His words were halted when she raised a gloved finger to his lips. "I cannot help but think you are offering yourself out of pity for me." Although she was curious as to what he might do in his position as an investigator, especially in that it required he work at night, she didn't ask. His nocturnal employment explained why he appeared tired, though.

He took the finger from his lips, his larger hand covering hers entirely. "Not pity," he whispered, his slight headshake reinforcing his reply. "For if you had readily agreed, I might have thought you felt pity for *me*," he reasoned.

"Because you are a widower?"

Randolph dipped his head. "A widower who is also the father of a babe."

Xenobia exhaled, her mind racing with possibilities. "You could have your pick of any number of women in search of a tryst—"

"I'm not interested in a tryst, my lady."

She furrowed a blonde brow. "An *affaire*, then?"

He shook his head. "I am not my father's son in that regard," he reminded her. "I thought I made that clear last night. If... *when* I take you as a lover, you will be the only one I bed."

Xenobia blinked at the comment, but her eyes widened at how he had couched the claim.

When I take you as a lover...

As if he had already decided they were going to *be* lovers. "You promise you do not pity me?"

"I promise," he replied. Then he remembered what he had discovered when he arrived at Bradley House that afternoon. Remembered the letter he had read.

Did Xenobia know there were hundreds of pounds of bank notes hidden in that one piece of furniture?

If so, did she have blunt stowed away in other furnishings in Bradley House?

If she didn't, did the servants know?

When he noted how she stared at him, he shook off the brief reverie. "After what I discovered today, I am of the opinion that you need a protector," Randolph added in a hoarse whisper.

Alarmed by the claim, Xenobia stared at him. "What did you discover?"

He gave his head a shake. "I'll show you when we return to Bradley House. In the meantime, would you be amenable to me acting as your protector?"

Xenobia stared at him. If Randolph declared he was her protector, then there would be gossip. "The entire *ton* will know we are lovers," she argued.

"Would you be embarrassed if they did, my lady?"

Xenobia took a moment to consider how she might feel if word got out she was carrying on with Sir Randolph. If Lady Pettigrew knew. If Lady Reading knew. If Lady Chamberlain knew. If Julia knew.

Well, Julia would be over-the-moon happy for her.

Lady Reading would be discreet. She wouldn't mention it to anyone.

Lady Chamberlain would want to know all the details, but she would only divulge them to her husband.

Lady Pettigrew would share the news in every Mayfair parlor on which she could possibly pay a morning call in the next fortnight. Despite her penchant for gossip, though, probably no one would believe her.

"I would not be embarrassed, Sir Randolph."

"Just Randolph, if you would. Or... or Rand when we are alone," he said as he dropped his forehead to touch hers. He had doffed his top hat the moment before, wanting nothing more than to kiss her senseless.

"Rand," she repeated, her gaze on his lips. Before she could stop herself, she kissed him.

Randolph returned the kiss, his arms once again wrapping around her shoulders to pull her close. When Xenobia finally released his lips, he allowed a grin. "I give you permission to do that whenever you wish," he murmured.

Xenobia grinned, her face reddening. "Surely only when we're alone," she countered.

His eyes darting sideways, Randolph allowed a chuckle. "Whenever you wish," he repeated.

The sound of a horse whinnying in complaint had Xenobia leaning to the side. "Was that Hermes?"

Randolph grimaced. "Probably." His subsequent curse came out as a whisper.

"Take me home, Rand. You can park the phaeton in the mews behind the townhouse, and we can warm ourselves next to a fire," Xenobia said as she stood. "You can even sleep if you wish. You look as if you could use a nap."

Randolph was quick to follow suit, standing before her. "As you wish, my lady. And the offer of a place to sleep is very welcome. You are right in noticing my lack of sleep."

"Xenobia," she countered as she threaded her arm through his elbow. "Or Xena, should you be so inclined."

Before he turned to lead them back to the King's Private Road, Randolph regarded her with awe. "A force of Zeus?" he inquired, referring to the meaning of her name. "You deserve to be called no less than your full name," he claimed.

Xenobia stared up at Randolph. If she'd been the least bit cold before, she was not now. "If you intend to worship me, then you best return me to Bradley House," she suggested.

Randolph hesitated, a wince appearing. "I really wish this was a Wednesday," he murmured. "So I wouldn't have to leave you."

Although she felt a wave of disappointment, Xenobia allowed a wan grin. "We'll merely spend what time we can together," she offered. "Until you must take your leave."

Randolph nodded before he returned his hat to his head. They made their way back to the phaeton, and he lifted her onto the phaeton bench, all the while Hermes snorted and stomped a hoof and a light snow fell around them.

Off in the distance, a pair of riders on horseback braved the chilly air as they made their way along Rotten Row, and Randolph was fairly certain he recognized the Welsh pony on which the female rider was seated.

Xenobia grinned as she settled herself onto the bench. She laughed as Randolph fairly launched himself onto the bench next to her. He had Hermes trotting into a tight U-turn and headed back to the Hyde Park Corner gate in only a moment.

Ten minutes later, and they were in the mews behind Bradley House.

Despite the late nights and early mornings leaving him feeling weary, Randolph looked forward to a few hours in her company. He would probably be asleep for two of them, but at least he wouldn't wake up alone.

CHAPTER 29
HORSE PLAY IN THE PARK

eanwhile, at The Queen of Hearts
Rachel regarded her reflection in the cheval mirror and winced. She hadn't worn her riding habit in nearly a year, and the creases from where it had been folded in her trunk were apparent in the wool skirts.

The color was still vibrant, though, the cobalt blue perfect with her eye coloring and her dark hair. She had opted to leave her hair as the maid had dressed it for her earlier call on Xenobia, deciding she didn't wish to bother a servant.

Nor did she have the time.

The clock on the mantel had already struck its half-past-the-hour chime, and no servant had knocked on her door to let her know anyone was waiting for her.

Then she wondered where Mr. Merriweather would even go to ask after her. Surely he wouldn't expect to find her in The Queen of Hearts, but it was doubtful he knew of the other entrance.

Or did he?

She quickly pinned her black and blue hat to her hair and pulled on a pair of black kid gloves before making her way down the stairs. From the quiet commotion she heard below, she knew someone had paid a call. A maid was speaking.

"Have a seat, sir, and I'll let her know you're here," the older woman said.

Rachel paused on the stairs, half-tempted to return to her bedchamber. The maid suddenly appeared, though, along with her brilliant smile. "Well, you look as if you're right ready for an outing this afternoon, Miss Roderick."

"I am, Mrs. Baker. Where might I find my caller?"

"Right here," Mark Merriweather said, at the very moment he appeared from behind the maid. His riding clothes fit him to perfection, his doeskin breeches tight around his thighs and his dark blue top coat a welcome change from the usual hunter green or scarlet red. Rather than wearing a white cravat, his was black, as were his Hessians. His valet had probably spent an entire day polishing them. Rachel was sure she could see her reflection in them.

Mark's mouth dropped open as he clutched his top hat and a riding crop between gloved hands. "Good afternoon, my lady," he added as he gave her a deep bow.

Stuck in the middle of the staircase, Rachel did her best to perform a curtsy on the carpeted steps at the same moment Mrs. Baker disappeared. "How do, Mr. Merriweather?" she replied before descending the rest of the stairs. She was blocked from stepping off the last one, though, as Mark stood staring up at her.

"Oh, dear, do I have something on my face?" Rachel asked as she lifted one of her gloved hands to her cheek.

"Great beauty is all," Mark replied. "As if Jupiter himself cast you in Aphrodite's likeness," he said in awe, apparently unaware he had mixed up his mythologies.

Rachel blinked and then had to stifle the urge to laugh in his face. "I do believe it was Zeus who fathered Aphrodite," she murmured. "But thank you for saying so." Even though he was taller than she was, Rachel still stood on the last step, giving her an inch or two height advantage.

"Nonetheless, he made you a classic beauty, my lady."

His words and the way he continued to gaze at her had

Rachel quickly sobering. "Thank you, sir. And although I appreciate you saying 'my lady', I am really not—"

"Nonsense," he interrupted. "You are the daughter of a marquess and a queen," he stated. "I shall always afford you all the courtesies." He offered his arm, and Rachel stared at it a moment before she finally placed her hand on it.

She had paled at hearing his words, and as they made their way out the door, she asked, "Who... who told you?" Would her father have mentioned her mother when the earl's son paid a call on him earlier that morning?

Her distress was replaced with awe the very moment she noticed three horses and a groom who stood holding their reins.

One was a Welsh pony.

A gray Welsh pony.

Mark angled his head to one side. "I paid a call on your father this morning. To do as you said and ask his permission. To take you riding." He noted how she stared at the pony and secretly thanked his good luck at having found Sir Randolph at the Reading stables preparing for his own ride in the park only the hour before. Explaining his need to borrow the Welsh pony for the afternoon was easier than he expected—and he hadn't even needed to show the short missive the Marquess of Reading had written on his behalf.

"Lord Reading mentioned you had been to see him when he paid a call this morning," Rachel replied as she moved to stand before the pony. "Richard?" she whispered, nearly bursting into tears when the pony responded with a quiet nicker. She smoothed a hand along his cheek and then his neck. "Oh, Richard, it's so good to see you again." She lowered her face and placed a kiss on his nose, which resulted in another soft knicker.

Mark offered her his handkerchief. "He said you might cry."

Blinking quickly, Rachel gave him a glance but waved away the offer of the hanky. "I'll be fine."

"When he told me who your mother was, I thought at first he was trying to dissuade me from my purpose—"

"Which is?" Hiring her to do his books couldn't be his only motivation for paying a call on her father.

"Courtship," he replied, his chin rising slightly. "That, and... well, I do require a bookkeeper," he added with a pained expression. "Here, let me help you up," he offered as he knelt and knit his fingers together to form a step.

Rachel stared at him. "Courtship?" she repeated in disbelief. She absently stepped onto his laced fingers. The extra boost he gave her was hardly necessary as she ended up well-seated on the sidesaddle. Richard was just a pony, after all. Spreading her skirts out along the side of the horse, she turned her attention back to Mark as the groom offered her the reins. "But... you're an earl's son."

"The second son. And no longer the spare," he reminded her. He mounted his own horse without seeming to expend any effort to do so.

For a brief moment, the shape of his bottom was quite clear in the doeskin breeches, and Rachel experienced the oddest sensation deep in her belly.

"Which is rather freeing, actually," Mark continued as he turned his horse in her direction. "It means I am not as bound by the dictates of Society as I might have been before my nephew was born." He gave a nod to the groom, who mounted his own horse and took off after tipping his hat in Rachel's direction.

"Mr. Merriweather—"

"Mark, please," he said as he waited for her mount to come up alongside his much taller Irish walker. Then they were heading east along Piccadilly toward the park.

"Society does not as easily abide illegitimate women as they do our male counterparts," Rachel stated. "By courting me—"

"With the intention of marrying you," he cut in.

"Means that your lot in life will be severely undermined."

"I don't see it like that."

"But Society will," she argued.

"Society can go hang—"

"Have you spoken with Middleton about me? Or your mother?"

Mark gave her a quelling glance, as if he wished they could

discuss something else. "I told Father of my intentions last night," he replied.

Rachel blinked, not expecting *that* particular response. "And?" she prompted.

"I think he's a bit jealous." Although the words were said seriously, he displayed a grin once they were out.

"Mark," she scolded. "I've never even met your father."

He glanced around to be sure they weren't about to be trampled by any carriages. "My parents did not marry for love," he said, his words barely audible. "They were incompatible from the beginning. Still are, in many respects. Mother prefers to rusticate in the country whilst Father stays here in town most of the time. I think the only reason Mother is here right now is because she wishes to spend the holiday with her grandchild, now that she has one."

Rachel grinned, deciding she would probably do the same if she were in Lady Middleton's shoes. "Are you saying your father is jealous because you will get to choose whom you marry?"

"Indeed," Mark replied as they came up to Park Lane. When traffic had cleared enough, they urged their horses forward and entered the park through the southeast gate.

"What are they building?" Rachel asked in awe. The beginnings of Greek columns were evident among a series of cubical blocks that were arranged on either side of the road.

"An arch and a screen of columns," Mark replied. "It will be quite the entrance arch when it's finally complete."

Almost immediately, the quiet of the park surrounded them, and conversation grew easier.

"Aren't you rather young to be considering marriage?" Rachel queried, trying a different tact in attempting to put him off of the idea of courtship.

"I am five-and-twenty," he replied. "I have reached my majority and have my inheritance. I have spent the last seven years attending all manner of entertainments—balls, soirées, garden parties, routs and house parties—all in the supposed pursuit of a wife," he added. "As it turns out, it merely took the suggestion of one of *your* friends for me to realize I have been looking in the wrong place."

Rachel inhaled sharply. "One of *my* friends?" she repeated. They maneuvered around an empty phaeton that had been parked near one of the crushed granite paths, and Richard suddenly increased his pace until he came up alongside the Cleveland Bay that stood in front of the phaeton. The two horses seemed to exchange greetings before Richard finally resumed his walk next to Mark's mount.

Having noticed the odd behavior—he and his horse had been left behind for a moment—Mark let out a chuckle.

"What is it?" Rachel asked.

"I do believe Sir Randolph must be in the park. That horse back there is one of your mount's stablemates," Mark explained as he indicated Richard. "Sir Randolph is your brother, is he not?"

"Oh, he is," Rachel agreed. "I have not yet met him, but I am friends with Lady Dunsworth. She thought we might see them today whilst they were on their ride." She glanced back at the phaeton and decided the occupants must be taking a walk.

Or perhaps they were enjoying a clandestine kiss.

"I was not aware Lady Dunsworth was out of mourning," Mark murmured.

"For only a few days now," Rachel replied. "Tell me, who is the friend of mine you referred to a moment ago? The one who put you up to courting me?"

Mark rolled his eyes. "If I tell you, you must promise me she will come to no harm."

Rachel scoffed. "If she is truly a friend, then she has nothing to fear from me."

For a moment, Mark continued riding as if he hadn't heard her, but then he turned an expression of amusement on her and said, "Lady Comber came to me yesterday afternoon."

Inhaling sharply, Rachel said, "Julia?" in disbelief.

"Indeed. She had just come from having tea with Lady Dunsworth where she had learned of your imminent arrival from the Continent."

As if Richard could sense her distress, the pony whinnied and Rachel leaned forward to press her hand against his neck. She took a deep breath in an attempt to calm herself. "What ever did she say that had you going to The Queen of Hearts last night?"

Mark chuckled. "I was already going to *be* at The Queen last night. I play cards with the Earl of Haddon there every Wednesday, and she knew that," he explained, his brows furrowing when he once again wondered how she knew. "What she said that had me seeking you out was the claim that there is a woman for every man, and she was sure you were the woman for me."

Rachel stared at Mark for several seconds before she let out a small cry. "Until earlier this afternoon, Julia hadn't even seen me in... in seven or eight *years*," she stammered.

"And yet, she was right. From the moment I laid eyes upon you—when you and The Queen were making your way through the dining room—I knew you were the woman for me."

"You hadn't even met me," she argued.

"True," he acknowledged.

"Surely you don't believe in love at first sight." She quickly put aside the memory of her father's claim that he had fallen in love with her mother in that fashion.

"Perhaps I didn't before," he replied, one of his brows furrowing. "But after our conversation last night... after I learned you weren't an insipid English miss, but a rather clever woman who could do arithmetic, well I... I was besotted."

Rachel scoffed again. "Besotted?" she repeated. "I wasn't aware men used that word."

"Have a care, my lady," Mark warned. "I was and still am besotted," he added, feigning offense.

"I am flattered," Rachel replied, deciding she really was flattered. Flummoxed as well, but after learning more about The Three Bells from her father, she had come to realize she had underestimated the earl's son.

"Enough to consider my offer?" he asked.

Rachel stared at him. "You mean the one of employment as your bookkeeper?"

He allowed a guffaw. "I was hoping for a bargain."

"Oh?"

"A one-for-two sort of arrangement," he said, his eyes twinkling with mischief.

"Arrangement?" Rachel repeated, wincing at having repeated the word. For a moment, she imagined an offer of *carte blanche* on top of the offer of a position to be the bookkeeper for The Three Bells.

"Marriage, actually," he clarified, his eyes on the road ahead. When she didn't immediately respond, he dared a glance in her direction and discovered she was no longer abreast of him. He pulled his mount to a stop and glanced behind him to discover she had halted her mount. She was staring at him. "A wife and a bookkeeper all in one beautiful woman," he added. "Why do you look so shocked?"

She scoffed. "We haven't even known one another for an entire *day*," she replied, her mouth left open in dismay.

"Yet I feel as if I have known you far longer. As if we were destined to meet. And marry," he replied, as he urged his mount to step backwards so that they could once again be side-by-side. "I have never known a woman to be so comfortable with me that she would tease me as mercilessly as you have done—"

"And will continue to do so," she warned, not bothering to add that her father had encouraged her in that regard.

He grinned, the look of mischief still apparent. "As I would hope you would, although not when we're intimate, of course," he murmured. "I have been in need of a good teasing for some time."

Wishing Richard weren't so short—she was forced to look up at Mark as she regarded him in disbelief at hearing his suggestion they would be intimate—Rachel gave her head a shake. "Why, pray tell?"

He allowed a shrug as he urged his mount forward. The pony followed suit without any encouragement from Rachel. "Owning a business has made me far too serious. I welcomed the responsibility at first. I needed something to occupy my time lest I spend it in the card room losing my allowance to Haddon," he explained. "But I have discovered there are trials at every turn. Unreliable vendors, rotten meat, limp vegetables, employees who do not always arrive on time—"

"An unsuitable cook," Rachel put in, one of her brows arching.

Mark inhaled sharply and then rolled his eyes. "He's not *bad*," he replied. "But he's not good."

Remembering her conversation with the maid, Gem Baker, the day before, Rachel's eyes widened. "What if... would you consider a *woman* for the position?"

Angling his head in her direction, Mark displayed a look of confusion. "You cook, too?" he asked in amazement.

Chuckling, Rachel shook her head. "No, but the woman who used to be the cook for my mother has been lamenting. Mrs. Baker used to do meals for twenty or thirty people every day, twice a day. Now that Mother has her French cook, Mrs. Baker has been relegated to housekeeper duties," she explained. "She misses what she calls the 'hub-bub of it all'."

Mark stared at her for a moment. "Where might I find this Mrs. Baker?" he asked, his manner most urgent.

Rachel grinned. "I can introduce you when you return me to my home."

Continuing to stare at her, Mark finally had to pay attention to the road. His horse had taken to wandering aimlessly along the King's Road, and Rachel's mount had simply done the same, as if recognizing the taller Irish walker as his leader. "I should like that very much," he said, once again paying attention to the reins.

"Is your public house far from here?" Rachel asked when she felt Richard pick up speed in an effort to keep up with the walker.

"Not even a half-mile," Mark replied. "I should like to take you there. On an afternoon such as this, it will be warm and smell of baking bread."

Rachel grinned. "I hardly think it would be proper—"

"There is a table in the back. Well hidden from the rest of the diners where we will not be seen," he said in delight.

"Mark!" she scolded.

At the sound of horse hooves and wheels, she turned to see that the phaeton they had passed now had two people on the bench seat. The equipage had turned around and was heading back toward the southeast entrance.

Disappointment settled over her when she realized she would not be meeting her brother on this afternoon.

"Are you up for a race back to the gate?" Mark asked, his grin of delight infectious.

Despite her momentary disappointment, Rachel set Richard into a run as Mark let out a shout and struggled to urge his mount forward. Despite his smaller size, Richard made it to the southeast gate only a head before the Irish walker.

From the look on Mark's face, Rachel knew he had deliberately tightened the reins on his mount in order to allow the Welsh pony to remain in the lead. "Sometimes, we must allow the small ones to win," he said in a hoarse whisper.

The strangest sensation gripped Rachel's heart. She nodded in agreement as they set off for The Three Bells.

CHAPTER 30
A SEDUCTION THWARTED BY EXHAUSTION

few minutes later, in Bradley House

Xenobia led Randolph to the back door of Bradley House. "I'm of a mind to take the servants' stairs to the second floor," she whispered as Randolph opened the door for her. She pulled her hands from her muff to remove her gloves and then shoved them into her pockets while Randolph followed suit.

When she reached for his bare hand with hers, Randolph's gaze went to the thin set of stairs that led to the upper floors. "Will it be warm enough in your apartments, my lady?" he queried. "I cannot help but notice, but your hand feels awfully cold."

Xenobia couldn't help the shiver that coursed down her spine just then. Was the man mad? She was far warmer than she would be on a hot summer day. "I rather doubt that's possible," she replied with a grin, almost embarrassed by what she thought they might be about to do.

Spend a few hours together.

In the afternoon.

In a bedchamber.

There was nothing about this tryst that could be considered appropriate, even if they didn't do anything scandalous. She was on the verge of feeling ashamed of herself.

Overcome by a yawn, Randolph struggled to cover it with

the hand that held his hat. "If you're not comfortable with this—"

"It's fine," Xenobia interrupted as she headed to the stairs. "There's a different bedchamber we can use. One where we won't be disturbed."

Xenobia lifted her skirts and made her way up the thin, wooden steps, her half boots barely making a sound. Meanwhile, she was well aware of his boots and the sounds they made directly behind her. The cadence of the slight tapping matched how fast her heart was beating.

About to reach for the door handle to the very first bedchamber along the second floor corridor, Xenobia gasped when Randolph's hand brushed past hers. "Allow me," he murmured as he opened the door.

Xenobia stepped in, relieved the darkened bedchamber was in good order. The heavy drapes were closed, no doubt to lessen the chill from the two windows. From the painting above the mantel and the dark blue fabrics curtaining the bed and covering the chairs in front of the fireplace, she remembered this room had been part of her father's apartments.

Randolph made his way to the room's fireplace, where a bucket of coal and kindling were on hand. He lit a fuzee, and soon the flames lit the room in a golden glow. Helping himself to a candle lamp, he lit the wick and returned it to the nightstand.

Xenobia noticed how he studied all the furnishings in the room. How his gaze darted to the clock and marble busts, to the objets d'art her father had collected. Remembering his comment about having to work at nights, she now worried that he might really be a thief, using his ties to the *ton* as a means to gain entry into ladies' homes to help himself to their jewelry and other valuables.

She quickly reminded herself of who he was—the son of a marquess and a friend to Julia's husband—and she tried to relax.

Randolph turned to regard her, his expression unreadable. "Perhaps you should come sit next to the fire."

"Of course," she quickly agreed and moved to take one of

the upholstered chairs. As Randolph helped her out of her redingote, she inhaled sharply when she saw that the curtains were open on the side of the bed that faced the fireplace. Had the bed linens been turned down, the expanse of white would have been an obvious invitation.

For a moment back in the park, she had wanted Randolph to accept such an invitation.

Now she was nervous.

Now she was trying to imagine what it would be like to be bedded by this man. What words he might murmur as her fingers slid down his chest, up his arms to wrap over his shoulders. What sounds he might make as he drove himself into her, filling her completely. What he might do when he experienced his ecstasy.

She tried to remember if there had been more to it and found her recollection of lovemaking a disappointment.

Perhaps this wasn't a good idea.

*R*andolph furrowed his brows as he stared at Xenobia, sure she must be having second thoughts. He was as well, but for a very different reason. "Would you lie with me while I sleep? I can warm the bed for you," he suggested. "I can undo your buttons, and you can join me when you're undressed. Otherwise, I fear it will be chilly in here for a time."

Xenobia wondered at the sudden excitement that came over her just then. Then she noticed his weariness. "What's wrong?"

Randolph angled the adjacent chair so it almost faced the one she was in, and he took a seat. He leaned forward, his elbows on his knees, and then reached out a hand to take one of hers. "I've not shared a bed with a woman since my wife's death," he murmured quietly. "And truth be told, at the moment, I do not have the energy to do more than remove my clothing and climb onto that bed," he said as he motioned with his thumb. "However, I can provide a warm body against which you can nap for a time." He paused and took a breath. "Do I have your permission to stay? Until I must leave to go to work?"

Xenobia was torn between asking him to leave and agreeing with everything he said. "You do," she finally replied, well aware he still held onto her hand. For the first time all day, her hand felt warm.

Randolph sighed. "Do you require help with buttons or... or hairpins?" he asked. "I promise I won't do anything to muss your hair."

She shook her head. "I can manage. I'll just go behind the..." She looked about for a dressing screen and discovered there wasn't one. "Into the dressing room."

And what? Undress while he did the same out here?

"Put on your favorite night rail," he finished for her, his gaze going to the door in the corner. Then he remembered they weren't in her bedchamber. This was probably a guest bedchamber. It was unlikely there was a night rail hanging in the dressing room. "Or a dressing gown, perhaps?" he suggested. Still holding onto her hand, he stood up and helped her to stand.

"I'll see what I can find," she replied as she turned her back to him.

The warmth of his fingers permeated the fabric as he undid the series of fastenings down the back of the gown. The bodice sagged forward, and when the tips of his fingers and then his entire hand settled onto her bare back to spread open the garment, Xenobia shivered. When he turned her around in his arms, he kissed her softly.

CHAPTER 31
THE THREE BELLS

eanwhile, at the corner of Duke and Charles Streets, Westminster

Riding on horseback in the streets of London was hardly the way in which young ladies and gentlemen were supposed to travel, but given the route Mark took, Rachel found she enjoyed the bucolic scenery.

Once out of Hyde Park, they were immediately on the edge of the Queen's Garden. When that ended, they rode through St. James' Park on their way toward the short streets that led to the Parliament buildings, Westminster Abbey, and St. Margaret's Church.

Mark dismounted at the corner of Duke and Charles Street and then hurried to help Rachel off her pony.

"Really, Mark, I could have managed," she scolded when his hands gripped the sides of her waist and he lifted her from Richard. "My feet were very nearly to the ground already."

"You would begrudge me the pleasure of holding onto you, if but for a mere moment?" he countered, his hands still resting at her waist.

Her feet had long since taken purchase on the ground, and she stared up at him in surprise. "Mark," she whispered. She glanced about, sure someone could have seen them.

A boy ran up to them, his clothes suggesting he wasn't a resident of any of the beautiful homes that lined Duke Street. "Hold your horses for you, guv'nor?" he asked as he reached for Richard's reins and then bowed to Rachel.

Mark regarded the urchin a moment and then angled his head in the direction of the buildings along Charles Street. "As usual, I'll be in The Three Bells. You can take them to the mews off the alley," he said as he offered the boy a coin. Then he pulled another, larger coin from his waistcoat pocket. "See to it they're given water and some hay?"

The boy's eyes widened and he nodded quickly. "Yes, guv'nor."

About to put voice to a protest, Rachel watched as the two horses fell in line with the boy, apparently well aware there was a treat in their future. She glanced over at Mark and gave a start when she noticed he had been staring at her.

"You needn't worry. He's done this for me before. Many times," Mark assured her. He offered his arm.

"He's so young," she murmured.

"And ready for another bath," Mark replied. "I think he's an orphan, but someone along one of these streets must look after him. He spends his nights in a room in the mews."

The scent of baking bread replaced the faint odors of the nearby river as they approached The Three Bells. The low stone façade topped by mullioned windows was broken up by columns that flanked the door, a triangular pediment above spanning the columns. Carved into the pediment were three bells. A sign mounted on the bottom of the second story bay wall adjacent to the pediment spelled out 'The Three Bells' in capital letters.

"This looks quite respectable," Rachel said in awe.

Mark furrowed a brow. "Did you expect otherwise?"

She inhaled as if to answer one way, but decided against her first thought to tease him. "Truth be told, I didn't know what to expect." When he pretended offense, she added, "I have seen many a public house that were not nearly as welcoming as this. Why, this looks like a restaurant."

"Given the patrons I wish to attract, it needs to be," he said as he opened the door. Instead of a dark interior lit only by a fire and a few candle lamps, the inside of The Three Bells was light, particularly close to the windows. The wooden tables were covered in linens, but the chairs weren't upholstered. Given the time of day, there were few diners, but there were a number of well-dressed gentlemen lined up at a polished wood bar, mugs of ale or glasses of amber liquid set before them. Conversations were muted, and their arrival barely elicited a turned head in their direction.

The level of noise was not nearly as raucous as the public house Rachel had frequented in Zurich, nor did the odor of stale ale and sweat permeate the air. She inhaled deeply and smelled only fresh, yeasty bread. "Surely your cook must be good at making bread," she whispered.

"He is not. The bread is made by one of the kitchen maids," Mark replied as he aimed them toward a table in the back. Farthest from the windows, a corner provided a small level of privacy. "Are you hungry?" he asked as he pulled out her chair.

Rachel was about to answer in the negative, but her stomach grumbled. "If I say I am, what am I to expect?" she asked as she took the proffered chair. She pulled her gloves from her hands and placed them on her lap.

"A decent meal," he replied with a grin. "A glass of wine?"

"Wine?" she repeated in surprise.

"Of course. This is a civilized establishment," he replied as he took the chair opposite. "Or you can have a glass of ale if you prefer," he offered at the same moment a server stepped up and gave a slight bow.

"Afternoon, sir," the young man said, obviously recognizing the public house's owner.

"Afternoon, Gilbert. What's cook got in the oven?" Mark asked as he removed his riding gloves.

"Shepherd's pie, beef roast, lamb chops, and roast potatoes, sir."

Rachel's eyes widened at the mention of beef roast, and Mark noticed. "The beef for us both and some claret. Bring the bottle. Oh, and some of that bread." He watched the server bow again before he turned his attention back to Rachel. "You'll have to let me know what you think of the meal. I wish for an honest opinion."

"It sounds delicious," Rachel replied. She glanced around, sure they were being watched. But those drinking at the bar were paying them no mind. The bits of conversation she could hear implied the men were members of Parliament, and yet she was fairly sure they had ended their sessions for the year. There were two gentlemen at a nearby table, their animated conversation clearly spoken in French. "It appears you attract members of the peerage," she commented.

Mark nodded. "That is my hope," he agreed. "Sometimes those who work in Whitehall will make the walk, but with two other public houses in the adjacent streets along with a coffee house in Duke Street, I have competition. Hence the need for an exceptionally good cook." He glanced about, wincing at seeing few patrons at the tables. "When Parliament is in session, it's far busier in here."

"The placement of the chairs at the smaller tables is all wrong," Rachel blurted, although she was listening intently to the men speaking French.

Blinking, Mark's gaze swept the dining area. "In what way?"

Rachel dipped her head. "Apologies, but... no man wishes to sit with his back to the door. If the chairs were placed as ours are, then no one except a single person at the tables for four would have to sit with their backs to the door." She furrowed a brow at hearing the word 'bank note' spoken in French.

Belgian French.

Names of gaming hells had her concentrating on the foreigners' conversation, sure they were making plans for that evening.

"I see your point," Mark murmured. "I'll have chairs moved after closing tonight. What else is wrong?"

About to mention the lack of a light on each table—the room had grown darker with the winter sun setting—Rachel held her comment when the server placed a bottle of wine and two glasses on the table along with a wooden board on which a loaf of hot bread sent up steamy and delicious aromas. Gilbert poured and then slipped a paper to Rachel. "From one of the gents at the bar," he whispered.

Rachel stiffened, and after the server stepped away, she opened the missive.

I'll see you home. Too dark to ride. R.

Furrowing her brows in outrage, Rachel scoffed until she realized the note was from her father. She glanced over her shoulder towards the bar and understood why she'd had the sensation of being watched.

The Marquess of Reading was drinking an ale as he conversed with another gentleman.

"What is it? Has someone... has someone *propositioned* you?" Mark asked in a hoarse whisper.

Rachel passed the note to Mark. "In a manner of speaking."

Mark glanced at the note before his eyes rounded. He glanced up and then had to quickly avert his gaze when he realized she referred to her father.

"His lordship is right, though. It will be far too dark to ride home," she murmured. Her attention briefly went to the two gentlemen who had been speaking in French. Words having to do with their last night in London and the need to exchange the bank notes for coin being of utmost importance had her remembering her brother's reason for being at The Queen of Hearts the day before.

She took a sip of wine, relieved it was of good quality, and then tore some of the bread from the loaf. "Do you have plans for later this evening?" she asked.

Mark stared at her. "I do not," he replied, his gaze darting to the bar. Truth be told, he had hoped they might spend the entire night together, although he knew it wasn't to be. Especially now that the Marquess of Reading was in the public house.

"Is there a chance you might locate my brother at a gaming

hell? Pass along a bit of information for me?" Rachel asked, trying hard to appear calm. Alarm had her heart racing. Whatever her brother was doing on behalf of the Crown might benefit from what she had just overheard.

Staring at her, Mark blinked. "Tonight?"

"Indeed. Would you like some bread?"

Mark swallowed, his gaze darting to the marquess. The two exchanged nods before Randall Roderick made his way to their table. Merriweather quickly stood up and gave him a bow. "How do, my lord? I would introduce you to my supper guest, but I believe you two have already met."

"Evening, Merriweather," Randall said and then bowed to his daughter. "Yes, we have. Twenty years ago or so?" he added as he favored her with a wink and a smirk.

"Good *afternoon*, Father," Rachel said, affording him a teasing grin before she took a bite of the bread. She wondered if her father had been following them whilst they were in the park, but she couldn't recall other riders on the King's Road—nor a town coach suitable for a marquess. "Mr. Merriweather has granted me an audience here in his place of business. I wished to see it first-hand before giving him my answer regarding his offer of a position."

Randall turned a steely gaze on the young man, one of his bushy eyebrows rising in surprise. "Position?" he repeated.

"My lord, I asked Miss Roderick to be my bookkeeper. For this establishment," Mark explained.

His brows now furrowing in confusion, Randall said, "You spoke of an entirely different proposal when we met this morning."

"I did," Mark admitted. "I was about to get to that, and, oh, dear. Here's our supper already," he stammered as the server set plates of sliced beef before Rachel and Mark. "Would you care to join us, sir?"

For a moment, the marquess looked as if he might pull up a chair from another table and help himself to one of their plates, but he gave his head a shake. "As good as it looks, I don't wish to spoil my dinner. My marchioness has seen to it my favorite meal will be served at seven o'clock. In the meantime, I'll see to taking Rachel home when she's finished here."

"But what of Richard?" she asked in alarm, remembering the horses were in the possession of a young boy.

Mark was quick with his reply. "He's in the mews now, sir," he said, his comment directed to the marquess. "I can see to it he's returned to your stables in the morning. Personally, sir."

"Very good. Enjoy your supper." Randall leaned down and kissed Rachel on the forehead. "You're going to vex me at every turn, are you not?" he murmured.

Rachel struggled to stifle a grin. "I'll do my very best, sir," she teased. In a quieter voice, she added, "In the meantime, there is important information that must be passed along to Sir Randolph."

Randall stared at her a moment before his head jerked slightly in the direction of the two men on which Rachel had been surreptitiously eavesdropping since she'd first heard their comment about bank notes.

She nodded.

"You can tell me all about it in the coach on the way home," he said.

Another moment passed, and Rachel was left alone with Mark.

Mark stared at her before daring a glance toward the bar. The marquess had rejoined a cluster of gentlemen whose conversation had grown louder now that the public house was darker. "You tease your father, too?" he asked in a quiet voice.

Grinning, Rachel nodded. "Are you jealous?"

Mark's eyes widened before they darted sideways. "I did speak with him this morning. About courting you. I didn't mention the position because..." He cleared his throat.

"You didn't wish to embarrass him," Rachel said, her opinion of the earl's son rising another notch. If he had mentioned wanting to hire her for the bookkeeper position that morning, Reading might well have tossed him out of his house.

"That, and self-preservation," he murmured.

Rachel grinned, deciding she rather liked the man who sat across from her. Whether she could abide sitting across from him every day for the rest of her life, she hadn't yet decided. Especially if she had to do so at a much longer table.

"Do you have a house in town?" she asked. She had already begun eating her beef, and from the lack of flavor, she was beginning to understand Mark's reservations about the cook.

Mark seemed hesitant to respond. "I have an agent looking into townhouses here in Westminster," he replied. "I thought something would come open when Parliament finished last month, but..." He gave a shrug.

"I understand Sir Randolph lives here in Westminster," she said. "Have you been to his house?" She struggled to overhear anything the two foreigners were discussing, but their conversation had turned to travel arrangements. A disagreement ensued about who would procure the tickets. There was something about boarding a ship bound for Calais in the morning.

"Your brother does live here in Westminster," Mark replied, unaware half her attention was on an entirely different conversation. "It's an excellent townhouse. Well kept. But since his wife's death, he's not there but three or four nights a week." His gaze darted to the marquess, and he saw that the man was still conversing with several others at the bar. "I believe your father bought it as a place in which to live when Parliament was in session. But then, when the townhouse next to my father's was put on sale, he bought it and gave the one here in Westminster to your brother."

Rachel nodded her understanding. "He wants me to quit where I am," she said in a quiet voice.

"Because you live in a gaming establishment," Mark guessed, apparently agreeing with her father on the matter.

"But I don't," she argued. "My bedchamber is in the private residence, wholly separate from the gaming hell." She casually glanced in the direction of the Frenchmen, dismayed that they had lowered their voices so she could no longer hear their words.

"If you accept my offer, I'll allow you to continue working for The Queen," Mark stated. "I'll pay you well. I'll pay you exactly the same as what I was paying Mr. Traynor... minus the amounts he embezzled, of course. There's an office upstairs where you can do the books, or—"

"Should I accept your offer, it will not be because I need the funds," she interrupted. "Reading has always seen to my expenses. From the moment I was born. But I sense it will not be easy for him to give up that responsibility."

"Even if he were to give it up to me?" Mark asked, perhaps too quickly.

Rachel considered the query a moment, torn between teasing him and considering his comment for what it was—another attempt at convincing her he was serious about courting her. About marriage. "You spoke with him. What was your sense?"

Mark inhaled slowly. "He wants you settled, of course. But he wants you safe. Wants you to be happy. *I* want you to be happy."

"Really?" she replied, displaying her surprise. She had never thought a man would consider her happiness when it came to her future.

All thoughts of the two Frenchmen left her head as she concentrated on Mark and what he had just said.

*M*ark let out the breath he'd been holding. "My mother hasn't been happy a day in her life. At least, if she has, I've not paid witness to it. But her poor nature taught me that when it was time for me to take a wife, I knew I should like to find a woman who would find joy in life and not strive to always find the... the *bad* in everything. To be vexed by every and all of life's minor irritations," he explained.

"You think I find joy in life?"

Mark stared at her a moment before a smile appeared. Then he chuckled. "From the moment I met you, I knew you did. I just paid witness to you teasing your father. You tease me mercilessly and have promised to continue to do so—"

"Except when we're intimate," she whispered.

Sobering, Mark stared at her for a long time before he swallowed. "You know it's a Leap Year," he whispered hoarsely.

Rachel blinked. "What has that got to do with anything?"

Mark glanced around, as if he wanted to be sure no one overheard him. "You know. Leap Years are when the women can ask the men to marry them," he explained. "If you're so moved."

Staring at him as if she didn't believe him, Rachel was about to giggle but quickly swallowed it when she saw how he stared at her. "What is it?"

"I really wish I could kiss you right now."

The oddest sensation shot down Rachel's spine at that moment. A combination of desire and arousal had heat pooling in her belly. Her nipples tightened behind her stays. Her heartbeats were suddenly audible, her pulse pounding in her ears.

She dared a glance over her shoulder, catching her father's eye.

Randall started to make his way to their table, his passage made harder since more diners had filled the tables.

When had that happened? Rachel had been so caught up in her conversation with Mark, she hadn't noticed the growing crowd.

She quickly stood, left her gloves on the table, and met her father halfway. Mark stood up as well, startled at her sudden departure from the table.

"Are you ready to leave?" Randall asked.

"Not yet," Rachel replied, daring another glance in the direction of the Frenchmen. "I wish to inspect the office in which I would be doing Mr. Merriweather's books. Before I accept the position, of course. We won't be long, but I wanted to let you know why I was about to disappear from the room."

"Office?" Randall repeated, his brows furrowing.

"It's just upstairs," she replied, her hand waving dismissively.

"Very well. If he tries anything—"

"He won't," she said with a wince. "He knows you're here."

When she turned around to go back to the table, she found Mark waiting for her, still standing and obviously nervous. "What was that all about?" he asked.

One of her eyebrows arched seductively. "Show me the office, Mark."

Mark blinked, but he didn't have to be told twice.

CHAPTER 32
WARMTH AND WONDER

*M*eanwhile, *at Bradley House*

Xenobia slipped out of her half boots and pushed the carriage gown down over her hips along with three layers of petticoats. For the moment she wore only her chemise, stays, and stockings, she thought Randolph might be peeking around the corner of the opened door. A quick glance into the bedchamber from her bent position showed only the high ceiling and the gilded plaster trim that rimmed the top of the wall covering.

She could hear the man undressing, although his movements were confined to the area next to the bed. Making quick work of rolling down her stockings, Xenobia plucked them from her feet and struggled out of her stays. When she pulled off her chemise, she was completely naked.

"I'm just going to get into bed," he said, his voice kept low lest it be heard by anyone outside her door. "Perhaps you should lock the door? I shouldn't want to frighten a maid if they come to service the room."

Xenobia blinked. "I will," she replied, just as she pulled on a huge dressing robe. Despite the thin silk of the banyan, she thought it a rather chaste garment.

If only her nipples weren't suddenly so cold. As she made her way to the door, she glanced down to find their silhouettes poking into the fabric. *At least they poke out and not down*, she considered. She threw the lock on the door handle.

Her bare feet barely made any sound on the Axminster carpet, but her gasp did when she rounded the curtained bed and discovered Randolph practically filling the bed.

She hadn't realized just how large he was.

"Are you... comfortable?" she asked in a whisper.

His eyes were closed, and he was lying on his side, facing the fire. Facing her.

"I am," he murmured sleepily. "This mattress is heavenly."

Xenobia blinked. Never having slept in this particular bed, she was relieved to know her guest was comfortable. Before she moved to join him, she was trying to decide how best to do so when he whispered, "Just back up, lie down, and I'll pull you against me."

Following his instructions, Xenobia still let out a squeak when his massive arm wrapped around her middle and pulled her against him. He moved back on the bed as he did so, and she was suddenly engulfed in warmth from below and behind and around her waist. The hand at the end of the arm settled against one of her breasts.

"Are you comfortable?" he asked in a whisper, his voice coming from over the top of her head.

Xenobia did her best to relax, despite how she sensed his knees had bent into the back of hers, that her bottom was resting into the bend of his body, and that his chest was at her back.

And then there was that huge hand that cupped her breast in blessed warmth.

"I am. I do hope I'm not causing you a chill."

The bed vibrated with his chuckle. "Another few minutes, and you will be warm enough to sleep," he promised in a whisper that was barely there.

"I apologize. This is probably not what you were expecting to be doing this afternoon," she murmured.

Randolph's eyes remained closed. If he hadn't been so tired, he would have lifted his head onto a hand and attempted to make eye contact with her. "I had no expectation," he finally replied. "So this is heavenly."

Although she had no intention of napping, Xenobia relaxed into his hold. That afternoon's jaunt in the fresh air had her more sleepy than she thought, and she closed her eyes. "Stay as long as you can," she whispered.

He angled his head so his chin rested atop her coiffure. "When I awake, will you still be here?"

Xenobia inhaled softly. "I will." She imagined the dimple appearing in his cheek, this time deeper. Curious, she turned over to face him. In the dim light from the candle lamp, she grinned as she reached out and touched it.

"You needn't be lonely any longer," he murmured.

For a moment, Xenobia was sure he was going to kiss her. His lips were that close. She already knew how they would feel pressed against hers—firm and commanding, delicious and demanding. "I suppose you say that to all the widows," she whispered, gently chiding him.

He shook his head in the pillow. "Actually, I've never said it before." Lowering his lips to her forehead, he pressed them against her cool skin and held them there for a moment. When he pulled away, her face lifted. He was sure her eyes darkened, sure he saw desire.

His lips were on hers in an instant, molding to the soft pillows that had begun to form a response he effectively silenced. When she didn't protest, he deepened the kiss at the same time he tightened his hold on her.

He had never been in the company of one so beautiful.

So broken.

He knew why, of course. He almost wished the late baron was still alive so that he might pound the cur to a bloody pulp.

But then Dunsworth would still be alive, and Xenobia would still be married and unavailable for this moment.

• • •

Xenobia allowed her body to mold against the front of his, her curves filling his voids until the two appeared as one beneath the counterpane.

Her response to his kiss could only be described as hungry, especially when one of her hands lifted to the side of his head while the other gripped a shoulder. When a slight moan sounded from the back of her throat, he gently pulled away but left his forehead pressed against hers. "I apologize. I've—"

"Don't you dare," she countered, her hoarse whisper barely sounding above the crackling fire. One of her hands touched his chest, and quickly pulled away, as if it had been burned.

He furrowed a brow. "Then I shan't," he murmured, as he grasped her hand in his and placed it against his chest, holding it over hers so it couldn't escape.

"Were you... were you planning to make love to me?" she asked, her whisper sounding loud in her ears. "When you came for me today?"

"I was not," he whispered, his arms tensing in anticipation of what she might do. He lifted his head at exactly the same time the flames in the fireplace increased in intensity, and the curtained bed was suddenly bathed in bright light. For a moment, his face was lit up in a golden glow, as was his bare chest. Everything below was covered by bed linens, but it was apparent he wore little if anything.

Xenobia's eyes widened and she gasped "Are you... are you naked?"

"I am."

Settling back into the mattress, he pulled her back against the front of his body and allowed a grin when he realized she no longer felt cold. Her heart was certainly racing, though.

Despite his hardening cock, he was asleep before his head was settled into the pillow.

CHAPTER 33
THE OFFICE

$\mathcal{M}$*eanwhile, back at The Three Bells*

Suddenly understanding Rachel's motivation for speaking with her father, Mark nodded at hearing her demand that he show her the office.

Show me the office, Mark.

He might have feigned misunderstanding her. He probably should have, given her father stood not fifteen feet away. But at that moment, Mark wanted nothing more than to kiss Miss Rachel Roderick. Since the marquess had every intention of seeing her home that evening, Mark knew he wouldn't have another chance at capturing her lips with his own.

Perhaps this would only be a chaste kiss. A kiss to seal their deal—she had apparently agreed to do his books.

But there was a possibility it would be much more. For a moment, he cursed himself for not having brought a ring he could use for a marriage proposal. He had one in his jewel box. One his grandmother had given to him in her will with the express instructions he was to gift it to the woman he would one day marry. The sapphire stones would look stunning with the riding habit Rachel wore.

Actually, they would look stunning no matter what Rachel wore.

Rachel would look stunning in nothing but the ring.

At that thought, Mark knew he had to get out of sight of her father. His imaginings had his cock responding in a manner that he wouldn't be able to hide much longer.

"This way," he said as he offered his arm. He led them to the door the servers used to access the kitchens. Once through it, Mark immediately turned to the right and indicated the staircase. "After you," he said, somewhat breathless.

Even before Rachel had made it halfway up the stairs, she knew the public house had at one time been a private residence. The stairs were carpeted, and the corridor walls at the top were lined with rose silk fabric and trimmed in dark wood baseboards and wainscoting. The office was more like a study, its floor covered with a Turkish carpet and the desk made of oak. Shelves filled with hundreds of leather-bound books lined one wall. The odors of vanilla and vellum surrounded her.

"Is there... an apartment on this floor?" she asked as she turned to regard Mark. "Or bedchambers and such?"

He nodded and indicated where the stairs continued to another floor above. "The kitchen maid—the one who bakes the bread—she lives up top."

"Does someone live on this floor?"

Mark shook his head as he moved to stand before her. "No, although I have been known to spend the night on occasion. There's a..." He swallowed, his gaze on her parted lips. "Parlor and a dining room. A bedchamber... and a..."

Rachel stood on tip-toe, her lips nearly colliding with his. He wrapped an arm around her waist and pulled her closer, capturing her lips in what should have been a quick kiss but soon continued far longer when Rachel gripped one of his lapels. When he finally ended the kiss, Mark lowered his head to her forehead. "I have been wanting to do that all day," he whispered.

Her eyes glazed, Rachel swallowed before she murmured, "You had all that time while we were in the park."

He blinked. "You might have said something."

"And appear fast?" she countered. "I think not."

Mark's expression showed his confusion until he noticed a

smirk forming at the edges of Rachel's lips. "You're teasing me again," he whispered.

"Am I?"

His lips captured hers, as if to scold her. When his tongue slipped into her mouth and caressed hers, she gave a start in his arms. He quickly pulled away, murmuring an apology.

"Please, do whatever it was you were about to do," she said in a breathy voice. "I wasn't expecting what you did is all, and it... it startled me."

Mark gave his head a shake. "I'll save it for when we're next together," he replied. "Your father will come looking for you at any moment."

Rachel's eyes cleared and she nodded. "You're right, of course. He needs to as I have information my brother may find useful."

Furrowing a brow, Mark asked, "What do you speak of?"

"His work. His investigation. Is there a chance you might see him later this evening? At a gaming hell?" she asked once again.

Mark stared at her a moment. "I wasn't planning to go out, but I can. For you," he offered.

"If you find Sir Randolph tonight, could you tell him I overheard something he might find useful? I cannot help but believe those Frenchmen downstairs are somehow involved in whatever my brother was speaking with my mother about yesterday. "

Nodding, Mark said, "I will," he replied. If he hadn't been told her mother was The Queen, he never would have guessed she was the daughter of a former courtesan. He supposed he should have known given her beauty. Given her playful manner.

Her manner was by no means playful at the moment, though. She seemed entirely serious as she relayed what she had overheard during their supper.

Too serious.

As if a life might depend on the information she possessed being passed along to her brother.

Mark leaned forward and lowered his voice. "If he's not at

The Queen, he'll be at The Jack of Spades. Plays billiards there some nights." He paused. "When can I see you again?"

Feeling as if she were arranging a clandestine meeting, Rachel said, "If you're at The Queen later tonight, I'll be in office. Doing the books."

"I'll find you," he whispered. "I have something for you, but..." He sighed.

"But what?"

"Not here," he said with a shake of his head.

Rachel displayed a pretend pout, but then glanced towards the desk. "Show me your ledgers."

Mark boggled. "Now?"

"Yes, now. Someone is coming up the stairs."

Mark's eyes widened, and he wondered how he hadn't noticed the subtle vibrations in the floor that indicated someone was indeed climbing the stairs. He moved to the desk and pulled the ledger from one of the top drawers. He opened it and flipped several pages until the last of the entries appeared, written in script. "Here is where Mr. Traynor was before I let him go," he said. Reaching into another drawer, he pulled out a stack of what Rachel recognized as bills of lading and invoices.

"I know how to match the invoices to the receipts and then enter the amounts of the invoices on the ledger," she said as she moved to stand by his side. "Would you like me to write your bank drafts and leave them for you to sign?"

Mark had to stifle a growl in the back of his throat. Her closeness had him wishing he could remove her riding habit so he might ride her. The desk would be entirely too uncomfortable, but the Turkish carpet would provide some padding for a turbulent tumble. He imagined her beneath him, her thighs gripping his as he saw to the creation of the next generation of Merriweathers. "You would do that?" he asked in a strangled voice.

Rachel gave him a quelling glance. "What did you expect me to do?"

He cleared his throat and bent slightly at the thought of

how his breeches were entirely too tight and someone was about to join them at any moment.

"I'd like you to..."

The door swung open, and the kitchen maid entered followed by Randall Roderick, Marquess of Reading.

"Father," Rachel said in mock surprise. "Has something happened?"

"The frogs have left the building," he said, his stern features relaxing when he noted how his daughter and the proprietor were bent over a ledger.

Rachel directed an apologetic glance at Mark. "My apologies, Mr. Merriweather, but I really must depart."

"No apologies are required, my lady," Mark replied, his cock having subsided substantially at the appearance of the marquess. "I will pay a call on you at another time so we can devise a schedule."

Rachel winked at him before she curtsied and said, "Thank you for the delicious supper and the ride in the park." She joined her father at the door. "And for seeing to it Richard is returned to the Reading stables."

All the while, the kitchen maid stood with her arms crossed over her ample bosom, watching the marquess and her employer with an arched brow.

*A*fter Randall and Rachel had left the office and were making their way down the stairs, the kitchen maid turned her attention on Mark. "Who was she, sir?"

Mark straightened and said, "My new bookkeeper. And with any luck, my future wife."

The maid rolled her eyes. "Next thing you'll be telling me is you've found a new cook," she said before she left the office, her cackle evident even behind the closed door.

Narrowing his eyes, Mark knew he had two... no, three calls to pay on this night.

CHAPTER 34
AN AWAKENING

*M*eanwhile, at Bradley House

The sound of a soft snore had Xenobia slowly opening her eyes. A heavy weight around her waist had her pinned to the bed, and the warmth at her back reminded her there was a man in her bed.

A naked man.

She could feel the hard planes of his chest against her upper back, his powerful thighs against the back of hers. In between, there was something else that was hard and pressed against her bottom.

Attempting to shift her hips in order to relieve the pressure, she stilled her entire body when it instead moved beneath the mounds of her bottom and came to rest between the tops of her thighs. Only the silk of the banyan separated her quim from what she realized was his engorged member.

She was unprepared for her body's reaction.

Arousal.

Desire.

Heat flooded her lower body. The space at the top of her thighs seemed to throb with need. Almost too warm, she spread open the top of the banyan's collar, baring her shoulders.

Embarrassed but intrigued, she reached back with one arm until her hand slid onto Randolph's body. The bare skin, even warmer than her hand, was smooth. She slid her fingers down, not sure of what she was touching.

Hips? Thighs?

The arm around her waist lifted, and his hand moved to cover hers, essentially ceasing its attempt at exploration. Randolph lifted himself onto an elbow and leaned over her.

"I did not mean to scandalize you, Xenobia," he whispered, just before he lowered his lips to her bare shoulder. With the banyan open, the top edge of its collar had slipped down her arm.

Allowing a prim smile, Xenobia found she rather liked how he said *Xenobia*. She remembered the shock she had felt at learning he was naked, though. Remembered how he had simply tucked her against his body and then fallen asleep.

"I am not in the habit of wearing anything to bed, and I could not afford to allow my shirt to wrinkle since I must wear it this evening."

"I am a grown woman," she countered. "I cannot believe that at my age, I have never seen a naked man, but—"

"You never saw your husband naked?" he half-asked, rising further on his elbow at the same time he bent a knee to better support his position on the bed.

Xenobia noticed how the bed linens slipped further down his body. "James always wore a nightshirt when he came to my bed."

This bit of information had Randolph blinking. "So... you've never seen a man's... member?" he whispered in disbelief.

"Only if you count the statuary in the British Museum."

Randolph frowned. "I do not," he replied. "For one thing, they're all a bit on the small side, and for another, none of them are... aroused."

Xenobia's eyes widened. "Is yours?"

He let out his breath in a huff. "It has been since the moment you came to bed." He placed his hand over hers and led it down to where his erection was hidden just below the edge of the bed linens.

At first tempted to pull her hand from his, Xenobia found she didn't want to as the warmth of his hand surrounded hers.

Once he had her hand over the engorged shaft, curiosity had her touching the smooth, warm skin that felt as if it were stretched taut over bone. His hand released hers, although his fingers still rested on her wrist.

She heard his inhalation of breath when her fingers slid down the shaft to a nest of crisp hair and then back up the other side. "It feels like velvet," she murmured in appreciation.

Randolph had to suppress a growl when she continued to explore, and then he finally wrapped his hand around hers and squeezed. "I want nothing more than to make love to you right now," he whispered.

Her eyes widening, Xenobia said, "I was afraid you would never offer. What do I need to——?" She let out a squeak when she found herself flat on her back and Randolph hovering over the top of her.

"You need do nothing. Just… lie back, and do not stop me."

Xenobia gasped as she felt one of his hands slide the banyan off of one breast as his head lowered to hers. His kiss on her lips was quick but thorough before he trailed his lips down her jaw to her neck and then to her throat.

His tongue delved into the hollow there before moving lower, to follow the contours of her collarbones and then to the top of a breast. His fingers moved to undo the banyan's tie, and soon her other breast was exposed to his hot mouth.

"Breathe, Xenobia. I should not want you to faint when I have so much more pleasure to bestow on you."

Xenobia did as she was told, which had her breasts rising, one of them right into his mouth. His lips surrounded her nipple, and his tongue laved over the hardened bud until she whimpered.

He moved his attentions to the other, spending a moment taking in the sight of her pink areola and the puckered nipple in the middle. "You have the most beautiful breasts," he murmured, just before he took possession of the nipple.

"I do?" she whispered. "You don't think them… too——"

"No," he replied before his mouth greedily continued its exploration, while his hands pushed the banyan's edges apart. The entire front of her body was exposed, her skin warm and tingling.

Xenobia felt sure he would enter her then. She bent her knees, stunned when they felt rubbery. Shaky. But his body continued to move down, his head following until it was between her thighs.

James had never done this.

She inhaled sharply. "Rand!" she managed to get out in a hoarse whisper when she realized his tongue had penetrated her body. Had begun circling her womanhood. Was making the throbbing she felt at the top of her thighs far more pronounced.

Her hands reached down, her fingers spearing his dark hair in an effort to find something to hang onto just as his lips joined his tongue in providing a pleasure that was as sweet as it was torturous.

And then the pleasure deepened and sharpened. She was blinded by white spots and left whimpering, doing her best not to scream lest she alert the entire household she was in residence.

"You taste of heaven," Randolph growled before he reappeared above her, his face a study in contrasts. Determination mixed with happiness.

And then he was inside her. Filling her with that velvet rod. Pulling it out a bit and then settling it deeper inside her.

She knew to lift her hips then. To grip his hips with her thighs, which had him murmuring something that sounded like a cross between a blessing and a curse.

Xenobia was unprepared for what happened then. The wave of pleasure that seemed to pass through her lower body had her holding onto him more tightly, just as he was attempting to pull himself back out of her body.

He groaned and quickly pushed himself back in, which only amplified the sensations Xenobia felt.

Pleasure.

Intense pleasure, followed by rolling waves of it that seemed to continue faster as his thrusts into her quickened.

She wasn't aware she made any sounds, but her breaths were suddenly loud in her ears, as was the word, "Yes!" she didn't remember thinking.

When his body seized and he stopped his movements, his face contorted into what appeared to be pain, Xenobia knew what to expect next. She thrilled at the sensation of warmth that flooded her lower body as her hands gripped his shoulders. When his arms seemed as if they could no longer hold him up, she guided him down to her body. Wrapping her arms around his back, she allowed a sigh of contentment.

His head settled into the space above one of her shoulders, and she felt his heavy breaths on her heated skin. "Do you have any idea how beautiful you are when you are in ecstasy?"

She inhaled and let out the breath slowly. "Having never experienced it before, I have absolutely no idea," she whispered.

He stilled in her arms and lifted his head, his gaze topped with a troubled brow. "On the one hand, I could pity you. But on the other, I am feeling rather proud of myself," he murmured.

Xenobia allowed a brilliant smile. "When we do this again, I wish to be naked. Like you," she whispered. "Does that scandalize you?"

Randolph blinked. "Why, yes, it does," he replied, as a grin brought the dimple to the base of his cheek. He leaned down and kissed her on the lips. When he pulled away, his arms seemed to lose all their strength. "Apologies, my lady, but I must..." He rolled off of her body, but managed to grasp her around the middle so that he pulled her atop one side of his body as he settled onto the bed. "Sleep."

Xenobia wondered how he could think of sleep just then. Her entire body thrummed with excitement. Thrummed with sensations she had never before experienced.

Her head ended up in the small of his shoulder, and she reveled in the warmth and feel of his pulse beneath her ear.

She placed a hand on his chest, feeling the crisp curls

beneath her fingertips. One leg slid between his, and she grinned at the thought of what rested against the top of her thigh.

She thought of all the years she could have been enjoying these sensations if only James hadn't treated her as a best friend and instead had treated her as his wife.

His lover.

Would Randolph be her lover now?

She closed her eyes and thought of what it might be like to have him in her bed every night.

Just before she fell asleep, Xenobia thought of Julia. The night before, she had been ready to curse her best friend. Now she was trying to decide what gift she might buy for her as a sort of 'thank you' for having sent Randolph Roderick to her door.

CHAPTER 35

A CARRIAGE RIDE TO A
DIFFERENT HOME

*M*eanwhile, in Charles Street, Westminster

Randall Roderick, Marquess of Reading, had offered his daughter an arm when they emerged from The Three Bells. With the other, he waved at a driver seated atop a coach pulled by two shires.

The traveling chariot, small and black, its wheels looking as if they had been recently cleaned, moved up the street until the driver halted the horses so its gold-crested door was directly in front of Rachel.

"This looks new," she remarked when her father opened the door. He gave up his hold on the door when the driver stepped down from his bench and saw to closing it.

"That's because it is. Tilbury finished it yesterday," Randall said as he settled onto the chariot's only bench. Facing the direction of travel, it was wider than a phaeton bench and far better padded. Across from them, where the front of another bench would normally be located in a town coach, was a lacquered wood panel that extended from floor to ceiling, and in the middle of it, a glass window.

Rachel was reminded of a sedan chair, only this was far larger and much more comfortable.

"Is this velvet?" she breathed as her gloved hands smoothed over the squabs.

"It is," Randall replied. "Royal blue. Do you like it?"

Chuckling as the chariot began to move, Rachel asked, "Isn't it more important what your marchioness thinks of it? I rather imagine she will adore such an elegant means to move about town. And so economical, given only two horses are required, and no groomsmen or tigers," she added as she studied the interior with appreciation.

"I didn't buy it for Connie," Randall replied. "I bought it for *you*."

Rachel jerked her head sideways to regard her father in shock. "Me?"

"Well, of course. You need a means to move about town. A way to get to The Three Bells," he said as he rolled his eyes. "Are you really going to be Mr. Merriweather's *bookkeeper*?"

Rachel ignored the disbelief in his query and placed a gloved hand on his. "Thank you, Father," she said. "This is entirely unexpected. And yes, I have accepted the position of bookkeeper for The Three Bells. Between Mother's books and those of Mr. Merriweather, I expect I shall never grow bored whilst living here in town."

Randall gave a huff. "I suppose not," he said, grudgingly. "But before I turn over this equipage to your care, I believe I should find your brother and relay what you overheard in the public house," he said.

"You're taking me to meet him?" Rachel asked hopefully.

"I am not. It wouldn't be proper for you to be seen in The Jack of Spades," he replied. Ignoring her sigh of disappointment, he said, "Now, tell me everything you heard. In English, though. My French is abysmal."

Rachel stared at her father a moment, finally deciding he hadn't meant to sound so stern with his demand.

For the next few minutes, she relayed the bits of conversation she had overheard, making sure she emphasized their plan to exchange all the bank notes with coin. "They leave for Calais in the morning," she said finally. "Late in the morning. I told Mr. Merriweather what I overheard, and he assured me he would try to find Sir Randolph as well, since they are friends."

"They are," Randall affirmed, before adding, "I suppose it will be better with two of us looking for him."

The coach slowed and came to a halt in front of a well-lit townhouse. Knowing it wasn't the private residence in Piccadilly, she glanced at her father. "Where are we?"

"My townhouse." He motioned to the house next door, a near identical copy of his. "Mr. Merriweather resides there with the Earl of Middleton and his countess, when she's in town, which is rare."

"So, you're taking a different coach to The Jack of Spades?" she asked.

"I am. But before you return to your mother's house, I insist you meet Connie, and your brother, and your nephew."

"Now?" she replied. "But... I'm dressed for *riding*," she complained. "I smell of horse. And it's well past the polite hour for paying calls."

"Connie won't care. But if she learns you were within ten feet of our house and I didn't insist you come inside, she will blister my ears with her rebuke." The chariot door opened and the driver set down the step. "Besides, I usually tease my son and toss your nephew a few times about now."

Rachel couldn't help the burble of laughter that erupted from her throat. "Apologies, Father. You said that as if you fear your marchioness, and yet you've had nothing but good things to say about her," she said as she allowed the driver to help her down.

Now that they were in a better lit street—gas lights lined Curzon Street on both sides—she could make out the details of the chariot. It was perfect for a spinster. Unlike a phaeton, it was enclosed and would protect her from the weather. The size and its need for only one or two horses meant it would be a quick means of getting about town.

A way to go from The Queen of Hearts to The Three Bells.

She could work in the mornings at The Queen, make her way to The Three Bells for a late luncheon, and then do the books there until...

The thought of Mark interrupting her work had her

inhaling softly. She imagined him leaning over to kiss her cheek. To tell her it was time she leave the books behind and to join him for dinner.

He had mentioned there was a bedchamber on the first floor, which had her wondering why he didn't just live at The Three Bells. Having the kitchen maid living above was no different than servants living on the top floor of a house.

"She won't bite, I promise," Randall said as he offered his arm.

Pulled from her reverie, Rachel gave a start. "Of course not," she replied.

The front door opened even before her father raised the brass knocker. A butler greeted them and bowed before stepping aside to reveal a brightly lit hall beyond the entry.

If any interior could be the exact opposite of The Queen of Hearts' gaming room, this was it. Walls of polished wood and deep green silk met white and black marble floors. The high ceilings were painted in the manner of the Masters. Gas-lit brass sconces illuminated the hall on either side of a central marble staircase. A round table in the center of the hall was decorated with a candelabra bearing red ribbons and flowers, reminding Rachel Christmas was only a week away.

"The Cupid in that corner up there—" Randall pointed to a painted cherub holding a bow with an arrow directed at a scantily clad maiden halfway across the ceiling—"looks just like my youngest son," he claimed. "He's nearly as chubby, too. And that little one looks like your nephew," he added as he pointed to another cherub.

The butler took Rachel's redingote and gloves and Randall's greatcoat. "I won't be staying long," the marquess warned. "And I'll need the coach brought 'round."

"Yes, sir."

The servant disappeared as Randall led Rachel up the stairs. "There are several extra bedchambers. Should you wish to move in, you'd be more than welcome," he said.

"I appreciate the offer, Father," she murmured as her gaze was captured by interesting curios and statuary. Given the elegance of the decor found in the main hall and along the first floor corridor, she could only imagine how beautiful the bedchambers might be.

They climbed a second set of carpeted stairs and emerged on a floor with a door-lined corridor. One door toward the end was open, and the voices of small children reached Rachel's ears.

"I used to do with you what I'm about to do with my grandson," he said with a smirk. "Vexed your mother as much as it does Connie."

He waited until Rachel nervously stepped into the nursery before he followed.

Two little boys let out squeals of delight, one toddling toward the marquess to hug his legs while the other fairly bounced with excitement on his mother's knee. "Dada dada."

"No need to get up, my sweet," Randall said as he hoisted the smallest boy into the crook of his arm and moved to kiss Constance on the forehead.

"Oh, but I will," she said as she lowered the boy she held to the floor and quickly moved to stand before Rachel.

"Connie, may I present my daughter, Rachel Roderick?"

"Oh, you most certainly can," Connie replied with a huge smile as she held out her hands to capture both of Rachel's.

Rachel dipped a deep curtsy. "It's an honor to meet you, my lady."

"Oh, there will be none of that," Connie replied. "I cannot tell you how happy I am to meet you."

Attempting to concentrate on the marchioness' greeting— she was sure she would detect jealousy in her words but did not —Rachel found her attention drawn to the marquess. He was tossing the smallest boy into the air, the white-gowned babe gurgling in delight upon being caught. She had to blink back tears, for the memory of him tossing her into the air came to her in a flash.

"This poor neglected babe is Randolph's son—your nephew —Charles," Constance teased as she indicated the boy who was currently mid-air but was on his way down so that he landed between Randall's crooked hands.

"He looks like a cherub," Rachel said with a giggle before her attention was drawn to her skirts, where the two-year old had his arms spread wide, as if he intended to hug her. "You must be my youngest brother," she murmured as she bent to lift the toddler into her arms.

Connie angled her head and grinned. "Indeed. May I present Robert Fitzsimmons Roderick? We're hoping he doesn't live up to his father's reputation, but as you can see, he's already a little flirt."

Rachel giggled as the babe rested his head on her shoulder and gazed at her, his long lashes dark against his chubby cheeks. "You do look like a little Cupid," she whispered. The boy's grin displayed his white teeth and a dimple in one cheek. "You are adorable," she added, just before her father let out an 'oomph.'

"I'm exhausted, and I must take my leave of you," he announced.

Connie gave him a questioning glance before he said, "Rachel can explain. I'll be back in time for a quick dinner." He gave the giggling one-year-old to her and kissed her on the lips before settling one on Rachel's cheek and another on his son's head.

Rachel's mouth hung open in shock for a moment as she watched her father depart. His behavior was so unexpected for a marquess.

"He was a surprise to me as well," Constance said as she turned her gaze back on Rachel. "But I cannot imagine a better match in all the world. I love him dearly."

"He feels the same toward you," Rachel replied as she absently patted the back of the boy she still held.

"Oh, where are my manners? Please, have a seat," Constance encouraged as she indicated one of the deeply upholstered chairs placed along the back wall of the nursery.

"Thank you," Rachel said as she positioned Robert on her lap after settling into a chair. "This is unexpected in a nursery, is it not?" she asked, as she patted the velvet-covered chair.

"Your father had them delivered after Raymond was born.

Before, there was a wooden chair in here, and he would find me sitting in it whilst I nursed Raymond. Vexed him to no end."

"That you nursed your son?"

"And that I wasn't in a more comfortable chair," Constance affirmed. "Oh, I would introduce you to my oldest son, but he's not yet home from Eton. Your father intends to collect him on the morrow."

"He's already in school?" Rachel asked in surprise. "I thought he was only... six?"

Constance nodded even as she displayed a look that suggested she was not happy with the arrangement. "He had a very good tutor after he was breeched, but your father insisted Raymond be educated as all his brothers were, so I had to let him go."

"I hadn't learned until yesterday that I'd been sent to school on the Continent because he insisted on it," Rachel murmured. "Do you find his manner... overbearing?"

A titter escaped Constance before she shook her head. "Not really. He has spoiled me, though, and I don't mind saying I don't mind one whit."

Rachel grinned. "Apparently, he has done the same for me without my knowledge."

"Oh?"

Hesitating, because Rachel wondered if the marchioness knew her husband had been supporting her, Rachel finally said, "He has paid all my expenses. For my entire life," she whispered.

Constance waved the hand that wasn't steadying Charlie as he sat on her lap. "As he's done with all your brothers," she replied. She furrowed a brow. "Well, except for the one, of course."

Rachel's eyes widened. "My twin, Richard?" she guessed.

Giving a quick shake of her head, Constance said, "I don't know who took him. Who raised him, but Randall insists he's doing well. Apparently he's at one of the universities and intends to complete the entire seven-year course of study."

Rachel quickly calculated Richard would be twenty-three or twenty-four when he finished university. "I do wonder if I'll ever meet him. Or if I'll recognize him without an introduction," she mused.

"He is the only one who doesn't have your father's name," Connie said in a quiet voice. "He can never know the truth of his birth."

Rachel dipped her head, her chin landing on the top of Robert's dark-haired head. "I understand," she sighed.

Robert lifted a hand to her cheek and bent his head back before kissing her jaw. Unintelligible words spewed forth as his hands waved about, which sent Rachel into a fit of giggles. Soon, Charlie joined in, his own arms lifting above his head as he gurgled and laughed.

"Whatever are they saying?" Rachel asked, unable to understand the baby-speak.

"I've absolutely no idea, but I merely act as if I do, and they seem fine with it," Constance replied with a huge grin. "Can you stay for dinner?"

Rachel's surprise showed. "It's very kind of you to offer. On any other night, I would accept, but I'm sure my mother must be wondering what's become of me. I left to go riding with Mr. Merriweather, and—"

"Another time? Perhaps you could join us Wednesday evenings? Your oldest brother comes for dinner nearly every week."

The oddest sensation coursed through Rachel just then. Dinner, with family. She glanced at the little boy who stared at her so intently she was sure he knew they were related. Then her gaze fell on Charlie, whose chubby cheeks were made more so with his wide grin at her sudden attention. "I will," she replied.

"I take it you haven't met Randolph yet?"

Rachel inhaled to respond and then gave a shake of her head. "I spent two minutes in his company yesterday, but we weren't introduced. I thought he seemed familiar." She paused before adding, "He took my best friend for a ride in the park today."

Constance straightened in her chair. "You refer to Lady Dunsworth?"

"Indeed," Rachel replied, her eyes rounding.

"Oh, your brother spent the night here, so of course I had to ask him about his meeting with her last night over breakfast this morning," Constance explained, an eyebrow arching with her amusement.

"I paid a call at Bradley House earlier today," Rachel said. "I hadn't seen Xenobia since she left Zurich a few years ago, but it was as if none of those years had passed."

Pulling Charlie up to her shoulder, Constance said, "I cannot help but hope those two begin a courtship. She wants children, and although I adore having Charlie with us, he needs a mother."

Rachel allowed a wan grin. "I think she favors Sir Randolph, and the thought of her married to one of my brothers makes me rather happy."

"Your best friend would become your sister," Constance said as she absently patted Charlie on the back. The babe's eyes had long since closed, and a thumb had disappeared behind his bow lips.

"Indeed," Rachel replied. She glanced down at Robert, who was watching her intently. "Well, young man. I suppose I should introduce myself. I'm Rachel. Aunt Rachel," she quickly amended as she caught his hand in hers and gave it a shake.

Robert struggled in her hold a moment, indicating he wished to get down. Rachel lowered him until his feet touched the carpet. He moved a couple of steps away from her, turned, and gave her a bow that nearly had him toppling onto his head.

Rachel suppressed a laugh as she rose and dipped a curtsy. "It's an honor to meet you, sir." She turned to Constance. "And you. And Charlie," she whispered. "But I really must get back to the office."

Despite the babe resting on her shoulder, Constance stood. "The office?"

"My mother's office, actually. I'm keeping her ledgers now," she explained. "And starting tomorrow, those of The Three Bells."

"Two days in London and you already have two positions?" Constance asked in disbelief.

"I do." Rachel was about to curtsy again, but paused and asked, "Pray tell, what is your opinion of Mr. Merriweather? Mark Merriweather?"

Constance allowed a shrug. "Given he's a second son, I admit I expected him to be a ne'er do well. I have discovered from having his mother for tea that he is nothing of the sort," she said. "Although he does gamble, he only does so one night a week. Apparently he spends his days seeing to something of import, but Lady Middleton knows nothing of it."

Rachel nodded her understanding but then wondered why Mark wouldn't have told his mother about his ownership of The Three Bells. "I suppose if his 'something of import' meant he was involved in running a business that might not be acceptable to her ladyship?"

Constance considered the query a moment. "Probably not," she agreed. "But then, she spends most of her days living in Wiltshire so she doesn't have to deal with the *on-dit* here in London." She reached out a hand to Rachel's arm. "Is he courting you? I could not help but overhear his conversation with your father this morning. They left the study door open, and I was in the breakfast parlor next door," she quickly explained, as if she feared Rachel would think she'd been eaves-dropping.

"He took me for a ride in the park this afternoon," Rachel admitted, a hand waving over her riding habit as if to indicate why she was dressed the way she was. "We had supper at The Three Bells where he asked if I would be the bookkeeper for the establishment. Then he kissed me." She sighed. "I don't think it was because I accepted his offer. He spoke of marriage. Several times, but I only just met him yesterday." Her eyes darted side-ways before she added, "I would implore you not to mention the kiss to my father."

A grin spread over Constance's face. "Oh, this is one secret I will adore keeping," she whispered.

"Thank you, my lady."

"Connie," the marchioness corrected her. "Come. I'll see you out," she offered as the nurse entered the room and ushered Robert off to his dinner. "Oh, and if you're concerned about Mr. Merriweather's quick regard for you, then might I mention it was the same for your father when it came to me?"

Rachel stared at the marchioness. "Love at first sight, you mean?"

Constance nodded. "And I was just as doubtful about it as you are." She paused a moment. "Or if you're not doubtful and Mr. Merriweather seems hesitant about actually proposing, you could do it. It's a Leap Year, after all, so you still have a fortnight."

Blinking in surprise, Rachel stared at the marchioness before she gave her head a quick shake. "Before today, I had not heard of such a thing," she whispered. "I do think I shall allow Mr. Merriweather to do the asking if he's still of a mind to do so."

*W*hen Rachel was settled into the velvet squabs of her new coach, she replayed the events of the day in her mind's eye, remembering most fondly the moments with the babes.

Remembering her time with Mark had her body reacting with a much different response. His manner had been sometimes serious and confident and at other times amusing and uncertain. How odd that she felt the same visceral reaction no matter which memory she brought forth.

She inhaled deeply and nearly giggled.

What a day this was turning out to be!

CHAPTER 36
AN INTERESTING EVENING ENSUES

Bradley House, seven o'clock in the evening

When Randolph awoke with a start, he held his breath while he tried to determine where he was, who was clinging to one side of his body, and what time it might be.

The bed curtains surrounding him on three sides explained the darkness. The scent of a guttering candle lamp accounted for the dim light that seemed to waver to his right.

"I didn't mean to wake you," Xenobia whispered.

The events of that afternoon came flooding back, and Randolph let out the breath he'd been holding. "Why did you leave the bed?"

Xenobia, now settled against his right side, smoothed a hand over his chest. "I had to use the chamber pot," she whispered. She didn't add that she had really just wanted to wash her nether region and rid herself of the banyan that had been bunched up around her middle.

Randolph's body acted as a much more efficient heat source than the fireplace, which was barely glowing from the lumps of coal Randolph had placed when he set the fire earlier.

He turned on his side to face her. "I don't suppose you noticed the time?" he asked in a hoarse whisper.

"Seven o'clock," she murmured, as she smoothed her hand down his side to his hip.

"I must take my leave," he said on a sigh. He didn't want to move, though. Didn't want to give up the comfortable bed and the warm, soft body that nestled against his and smelled faintly of flowers.

"I don't want you to go, but I understand if you must. You're welcome to return when you have completed your work for the night."

Randolph cleared his throat. "My lady, I fear we may have already scandalized your servants—"

"Oh, I hope so. They could do with some excitement."

Furrowing a brow, Randolph regarded his hostess for a moment until he saw she was grinning. "For a moment, I thought you were quite serious."

"For a moment, I was, but I rather doubt they even know we're here." After a pause, she added, "I do not want you leaving under cover of darkness, as if we've... as if we've done something tawdry."

Her hand had moved down to wrap around his tumescence, and he sucked in a breath as she squeezed.

"If you are not careful, I shall lay claim to you again," he warned, as if he thought his words would have her cowering.

They only made her more bold, though, for she lifted her lips to his and kissed him.

Randolph had her up and over the top of him, forcing her to straddle him. He trailed the backs of his fingers down the front of her body, their tips setting off frissons of pleasure in their wake. When they reached her mons, he was stunned to find she was already wet, her honeyed folds opening as his thumb sought her womanhood.

The nubbin was already swollen, and when he circled it with the tip of his thumb, he thrilled at hearing her sharp intake of breath, at seeing her chest rise and her breasts quake. Desperate for his own release, he slid his thumb over her womanhood and pressed it.

He was about to apologize for the cheat. He knew her resulting pleasure was sharp and quick, almost painful, as opposed to the slow, rolling pleasure she would have felt had he taken his time with his ministrations.

Xenobia didn't seem to mind. Her hips lifted in an overt invitation, so he entered her slowly and then pulled her down. He slid a hand up to one of her breasts, circling the nipple with a finger as he guided her hip with his other hand to slowly rise off of him. Then just as slowly, he pulled her down. Xenobia understood what to do, and she continued the slow rhythm, grinning when her hips lowered to meet each of his languid thrusts.

When a mewl sounded and she gripped the tops of his shoulders, he quickened his thrusts. She continued to meet his every upward thrust with a downward push of her hips until he felt undulations surrounding his turgid manhood. Undulations that seemed to pull him in deeper, that had him pushing harder until her mewling increased and she threw back her head and her back arched.

He used an arm to pull her down to him so that her breasts would be pressed into his chest as the intense pleasure of their joining took him.

Took her.

He knew she was in ecstasy from the way her breaths caught, from how her lower body gripped him, how her fingernails dug into his back.

His own head, thrown back so the cords of his neck strained against his skin, was nearly buried in a pillow before the last vestiges of his orgasm finally released him.

Xenobia collapsed atop Randolph, her head ending up on one of his shoulders. When her arms wrapped around the sides of his chest and her hand smoothed over his knotted muscles, he relaxed completely. Before he fell asleep, he murmured, "Please wake me if I'm not up by eight," and fell asleep.

*X*enobia allowed a sigh of contentment as she slowly unbent her legs until she was stretched out atop him. Despite her bare back, she was warm, and her entire body felt alive. Still inside her, his member no longer throbbed, but it managed to set off little darts of pleasure as it subsided in size.

She turned her head and kissed the whorl of an ear. "Thank you," she whispered, just before she closed her eyes.

Randolph merely made a humming sound in the back of his throat and wondered if he would ever regret this night.

As for work, he had a duty to perform. With any luck, this would be the last night he would have to engage the counterfeiters. Perhaps his next assignment would not require so many nights spent in gaming hells.

Now there was some place else he preferred to be.

Fifteen minutes later

Pulling on his clothes and coat as quietly as he could manage, Randolph moved to place a kiss on Xenobia's cheek when she said, "Give me a moment to dress, and I'll go down the front stairs. Provide a distraction whilst you go out the back," she suggested.

Randolph chuckled. "Are you quite sure you've never done this before?" he asked in a tease. He watched as she stood from the bed, goose pimples forming on her naked skin. He reached out and pulled her close for a quick kiss before allowing her to make her way to the dressing room. His gaze stayed on her retreating backside as a growl formed in his throat.

Damned counterfeiters.

He leaned down and pulled on his boots. When he stood, he was stunned to find Xenobia mostly dressed and turning her back for him to do up the buttons.

"You'll return later tonight?" she asked. "I'll be sure to leave the back door unlocked for you."

He hesitated before answering. "It all depends, Xenobia," he hedged as he did up the buttons.

"On what?"

Randolph furrowed a brow. "I cannot say. That is—"

"Is it because what you do at night is a secret?"

"It matters not the time of the day. It's simply the nature of my... of my position," he stammered.

She turned around to face him. "Is your position why you were knighted by the king?"

Randolph realized they had never spoken about why he had introduced himself as a 'sir'. "It is," he finally admitted.

She inhaled softly as her eyes widened. "You work for the Crown." She didn't make it a question.

He dropped his forehead to hers. "One of its many offices, yes," he admitted on a sigh.

"The Foreign Office?" she guessed.

He blinked.

"Are you chasing counterfeiters?" she asked on a gasp.

Giving a start, Randolph furrowed his brows. "How do you...?"

"Lady Chamberlain paid a call yesterday. She spoke of the problem. Said her husband had agents assigned to the case because there were *foreigners* involved." She leaned closer and lowered her voice even more. "*Frenchmen*, she implied."

Randolph struggled to keep an impassive expression on his face. He couldn't decide if he should be angry or laugh at the strange circumstance in which he found himself.

"Xenobia, I must ask you to keep this a secret."

"Who would I tell?"

He was about to mention Lady Comber, but realized Alistair's wife was probably in the parlor with Xenobia when Lady Chamberlain mentioned the counterfeiters. "Just—"

"I won't tell a soul," she said with a shake of her head. "You can trust me."

Randolph blinked, suddenly convinced that she would indeed keep his confidence. He leaned down and kissed her quite thoroughly. "I believe you," he murmured. "Now you really should go down for your dinner. I'll wait for a full minute before I make my way down the back stairs."

She nodded her understanding as she sneaked out the bedchamber door and calmly made her way to the main stairs.

• • •

minute later and Randolph was down the servants' stairs and about to head toward the back door when he overheard one of the footmen say something about The Queen of Hearts.

"We're not going anywhere if her ladyship doesn't come down for dinner soon."

"Och, we have to," another said. "I got us the last of the ten pound notes from the gaming table. 'Bout time we beat those frogs."

"I was just up in my mistress' room, and she ain't there," a female voice said. "Chesterfield says she hasn't returned from her ride in the park." Randolph sorted this last comment was made by Xenobia's lady's maid.

"She's out of mourning, and it's almost Christmas," the first footman countered. "She's pro'bly at Crocky's."

A round of laughter ensued followed by a lone comment in the voice of the lady's maid lambasting the notion that Lady Dunsworth would engage in gambling.

Randolph bristled at how the footmen talked about Xenobia. A meek and mild baroness who probably never spoke poorly of her servants or anyone else. Despite her displeasure with her late husband, she never spoke of him in anger. Instead her voice had been filled with hurt.

Once he was lord of the house, Randolph would see to it these servants were replaced.

Randolph blinked, stunned by his thought. He couldn't give it much consideration, though, when he heard the sound of Chesterfield clearing his throat. "Her ladyship is waiting in the dining room. For her dinner."

Relieved Xenobia had made her appearance, Randolph took advantage of the servants' sudden attentions to their duties and quickly made it to the back door. He slipped out, determined to find the footmen at The Queen of Hearts later that night.

CHAPTER 37
A MAN ON A MISSION

eanwhile, back at The Three Bells

From the sense of disappointment he felt at watching Rachel Roderick leave his public house, Mark Merriweather knew his heart had been captured by the young woman.

Only a day had passed, though.

How had she managed such a feat?

How was it the beautiful brunette could have him imagining an entire life in her company?

At first, Mark had thought he was merely smitten. From his initial conversation with her, he knew she wasn't insipid, and he thought he liked her well enough to consider her for matrimony.

He had known from the moment he saw her that she was beautiful. That he looked forward to bedding her. His rigid cock had made itself apparent at least twice whilst in her company.

Now that he had kissed her, he knew so much more.

He didn't believe in "love at first sight." Lust, yes, which explained what had him approaching her when she had been about to dine with The Queen the evening before.

That and Lady Comber's enthusiastic recommendation.

But after that? After learning Rachel was at The Queen of Hearts to apply for a position?

Under any other circumstances, Mark would have walked away. Her need for employment meant she was a young, unattached woman, requiring the position in order to pay her way in life.

Appearances suggested otherwise. The gown she had worn was far too expensive for someone in need of a job. Her manner of speech was that of someone to the manor born. The way she conversed with The Queen had him realizing they knew each other—had known one another—a long time.

The idea he could hire her as his bookkeeper had him thinking twice about simply walking away. Once he'd finally found her in The Queen's office—he had managed to traverse a good deal of the residence in search of her—he found her so intent on her numbers that she didn't even notice his presence. He was positive he was making the right decision in offering her a position.

And then she had teased him.

The delight in her eyes had ensnared him. Convinced him there was far more to the young woman than beauty and a talent for arithmetic. Had him remembering Lady Comber's earlier call regarding his need for a wife, which meant Rachel had need of a husband.

The idea of courtship was easy to consider. He probably should have been cowed when she admitted her relationship to the Marquess of Reading, but the added comment that she was born on the wrong side of the blanket helped to temper that particular issue. That she was the sister of one of his friends certainly didn't hurt. That she knew of a woman who might solve the problem of finding a competent cook for The Three Bells only endeared her to him more.

Then she had kissed him. Kissed him with a sort of fervor he felt to his bones. His cock hadn't been the only body part to react. There was an ache in his chest that would only be allevi-ated once he knew she would be his.

Shaking himself from his reverie, Mark knew he best be on his way to Mayfair.

His first stop had to be the mews in the alley, though. There was a pony that needed to be returned to the Reading stables, and he needed a means of transport to St. James Street.

An hour later
His first errand complete—a Reading stables groom had seen to taking the Welsh pony from the tether attached to the back of a slow-moving hackney—Mark ordered the driver to take him to Curzon Street. Given there was no moon on this night, the inky blackness surrounded the hackney until they reached Mayfair and streets lined with gas-lit street lamps.

After studying the coin he tossed in his direction, the driver was happy to maneuver the hackney around a chariot that was parked in front of the Reading townhouse. The hackney waited outside the Middleton townhouse while Mark raided his jewel box for the ring his grandmother had insisted he bestow on his bride.

Mark managed to sneak out of the house by going down the servants' stairs at the back of the house and then hurrying through the front hall, effectively avoiding his parents as they sat down to dinner.

The chariot that had been parked behind the hackney was no longer there, which had Mark thinking the marquess was off in search of his son.

His next stop was The Jack of Spades. Mark wasn't positive that's where he would find Sir Randolph, but it was the best place to start.

Perhaps the upcoming holiday had more than the usual revelers and shoppers out on the streets, but Mark was sure he had never seen so many pedestrians along St. James Street. Due to the number of vehicles that crowded the intersection with Jermyn Street, the hackney driver was forced to drop him before they reached it. Mark gave the driver another coin and sent him on his way.

Mark was happy to join the shoppers and club-goers who crowded the pavement, their general good cheer adding to his own. He had been kissed on this day, and he had plans to propose marriage.

The thought of Rachel Roderick had a grin splitting his face as he made his way past the dunner at the door of The Jack of Spades. The faro tables were already occupied, so Mark forced his steps to slow as he made his way around the perimeter of the gaming hell. When he didn't find Randolph, he approached the dunner.

"I'm in search of Sir Randolph. Has he arrived?"

The dunner frowned, his expression suggesting he might land a facer somewhere in the vicinity of Mark's left cheek. "Haven't seen him. Who's asking?"

Mark sighed. "Merriweather. He is expected, is he not?"

Before the dunner answered, his gaze was drawn to the door, where the two men who had dined at The Three Bells entered and then paused before continuing into the gaming hell.

His attention drawn to the same two gentlemen, Mark arched a brow. "Damned frogs," he murmured, loud enough for the dunner to overhear him.

"How do you know they're French?"

Given the dunner had at least six inches on him, Mark had to look up. "One is from Belgium. The other from France. They're uttering counterfeit money. I have news Sir Randolph needs to know."

The dunner's brows rose in surprise. "When he arrives, he'll go straight to the billiards room," he said as he indicated a door at the back of the gaming hell.

"The smoking room?" Mark asked, obviously unaware the proprietor had repurposed the space.

"Aye," the dunner replied, his gaze still on the foreigners as they paused to watch the play at one of the faro tables.

"I'll be in there," Mark said. From the dunner's lack of response and the direction of his gaze, Mark knew the oversized hulk of a man was familiar with Sir Randolph's mission.

Wanting to impress his future bride by helping her brother, Mark saw to acquiring a drink and made his way to the billiards room.

CHAPTER 38
BURIED TREASURE
DISCOVERED

Meanwhile, at the front of Bradley House
As quietly as possible, Xenobia skulked down the main stairs in the hopes she could make it to the ground floor without being noticed by a servant.

At no point had she heard the chime for dinner—she was sure it was around eight o'clock—nor had she spotted Chester-field on the hunt for her. She supposed since he hadn't let her in the front door, he thought her still out with Sir Randolph.

When she reached the first floor, she dared a glance over the stair railing until the roses on the gaming table came into view. Also in full view was the footman, Smith. He was bent over, pulling out a drawer from the table.

Xenobia watched as he extracted what appeared to be several sheets of parchment before he quickly glanced around and then carefully closed the drawer. He stuffed the parchments into a pocket and made his way toward the back of the house.

Curious, Xenobia made her way down the last set of stairs. The hall was empty of servants—not unusual given the time of day nor the fact that she employed so few—so she moved to the table and opened the same drawer as the servant had.

Finding it empty, she furrowed a brow and dared another glance down the hall. She knelt and studied the edge of the table, stunned to discover that the inlaid wood pattern on the sides outlined a series of drawers encircling the table.

She moved to one that better hid her from the hall leading to the kitchens and pulled it open. Stunned at finding a stack of twenty pound notes, she nearly shut the drawer. Instead, she extracted one of them and absently closed the drawer as she stared at the bank note. "Bank of England" was printed at the top, and the year "1817" was shown as its date of issue.

Hearing an outburst of laughter from down the hall, she quickly hid the note in her gown's pocket and made her way to the dining room. She had just entered when Chesterfield appeared from the butler's pantry.

"My lady," he said in surprise. "Apologies. I did not know you had returned."

"Obviously," she replied, deciding she owed him no explanation. "I'd like my dinner now." When she noted the table had not been set, she added, "In here, if the footmen can be bothered to serve."

Chesterfield's eyes widened at hearing the rebuke in her voice. "Right away, my lady."

Xenobia watched as the butler hurried from the room, heading back toward the kitchens. She used the time to return to the gaming table, where she opened every drawer. At first tempted to leave the bounty where it was, she instead began stuffing the bank notes into her carriage gown pockets until she had emptied out all the drawers except the one containing a deck of playing cards.

She was about to place the colorful pasteboards back into the drawer when she noticed the corner of a sheet of paper peeking out. A tug on it had it finally loosening, as if it had at one time been caught in the drawer and then bent upon the drawer's closing.

About to unfold the parchment, she paused when she heard the sounds of footfalls moving closer. She shut the drawer. Acting as if she had just descended the stairs, she made her way into the dining room. "I've changed my mind," she announced to the two footmen who were seeing to the place setting. "I'll take my dinner in the parlor."

"Yes, my lady," Smith and Colburn replied in unison.

Xenobia knew that once dinner had been taken up, neither one of the footmen would return to the parlor, ensuring she would be left alone. She was about to take her leave of the dining room when she paused. "Pray tell, how long did you work for my father?"

The two footmen exchanged quick glances before Smith said, "Just a year, my lady."

"Two for me, my lady," Colburn replied.

"Tell me, did he entertain often?"

The two showed expressions of confusion. "If you mean hosting a dinner party or the like, very rarely," Colburn offered.

"No balls or soirées during my time, but then he didn't have a hostess," Smith chimed in.

"No... gentlemen callers?"

The two footmen blinked. "He wasn't like *that*, my lady," Smith said in a hoarse whisper as his head shook.

Her face coloring when she realized what he had thought she meant, Xenobia quickly added, "Men he might have hosted in his study, perhaps? Tradesmen or bankers or...?"

Colburn furrowed a brow. "Chesterfield would know more, but the captain did have an occasional caller. His solicitor, I think he was. Especially towards the end, when his wound was bothering him so much, he could hardly get down them stairs."

Xenobia winced, remembering when her mother announced that Captain Alton Bradley was on his deathbed and they best pay a call. At the age of eighteen, Xenobia had never experienced a death in the family, so the captain's passing hit her especially hard. Learning he had been generous with her in his will had been an unexpected surprise.

Now finding hundreds of pounds of bank notes in his gaming table had her astounded.

"Well, I appreciate your insights. I'll be in the parlor."

"Yes, my lady," the two replied as they watched her go.

Xenobia made her way up to the first floor, determined to

keep her steps unhurried. She entered the parlor and found the book on Thoroughbreds on the side table where she had left it the night before. Placing it on the card table in the back of the parlor, she opened it and pretended to read. Instead of reading the book, though, she read the note she had found in the table.

To my dearest daughter Xenobia,

If you are reading this note, you've no doubt come into possession of it by way of your husband—if you have one—or perhaps my solicitor. I cannot imagine you will find it where I intend to leave it.

Despite having told you that any buried treasure you might discover in the house belongs to you, I don't recall your curiosity piqued enough that you actively searched for it. Five-hundred pounds can go a long way towards a trip to Italy or a new wardrobe, jewelry, or a new coach-and-four.

Perhaps this note will ignite your curiosity, for its resting place is just the beginning of where to find the first treasure.

Hopefully before the servants do.

Treasure hunts are always the most entertaining during the holidays. Share your finds with others for the happiest of Christmases.

Your father,

Alton Bradley

P.S. As much as I loved her, your mother could never keep a secret, so I have not told her about this. She was always good about sharing, though—her friendship, her possessions and— perhaps too much—her body.

By now, you have already learned this about her.

Do not find fault with her over her affaires of the heart, though. One day you may discover a deep and abiding love with someone who, like you, least expects it. Return it and live a full and happy life. You deserve no less.

Father

Xenobia reread the missive three times as tears welled in her eyes and finally streamed down her face.

Five-hundred pounds?

Had anyone else found this note before she did? Had they discovered the bank notes in the other drawers from having read the note? Or did the footman only find the bank notes by accident? Perhaps from having moved the furniture?

She moved to pull a hanky from her pocket, her hand rifling past a wad of bank notes on its way to the bottom of her pocket.

At that very moment, Colburn appeared on the parlor threshold carrying the tray with her dinner.

Afraid the notes would spill out of her pocket, Xenobia left her hand where it was and called out, "I'll take it back here, Colburn."

"Yes, my lady," the footman said as he stepped up with the tray and set it on the table. Xenobia pushed aside the book to give him more room. "Will there be anything else, my lady?" he asked as he finished pouring a glass of wine.

Xenobia shook her head but then asked, "Tell me, Colburn, do you gamble?"

Colburn furrowed a brow, but then noticed the illustration of a horse in the open book. "Not on horses, my lady. Too rich for my blood."

"But do you play hazard or...?"

"Vingt-et-un," he admitted. "Not often, of course. Mayhap a few times a year."

"Do you have a favorite gaming hell?" She deliberately used the word "hell" as a means of determining how the footman would react.

His eyes darting to one side, Colburn seemed hesitant to answer. "Depends on how much blunt I have."

"Say you had... fifteen pounds." She noted how his eyes widened.

"Uh... I wouldn't gamble *that* much, my lady. Might use half or more for a new suit of clothes or... or a good pair of boots. Save some, too."

"And the rest?" she asked, admiring how he responded.

"I suppose I would go to The Queen of Hearts or... or The

Jack of Spades. They're both close. In St. James Street and Stafford Street. Not as disreputable as the hells over in Cheapside." His eyes darted sideways. "Excuse the language, my lady."

"Of course. Tell me, Colburn, were you planning to go gambling this evening?"

Colburn shook his head. "I wasn't. But Smith asked me to go with him. Says he recently came into some blunt. Must be burning a hole in his pocket, 'cause he's anxious to leave when our duties are done this evening."

Xenobia thought of the denominations of bank notes she had retrieved from the table.

Ones, fives, and twenties.

No tens.

Smith had removed three notes from the only drawer that she had found empty. She dared a glance at the letter from her father. Had Smith found the note? If so, had he read it?

Could he even read?

The words her father had written with respect to sharing caught her eye, and she allowed her initial anger at Smith to subside. "Then both of you should change your clothes and be on your way," she said. "Do tell Smith he needs to share the thirty pounds with you he took from the gaming table in the hall. Fifteen pounds each. An early Christmas present. Do you understand?"

Colburn looked as if he might faint. "Uh, yes, my lady." He bowed and was about to take his leave when he asked, "Are you firing us, my lady?"

Xenobia shook her head. "I am not. You can thank my father for that. Besides, who will cut and bring in the evergreens for the mantel and the staircase on Christmas Eve if not you two?"

Furrowing a brow, Colburn finally nodded. "Thank you, my lady. Happy Christmas."

"To you, as well. And good luck tonight."

Colburn bowed and took his leave.

Xenobia waited a few minutes before she hurried to the parlor door, closed it, and threw the bolt to lock it. She quickly returned to the card table, clearing away the book and setting aside the dinner tray before she emptied her pockets of all the bank notes.

Lining them up by denomination, Xenobia counted the number of each and sat down.

Hard.

Four-hundred and sixty-three pounds were neatly stacked before her, which meant that only seven pounds—besides the thirty Smith had taken earlier that evening—had gone missing. She might have laughed if she wasn't so overcome by her father's generosity. His love of buried treasure.

She ate her dinner and drank the wine, quite unable to wipe the smile from her face.

CHAPTER 39
A COUNTERFEIT CRIME

*M*eanwhile, at *The Jack of Spades*

"You're late," the dunner said as Randolph made his way into The Jack of Spades.

"I am actually here a few minutes earlier than I planned to be," Randolph countered. "Have the frogs arrived?"

"About fifteen minutes ago. They've mostly been watching the play at the faro tables, though."

"Have they played?"

The dunner shook his head. "Not that I could see."

"Is Frank in his office?" Randolph opened his chronometer, confirming it wasn't yet nine o'clock.

"He and a few others. Official looking, they was. And there's another bloke waiting for you in the billiards room. A gentleman, given his clothes looked expensive."

Randolph inhaled sharply. Perhaps he was late. "Another?" he repeated.

"Some bloke arrived just before the frogs. Said he was looking for you. Knew all about them," the dunner relayed.

Giving his thanks, Randolph decided the man in the billiards room would have to wait. He quickly made it to Frank O'Laughlin's office and rapped a knuckle twice on the wood door before letting himself in.

To find five men turning to stare at him.

"I apologize. I thought I was *early*," Randolph said as he closed the door behind him.

"Relax, Roderick. We've only just arrived a few minutes ago," Viscount Chamberlain said from where he was ensconced in what was usually Frank's chair.

Frank stood off to the side, his arms crossed over his chest. He was displaying an expression that suggested he wished he were somewhere else.

Chamberlain motioned to the others in the room. "These two are agents from the bank, Fields and Gabler, and this..." He indicated a burly bald man who stood nearly six inches taller than Randolph. "Is Mr. Morton. Home Office."

"Home Office?" Randolph repeated. "Aren't we dealing with foreigners here?"

"I asked him to join us in the event a bit of muscle might be required," Lord Chamberlain said. "Did you happen to see if the frogs have arrived yet?"

Randolph nodded. "They're watching the faro tables, but the dunner at the door said they hadn't yet played."

"Probably waiting for you to make an appearance in the billiards room," Frank murmured.

"I didn't realize I would be playing this evening," Randolph said, his attention going to the two agents from the bank. "Have the bank notes we turned in last week been examined?"

Lord Chamberlain indicated the agents had the floor. Fields opened a satchel and pulled out stacks of bank notes that had been tied with string. One after another, he set them on Frank's desk in neat piles. It was clear from the corners that the bills had been marked so they could be pulled from play and turned over to the Bank of England to determine their authenticity.

The very last stack was made up of individual one-pound bank notes.

Randolph helped himself to one of them. He stared at the date of issue—1817—and then quickly splayed the rest in the stack. All of them displayed 1817 as their date of issue. "I didn't realize you were concerned about one-pound notes," he remarked, sure these were from the gaming table in Xenobia's hall. All the banking notes he'd had a chance to examine in the table's drawers were from 1817.

"We are when they have that particular date on them," Gabler replied.

"Why?"

Fields cleared his throat. "A particularly bad year for counterfeiting," he stated. "We have since pulled legitimate eighteen-seventeen notes from circulation—most are too worn to be of use anyway—so when these were included in your haul from last week, we took notice."

Randolph stiffened, remembering the letter he had found in one of the drawers of the gaming table. A note penned by Captain Bradley to his only daughter. A note that described a buried treasure of five-hundred pounds.

He had been embarrassed at reading the rest, but his opinion of her late father had risen several notches after reading the missive. Bradley made no apologies about loving a woman who would never be beholden to only him.

Neither did he make excuses.

But he had seen to it his daughter had a small fortune, and apparently others scattered about the house. Randolph briefly wondered just how much money the captain had hidden for her to find.

His thoughts once again went to his father's comments the night before. The story he told of Constance finding money hidden about her home at Fair Downs in Sussex. About how that money had been used to run the household, pay the staff, and put food on the table—all because her cousin knew she wouldn't have accepted it if he had given it to her directly.

Had Alton Bradley known Xenobia was a skinflint when he hid the money for her? Had he known she wouldn't spend it on frivolity? He had encouraged her to share the largesse. To give some of it away.

For a moment, Randolph wished he had made the captain's acquaintance. He would have liked to meet a man with such a unique means of sharing his wealth.

If in the next week Xenobia made no mention of the letter

from her father, he would see to it she would discover it of her own accord.

She was more curious these days.

Randolph's attention went back to the seven one-pound bank notes and his opinion of the captain entirely changed. The thought that Bradley might have left his daughter a treasure of counterfeit bank notes had his expression darkening. Had bile rising in his throat. Had anger replacing his usual calm manner.

So he was entirely unprepared when Fields said, "However, these are legitimate."

Randolph blinked. "Wh... What?"

"Due to their age, they're unusual to find these days, but they were issued by the Bank of England," Fields explained.

"Something tells me there will be three ten-pound notes from eighteen-seventeen in play this evening," Randolph said. "Either here or at The Queen of Hearts."

"Oh, please let it be at Violet's gaudy gold emporium," Frank moaned in disgust. "I just want my business back."

Randolph struggled to keep a straight face as Gabler regarded him with a frown. "What do you know, sir?"

Rolling his eyes, Randolph said, "There are hundreds of pounds of bank notes from eighteen-seventeen in a house in Curzon Street. A buried treasure, so to speak. The owner, Alton Bradley, hid them for his daughter to eventually find—"

"Bradley's daughter?" Lord Chamberlain interrupted. "Are you referring to Lady Dunsworth?"

Wincing, Randolph nodded, hoping the viscount wouldn't ask how it had come to pass that he had been in Bradley House. "I am. One of her footmen has pilfered these—" He pointed to the one-pound bank notes—"As well as three ten-pound notes that I know of. He may have taken more in the past."

"We'll arrest him if he shows up this evening," Fields said, his attention going to Mr. Morton.

Randolph considered justice would be served should the servant be caught, so he held his tongue.

"If this 'buried treasure' could be brought to the bank and

exchanged for newer notes, it would be most appreciated," Gabler suggested.

Nodding, Randolph said, "I will see to it." His attention went to the stacks of other denominations. "And what of those?"

Fields displayed a wince. "All counterfeit but these," he said as he tossed a stack of five-pound notes to Frank.

The gaming hell owner caught the stack of tied bills in his hands and frowned, his attention going to the piles of ten- and twenty-pound notes. He made a sound of disbelief.

"Fear not, O'Laughlin. We will compensate you for your troubles," Lord Chamberlain said. "In the meantime, Roderick, I do believe you need to challenge the frogs to a game of billiards. Just act surprised when they're escorted out the back door by Morton here, won't you?"

Randolph allowed a chuckle. "It will be my pleasure."

He left Frank's office and kept his head low as he made his way back to the dunner at the front door. "Anything new on our frogs?" he asked in a whisper.

"They moved over to the hazard table. Haven't played, but meanwhile, a high and mighty lord was here asking about you. I sent him back to the billiards room 'cause I thought you was already in there."

Randolph grimaced at the thought that some aristocrat might have come to challenge him to a game. Why else would a lord come to The Jack of Spades in search of him?

He kept his head low as walked to the billiards room, making sure to avoid the hazard tables on his way. Once inside, his attention fell on the only two men in the room.

His father and Mark Merriweather.

"About damned time," Mark said as he abandoned his queue on the felt-topped table and moved to join Randolph. "Your father has beaten me three games in a row, and I've only been here half an hour," he complained.

"Good to see you, Merriweather, Father," Randolph said, his manner guarded.

"We have news about your prey," Randall said as he moved

from the other side of the billiards table to join Randolph and Mark. "Thanks to your sister."

Randolph furrowed a brow. "Rachel?"

"My future wife," Mark whispered. "She kissed me after supper tonight." He pulled a ring from his waistcoat pocket. "So I'm going to marry her."

Exchanging a quick glance with his father, who merely shrugged and seemed rather pleased with the arrangement, Randolph asked, "How much have you had to drink tonight, Merriweather?"

Mark allowed a shrug. "I shared a bottle of wine with Rachel over supper," he replied before his eyes rounded. "I am not *foxed*. And just as soon as I tell you what you need to know about those damned frogs, I'm going to The Queen of Hearts to propose."

At the mention of frogs, Randolph gave a start. Thoughts of his sister flew from his head. "What do you know?" he asked before his gaze once again darted to his father.

"Miss Roderick overheard them planning their evening. They're going to exchange all the counterfeit notes for coin and depart for Calais late in the morning," Mark replied. "This is the last night they will be in London."

A sense of alarm coupled with relief settled over Randolph as he turned his attention on his father. "Aren't you supposed to be having dinner with my stepmother about now?"

"I already did," the marquess replied. "A quick one. This is my second visit to The Jack on this night, and the half-hour I spent at The Queen earlier will no doubt have tongues wagging," he complained.

"Why have *you* come?"

Randall jerked his head in the direction of Mark. "Same reason as him. Your sister's command of French and a penchant for eavesdropping is how we learned about their plans for this evening."

Nodding his understanding, Randolph said, "I'm looking forward to meeting Rachel. But we have arrangements in place to see to arrests on this night. If you wish to pay witness to them, then you're welcome to stay in here. Otherwise... you may wish to find another game."

Mark frowned. "You mean our information is of no use to you?" he asked with a good deal of disappointment.

"That's not what I mean at all," Randolph replied. "Your information means time is of the essence. Your information means I need to gain their attention and attract them to this very table, if they are not already on their way." He paused to indicate the billiards table and, upon seeing the few balls still scattered about the felt, he immediately understood how his father had beaten Mark.

"Well, then. I'm off to The Queen of Hearts and the owner of mine," Mark announced as a fist collided with his chest. He turned his gaze onto the marquess. "I still have your permission to ask for her hand, my lord? Despite my terrible play on this eve?"

Randall rolled his eyes. "You do, Merriweather. But if I discover you allowed me to win, there will be hell to pay."

Mark shook his head. "Oh, no, sir. You are a far better player than I," he replied.

Attempting to stifle a grin, Randolph's gaze went from his friend to his father and back to Mark. "Have a care, Merriweather. I haven't yet been introduced to the young lady, but she seems... perfect."

"That's because she is," Mark replied. He gave the marquess a bow and slapped the palm of his hand against Randolph's arm. "Perhaps you and your new lady can join us on a ride in the next day or so? Our ladies are best friends, you must know."

Randolph cleared his throat. "As I learned earlier today. I'm sure we can work something out."

"Good. I'm off," Mark said before he disappeared through the door.

Turning his attention back to this father Randolph asked, "How much did you take him for?"

"I didn't. We were just... practicing," Randall replied. "He is *terrible* at billiards," he said with a wince.

Randolph cleared his throat. "And yet you gave him permission to marry my sister?"

A grin split the marquess' face. "Oh, yes. I just discovered today that the man owns The Three Bells," he claimed. "And Rachel has agreed to keep his books."

Apparently unimpressed, Randolph merely arched a brow.

"What is it?" Randall asked. "What do you know?"

"The Three Bells could certainly use a different cook," Randolph groused.

A grimace appearing on his face, the marquess was quick to agree. "But I'm quite sure with my daughter's help, Merriweather will have that sorted in short order."

Randolph nodded his understanding. "In the meantime, I have my own issue to sort. I'll see you Wednesday night?"

Randall nodded. "If not, before." With a quick glance back at the billiards table, the marquess took his leave.

Pausing for another minute before he departed, Randolph made his way back to the entrance of The Jack of Spades. Waiting until a wave of new gamblers made their way through the front door of the gaming establishment, he merged with them to make it look as if he had just arrived.

Finding his marks was easy—they were still watching the hazard tables with looks of boredom. "Ah, you're back," he said as he clapped the Frenchman on the back. "Care for a game of billiards?"

The one from Belgium gave him a shrug that suggested he had nothing better to do while the Frenchman seemed entirely too eager. The three of them made their way to the now-empty billiards room.

Ten minutes later, Randolph sunk the last ball in what would have been just the first match against the Frenchman, had he and the Belgian not been removed by Mr. Morton and the bank agents.

Now Randolph was the only one left in the room.

He reached into his waistcoat pocket for his chronometer,

his fingers brushing against the other object he had deposited there the night before.

Pulling it out along with the watch, he stared at it and then checked the time. He gave a sigh when he remembered what he'd been doing twenty-four hours earlier.

What he'd been doing six hours earlier.

What he'd been doing just three hours ago.

How was it so much could happen in only a day?

Knowing they were probably counterfeit, he left his winnings on the felt and took his leave of The Jack of Spades, intending to go across the street to The Queen of Hearts.

Before he stepped from the pavement, though, he paused when he recognized one of Xenobia's servants in the company of another man. When he heard him speak, he knew it was one of the footmen he had overheard earlier that evening at Bradley House.

The one who had said he had taken the money from the gaming table.

"You're quite sure she's not going to fire us?"

"I swear it. She said we could each have fifteen pounds as an early Christmas present," the one he knew as Colburn claimed. "I was sure we was done when she said she knew you had taken the blunt from the table. She must have seen you do it."

"I suppose it was too good to last," the other one said. "Just think if we'd never had to move that table, we'd never have found the one-pound notes."

Despite a desire to wallop the footman before he could make his way into The Jack of Spades, Randolph resisted the urge.

There was a stop he needed to make across the street and somewhere else he wanted to be.

CHAPTER 40
THE LITTLE THINGS

*M*eanwhile, in the private residence at *The Queen of Hearts*

The driver held out his hand as Rachel took the single step down from her new equipage. "Have you lodgings, sir?" she asked. She hadn't been introduced to the man earlier, and now wondered from where her father had hired him.

"I do, my lady. In the mews next to The Queen of Hearts. Name's Baker."

The reply was entirely unexpected. "Do you work for my... for my employer, Mrs. Higgins?" Rachel asked in surprise. She had almost said "my mother" but caught herself in time.

"I work for The Queen, my lady. Don't know any Mrs. Higgins. But I'll be seeing to your chariot and horses. When you're in need of a ride, you only need to let one of the footmen know, and I'll come right around to this door here," he explained, as he motioned to the entrance to the private residence. "Will you be needing to go out again this evening?"

"Oh, no. Good night, Mr. Baker."

The driver hurried up to the door and opened it for her, which had Rachel wishing she'd had some coins with her. She was still dressed in her riding clothes and hadn't taken a reticule, though. "Thank you, sir."

She stepped into the vestibule to discover The Queen of Hearts' former cook, Gem Baker rushing to meet her.

"Oh, Miss Roderick, we've been so worried. The Queen was looking for you—"

"I left a note," Rachel replied.

"Which she found. And then his lordship came and said he'd made arrangements for you to get about town. I see my husband got you home all right. He's been so excited about driving that fancy coach of yours."

Rachel's gaze darted to the door to discover her driver had already set off for the mews. "I just met Mr. Baker a moment ago. I didn't realize he was your husband," she replied.

"Goin' on fifteen years," Gem said with a wave of her hand.

"He seems very nice."

"Oh, he is. Smells like horse all the time, though."

"As I rather imagine I do," Rachel said as she made her way to the stairs. "I'd like to take a bath if I might."

"Water's already hot. I'll get it into the tub for you," Gem said as she hurried alongside Rachel. "And help you with your buttons."

"That's very kind of you."

Once Rachel was in the tub, she told the maid about her afternoon ride as she admired a cake of soap. Lifting it to her nose, she sniffed it.

"The Queen buys that in Jermyn Street," Gem said when she noticed Rachel's perusal. "Floris, I think is where she gets it. Only the best for her girls, she says."

Arching a brow in appreciation, Rachel began washing as she told the maid about the supper at The Three Bells.

"I've heard of that public house," Gem said as she busied herself with seeing to Rachel's riding habit. "Good neighborhood. They say they put linens on the tables like in some restaurants. Word is the place could use a new cook, though."

"Are you interested in being that cook?" Rachel asked as she reached for a bath linen.

Gem stood staring at her, the riding habit hanging from her hands forgotten. "Pardon me, miss, but did I hear you right?"

Rachel wrapped the linen around her body. "Mr. Merri-weather knows he needs a better cook, so I mentioned your name to him whilst we were eating supper. I'll be keeping the ledgers there, you see. Mornings here, afternoons there." She didn't add that she might be marrying the proprietor.

"Why, I do miss the cooking," Gem replied. "But..."

"What is it?" Rachel asked as she pulled a day gown from a peg in the dressing room. Despite the hour, she still intended to go down to the office before retiring for the night.

"I would miss working for The Queen," Gem said. "You don't think she'd be angry with me? Question my loyalty, and all?"

Rachel considered the circumstances as she moved into her bedchamber. "I think she would be happy to know that you will be doing what you love to do, especially since I have every intention of enjoying one of your meals every day."

"What's this?" Violet Higgins asked. She had slipped into the bedchamber at some point during their conversation, dressed in her usual red satin costume and large, white wig.

"Good evening, Mother," Rachel said as she hurried over to kiss Violet on the cheek.

"And to you, darling."

"I was just telling Mrs. Baker that I think you would be happy for her if she were to accept the position of cook at The Three Bells."

Violet exchanged a quick glance with Gem. "I would indeed," she said. "Having had a luncheon there last week, I have to agree they could use a new cook," she added. She turned her attention back to Gem. "I felt horrible about replacing you with Jean Claude—"

"Oh, you needn't, your highness. He is an excellent chef," Gem said. "Where as I just know how to cook the standard fare."

"Well, don't be thinking you need my permission to accept the offer. And I'm happy to supply a character for you," Violet said.

Gem's look of surprise had Rachel suppressing a grin.

"Thank you for your help this evening. I shan't be needing you for the rest of the night."

"Yes, my lady," Gem said before she dipped a quick curtsy and made her way out of the bedchamber. "I'll just be seeing to giving this a good brushing."

Violet turned her gaze back on Rachel, who had pulled on a day gown and was seeing to some slippers. "How is it *you* know about The Three Bells' need for a cook?"

Rachel sat on the edge of the bed, a slipper in her hand. "Mr. Merriweather took me there for supper after our ride this afternoon," she replied.

"Without a chaperone?"

Rachel inhaled as if she were about to respond and then let out the breath of air. "We didn't have one for our ride, but Father was at The Three Bells."

"Rachel! Were you seen by anyone?"

Managing to display the appropriate amount of contrition, Rachel said, "Besides Sir Randolph and Xenobia, we were practically the only ones in that part of the park."

Violet visibly relaxed. "So you've finally met your brother?"

Wincing, Rachel shook her head. "No."

About to ask why, Violet saw the disappointment on her daughter's face and decided not to press the issue. "I was going to admonish you for having disappeared for so long—"

"I left a note."

"Which I discovered and read. Thank the gods your father found me to let me know what had become of you. Sounds as if there's a bit of excitement happening across the street?" she hinted.

Rachel's eyes widened, remembering that both her father and Mark were in search of her brother. "Hopefully not too much. I would hate to think Sir Randolph might be in any danger from those foreigners."

"Sir Randolph can handle himself," Violet assured her. Her brows furrowed when she noticed how Rachel was dressed. "Where are you going now?"

"The office."

"Well, you needn't. There are only a couple of items I dropped off in there on the way up," Violet countered.

"I want to," Rachel said. "Besides... I... I may have a caller."

Violet's eyes widened. "This late?" Then her mouth dropped open. "Already?"

"What?" Rachel asked, not sure to what conclusion her mother had just jumped.

Slumping into the nearest chair, Violet regarded her daughter with a look of sadness. "Yesterday I was under the impression you wished to remain a spinster."

"I did," Rachel agreed.

"Earlier this evening, your father informed me Mr. Merriweather had asked his permission to court you."

"He did, which is part of the reason Mr. Merriweather asked me to go riding with him."

Violet looked as if she were about to cry. "Has he already proposed marriage?"

Rachel's eyes darted sideways. "He speaks as if he has, but..." She held out her hands. "He hasn't asked, and he's not yet given me a ring. He has offered me the position of bookkeeper for The Three Bells." When she saw her mother's expression of hurt, she said, "Oh, please don't be sad."

"I am not."

"I like him. He's... he's not like other gentlemen, Mother. He actually owns a business, in a property that seems rather expensive, and he seems intent on wishing to run it rather than have a man of business see to it."

Violet rolled her eyes. "After what our man of business did, I cannot blame him," she muttered, referring to Mr. Traynor. A brief mention of the man's crimes to Randall had the marquess assuring her the man had already been tried and transported. "Now I am glad to know there is more to Mr. Merriweather than a game of cards every Wednesday night. If you really do like him, it's within your power to see to it a proposal happens."

Rachel gave a start. "Are you referring to it being a Leap Year?"

Tittering, Violet said, "If only you could have seen your face a moment ago. I didn't realize you would already be familiar with the custom."

Deciding not to mention that Mark had been the one to bring it up first, Rachel leaned over and kissed her mother on the cheek. "I shall let Mr. Merriweather do the proposing," she said. "If you happen to see him, you might mention I'm in the office."

"If I happen to see him and tell him you're in the office, then I shall be joining him in the office," Violet warned.

Rachel grinned, as if she looked forward to it. "Understood." After another moment, she added, "You do realize that if he hires Mrs. Baker to be his cook, he will no longer pursue the services of your Jean Claude."

Violet's eyes rounded before a grin lit her lips. "Oh, all right. If I see Mr. Merriweather, I'll tell him you're in the office," she murmured. "And I won't join him."

Rachel gave her a nod and made her way to the office.

CHAPTER 41
A LEAP OF FAITH IN A LEAP YEAR

eanwhile, at Bradley House
Having consumed her dinner and two glasses of wine, Xenobia collected her treasure into a trinket box she had found on the fireplace mantel in the parlor.

She had nearly laughed out loud when she discovered five twenty-pound bank notes already in the bottom of the box. Adding the bank notes from the gaming table—all except for a single twenty-pound note—she shut the box and tucked it under her arm before she made her way to her bedchamber.

Sullivan was already there, ready to take the pins from her hair and help her into a night rail.

"I'll warn you now. I'm not wearing my stays at the moment," Xenobia said as she set the box on her dressing table and took a seat.

"My lady?"

"I removed them when I took a nap before dinner."

"Oh," Sullivan responded before she undid the buttons down the back of the carriage gown.

"Do you know if Smith and Colburn have left for a gaming hell yet?" She wasn't disappointed to see her lady's maid's look of shock reflected in the mirror.

"They've been gone at least an hour. Tail betwixt their legs,

288

too, my lady, if you ask me. Like they knew what they was doing was wrong."

Xenobia allowed a prim grin as she pulled the twenty-pound bank note from her pocket and held it up. She watched Sullivan's reaction in the mirror and smiled. "Happy Christmas," she said.

"For me, my lady?"

"Indeed. Just don't tell the footmen you got more than they did," she said in a whisper as Sullivan gingerly took the parchment from her.

"Thank you, my lady. I don't think I've ever seen this much blunt in all my life."

"Spend it wisely, but do have some fun with it, too," Xenobia encouraged.

"I shall," the lady's maid replied as she quickly stuffed the bank note into a pocket. Her expression grew curious. "Did your ride in the park go well?"

Xenobia nodded. "It did. Sir Randolph is the son of a marquess and a widower," she said, enjoying the thrill she felt at seeing Sullivan's expression. "Why, I think I shall have to propose marriage if he does not." She paused as she watched Sullivan's eyes widen. "Have I thoroughly scandalized you?"

The lady's maid stared back at her reflection and then grinned in delight. "Not at all. It's a Leap Year, my lady, so you are entirely within your right to propose marriage."

Blinking several times, Xenobia stared at Sullivan. "It is? I am?"

Sullivan angled her head to one side. "Aye. I don't think it only applies to the Scots or Irish," she replied. "Besides, it's not fair they have all the fun."

Xenobia whirled around and looked to the clock above the fireplace. "How late would a goldsmith's shop be open tonight, do you suppose?"

It was Sullivan's turn to blink. "I'm sure I wouldn't know, but I expect ten o'clock, my lady. Especially this close to Christmas."

"Have Chesterfield hail a hackney."

"*Now?*"

"Yes, now. I need to purchase a ring if I'm to propose marriage," Xenobia countered.

Sullivan rushed from the room, and Xenobia nearly giggled at seeing how quickly her lady's maid moved. Unfortunately, Sullivan had already undone several of the buttons down her back.

Xenobia did what she could to refasten the top buttons before she plucked a number of twenty-pound notes from the trinket box. Then she made her way to her father's bedchamber and the dressing room, where her redingote and two sets of petticoats were strewn about the floor. She pulled on the garments and descended the stairs.

"You're coming with me," she said to Sullivan as she entered the vestibule.

Sullivan's delight matched her own as they made their way to the curb and into a hackney. "Rundell and Bridge, as fast as you can," she said to the startled driver.

"Yes, my lady," he replied when he saw the bank note she held up. His expression turned to one of delight. "Because it's Christmas? Or a Leap Year?" he asked with a roll of his eyes.

"How about both?"

She and Sullivan climbed into the equipage, giggling as it raced toward Ludgate Hill. "I do hope we're not too late," she said as they bounced along Oxford Street.

"This close to Christmas? Of course they will be open, my lady," Sullivan replied, pulling her cape closed. "Have you something in mind for your son of a marquess?"

Xenobia took a steadying breath. "A gold band, certainly. Perhaps they have one with a small gemstone. A sapphire, mayhap?"

"Do you know what size to buy?"

Blinking, Xenobia remembered how his hand had held her breast. How his fingers had fondled her. "Large?" she guessed.

Sullivan giggled. "They may require a more exact measurement."

Xenobia couldn't help but laugh at the comment. "Perhaps they already know," she murmured.

When the hackney slowed and stuttered to a halt in front of the goldsmith's shop, Xenobia could barely wait for the driver to step down from his bench and open the door.

"Will you wait for us, please?"

"My lady, you gave me enough blunt to drive around London five times," he replied. "I'll be right here when you've completed your shopping."

Xenobia was about to kiss him, but she thought better of it and instead made her way into the shop.

Despite the hour, the gift shop was brightly lit. She made her way to the back, past the array of oddities and bright gilt gifts. Several gentlemen had the attention of an older man, a jeweler who held two trays of rings for their perusal. Her attention went to a glass case where larger rings were on display.

"My lady? Is there something in particular I might show you?"

Xenobia looked up to find a young man regarding her with a curious expression.

"I wish to propose marriage," she blurted. "I need a ring for a man who has rather large fingers."

"Ah. Leap Year," he replied happily. He pulled a tray of gold bands from the glass case and placed it in front of her. "Haven't had a query like this for several months," he added as he pulled another tray of silver bands from the case. "Are you looking for a particular gemstone?"

Xenobia blinked. "He's the son of a marquess," she replied.

"Oh," the young man responded, his 'oh' sounding in three syllables. "A sapphire, then. Mayhap with a diamond or two or three?"

Frowning, Xenobia examined the tray of gold rings while Sullivan busied herself admiring the array of gold and silver gifts on display in the rest of the shop.

Taking a deep breath, Xenobia imagined Randolph's typical day. His mornings were spent in the stables with horses. He drove in the park in the afternoons to exercise horses. His evenings were spent in pursuit of threats to the Crown.

With those images in mind, she surveyed the gold offerings and grinned when she found a simple gold band with a single square gemstone between two smaller diamonds. "Might I see that one?" she asked as she pointed to it.

The shopkeeper plucked it from its black velvet bed and handed it to her. Xenobia examined its size, sliding it onto her thumb to discover it was far too large. "This one, yes," she murmured. "How much?" she asked as she pulled a wad of bank notes from her carriage gown.

"One-and-twenty pounds, my lady," the young man said as he studied a tiny slip of paper still embedded in the black velvet. "One sapphire and two diamonds in gold."

Xenobia grinned as she peeled off the bank notes and handed them to the startled shopkeeper. "Do you have a box for it?"

"Of course, my lady," he replied. He disappeared and then returned with the ring encased in a black velvet box. "I hope he says yes, my lady."

Her eyes widening in alarm, Xenobia said, "Me, too."

She turned to find Sullivan holding a silver candlestick in one hand. "What's this?"

"My Christmas gift from you, my lady," Sullivan replied happily. "I've always wanted one of my own for my quarters. An ornate one, like this."

Xenobia resisted the urge to wince at seeing the gaudy candlestick. "Do you have enough money to buy it?"

Her lady's maid nodded. "Oh, more than enough." The servant moved to the counter to pay for her find.

Reminded she wanted to give a gift to her cousin, Julia, Xenobia moved to regard a collection of silver items on display. Her gaze passed over the tea sets and salvers, trinket and snuff boxes, vinaigrettes and chatelaines to come to rest on a calling card case.

Grinning, Xenobia plucked the ornate case from its shelf, imagining it holding calling cards printed with Julia's name followed by the word, "Matchmaker." She joined Sullivan at the counter, giddy with excitement. "This will be perfect," she told her maid before she paid for the gift.

Once they had their purchases in hand, they hurried out to the hackney. "Bradley House, as quickly as you can," Xenobia said as they climbed in.

A half-hour later, they were giggling as they made their way past a startled Chesterfield and up the stairs.

Meanwhile, Randolph Roderick was making his way into the back door of Bradley House.

CHAPTER 42
A PROPOSAL

*M*eanwhile, in the office at *The Queen of Hearts*

Having settled into the chair at her mother's desk, Rachel wasn't prepared to find another small stack of posts on the corner. She rifled through the envelopes, setting aside what appeared to be private letters for her mother while pulling out those that were addressed to the business.

The one on the very bottom was addressed to her, and Rachel stared at it for a long moment before breaking the wax seal and unfolding it.

My Dearest Daughter,

Rachel rolled her eyes, her gaze having gone to the bottom of the missive to discover it had been sent by Randall Roderick, Marquess of Reading.

Dearest Daughter, indeed.

She was his only daughter.

Rachel grinned as she returned her attention to the first lines of the missive.

I wish to thank you for accompanying me to meet my marchioness on this day. During our brief dinner this evening, Connie entertained me with stories of your formal introduction to your youngest brother. I am told his bow was a deep one, nearly resulting in his tumbling onto his head. I have been tutoring him on the niceties and will have him work on the depth of his bows.

Rest assured I will find your oldest brother and see to it the information you overheard is passed along. At some point, perhaps tomorrow, I shall see to a proper introduction for the two of you.

I have a confession to make regarding your ride with Merriweather. I was watching from afar. I followed you to The Three Bells. It is how I ended up enjoying a drink at the tap along with conversation with one of my colleagues. I thought to keep this from you and hope you would consider it a coincidence, but you are too clever to believe it.

It is not that I mistrusted Merriweather.

I do not.

He is an enterprising young man who understands his place in the hierarchy of his family. He will never inherit the earldom and is therefore superfluous. That he has seen to purchasing and running a business is a testament to his having been raised with a sense of responsibility by his father. I believe this sense of responsibility extends to matters beyond the business—family, for example.

If you have not yet proposed (my Connie tells me it would be within your right to do so given this is a Leap Year, even if you are not Irish), then I expect Merriweather to do so.

You have my blessing no matter your answer.

In the meantime, you will have a decision to make as to what you want for your future. I would tell you to choose wisely. To consider all your options. But, alas, you are a young woman, and therefore have few. So I will instead tell you to choose based on what your heart tells you to do. Take your time. Put off Merriweather if you don't wish to marry him. Do what you must with the knowledge that I will see to your expenses until another, more worthy gentlemen takes them on.

I would merely ask that you not follow in your mother's footsteps. Her life has been far lonelier than it should have been, and I do not wish that for you.

Nor do I wish that life for your best friend. Your mother tells me Lady X deserved better than she got with her first husband. I believe with the right nudge, your brother could be her next husband. If not, they will at least be friends.

Please know you are welcome for dinner any day we are in residence. Breakfast, too, should you be awake early.

I must depart for St. James Street. Enjoy your chariot and have your invoices from your shopping trips sent to my attention.

Your father

Tears streamed down Rachel's face as she set the letter onto the middle of the desk. She would have continued to stare at the even script written on a sheet of high-quality parchment, but a square of linen appeared in her watery line of sight.

She glanced up to discover Mark Merriweather regarding her with a look of concern. "Mark," she whispered.

"Tell me who has broken your heart so completely, and I shall challenge him to a duel," he said in a hoarse whisper.

Rachel pressed the linen against one cheek and let out a snort before she stood. "You idiot," she whispered before she hurried around the desk and lifted her arms to his shoulders. "It's a letter from my father," she said as she settled her head against his chest.

Shocked at how she practically ran to him for comfort, Mark wrapped his arms around her waist. "Your father has made you cry?" he asked, his response a combination of surprise and censure. His hold on her tightened as he moved a hand to the back of her head.

"He writes a rather eloquent letter," Rachel replied. She straightened and regarded him with a watery grin. "You changed clothes."

"I did. Your father and I ended up at The Jack of Spades in our pursuit of your brother. Seems as if our intelligence was not required on this night."

"Oh," she replied as a look of worry settled on her face.

"Oh, do not fret, for I was able to locate Mrs. Baker. We spoke for a time, and she has given me her assurance she will accept my offer. She will not begin her duties at The Three Bells until a week has passed, though."

"So… just after Christmas?" Rachel reasoned.

"She wishes to provide The Queen with a 'suitable notice' is how she put it," Mark explained. "I cannot fault her loyalty, for I hope she will show the same with me."

"She will be a loyal employee," Rachel assured him.

"And I gave some thought to your suggestion that I live above The Three Bells. The idea has a good deal of merit. There will always be meals, and the location is unmatched by most properties."

Rachel furrowed a brow. "Yet you are not convinced you should live there."

He shook his head. "There are other considerations," he murmured.

"Such as?" she asked gently.

"You," he whispered.

For a moment, Rachel imagined a life with Mark Merriweather. What it would be like to live and work above the public house in Westminster. To ride in her chariot to her mother's private residence to do the books for The Queen of Hearts. To share meals with Mark at the table in the back of The Three Bells. To kiss him in the mornings upon waking and fall asleep in his arms at night.

Only the day before, she could not have imagined such a life. She had thought she could only look forward to life as a spinster.

"Will you marry me?" she asked in a whisper.

Mark blinked before his eyes darted sideways. "Of course, I will," he replied before his eyes rounded. "Oh. It's a Leap Year, isn't it?" he murmured in awe.

"So I've been told," she replied. "Are you quite sure?"

He nodded. "Quite. Why would I not be?"

Rachel inhaled and said, "My father is a marquess, but my mother was a courtesan, and now she owns a gaming hell."

Mark angled his head to one side. "Rachel, my darling, I'm not about to hold your father's status as an aristocrat against you," he murmured, the barest hint of a grin teasing the corner of his lips. "I can only hope your mother does not hold against me my ownership of a business and my determination to run it myself, especially now that I'll have you doing the books."

A slow smile appeared on Rachel's face. "She will not, nor will she hold it against you that you are hiring away one of her best employees."

He winced. "At your behest."

"Since you will be giving up your pursuit of Jean Claude."

His wince turned into a grimace. "Oh, must I?"

She grinned at that. "You must. And thank you for not dismissing the idea of hiring Mrs. Baker out of hand."

"Why would I?"

Rachel once again rested the side of her head against his shoulder. "Because I am a woman."

He held her a moment, his head dropping to the top of hers. "Which is such a relief, since I plan to wed you as soon as I can procure a license."

"I'm sorry I don't have a ring for you."

Mark lifted a finger. "Ah, but I have one for you," he said as he reached into a waistcoat pocket and pulled out the ring he had plucked from his jewel box. He held it up. "My Grandmother gave it to me. She insisted I give it to—"

"Oh, it's beautiful," Rachel said before she sniffled.

"You would wear it? For me?"

She held out her left hand. "Of course," she whispered, watching as he threaded it onto her fourth finger before he lifted her hand to his lips and kissed the ring. "It fits perfectly." She glanced up at him and exhaled. "Oh, dear. Did you have a proposal all prepared? My father thought you might."

"I did," he admitted. "But you saved me from making an utter fool of myself," he added before he kissed her on the forehead. "And for the rest of our lives, I shall tell everyone I know that *you* were the one to propose marriage," he added with a teasing grin.

"You wouldn't!"

His brows furrowed. "You're right. I won't, merely because no one would believe me."

"They would," Rachel murmured.

"They might," he hedged.

"*I* will know the truth," she said as one of her brows arched.

Mark took an unsteady breath before he captured her lips with his.

The kiss, hard and unrelenting at first, had Rachel moaning before he finally, slowly, pulled away. His forehead dropped to hers. "However am I to wait until we are wed to make love to you?" he asked in a whisper. "Until I can wake up next to you and kiss you in the mornings? Until I can send you to slumber with a good-night kiss?"

Rachel gave a slight shake of her head. "We can wed when you wish," she whispered.

The quick halt of footsteps on the carpet had her glancing around the side of Mark's arm. "Sir Randolph!" she said with surprise as she quickly let go of Mark and dipped a curtsy.

Randolph gave a start, not only at her greeting but at recognizing his friend when Mark turned to regard him with surprise.

"Did you beat them at billiards, then?" Mark asked, thinking the knight was there to speak with him. "Have they been arrested?" He stepped up next to Rachel and held out his right hand to their intruder.

His attention on Rachel, Randolph shook Mark's hand and said, "I did, and they have been." He gave a bow. "Rachel Roderick, I presume?" He reached for her hand and lifted it to brush his lips over the back of her knuckles.

A brilliant smile lit Rachel's face before she said, "How do you do, brother? It's a pleasure to finally meet you."

Randolph still held onto her hand and was regarding the ring on her finger with fascination. "And you, sister." His attention went to Mark. "You proposed marriage?"

Mark shook his head. "I didn't," he replied, as if he thought his life might be in danger.

"It's a Leap Year, so *I* did the honors," Rachel said. "I do hope the information I overheard over supper tonight helped you with your investigation of those foreigners?"

Randolph turned his attention back to her. "It did. In fact, I would mention your skills to my employer, but I fear he might offer you a position, and I rather doubt your future husband would like you working for the Crown," he murmured.

"I would not," Mark agreed.

Ignoring his friend's comment, Randolph said, "I came to let Mrs. Higgins know that the arrests had been made and that we don't expect to insert any more investigators into her games in the near future."

"I will tell her when next I see her," Rachel replied. "I'm sure she'll be glad to hear it. In the meantime, did you enjoy your ride in the park with my dear friend, Xenobia?"

Jerking at the unexpected query, Randolph allowed a slow grin. "I did. Pray tell...?"

"Mark and I were riding horses in the park whilst you were... not," she replied as an impish grin appeared on her face. "And thank you for taking care of Richard for me all these years. He was a joy to ride, even if I felt a bit too close to the ground."

Clearing his throat, Randolph merely nodded. "I hope to have news of my own regarding Lady Dunsworth on the morrow. In the meantime, do not let this man talk you into anything... at all," he said as he took a step backwards.

"At all?" she repeated, her impish grin still in place.

"Now see here, Randolph," Mark started to say in protest.

Randolph arched a brow as Mark's fists went to his hips. "At all," he repeated before he gave her a wink.

"Understood, brother. Now go make my best friend a happy woman, won't you?"

A dimple appearing in his right cheek, Randolph nodded. "I shall do my best." He gave a deep bow and made his way out the door.

Mark watched him go, an odd expression settling on his face.

"What is it?" Rachel asked as she turned and moved to stand before him.

"Do you intend to follow his advice?" he asked, his manner rather sober.

Rachel pretended ignorance. "That man? Why I only just met him. Why would I follow his advice?"

Mark stared at her a moment before he grinned and pulled her close. "Why Rachel Roderick, I do believe I love you."

Staring at him in wonder, Rachel inhaled softly. "Will you make love to me?"

Blinking, Mark glanced around the office. "Here?" he asked in alarm.

"No, of course not. My bedchamber is upstairs. There's a lock on the door. We shan't be disturbed." For a moment, Rachel thought he might decline, the look on his face making his indecision apparent.

"I don't have a mistress," he blurted.

Rachel's eyes widened. "I'm rather glad to hear it," she replied.

"If you're expecting me to have a good deal of experience, then you will be sorely disappointed," he went on. "In fact, we may have to rely on yours if we're to... to..." He let out the rest of his breath on a sigh.

It was Rachel's turn to blink. "*I* don't have any," she said. "Wait. You thought I had been with another man?"

Mark shook his head, immediately realizing his mistake. "Of course I hoped you hadn't, but... as you said, your mother was a courtesan. From the way you said it, I thought you were telling me that you... that you... oh, I'm a prize idiot."

For a moment, Rachel's ire nearly had her slapping the young man across the face, but from the expression of remorse he displayed, she allowed the momentary anger to pass. "My virtue is intact," she whispered.

He nodded his understanding. "My father took me to an expensive brothel once. Paid for me to spend the night with a courtesan. She was much older than me," he stammered.

Rachel struggled to suppress a grin. "Did you visit her often?"

He shook his head. "Just the one night."

"But you remember what to do?"

His eyes widened. "Oh, oh, yes," he assured her. "But I'll be terribly nervous."

"As will I," she replied, her own eyes rounding.

He tightened his hold on her. "Then we shall be nervous together," he whispered. "Lead the way to your lair, my lady, and I shall do my best to prove my love and affection."

Rachel tittered. "You needn't say it as if there will be dragons to slay."

"If there were and I did, then I could be a knight, like your brother," he whispered as they made their way out of the office. She turned down the gas lights and closed the door before they headed up the stairs.

"'Sir Mark' does have a nice ring to it," Rachel teased. "Perhaps I shall make you my personal knight."

"I would be honored," he whispered.

She led the way to her bedchamber and slipped in. Once Mark was inside, she closed the door and threw the bolt.

An n hour later Despite the awkwardness of undressing one another for the first time, of attempting to climb onto the bed without bumping into one another, of Rachel's ticklishness and Mark's insistence that he kiss every square inch of her body, the betrothed couple finally found their rhythm in the simple acts of kissing and making love.

Mark remembered what to do—where to touch, how to kiss, what to lick—before he finally laid claim to his future bride.

Beneath him, Rachel watched in fascination when Mark's release had his entire body ceasing movement. For a moment, in the dim light from a single candle, he was frozen in ecstasy, the cords of his neck strained, his head thrown back, the fingers of one hand laced with hers.

Despite the chill in the air, her entire body warmed all at

once, and she lifted her free hand to the back of his head so she could pull it down to her shoulder.

His breathing labored, his murmurs incoherent, Mark finally relaxed atop her body before kissing her on the cheek. "Would it be all right with you if I were to stay here for the rest of my life?" he asked, his hand cupping her left breast.

Rachel tittered as she slowly lowered her legs to the bed. "If you mean in my heart, then you best plan on it," she whispered.

From his even breathing, she knew he had fallen asleep. Slumber soon took her, too.

CHAPTER 43
TWO HEARTS OF A
SINGLE MIND

eanwhile, at Bradley House
Sullivan sighed as she undid Xenobia's gown and helped her out of it. "Thank you again for the generous gift, my lady."

Xenobia's smile widened. She couldn't seem to stop smiling from all that had happened this day. "You're welcome. Do help yourself to a taper from the stores. I rather imagine you'd like to put your candlestick to use this evening."

"Oh, not until Christmas, my lady."

"Saving it, are you?" Xenobia teased.

"Something like that." Sullivan held open a night rail, and Xenobia pulled it on followed by her dressing gown. "Given the late hour, I expect I shall wish to sleep late on the morrow," she said. "Why don't you do the same, and I'll ring when I'm ready to dress?"

Sullivan looked uncertain for a moment but finally dipped a curtsy. "Very well, my lady."

Xenobia watched the servant take her leave, counted to twenty, stuffed the ring box into a pocket in her dressing gown, and then sneaked out of her bedchamber. She hurried to the end of the hall and paused before pushing down the door handle of the bedchamber she and Randolph had shared earlier that evening. Just the memory of what they had done had her excited. Had her hoping they might do it again.

She grinned in delight when she discovered Randolph already in the room. He was untying his cravat. "I'm so glad you've come," she whispered as she rushed to him.

Randolph captured her in his arms and kissed her. When he finally loosened his hold on her, he regarded her with a grin. "Careful, my lady, or I will expect a similar greeting from you every night," he warned in a teasing voice.

"I would be happy to comply." Her smile faltered as she lost some of her resolve, remembering just then the shopkeeper's last words. "Do tell me about your night. Did it go well?"

Randolph's expression changed as he nodded. "Very well, actually. As it happens, most of the bank notes I turned over to the investigators last week were indeed counterfeit. The culprits have been arrested, though, which means I have a few days before I gain a new assignment."

Xenobia's eyes widened. "That's good news, is it not?"

He pulled her into a loose embrace. "It is," he agreed. "There's a small matter of about five-hundred pounds that still needs to be resolved, but it's nothing urgent," he added when he remembered the bank's representatives requesting that her buried treasure be exchanged for newer bank notes.

"What is it?" she asked, her curiosity piqued at the mention of five-hundred pounds.

"Nothing that can't wait until morning," he murmured as he held her. "I met Rachel this evening."

"Not at a gaming establishment, I hope?"

Randolph grinned. "In her mother's study, as it happens. I was there to let the owner know the men who had been passing the counterfeit notes had been arrested."

"So you've met Rachel's mother?" Xenobia dipped her head, worried he might disavow his half-sister given Violet Higgins' occupation.

"I have, although she was not there tonight. It seems I may have interrupted a marriage proposal, though."

Xenobia sucked in a breath. "Mr. Merriweather did not waste any time. Are you... concerned?"

Randolph shook his head. "He is a friend, and he is honorable, and he had my father's permission." When he saw how Xenobia regarded him, as if she seemed nervous, he asked, "Did you have a good evening?"

"I did, although it's been very strange. In a good way." Although his query was the perfect prompt for Xenobia to put voice to a marriage proposal, she hesitated. "Please don't think me any more wanton than you probably already do, but I'd like for you to know that you are welcome here at Bradley House. Any night—any day—should you wish," she said as she waved a hand to indicate the bedchamber. "This can be your room if you'd like."

Randolph regarded her with a quizzical expression before he once again pulled her into an embrace. "Whether or not I accept your offer will depend on whether or not you're here."

Her eyes darted sideways as a grin slowly appeared. "I wouldn't wish to be anywhere else," she whispered, rather enjoying how his hands slid across her back and down and over the curves of her bottom.

When his hand smoothed over the slick fabric of her satin dressing gown to her hip, it brushed over the ring box she had stuffed into her pocket. Xenobia felt the box bump against her thigh, and she inhaled softly.

"What do you have there?" he asked as his hand molded over the cubical shape.

"Your Christmas gift," she blurted.

Randolph blinked. "This is unexpected. When did you—?"

"Tonight. I went to Rundell and Bridge with Sullivan." She pulled it from her pocket and held it up. "You can open it now, if you'd like."

His gaze settled on the black velvet box and his eyebrows shot up. "You're sure you do not wish for me to wait until Christmas morn?"

"Oh, open it now, please. I'll be terribly vexed if you don't."

Randolph allowed a chuckle at seeing her anxious expression. "All right."

Before he had the lid opened, though, Xenobia said, "Since this is a Leap Year, I wish to exercise my right to ask for a man's hand in marriage. Your hand," she said. "I think we suit rather well. And not just because..." Her attention turned to the bed and then back to him. "Well, you are an excellent lover."

His eyes darting between the gold ring and her wide eyes, Randolph was left speechless.

"Well, do you... do you like it?" she asked, her moment of courage quickly passing.

Randolph blinked. "I do. Very much," he replied.

When he didn't remove the ring from the box, Xenobia said, "If you're concerned about a dowry—"

"I am not."

"—I come with a house and a small fortune that seems to grow if I merely open drawers and boxes."

Randolph blinked. "The gaming table?"

Xenobia sucked in a breath. "You knew?"

Randolph furrowed a brow. "I was going to tell you tonight. I discovered it quite by accident while I was admiring the table this afternoon," he admitted. "There is quite a fortune tucked away in there."

"There was," she agreed. "I've tucked it away in a safe place in my bedchamber," she added. "But that's not all. Apparently my father has left little treasures for me all over the house. For example, Rachel found a twenty-pound note in a music box in the parlor, this afternoon." Xenobia's attention went to a jewel box on the tall bureau. She hurried over and opened it. "See what I mean?" she asked as she pulled a wad of bank notes from the box. "It seems there is buried treasure all around. I just never bothered to look."

"1817?" Randolph guessed as he moved to examine the notes she held.

Her attention went to the top bank note. "How did you know?"

"According to the men from the bank, these have been

removed from circulation, which is why the seven one-pound notes one of your footmen lost at The Jack of Spades last month were flagged as possibly counterfeit."

"That would have been Mr. Smith," Xenobia remarked. "While you were making your way out the back door tonight, I spotted him lifting thirty pounds from the table."

Randolph made a sound of disgust. "Yet you didn't fire the cur," he accused.

"How do you know?"

"I eavesdropped on a conversation he was having with the other footman. When they were about to go in The Jack of Spades. You were terribly generous."

"Even so, I think they both know they're on report," she replied. "Anyway, I'll allow you to deal with them however you wish once you're master of the house," she said as she reached over and plucked the ring from it's bed of velvet. "Which can only happen if you agree to marry me."

Randolph had to suppress a chuckle. "What's become of the timid filly I met only one day ago?"

Xenobia inhaled softly. "Did you prefer her?"

He shook his head. "I pitied her," he remarked.

"And now?"

"I don't. In fact, I'm rather charmed by what she's become. I cannot imagine it's only because she's discovered a small fortune, though."

"All that fresh air and a couple of tumbles might have helped," she whispered, her cheeks blooming with color.

"Ah, I shall keep that in mind," he teased before he turned his attention to the ring.

Xenobia set aside the bank notes and then took his free hand in hers. Once she had the band slid onto his fourth finger as far as it would go, she frowned at how snug it fit. "Oh, dear," she whispered, her hands gripping his. "I insisted it had to be large—"

"It's fine, Xenobia," Randolph murmured in awe. "And rather elegant."

"You haven't given me an answer."

Randolph dropped the ring box onto the chair next to where he stood and used that hand to search in a waistcoat pocket for the ring his father had given him the night before. "I had a plan for this evening, my Lady X, and it had nothing to do with Christmas," he said as he held up the garnet and diamond ring. "But it seems you have beaten me to the proposing part of it."

Xenobia stared at the ring. "For me? Rand!"

"Will you marry me?"

She nodded as she squeezed the hand she still held. "Yes. Yes, of course," she replied as she very nearly bounced on the balls of her feet. Offering her right hand, she watched as he slid the gold ring onto her fourth finger. "A garnet," she breathed. "And are those diamonds? Oh this is the most perfect Christmas gift."

Randolph chuckled. "I'd like to think it's our hearts joined as one," he murmured, wincing at hearing the sentiment out loud. He remembered he had thought the symbolism entirely different when his father had handed the ring to him the night before. Then he had been reminded of the flowers in Xenobia's parlor, imagining it a rose with leaves on either side.

Xenobia inhaled. "And the diamonds are us?"

"And everyone with whom we are close."

"Your side might require more diamonds," Xenobia teased.

He regarded her for a moment, his expression unreadable. "Speaking of my side, there's someone you must meet before we—"

"Your son, I hope. I've only ever held him the one time, and that was when he was just a tiny babe."

"You've held my son?" Randolph asked in surprise.

Xenobia nodded. "I was invited to Lady Reading's parlor for tea last year, just before Dunsworth died. When she spoke of Charles, I asked if she might show me the nursery."

"Which she was glad to do, I suppose."

"Her second son had just started walking, and the oldest had already been breeched but he hadn't yet gone off to school."

"He's already at Eton," Randolph murmured as he slid the

flat of a hand down Xenobia's front. "Although I admit to feeling some fright at what might happen should we have a babe—"

"I want as many as I can have."

Randolph admired her enthusiasm and allowed a nod. "You wont mind if they're all boys?"

Xenobia giggled in delight. "You're forgetting you have a sister," she chided.

"Well then, shall we see to a sibling for Charlie?" he asked, his gaze darting toward the bed.

"Are you sure you're not too tired?" She doffed her dressing gown and moved to undo the buttons of his waistcoat.

Randolph's expression darkened. "I find I'm wide awake."

Xenobia grinned, remembering how he had fallen asleep after they made love earlier that evening. Three times. "Not for long," she teased as she pushed the waistcoat from his shoulders and started undoing the buttons on his fly.

"Minx."

To his credit, Randolph was awake for at least half an hour.

CHAPTER 44
EPILOGUE

*D*ecember 26 (Boxing Day), 1824, Westminster
Squealing in delight, Xenobia stepped down from a Reading-crested town coach, her arms filled with a white-gowned Charlie. She rushed to where Rachel Roderick and Julia Comber stood in front of the townhouse in Westminster that Randolph had called home for several years.

"You look so elegant," Xenobia said as she hugged her friend and now sister-by-marriage. Then she turned to Julia and continued to grin. "I would hug you, but I'm not sure how close I could get."

Julia grimaced as a hand rested on her rounding belly. "Alistair made a similar remark last night."

"Oh, dear. Did you banish him to his own bedchamber?" Xenobia teased.

Julia gave a pretend pout. "The thought crossed my mind, but he's like having a large, hot brick in bed with me, so I put up with his teasing."

"What have you done with him today?"

Julia waved a hand toward the front door of the house. "I believe the more appropriate question is 'what is Mr. Merriweather doing to him?' They've been up in the billiards parlor since our arrival."

A blush appearing at hearing Julia's remarks, Rachel

regarded Xenobia and said, "You look far too happy to be married to one of my brothers." Her attention went to Charlie, and she poked a finger into his dimple.

"I heard that," Randolph said as he made his way from the coach. He grinned when Charlie's squeal of delight had the three women giggling.

Rachel was quick to move in front of him, giving him a brief hug. "I do love being an aunt, so thank you for bringing him."

Randolph gave her a quelling glance. "As if my wife would have left him behind."

"Well, I wouldn't have, either," Rachel replied. "Remember, I didn't have any siblings growing up."

Although they had known one another for over a week, the siblings were still hesitant around one another. Xenobia thought today's visit would help the two grow closer. With the servants off for Boxing Day, they had all agreed to assemble at the town-house for a post-Christmas tea to talk about Rachel and Mark's wedding and their plans for the future.

"I suppose your mother is missing you?" Randolph asked as he offered his arms to his sister and wife. Julia linked an arm with Rachel.

"I've seen her every day since I moved here," Rachel replied. "We usually have an early luncheon together when I've finished her ledgers."

"And your coach?"

"It's perfect for me and for Mr. Baker. He takes his wife to The Three Bells in the morning so she can get started in the kitchens. He takes me to The Queen, and when I'm done there, he takes me to The Three Bells and then has his luncheon. He comes for me after dinner and brings me back here," she explained.

"I'm glad to hear it's working," Randolph said, darting a glance at Xenobia. So far, their arrangements had been easy. They had married the Saturday prior on a special civil marriage license he had procured the day before. He had moved into Bradley House after their vows were said, and Charlie had joined them a few days later—once Xenobia had acquired all manner of nursery accoutrements, gowns, and a perambulator. He made his daily sojourn to the Reading stables, and in the afternoons, if it wasn't too cold, he stopped at Bradley House to take Xenobia and Charlie for a ride in the park.

Randolph and the three women made their way up the front step and into the townhouse he had called home until the week before. Now that he was master of Bradley House, Randolph had insisted Rachel take up residence in the Westminster townhouse.

Meanwhile, Mark had moved into the rooms above The Three Bells and told anyone who asked that he was living there until after his wedding.

In reality, he was spending his nights with Rachel at the townhouse.

"I hope the house is working for you?" Randolph half-asked.

"It is. I do like having my own household," Rachel replied as she led them to the parlor. "Until Mark moves in, I don't yet have a need for many servants."

"Has a modiste started a trousseau for you?" Xenobia asked.

Rachel nodded. "Mother insisted, and Father is paying the bill, so some poor seamstresses are stitching up a storm this very moment. Have you ordered anything for the Season?"

Xenobia shook her head. "I wore widow's weeds for a year, so I have an entire wardrobe I've barely begun to wear."

"But is it still fashionable?" Julia asked. Charlie was perched on what was left of her lap given her pregnancy, his splayed fingers gently patting her belly.

"It will be fine," Xenobia insisted, waving off the idea of employing a modiste. "I expect you'll wish to be married before the start of the Season?" she added, her attention on Rachel. "There are only two months before the first ball."

"If Mark had his way, we would already be wed," Rachel replied. "But Father wants me wed in St. George's, which I didn't even think was possible, so we'll say our vows next Saturday."

Julia and Xenobia exchanged quick glances, and Rachel

noticed. "Father has been using his influence to great effect," she murmured as she rolled her eyes.

"He does that," Randolph agreed. "But it will be a fitting way to end the year. I should like to be one of your witnesses," he offered.

"As would I," Xenobia said.

"Alistair and I will be there, of course," Julia said before she returned her attention to Charlie.

"I would like that very much," Rachel replied. "I always thought having a madame for a mother meant an advantageous match would be hard to come by. But Mark's parents don't seem the least bit bothered. I have already been invited to tea three times by the countess." She gave Xenobia and Julia cups of tea. "Since Mrs. Baker has already proved herself as an excellent cook at The Three Bells, Mark would like us to go to the Continent for our wedding trip. He believes I know enough about travel there so we shan't get lost," she added. "I haven't the heart to tell him otherwise."

"We may join you," Xenobia said. "Especially since my treasury continues to grow."

"Where from now?" Rachel asked as she served tea to her brother.

"I found the latest bank notes under a marble bust, and only because Charlie nearly toppled the caryatid on which it was sitting. He's learned to walk."

Randolph cleared his throat. "Then I discovered a stash in a false bottom of a drawer in the desk in the study," he said as he helped himself to a biscuit. "The bank was sure all the notes from eighteen-seventeen were accounted for, but we just keep finding more."

"I take it you're not spending it all in one place?" Julia asked, fascinated by the thought of finding money that had been hidden away for years. She had already scoured her own townhouse in search of hidden money, discovering only a couple of coins in the cushions of some chairs in the parlor. After she complained to Alistair of her paltry finds, he had begun leaving a few farthings and pennies in her jewel box, under her pillow, and in her shoes.

Xenobia shook her head. "Except for a few items for Charlie, we haven't spent any of it."

Rachel looked to her brother for confirmation of Xenobia's claim. He gave a shrug. "I've married a cheap woman," Randolph said in his most deadpan manner.

Rachel burst out laughing at the same moment Xenobia leaned over and said, "Don't you dare tell him!"

"Tell me *what?*" Randolph asked, his eyes darting between the three women.

Honoring Xenobia's insistence that she not say anything, Rachel kept quiet, but Julia whispered, "She's a skinflint, Randolph. Frugal. A penny-pincher."

"And now you know her little secret," Rachel whispered.

"Julia," Xenobia whined in protest.

"Actually, I should amend my opinion given the gift she bestowed on me for Christmas," Julia murmured. She reached into her reticule and pulled out the silver calling card case Xenobia had purchased at Rundell and Bridge. Inside were the cards Xenobia had ordered from a stationer. "Lady Julia Comber. Matchmaker," Julia recited proudly. "Every man needs a match."

"I would agree with that," Mark said as he and Alistair joined them. Mark hurried over to Rachel and bussed her on the cheek while Alistair took Charlie from his wife and hoisted him into the air. As the boy giggled, Alistair settled into an upholstered chair next to Randolph and greeted him.

"So sorry we're late to the party," Mark murmured. "Despite having practiced this past week, Alistair beat me in three games," he complained.

"How many did you play?" Rachel asked.

"Three," Alistair said as he lifted Charlie above his head, much to the boy's delight. "I forgot how heavy they are at this age," he added as he feigned exhaustion. He passed the boy off to Randolph, who settled him onto his shoulder.

"It won't be long before you'll be tossing the next one into the air," Randolph said.

"I hear you're going to have a new brother before this time next year," Alistair countered.

"Or a sister," Rachel said with a grin as she gave a cup of tea to Alistair.

"What have I missed?" Mark asked as he took a chair and then the cup of tea Rachel offered.

"These two have been accusing my wife of being a cheap woman," Randolph said as he indicated Rachel and Julia. "But I happen to know they are wrong."

Mark's brows arched in curiosity. "Do tell."

Randolph held out the hand which sported his sapphire and diamond wedding band. He considered what he had learned about it when he had shopped for a Christmas gift for Xenobia the day after her proposal, and he raised a brow. "Well, she isn't a penny-pincher when it comes to me," he said rather proudly. "And she certainly hasn't been with Charlie. You should see his nursery in Bradley House."

Julia and Rachel both glanced at the ring before turning their attention to Xenobia. "What changed?" Rachel asked in awe.

Xenobia shrugged. "I suppose it's because I was a rich widow, and I didn't even know it," she replied. "But after reading a letter I found from my father, I've also discovered I rather adore buying gifts for the men in my life."

"And we like receiving them," Randolph said, directing a wink in his son's direction. "Don't we?"

Charlie giggled in delight as his head bobbed in agreement.

Mark's eyes suddenly rounded. "That reminds me," he announced as he stood up and moved to stand before Julia. He extracted a ten-pound note from his waistcoat pocket and handed it to her before returning to his seat.

Alistair straightened in his chair as Julia displayed a look of satisfaction. "What was that for?" he asked in alarm.

"Why, my services, of course," she replied happily.

Mark was prepared when Alistair's frown turned onto him.

"Matchmaking services, sir. Her ladyship was the one to tell me about my Rachel," he explained, his attention turning to his betrothed so he could give her a wink.

"How much did you give her?" Alistair asked.

"Ten pounds," Mark replied, his manner nonchalant.

Alistair's shocked expression lingered until Randolph leaned over and said, "I wouldn't worry about it. It's probably counterfeit."

A growl emanated from Mark before he said, "I heard that," and the women feigned shock before they burst out in a fit of giggles.

AUTHOR'S NOTES

Counterfeit Money

Funny money, as it turns out, was huge a problem in England! Many despised the Bank of England's insistence on paper money to replace coins. Forgers loved it, though. By 1817, the number of forged notes and coins in circulation reached record highs in London.

The Bank's determination to punish those convicted of forgery led to public outcry after a series of high profile trials at the Old Bailey. An unprecedented number of people were convicted of forgery and sentenced to death. Technically a form of treason, the crime of counterfeiting was a capital one. The vast majority of those convicted were poor and in many cases women. Their crime was often not the manufacture of forged notes but 'uttering'—being in possession of or putting into circulation the forged notes.

Paper money was supposed to be tied to gold reserves. With England's growing debt due to expensive wars against France, the convertibility of the paper into gold couldn't be ensured. To ward off financial collapse due to money becoming scarcer as its value increased, the government empowered the Bank of England to print large quantities of small-value paper notes—and forgers took advantage.

The situation was made worse because of London's size and

the amount of money circulating along with ready materials and skills. Country banks, which were independent of the Bank of England, issued their own notes and their circulation was limited to a regional area. Given their close-knit environments, it was more difficult to utter forged notes as people were more suspicious of strangers bearing bank notes.

Despite the increasing convictions for forgery, by 1817 more than one in twenty £2 or £1 B of E notes were forged—and those were just the ones they knew about! Bank of England removed 28,648 forged notes from circulation in 1817 while only 2000 5£ notes were removed from circulation in 1816.

Not even the threat of death could deter counterfeiters. By December 1917, the Bank of England adopted a combination of special inks, watermarks, artistry and chemistry to out-skill the forgers.

In order to prosecute forgers, the Bank of England built up an impressive network of detectives and informants to one of the most organized private prosecution agencies in British history. Masterminded by Freshfields (their solicitors), the Bank of England employed vast sums in prosecuting forgers. No expense was spared. Rewards were provided.

From where were most counterfeiters operating? In 1820, one of the prosecuted, Edward Ewer, described in great detail how markets and fairs were the operational center of counter-feiting.

It wasn't until 1836 that the crime of counterfeiting was declassified as a capital offense, which meant conviction rates soared—juries were more likely to return guilty pleas if the defendant wasn't going to hang. Judging by the number of trials at the Old Bailey, the number of offenses in 1817-1821 were surpassed in the mid-1830s (there were 90 in 1835 alone). With conviction rates at 99%, the Bank of England had begun to turn the tables in its favor.

Gaming Hells

One of the most famous gaming establishments mentioned in **THE KNOT OF A KNIGHT** is Crockford's. The current gentlemen's club of the same name in London was named for the gaming hell that was founded by William Crockford and originally located at 50 St. James's Street in 1823.

Crockford's featured a varied clientele and existed for the sole purpose of separating their players from as much of their money as possible.

Although a sharp eye could catch Crockford's operators' frequent attempts at cheating—their *operators* employed slight of hand along with *waiters* that made sure to distract a player's attention when a cheat was in progress—there were few when the drinks were encouraged and kept full.

A number of *crowpees* were employed to watch the play, not only to catch customers who might be cheating, but to keep an eye on the employees as well. Then there were *puffs*—essentially decoys—who were employed by the house to play with high stakes as a means of encouraging other players to raise their bids.

Music Boxes

Probably invented about 1770 in Switzerland, the earliest music boxes were small enough to be enclosed in a pocket watch, but they were gradually built in larger sizes and housed in rectangular wooden boxes.

A music box makes its sound when tuned metal prongs, which are mounted in a line on a flat comb, are made to vibrate by contact with a revolving cylinder driven by a clockwork mechanism. As the cylinder revolves, small pins pluck the pointed ends of the metal prongs, causing them to vibrate and produce musical notes. The sequence of notes is determined by the arrangements of the prongs on the cylinder.

The deeper the prongs are cut into the comb, the lower their pitch when plucked. A watch spring and clockwork move the cylinder, and a fly regulator governs the rate.

Music boxes were especially popular from about 1810, but they were eventually rendered obsolete with the introductions of the player piano and the phonograph.

Fashion and Jewelry

To accommodate the interesting colors of Regency fashions,

a number of gemstones were used by goldsmiths in the creation of their jewelry.

Xenobia's coquelicot gown was a saturated poppy red with hints of pink and orange. Her matching jewelry would have been made of red coral, rubies, or garnets.

Like the blooms for which they are named, jonquil, primrose and evening primrose were all varying shades of yellow. These colors added warm and optimistic hues to the Regency palette, and they were frequently paired with amber and citrine or sapphires or emeralds for contrast.

Named for the Greek goddess of fruiting orchards, Pomona, a dark shade of apple green, paired well with emeralds. Paris green was the first colorfast green available, so it was quite popular and worn with chrysoprase and jade. Unfortunately and much like the verde paints popular for Victorian parlors walls, it was produced by mixing copper arsenic powders and other toxic chemicals. Your gown—and your parlor—could literally make you sick!

Puce, the French word for flea, was similar to the brownish purple-red of old blood that could be found in the pests. Despite its name, puce was one of the top fashion colors and was worn with jewelry that included garnet, pearls, and rubies.

The everyday wardrobe colors of the time—white, Spanish brown, dove grey, powder blue, pale lilac, peach blossom and wild rose—were incorporated in great abundance. Both freshwater and saltwater pearls, amethysts, sapphires, emeralds, black onyx, jet, aquamarines, "Persian blue" turquoise, periodot, topaz, rubies and citrine.

ABOUT THE AUTHOR

A self-described nerd and student of history, Linda Rae spent many years as a published technical writer specializing in 3D graphics workstations, software and 3D animation (her movie credits include SHREK and SHREK 2). Getting lost in the rabbit holes of research has resulted in historical romances set in the Regency-era as well as Ancient Greece.

A fan of action-adventure movies, she can frequently be found at the local cinema. Although she no longer has any tropical fish, she follows the San Jose Sharks and makes her home in Cody, Wyoming.

For more information:
www.lindaraesande.com
Sign up for Linda Rae's newsletter:
Regency Romance with a Twist
Follow Linda Rae's blog:
Regency Romance with a Twist